D0005084

WHEN THEY FADE

JEYN ROBERTS

Alfred A. Knopf
New York

THIS IS A BORZOI BOOK PUBLISHED BY ALFRED A. KNOPF

This is a work of fiction. Names, characters, places, and incidents either are the product of the author's imagination or are used fictitiously. Any resemblance to actual persons, living or dead, events, or locales is entirely coincidental.

Text copyright © 2016 by Jeyn Roberts
Jacket photograph (girl) © 2016 Terry Vine/Getty Images

All rights reserved. Published in the United States by
Alfred A. Knopf, an imprint of Random House Children's Books,
a division of Penguin Random House LLC, New York.

Knopf, Borzoi Books, and the colophon are registered
trademarks of Penguin Random House LLC.

Visit us on the Web! randomhouseteens.com

Educators and librarians, for a variety of teaching tools,
visit us at RHTeachersLibrarians.com

Library of Congress Cataloging-in-Publication Data
Names: Roberts, Jeyn, author.
Title: When they fade / Jeyn Roberts.
Description: First edition. | New York : Alfred A. Knopf, [2016] |
Summary: "Brutally murdered in the early 1970s, Molly can fade back to earth
for a few fleeting moments as a teenage hitchhiker who can see the future. When
Tatum, bullied at school and dumped by her best friend, picks up Molly and
hears 'You're going to die. It will hurt and you'll be alone. And no one will help
you,' Tatum and Molly must figure out how to help the other in order to save
themselves." —Provided by publisher
Identifiers: LCCN 2016001074 (print) | LCCN 2016026347 (ebook) |
ISBN 978-0-385-75413-2 (trade) | ISBN 978-0-385-75415-6 (ebook)
Subjects: | CYAC: Ghosts—Fiction. | Bullying—Fiction. | Love—Fiction. |
Horror stories. | BISAC: JUVENILE FICTION / Horror & Ghost Stories. |
JUVENILE FICTION / Love & Romance. | JUVENILE FICTION /
Social Issues / Bullying.
Classification: LCC PZ7.R54317 Wh 2016 (print) | LCC PZ7.R54317 (ebook) |
DDC [Fic]—dc23

Printed in the United States of America
September 2016
10 9 8 7 6 5 4 3 2 1

First Edition

Random House Children's Books supports the First Amendment
and celebrates the right to read.

For Jasmine.
One more time through the cracks.

MOLLY

When I died . . .

- I was sixteen.
- I was in love.
- It was the spring of 1970.
- Until the very end, I thought I'd live forever.
- My death wasn't peaceful or bittersweet. I never saw a white light. I didn't pass away quietly in my sleep. My family was thousands of miles away.
- My death was pain. Fear. Helplessness. Begging.
- I knew my killer.
- My death was slow.
- I didn't see my life flash before my eyes. I didn't see my grandmother, my aunt, or my pet hamster that died when I was seven. I didn't think about the things I still had yet to do. The places I hadn't seen. The people I should have forgiven. All I could think about was how stupid I was.

- I wish I could have talked to my father one last time or at least written him a letter.
- Such a foolish, foolish girl.
- Now I'm dead.
- I'm not in heaven.

* * *

My name is Molly.

The lake is neither cool nor warm. If I had to define it as something, I guess I'd say it's average. It's never overheated or chilled. Never boiling or frozen. I haven't waded into its depths, but once I reached down and ran my fingers along its surface. The water felt foreign against my skin. Different. Not the way water is supposed to feel. I remember childhood, jumping from the dock at my grandparents' cottage. That heart-stopping moment when cold water meets hot skin. Gasping. Giggling. Screaming at my brother for pushing me in. I miss that.

I'm not even sure if I have a body temperature to worry about anymore.

I miss a lot of things.

The way an apple tastes when you first bite into it. The sweet, juicy flesh that explodes across your tongue. The stickiness that tickled my hands. I used to wipe my juice-covered fingers on Julian's lips so I could have an excuse to kiss him. I miss the times I stayed up so late, the sun began to peek through the shadows. The world smells best first thing in the morning. Clean and crisp, like walking on a mountaintop. Like a newborn baby. Before the heat, traffic, shops, and people add their own scents to the air. Before everyone's love, pain, boredom, happiness, sadness, and a thousand other emotions add to the earth's gravity and weigh everything down.

I miss music. The freedom it represented, the bass vibrating through my stomach, and especially the way it got beneath my skin and made me glow. Dancing. Spinning, twisting, arms spread out, toes stepping on top of each other, imagining every dream there ever was. Falling down. Laughing.

I miss the way Julian used to hold me, as if nothing mattered in the world other than the two of us simply existing. Sitting out in a field, covered in that old blanket of his, red and white like a checkerboard, smelling faintly like horses. We'd watch the sun set. Listen to the crickets serenading each other in the grass. I'd press my head against his chest, feeling the warmth of his skin beneath his shirt. Taking my hand in his, he'd whisper into my ear. He'd pull me close just to hear each breath I'd take.

I miss love.

All those things are memories.

But not forgotten. Never forgotten.

In this world, nothing changes. The lake spreads out before us, a gigantic body of brilliant blue. The water might be deep or it might be shallow. No one ever goes in. It's clear and practically unmoving, except for the gentle lapping of waves against the pebbles that make up the shoreline. I've never seen whitecaps or even driftwood. There are no storms or even soft breezes.

We are deep in the valley of nonexistence. Mountains enclose us; bold, bare rocks stretch upward toward a solid blue sky that never turns dark. No clouds. There are trees—thousands, if not millions, of silent sentinels: pine, red cedar, Douglas fir, and dozens of others. I couldn't possibly identify them all. They never change colors because seasons don't exist. No wild animals, either. No eagles scanning the ground for dinner as their gigantic wings spread outward in a straight line. No squirrels, with their big baby eyes, hoarding nuts. No fish. No spiders. Not even an ant to crawl across my skin.

Sometimes when Parker is bored, he'll try and go for a walk. But he always comes out the exact same place he enters, and he's never sure how he manages to go in such a roundabout way.

We live on the shore of our lake. There are no houses because we don't need to go inside. No one sleeps or even rests their eyes. Our bodies are never exhausted. They don't age, get worn, change from the climate, or even get paper cuts. No one ever falls ill from a cold or flu. No burst appendixes or severed limbs.

We don't eat or drink. No one ever complains about being hungry because such things are in the living past.

We are ageless.

Perfect.

So is our world.

Parker says that sometimes things do change. The décor, for example, wasn't always the black metal benches with their curls and fancy designs. Thin, French-style patio tables with bright-colored parasols give the place a dated, early-1900s feel. Patio lanterns made of tissue paper are strung from the pines— useless, since the small candles inside have never been lit. Parker says that one day the tables were simply there, replacing the wooden benches that preceded them.

Just like the sparse outdoor furniture, we are outdated too. Most of us are still wearing the clothing we died in. Parker wears his lounge suit and bowler hat. The jacket rests on a tree stump, and a long time ago he rolled his shirtsleeves up and unbuttoned his collar because I told him he looked too uptight. What I'd really like to do is convince him to grow his hair long so I could weave it with flowers. I'd like to run my fingers through it and feel its thick coarseness. Sometimes I think I'd like to kiss him. But hair no longer grows, and there are no blooms around to be picked. And love is just a memory to prove I was once alive.

I sit on a wood log with Parker and sometimes Mary. She wears her corset and often complains how hard it is to breathe. But of course she's simply exaggerating. She no longer needs air. She once tried to rip away the layers of her long dress, exposing her legs for everyone to see. But she had a change of heart, and in the blink of an eye, everything returned to normal.

As for me, I wear the clothes I died in: a yellow peasant blouse and a long white cotton skirt. Thankfully, the bloodstains are gone. My feet are in sandals, and I have beads around my neck. They annoy me sometimes, the way they clack when I move. It makes the others notice. It makes *me* notice. I'd take them off, but without them I'd feel wrong.

On my finger is the silver band with the tiny diamond, the last thing Julian gave me before I died. His promise to take care of me forever. To love me until death did us part.

Sometimes I wonder if he looks up at the sky and thinks about me. Maybe late at night he wakes from a dream with my name on his lips. Or he'll see something that helps him remember, sending a brilliant flashback to an older time and place. Would such things still make his heart ache? Did he ever come to terms with what happened to me? Did he find a new love? Sometimes I worry that he's passed on and found his own lake. Wherever he is, he's not here.

Because we are in a certain type of afterlife.

We are the restless. We are the dead.

And as far as I can tell, there's no way out.

TATUM

I've got a secret!

Evil words. Evil. Evil. Evil.

Tatum shouldn't have listened. She should have told Claudette that she was busy and didn't have time for such trivial things. She should have worried about the D she'd gotten in biology, or about her mother complaining that she never made her bed anymore. But she didn't. No, she allowed Claudette to tell her the secret. She wanted to hear it. And it was quite shocking. Tatum giggled at first. Then she blushed and gasped at every word. But when the laughing turned to concern, and then to fear, she still had to hear every single last word.

So why hadn't anyone listened to her?

The words are waiting for her on her locker. Bright red lipstick, from the looks of it.

SNITCH

BITCH

Nice.

She could spend time wondering who did it, but the effort would be fruitless. There are sixteen girls in her grade, and every single one of them hates her. At least half of them wear red lipstick. She's pretty sure most of them can read and write. Even if she managed to thin the herd and come up with a name, she's positive none of the school officials would do anything. They'd just frown and tell her to head to her next class.

So she grabs tissues from her locker and wipes off the words, ignoring the laughter from down the hall as Graham Douglas and his ogre friends watch her. Sweat beads on her forehead and she wipes that away too, but with the back of her hand. Her mousy brown hair falls into her eyes, and she doesn't bother brushing it away.

Tatum drops the tissues in her purse even though there's a garbage bin just a few feet away. She won't turn her back on her open locker. The last time she did that, they stole her car keys. Then her car. And when it was found, her father screamed at her for the four hundred dollars he'd have to pay to paint over the words they'd scraped across her hood.

Words much worse than *snitch* and *bitch*.

"It's your own damned fault, and you're paying me back for all of this."

"You're going to blame me for their vandalism?" At that point only a few weeks had gone by, and Tatum still didn't quite understand her new world. Her father, of all people, should still have been on her side.

But he'd only looked at her and frowned. "You opened your big mouth and told stories. You brought this on yourself."

That was the final realization: No one believed her. Not even her own father.

The worst part? She was telling the truth.

Tatum grabs her books for the final class of the day and slams her locker. She looks up just in time to see Claudette barreling down on her. The bigger girl slams her shoulder into Tatum, knocking her books from her hands. Her pencil case bursts open, sending pencils and pens spiraling across the tiles. Kids begin to kick them.

"Oops."

Tatum ignores Claudette, reaching down to collect her items. She doesn't even bother with half the pens; she refuses to spend more time than necessary on her knees. She can always get new ones. There's no point in trying to stand up for herself. All the fight inside her is gone.

Best to just try and get through the next few months. Then high school will be over and she can move on. Preferably somewhere far away where she never has to see Claudette or Mr. Paracini ever again.

* * *

Someone let the air out of her back tires again.

Tatum doesn't bother to look around to see if the guilty party is watching. They're all watching. She's used to it. Tossing her backpack into the passenger seat, she goes around to the back and opens the trunk, grabs the air-compressor pump she purchased a few weeks ago. Ignoring a few nasty shouts from some sophomore girls, she starts the ignition and plugs the cord into the cigarette lighter.

Only two tires flat. She should be thankful. Most of the time they do all four. They must have been in a hurry.

When she reaches down to attach the valve to the tire, she pulls back her hand in surprise. The smell reaches her nose as drops of liquid drip off her fingers and onto her shirt. Someone's urinated all over the tire.

"Wet yourself, bitch?"

Tatum looks but can't tell who spoke the words. The parking lot is full of students, most of whom are glaring at her. No one bothers to hide the fact that they hate her.

Graham and some of his buddies are standing by his car. He says something and they all start laughing. Levi Tessier, a boy who bought her flowers in seventh grade, grabs his crotch and grins. Tatum quickly looks away, refusing to give them any satisfaction.

"Here."

Her head whips around, arms going up in defensive mode, but it's just Scott Bremer handing her some napkins. His car is parked next to hers.

"Thanks."

Scott tosses his backpack into his passenger seat without giving her a second glance. He doesn't even look back at her as he pulls out of the parking spot. But the nice thing about Scott isn't that he ignores Tatum. It's that he ignores everyone in general.

Tatum uses the napkins to clean around the rubber valve. She inflates the tires as quickly as she can, thankfully without commentary from the watching group of boys, and throws the air compressor back in the trunk.

She slams the car into gear. She can't get away fast enough.

Supper is quiet. Mom and Dad don't talk to her much these days. They push food around on their plates silently. Mom occasionally scrapes her teeth with her fork, something that drives Tatum crazy, but it isn't worth complaining about.

Not that it matters. Tatum has nothing to say to them, either. They are traitors.

When Claudette first told her she was dating Mr. Paracini, Tatum was both thrilled and a little disgusted. He was a teacher and married. Yes, he was by far the most attractive man at Hamilton High, and yes, he did tend to give better grades to girls who flirted with him, but to actually date him? The idea was scandalous.

And that was why Claudette entrusted Tatum to keep her little secret.

At first it was fun and games. Tatum covered for her friend, allowing Claudette to say she was spending time with her, in case her mother called. She even faked a sleepover when Mr. Paracini's wife was out of town for the weekend.

"He's just amazing, Tatum," Claudette told her in the early days. "He picked me up at the Shell station out by the highway. I had to keep my head down until we got out of town, but it was worth it. We spent the day walking around Seattle. He bought me flowers at Pike Place Market. And dinner. Oh man, this place was super cool and totally expensive. The waiter spoke French!"

"What time did you get home?"

"After ten. Barry had to be back before his wife. She'd taken the kids to Bellingham to visit their grandparents.

Driving back on the highway, Barry was getting nervous. He was worried that we might see her car. Could you imagine?"

Mr. Paracini, aka Barry, had a wife and two small children. According to Claudette, they didn't get along and hadn't had sex in two years. He planned on divorcing her as soon as he got his boat in the marina.

"We're going to live on the boat. It's a twenty-five-footer," Claudette said with dreamy eyes. "And we'll sail to Hawaii next summer. I swear, Tatum, you need to find yourself an older man. High school boys just don't cut it."

Tatum smiled. She was jealous, of course. Any girl would be. Not only had Claudette captured the heart of Mr. Paracini, but she was making all sorts of romantic plans for when she turned eighteen. She was leading the super-cool secret romantic life that everyone else dreamed about. An older man. A really hot older man!

"Of course, we'll have to keep it a secret a bit longer," Claudette said. "Barry's right. This town is full of snooty old ladies who wouldn't understand. Once we get out of here, it'll be so much better."

And that was it. The big secret. The one that should not be told.

* * *

Tatum's bedroom has become her sanctuary. Gone are the photos of her and Claudette hanging out at the mall. Gone is the trophy they won when they were six years old and things like sack races were still cool. Gone are the countless selfies of the two of them on Tatum's bed. In Tatum's car. At the rock-and-roll museum. On the trail at Mount Rainier. All of Claudette's clothing has been bagged up and is waiting in the garage if she ever decides she wants it back. Her nail polish and hair bands, all the little things she left behind and never bothered to retrieve. The things they openly shared. The pictures went in the trash. The trophy was broken in two. The friendship bracelet had been burned up in the bathroom sink.

The price of memories that just can't be forgotten.

Tatum sits on her bed cross-legged, her laptop closed. Once upon a time, she spent countless hours on Facebook and Twitter. Playing games, gathering farming neighbors, discussing rumors about who had done what to whom, and basically just having a blast. Looking at goofy pictures and cute kittens. Laughing and swooning over celebrities. Watching James Franco get roasted. Sharing Skype conversations that went late into the night when she was supposed to be studying.

Tatum doesn't bother anymore. She closed her Facebook page ages ago. Claudette started a hate page in her honor. Hundreds of comments discussing how much people loathe her. Some of them are simple: name calling or making up lies and theories to make Tatum look bad. Others go darker: old friends and new enemies advising her to drink bleach, slit her wrists, and drive off cliffs. In the beginning she read them all obsessively.

Claudette Nesbitt: Yah, she needs to die. Mouthy bitch, jealous of my life. Right? B careful. She might make stories up of you next.

Juniper Hafner: Yeah, whatevvvaaaaah! She's fat and ugly. Virgin suicide to be.

Levi Tessier: What u expect? No one wants to fuck her. She's one ugly hoe.

Juniper Hafner: LOLs. Didn't you date her?

Levi Tessier: Like 3rd grade. Dumped her ass cuz she wouldn't suck my dick.

Claudette Nesbitt: Lol. She has no life. Someone should end it 4 her.

Ignore it. Ignore it. Ignore it.

Three more months. Then she'll graduate and get the hell out of Dodge. It doesn't matter that she and Claudette planned to take the year off and travel across Europe together before applying to college. Tatum has the money saved. She'll still go away. A big city is what she needs. A place to escape. Somewhere no one has ever heard the name Mr. Paracini, aka Barry. Once she's settled and far away, she'll find a job and eventually start applying to school. She'll never come back.

Tatum tries to turn her attention to her history essay, but her phone vibrates. She's changed the number twice since all this happened. It cuts down on the texts and late-night hangups, but still, they always manage to find a way through.

Sure enough. Unknown number.

Die ugly slut

She pushes the history book off her bed, watches it drop to the floor. The phone vibrates again. Then a third time. She turns it off without looking. Tosses it in her bag. Gets off the bed and heads down the stairs.

"Honey?"

Her parents are watching television in the living room. Tatum passes them to get to the front door.

"What?" She slips her feet into her shoes.

"Little late, isn't it?" Mom glances back at her.

Tatum looks at the clock. It's only a bit after eight. "I've got a bunch of work to do tonight. Thought I'd go get a coffee first."

"You can't make one here?"

"Not a mocha." She grabs her coat from the hook.

"Okay," Mom says. "Don't be too late. You've got your phone?"

Tears blur her eyes, but Tatum won't let people see her cry. Not even her parents. She won't waste a single tear on anyone again. It only makes her weak. And Claudette can smell weakness a mile away.

"Yeah, I've got it," Tatum says. She shakes her bag to emphasize. Mom doesn't need to know it's turned off.

"Call if you need us."

Good old Mom. She's never actually come out and said she doesn't believe Tatum. In fact, she spent a lot of time in the beginning defending her to everyone: *Tatum's a good girl. She'd never tell a lie like that. I honestly don't know what's going on with the girls. They've been friends since they were toddlers. You know how they can get. They have their little snits. But they always come back around.*

Yeah, except this isn't a little snit. Tatum will never forgive Claudette.

It was good to have Mom on her side. But as the days went by and the accusations continued, Tatum watched her start to hold back. And since Dad's outburst over the car-keying episode, and Mrs. Paracini's threat to sue, Mom's been acting like the whole thing is better off pushed into the closet. She wants to close her eyes and pretend everything is behind them. Now her criticisms are thinly veiled attempts to avoid the real truth.

Are you sure you didn't say something to make her mad? Really, honey. You can tell me.

Don't worry. Once you graduate, no one will ever remind you of it again.

But Mom doesn't know about Facebook. Or the phone calls. The hell that has become school. She doesn't know because Tatum stopped talking about it. Otherwise Mom might try and get involved again, and that's the last thing Tatum needs.

Tatum walks around her car before she gets in. Four tires. Check. Still full of air. Check. No foul body odors to suggest she look for wet spots. Check. Doors locked. Check. No windows broken or insults scratched in the paint job. Check.

Normally they don't bother attacking in her driveway, but she figures it's just a matter of time till they show up with rotten eggs or dozens of toilet paper rolls just to give themselves a good time. There's not a lot to do in Hannah, Washington. Having a car is the best thing because it means getting out. Day trips to Seattle. Hop, skips, and jumps to bigger places where Taco Bells, Jack in the Boxes, and massive outlet stores litter the I-5. Drive-through Starbucks. Twenty-four-hour Walmarts.

And for Tatum, her own car means small escapes.

Escape she does. Her secondhand Yaris starts on the first try. Looking at the illuminated clock on her dashboard, she figures she can get away with about an hour before Mom starts calling to check up on her. She puts the car in drive and goes.

Driving. Such simplicity. Bliss. A chance to forget all her problems by simply pointing the car in one direction and pressing the accelerator. Opening the window and letting the wind tickle her ears. Tatum is positive she was an explorer in a previous life. Someone who made a living plotting her way through forests and valleys to find the open sea. There is nothing greater in the world than the experience of simply moving forward.

Driving does this. Tatum almost wishes her parents would stop pressuring her to apply to college. She'd love to be a truck driver. The open road. A thousand miles of gravel. A car stereo to keep her company. Now that's heaven.

But not enough tonight. As much as she'd just love to disappear, that probably wouldn't go over well with her parents. They'd find her and drag her back. So for now she'll barely get to wet her whistle, as Dad likes to say.

Tatum pulls to a stop at the bottom of the hill. If she turns right, it'll take her toward Main Street. She's more likely to come across enemy territory. And if they follow her like they did last week, the only safe way is to head back home. Left takes her toward the old highway. A small, almost-forgotten interstate that no one ever travels. It's the long way around to the next town, shadowed by the new and improved Interstate 90. The state doesn't even bother repairing it these days. Eventually it'll turn to crumbling gravel, and the only people who will complain are those in the few remaining acreages where city folk love to retire.

The route may be forgotten, but for Tatum it'll take her to Frog Road.

Perfect.

Tatum heads left.

Frog Road isn't its actual name. It's just what Tatum's dad has called it ever since Tatum once caught him driving over an aforementioned amphibian when she was a little girl. She made him stop the car so she could get out and try and rescue its little frog body before another car came along. Luck must have been on that frog's side that day (or perhaps it was stuck to Dad's front tire) because she never did find the remains.

Frog Road goes along part of the twisting Snoqualmie River. And if Tatum hurries, she can turn up the music and drive for a good twenty minutes before reality makes her head back home.

It's a cool night for spring. Thankfully, there's no rain in sight, but as she drives along, Tatum notices the first few wisps of fog settling in. She's not overly surprised, nor does it worry her. She's driven in fog heavy enough to barely see past her dashboard. She knows the rules: Slow down and never turn on your brights. Watch for animals, especially small amphibian types.

Ten minutes in and she's almost ready to turn around. The whiteness has taken over everything. She can barely see the pavement anymore. And when the road gets that dangerous, Tatum stops having fun. She's even turned off the radio in order to concentrate.

When she sees the girl by the shoulder, she nearly swerves into the middle of the road.

A girl who calmly holds her thumb out.

Tatum's never picked up a hitchhiker. She's been heavily influenced by the stories her parents have told her. Couples who will rob her and steal her car, leaving her stuck in the middle of nowhere. Men who will butcher her. The names of famous serial killers float through her mind. The Green River Killer. Ted Bundy. Surely they must have preyed on girls foolish enough to stop their cars? Or picked up girls on their own. Or prostitutes? She can't remember.

Not that it matters. This girl certainly can't be a killer. She looks to be about Tatum's age, although Tatum doesn't recognize her. She definitely doesn't go to Tatum's high school.

And the way she's dressed, she must be freezing.

Tatum puts her foot on the brake and pulls over. The seconds move slowly as she watches the girl jog toward her. If she's going to flee, now's the time.

Instead she hits the unlock button.

The door opens. The girl bends over to check Tatum out. Her hair is long and perfectly straight. Dark chestnut, the kind of hair color Tatum wishes she had instead of her own mousy brown.

"Thanks," the girl says. She smiles and gets in.

MOLLY

I'm sitting with Parker and Mary when I feel it coming.

We call it the Fade.

Stupid name, but I guess no one's bothered to try and come up with something better. It's the moment when one of us travels back into the real world.

The haunting.

We're all ghosts here.

And contrary to popular belief, it's not always by choice. It's not like we saw the white light and said, "No thanks, I'll stay here." None of us thought with our dying breath that we'd like to spend eternity haunting some boarded-up house or darkened alley. The whole ghost thing is massively distorted. Yes, we all have unfinished business. Show me a single dying person who didn't. Even if you've convinced yourself that you're ready, there's always something you still desire. One more sunrise. One more piece of cake. One last goodbye. The list is limitless.

As the years go by, the unfinished business is forgotten. Loved ones die. Bodies are found and buried. Secrets are taken to the grave or discovered in diaries hidden in attic trunks.

But we stay here.

We don't want help, either. We're not appearing over and over again to try and point out who killed us or show someone where our body is so we can get a proper burial. We're not looking for the diamond ring torn from our finger or a missing kneecap that some criminal kept as a trophy. The stories people make up to simply justify our existence? Total garbage. Even if we could talk to the living and tell them our tales of woe, I doubt it would be of any help. Some of us have been haunting for centuries. The people who wronged us are long gone themselves.

We're not lonely. I've got Parker and Mary and a host of others to keep me company. Yeah, it's not the most exciting place to be, but I'm sure there are worse. Because if this place exists, other places do as well. And all I can hope for is that the man who harmed me went somewhere a lot warmer.

Okay, yes. That's one thing we have in common: We all died before our time. It was always violent, sudden, and painful. Although there are a few here who try and pretend otherwise, I have never met anyone in our valley who went peacefully in his or her sleep.

We share our stories.

Parker died in 1923. He was eighteen years old. He'd moved to London, England, from his home in Stoke-on-Trent to study medicine. One night, while walking home to his small one-bedroom flat, Parker was mistaken by a drunken man for his wife's lover and stabbed through the stomach with a sharpened fish knife. Parker lay in the darkened street while the drunk realized his mistake. Instead of going for help, the man dragged Parker into an alley, where he covered him up with newspaper and garbage. Parker spent the next few hours weakening, dying, unable to cry loudly enough to get any attention from the early-morning longshoremen as they headed to the docks to begin work.

Funny enough, Parker doesn't haunt the alley in which he died. He says he often appears in more than one place. Sometimes it's the hospital where he interned; other times it's the pub where he had his last drink. His haunting routine is mostly quiet. He doesn't have a voice with which to speak. Only an image of him coated in blood. So far, he says, he's scared more than one nurse out of her knickers.

Mary also died in London, but her story is much worse. In 1888 she was twenty-five and a prostitute. She'd been through a marriage that went nowhere, and she'd left the man. According to her, there weren't a lot of respectable jobs for a woman such as herself. One night a man followed her home and did all sorts of unspeakable things to her body with a knife. She stayed alive through a fair amount of it.

Mary only goes back into the world on rainy nights. She doesn't appear as a victim all torn and bloody, but just as herself. She materializes in the small room where she died, or sometimes on the stairs. Once, she found herself walking down the alley. She says it's quite boring, actually. Every now and then she'll come back bragging about how she freaked someone out, but mostly she says it's just the owners' cats that run and hide.

We come from all over. All places. All nationalities. A Canadian girl haunts a music studio, floating down the halls each night at midnight. Her lover, a famous musician at the time, strangled her over an argument about who got the last bit of cocaine. The other band members took her body and dumped it in the trash several blocks away. She heard the men talking about it the first few nights she returned. Listened while they patted each other on the back for removing her body from the scene of the crime. Watched when her lover showed up with a new girlfriend. She's quite angry most of the time, so we don't talk to her much. I can't blame her. I wouldn't want to Fade every night either.

A Chinese man, killed by his wife, haunts a rice field in Sichuan.

We have someone from Brazil who only Fades during Carnival.

A boy from Germany haunts the street where his house was bombed during the war. His cheeks are still hollow from lack of food.

An old lady from Boston drowned along with her dog. She's the only one here who managed to bring her beloved pet. She sits over by the corner of the lake and chats with her furry friend all day long. And if you try being polite, she'll talk your ear off for hours. Mostly about her poodle. Sometimes she'll talk about the two children she left behind, but not as often. After all, it was her son who killed her.

Every one of us has a story. We have a death. We have a haunt. We all Fade.

We do different things. Mary walks around and spooks cats. Parker gives nurses something to gossip about. And me? I hitchhike.

I have no idea why. It wasn't something I was doing before

I died. Actually, I had caught a ride with Walter, but I knew him well. He was part of our community. Our family. He was someone I trusted.

The first time I Faded, I couldn't have been more spooked. Isn't that hilarious? A ghost who gets spooked? I suppose stranger things have happened. One minute I was sitting with Parker and Mary, staring off into the trees; the next, my body simply disappeared. I'd been ready for it, considering I'd been at the lake for some time, and pretty much everyone wanted to talk about it. Everyone wants to be the first to explain the Fade to the new kid. Some of the others even tried to predict what I'd do. If money had meaning, they would have bet on it.

The Fade isn't much of anything. Have you ever had that feeling when you get dizzy stepping out of the shower? That moment where everything tilts awkwardly on its side and your brain gets all light-headed. Sometimes the edges of your vision darken and you have to reach out to steady yourself. That's what the Fade feels like. A quick moment of dizziness followed by a complete change in scenery.

People here enjoy Fading. Well, most of them do. I quickly figured out why. As I found myself standing in knee-high grass, a gust of freezing wind nearly blew my skirt up over my head.

Wind.

Feelings.

I was standing in the middle of a ditch. Looking around, I tried to take in my surroundings. There was nothing familiar, or so I first thought. In the darkness I couldn't see much. I stepped forward and climbed the steep embankment to the road. Dirt dug into my hands as they pressed against the cool ground. I brushed them off, marveling at how my skin burned slightly from where the pebbles dug in. I waited for my eyes to adjust. Slowly the dark shadows became trees.

This could have been any road in America. The pavement beneath me stretched out into darkness, leaving me unable to fully take in my surroundings. But I didn't need to. I knew exactly where I was. Call it instinct, or perhaps something in my ghostly mind had clued in. It was the road Walter and I had driven down not that long ago. I knew that if I were to continue walking for a few miles, I'd come to the place where he'd dumped my body.

The field.

Was my body still there? Decomposing beneath the moonless sky?

As he killed me, the last thing I smelled was the wildflowers. The meadow was full of them. Millions. Seeds stuck in my hair. Flattened beneath my back, tickling my bare arms and legs, as my blood dripped down to nourish their roots. They'd be dead now. Wilted away as winter sucked the warmth from their stems.

Another gust blew through my blouse, causing me to shiver. It was cold, but not quite snow-cold. I shivered, wishing I had something warmer to wear. But at the same time, it felt so good to feel, even if what I felt was nothing but biting air. Looking up at the sky, I could see stars. More like late autumn. I'd died in the spring. In May. One month after my birthday.

Had two seasons passed? Or more? It didn't seem like that long. In fact, I could have sworn I'd only been at the lake for a few days. But it's hard to tell when nothing changes. An entire year could have passed and I wouldn't have known.

From a distance I could see headlights coming my way. I stepped over to the side of the road, determined to go back into the high grass and hide. But something wouldn't let me. An unseen force held me back, pressing gently against my body, showing me where to go. No. Hiding wasn't my purpose. Neither was jumping out onto the road and screaming like a banshee. Slowly, I watched as my hand went up. Then I stuck my thumb out for a ride.

The car slowed as it approached. The headlights flashed over my body momentarily, and I was too blind to see who was inside.

I had no fear. Impossible. Fear is the unknown. It's the uncertainty of what bad things could happen. It's pain. Despair. Horror. I'd already been through the worst mankind had to offer. I was no longer part of the world. I was pretty sure no one human could ever hurt me again. Unless of course this car held my killer and I would be forced to relive my death over and over again like the tiny Cambodian girl no one liked to talk to. She shook constantly and stammered with broken English, begging for God to help her. I avoided looking in her direction. Hers was a suffering even the dead found difficult to face.

I studied the car as my legs began walking toward it. No, it wasn't Walter's. He drove a VW bus. This car was a Ford, early-sixties style with a hardtop roof. Double headlights. The kind of car Julian wanted to buy if he ever got the money.

The driver leaned across the passenger side and opened the door a few inches. My fingers reached out and clasped the handle.

"Where ya goin', cutie? Next town?"

I nodded. I had no idea where I was going or if there even was a next town to worry about. But it must have been the right thing to do.

"I can do that. Hop in."

My body agreed to that. I climbed inside and closed the door. Rubbed my hands over my bare shoulders. The interior was still cool, but without the wind it was a huge improvement. I looked at the dashboard, which rattled along with the engine. I reached out and ran my fingers across the surface, feeling the vibrations from the engine. I grinned at the Hawaiian hula girl who bounced along in rhythm. The cheesy dice hanging from the rearview mirror. I touched everything, not caring if I looked weird or not.

"Good thing I seen you," the man said as his foot pressed down on the gas pedal. The car lurched forward, and I reached out and placed my fingers against the dash. I glanced over at my driver. An older man in his late forties or early fifties. Conservative. His hair didn't have a strand out of line. He didn't look like the sort of man who might pick up young hippie girls in the dead of night. But there was something in his eyes that suggested he was the type who saw things for how they really were. That maybe he understood that once in a while a girl needs to catch a ride with a decent stranger. Someone decent who doesn't have roaming hands or darker plans.

"It's cold out," the man continued. "Not really a good place to try and thumb a ride. Most people would probably drive on past ya without seeing. I almost didn't stop myself. Don't normally pick up strangers. But being it's so nasty outside, I was worried you might not get another ride till morning. This ain't a busy road."

It was time to find out if I could really talk. What kind of words might I be allowed to say?

"It's where I got left behind." My voice came through clear and loud over the engine. A large smile came to my lips. Thankfully, the darkness concealed it. Sweet words! Most ghosts couldn't talk. I wondered what the powers-that-be would allow me to say. Would they control my vocal cords the way they forced my limbs? Would it always be this way? Was I destined to play puppet, or would they cut my strings when I didn't fight back?

"Last guy give you problems?"

"No," I said a bit too quickly.

"That's good. I've got a daughter 'bout your age. She don't hitchhike—hell, I'd tan her hide if she did. But I pray she don't get taken in by some creep. Some girl died here not too long ago."

I looked over at him in surprise. He must mean me. How many girls died along this road?

"Who was she?"

"Not sure. Papers didn't say much. She belonged to this traveling hippie commune. Fifteen? Sixteen? Not pretty what that guy did to her."

They'd found my body. Part of me was happy to hear that. They'd probably returned the remains to my father. I wondered where they'd buried me. The other part was a little sad, wondering if it would have been better for Julian if he'd never found out what happened.

"Did they catch the guy?" I asked.

"Yep. Big manhunt. He was one of the people in that commune. Fatherly type. Saw his picture in the papers. Big beard.

My mama always said you can't trust a man who wears a beard, but I always thought that's a bunch of hogwash. Guess maybe she was right somewhat. But this guy didn't look like the type to hurt a fly. He had nice eyes. I remember saying that to my wife: 'He's got nice eyes, Ethel.' That's the problem with people, innit? Can't always tell the good from the bad."

"Yes," I said. I'd certainly been fooled by Walter. I could easily understand why others could be too.

"I get that you kids like to be daring and all sorts," the man said, "but where on God's green earth is your jacket? You must be freezing to death. I was young once myself, and I remember all trying to pretend I wasn't cold. Grew up in the north. Used to go out with the coat undone and my lips bright blue."

I smiled and tried not to shiver. "I'm fine," I said, but my face must have given me away.

"Hold on," the man said. He pulled over to the side of the road and opened the door. "I've got a blanket in the trunk."

I watched him as he went around to the back and popped the trunk. How trusting he was to walk away from his car with the ignition turned on. Or maybe he was one of the bad guys, going to grab his tire iron to try and smash my head in. I paused in midthought. What if that was my destiny? To be brought back to earth to be killed over and over by strange men? There couldn't be that many terrible people in the world, could there? Would the afterlife kick me even further now that I was in the dirt?

But no, when he closed the trunk, I could see a thick wool blanket in his arms. He handed it to me from across the driver's side, and as I reached for it, our fingers touched.

Emotions. Memories.

He did have a daughter my age. He worried about her because she didn't have a boyfriend yet when all her friends did. She was a pretty girl (even though all fathers think that) and she dressed well enough, but she lacked confidence and was too shy around strangers. Instead of talking to the boys, she ran from them. She spent her nights babysitting and refused to talk about it.

He worried about his bills and the mortgage that was slowly getting out of hand. Business was slow, and he didn't know how much longer he wanted to spend on the road. Twenty-five years of hitting the pavement made him yearn for simpler times. He couldn't afford to retire, and he didn't think there were other jobs he could apply for. No one would give him a desk job when there were all those fresh, shiny faces of the younger workforce.

He knew these things, and after touching him I knew them too. A jumble of thoughts and feelings washed over me. Summer at the beach when he was sixteen years old. The year he met his wife. She'd looked so cute in the pink bathing suit. Fast-forward to their wedding day. When he removed the veil from her face, tears burned her eyes, but the smile never left her face. Kissing her. The birth of their child. The death of his father. All these memories flooded my mind.

When he looked at me, a small spark of desire filled his body. It made him ashamed and excited at the same time. He loved his wife, and I *did* remind him of his daughter. But I was young and pretty to look at. Nothing wrong with taking a peek once in a while. But he was a God-fearing man and took his vows seriously.

Too bad his wife didn't. She was cheating on him right that very second with her neighbor's husband. That he didn't know.

I gasped in surprise.

"Go on, take it," the man said. "You'll be nice and warm. The heater don't work so well on the car these days. Taillights burned out too. Keep meaning to take it in, but times are hard."

"Thank you," I said. I pulled the blanket around myself, and the scratchiness of the wool brushed against my skin. I felt warmer instantly.

I felt that spark of desire inside him disappear, replaced with a fatherly pride in doing the right thing.

And I saw his wife kiss her lover.

What on earth was going on? Was this my curse? It was bad enough that I had to spend my eternity haunting, but was I going to be forced to see things I didn't want to see? Secrets? Did this happen to the others, too? I would have to ask around when I got back.

The man hit the gas and we began to move.

"I'm John Gershwin."

"Molly," I said, instantly regretting it. What if my name had recently been all over the papers? What if he recognized it, realized exactly what I was, and drove us off the road in fear?

For a ghost, I was awfully paranoid.

Thankfully, none of that happened. We drove along for a while with John talking away, chatting about nothing in general. I listened and watched the darkened woods speed by, the vision of his wife with another man stuck in my brain.

I had to say something. Why else would the powers-that-be show me such a thing? But how could I tell a nice man such awful news? I remembered how devastated my father had been when my mom ran off with another man. He'd spent weeks sitting in his chair, a bottle of beer in one hand, listening to the saddest country music ever created. All I could do was try and force dinner down his throat and set the alarm beside him on the nights he fell asleep before heading off to bed.

"We're not that far now," John said. "'Bout two more miles till we reach town. Is there somewhere specific I can drop you off?"

My body suddenly tilted on its side, or at least that's what it felt like. I was Fading. The lines of my vision darkened.

It was my moment. I had to do something. It was bad enough that I was about to scare the socks right off John by disappearing in his front seat. But could I hurt him too? What was worse? Not knowing the truth or being forced to hear it?

I decided to be coy.

"You should talk to your wife," I said. I let the blanket drop from my shoulders. Already the skin on my hands was disappearing. "You need to ask her if she's got something to tell you. A secret. Thanks for the ride."

And I was gone. I didn't even get to see the astonished look on his face or whether he drove smack into a tree.

Hopefully not the latter.

Then I was back at the lake. My nose no longer felt cold. Neutral again.

"How was it?" Parker asked.

I told him everything.

"That's impressive," he said when I finished. "You can see things. Only a few of us can do that." He pointed over to the corner where a young Japanese girl in a white-and-green school uniform sucked her thumb. "Yuriko has that too. She can foretell disasters. Sadly, no one ever listens."

"I wish I could talk to the lifers," Mary said. "I'd do better than that. I'd sing at the top of me lungs and scare 'em all to death." She laughed and started belting, off-key, an old song about a man going to sea and the bonny lass he left behind. As she clapped her hands together, her petticoats shuffled and swayed.

"You're scaring me right now," Parker said, but I saw the small smile on his lips.

That was more than four decades ago. Since then, I've Faded more times than I can count, and I've learned more secrets than I care to remember. I've told people all sorts of things. Some have been innocent and cute: I've discovered the hiding spots of treasured items. Others have been darker: Failed relationships. The last words of loved ones, people I'm assuming have left this earth and traveled to places where they aren't forced to come back.

And now, sitting on the log, listening to Mary brag about how the men used to whistle at her on a good night, I feel the beginnings of the Fade. The uneasiness in my body as the ghostly blood rushes to my face.

"I'll be back," I say with a smile.

"Hope it's a good one," Mary says. "Something wicked. No more of those lost pets. The last few have been downright dull."

I smile. Mary loves to hear about my visions. They're the most exciting things in a world that never changes.

Even the dead enjoy a good story.

A soft brush of air caresses my face and I open my eyes. I'm back at the side of the road, the exact same spot. My starting point.

It's a lovely night. Foggy. But not overly cold. Springtime, I think. March or April. I instinctively look down at the ground beneath my feet. No flowers. Just a lot of dewy grass and a few stones. Too bad. I curl my toes up in my sandals, hoping to keep my feet from getting wet.

I work my way up the embankment and onto the road. No such luck. My feet are now soaking, and so is the hem of my skirt. I have to admit, I much prefer to Fade in the summertime. I pull the ends of my skirt up and give it a quick shake. My legs are pale and look like thin white sticks. I wonder if my face is just as pallid. I can't remember the last time I looked in a mirror.

Glancing in both directions, I admire the way the low clouds close in on everything. It's been a lifetime since I've seen fog. We didn't get much of it when I was growing up in North Carolina. I had never experienced it this thick until I came out to the West Coast.

In the distance I hear the rumble of an engine. Unhooking my skirt from a bush, I step onto the side of the road, where I'll be both visible and safe. It's taken me a while to get the right position. There have been a few times where I've almost been hit. No need to scare the drivers until I've had a chance to personally do it with my stories.

A small gray car comes into view. The headlights flash against me, engulfing me in light. The car is curved and simple—I can't help but think about how different cars look these days. They're a lot quieter and less bumpy when you ride in them too. It comes to a complete stop about thirty feet away.

I jog toward it, my body urged on by the now-familiar unseen presence. Just like a hand on my back, guiding me to my destiny.

I open the door and peer inside. A girl. She looks about my age, maybe a bit older. Medium-length hair and a heart-shaped face. She's wearing a fleece jacket with a hood and a pair of jeans. Black boots. I always look at the clothing first. I like seeing how everything has changed over the years. I rarely get picked up by females. So something like this is a bit of a treat, especially since she's young. I wonder what decade this might be. A few Fades prior, I got a glimpse of a newspaper. The date was 2011. I wonder how much time has passed since then. Maybe tonight I'll get a clue.

"Thanks," I say as I climb inside.

She smiles, a little wary, but not overly. She's a very pretty girl, but there's something in her eyes that says she's unhappy. Boyfriend troubles, probably. It often is.

The girl puts the car in gear and the tires start to roll. The fog moves around us, brushing up against the car, keeping everything strictly between us and the outside world.

"Where are you going?"

"The next town," I say. My standard reply. I know that Evander is a small community about ten miles ahead of us. "You can drop me off anywhere." I smile slightly. That lie always makes me want to break out in a grin.

The girl hesitates for a moment. "Yeah, sure," she says. "I wasn't planning on going that far, but why not."

"Where are you going?" I ask.

"Nowhere. Just out for a drive. Didn't realize it was going to be this foggy."

"It's beautiful," I say.

I remember when I went down to San Francisco with the group. Julian woke me up early one morning and we snuck away. We walked across the Golden Gate Bridge in the fog, admiring the way the whiteness swallowed up the ocean beneath us. It was like we were walking across the clouds. I told Julian that it looked like we could jump right into all that softness. He laughed and held my hand tighter.

All that reminiscing makes me look down at my hands. I swear, I can almost feel his touch. It's been so long since anyone held my hand. I look over at the girl and wonder what I'm going to see when I touch her skin. Should I do it discreetly or just reach out and get it over with? It's hard to tell. I'm not sure what sort of reaction I might get.

She notices me watching her, and her fingers dig deeper into her steering wheel. Her face hardens. There's something there just beneath the surface.

"Is something wrong?" I ask.

"No," she says, but her tone suggests otherwise. She glances over at me, looking at my face. "Are you from around here? I've never seen you before. I thought pretty much everyone in this area went to my school."

I shrug. I could tell her I'm visiting friends, but she might ask which ones. She's right: this is a small community, and everyone knows everyone. The teenagers are probably a tight-knit crowd. I have to be careful. I don't want to spook her—well, at least not yet.

"I'm passing through," I say. "My name's Molly."

"I'm Tatum."

We sit in silence for the next minute or so. I look at the

sun visor above my head, wondering if there might be a mirror there. Would she think I was weird if I checked? Would I even recognize myself?

"You don't have any luggage." The girl pulls me from my vain thoughts.

"What?"

"Luggage. You don't have any." She eyes me again, suspiciously. She's got a good point, too. If I'm passing through, a hitchhiker trying to see the country, I should at least have a change of clothing or maybe even a sleeping bag. I look down at my empty arms. I don't even carry a purse.

"It's in a locker at the bus station," I say quickly. "In Seattle. I used to have an old friend here, so I just came down for the day. But he's moved away."

She nods, obviously buying my story. There is a bus station in Evander, so she's probably thinking that's where I'll want to be dropped off. I turn to look out the window. After all these Fades, I've grown to recognize this road and its bumps and curves. The burned-down barn on the right that was standing until around my third Fade. The small lake across from it. I can't see it in the dark, but I know it's there. I swam in it, three days before I died. I know this road better than any other. Even the fog doesn't trip me up. We drive past the field where Walter dumped my body. Only a few more miles to go and we'll reach the town limits. At the rate the girl is driving, I'll be Fading in about two minutes.

Time to make my move.

When she puts her hand on the gearshift, I reach out suddenly and run my fingers across her skin. She instantly pulls back. So much for being discreet.

What comes next makes me even more obvious.

A wave of emotions crashes against my brain, making me cry out in horror. Pain. Sadness. I see flashes of events: people slamming against her in the hallway, computer messages filled with mean words, a girl with long curly hair screaming, angry feelings toward an older man, possibly a teacher. I see the girl crying in her bedroom, wiping away the tears, trying to pretend nothing's happening. All these horrible moments. A terrible loneliness.

That's only the beginning. What comes next is a million times worse.

Darkness. Shoes. Kicking. Blood. Water. Metal. A face being pushed under the surface, lungs screaming for air. Laughing.

Betrayal.

Something is about to happen. Something that will make my death look like a walk in the park. The images assault me. I can't make them stop. It's like watching a movie in fast-forward, only I'm hearing every single scream, feeling every single emotion. I double over, hands clenching my stomach as a stabbing pain cuts through me like a knife.

"Are you okay?" The girl begins to slow down.

I start to Fade. It's happening too quickly. I need to get this message out. I have to warn her. I reach out and grab her wrist. She tries to pull away, but I hold on tighter. I have to tell her.

"You're going to die. It will hurt and you'll be alone. And no one will help you." A sob catches in my throat as the words leave my lips.

"What? What do you mean?"

But I can't answer. I'm fading away into the gray upholstery.

I see her face. Eyes wide and terrified. Curious. She can't believe what's happening. Reality just won't allow her to believe.

Later, she'll find ways to convince herself that she made the whole thing up.

I pray with all my heart that she doesn't.

TATUM

What the hell?

Tatum's foot automatically slams against the brake. Twisting the steering wheel, she brings the car to a stop by the side of the road. Tires crunch gravel, and for a horrifying second she thinks she's heading straight into the ditch. Thankfully, it doesn't happen; no need to call a tow truck tonight. That would be one more proverbial backbreaking straw to send her father further off the deep end.

What the hell just happened?

The girl, Molly—that was her name—is gone. Tatum looks at the empty passenger seat, not believing her eyes, her brain frantically running on overdrive to try and find an explanation. Anything.

No one disappears into thin air. It's not possible.

Unless they're a ghost.

Or Tatum is completely crazy.

No such thing . . . I mean the ghost thing. Insanity's still up for debate.

The door. She must have opened it and slipped out. Jumped and barrel-rolled into the bushes. *No, that's not possible.* Tatum knows that didn't happen. She would have seen that. You can't just climb out while the vehicle is moving. You'd have to be a stunt person or some sort of acrobat. Can you even open a car door while it's moving? Tatum tends to automatically lock the car at night. Did she after Molly climbed in? She can't remember. Besides, the warning system would have gone wild. She looks up into the rearview mirror. Nothing moves in the fog behind her. Her brake lights blaze red, making the whiteness glow slightly pink.

This is stupid. No one disappears into thin air. But I know she didn't open the door and jump out. There's no way I wouldn't have noticed that. I'm not that self-centered. And I'm not going crazy. I didn't imagine the entire thing. I have no history of mental illness. No strange obsessive behaviors. I've never had any desire to cut myself or jump off bridges.

Do insane people know they're crazy?

That leaves ghosts and goblins and whatever else goes bump in the night. I left all those fantasies around the time I got a training bra.

She should get out of the car to check. Just in case. Maybe it happened so fast, her brain just didn't have time to process it. That has to be it. All the other ideas are too preposterous for Tatum to even want to consider. She turns the ignition off and opens the door. A blast of cool wind slips into the car, making her shiver.

"Hello?"

Nothing. Not even crickets. Tatum climbs out of the car, the security system beeping at her, letting her know the keys are still in the ignition. She snatches at them, shoves them in her pocket. Remembering there's a flashlight in the trunk, she reaches back into the car and presses the button. She closes the door quietly. The interior lights blink out, and she's left in the darkness.

Slowly she makes her way around to the trunk and pulls out the flashlight. Turning it on, she holds it in front of her, looking back down the road.

Nothing.

"Hello?"

Nothing but pavement and fog. She checks the ditch and shines the beam along the trees and bushes.

"Molly? Are you out there?"

If there really was a girl in her car a few minutes ago, she's done a good job of disappearing.

But how?

Tatum walks around the length of the car, even checking the backseat twice to make sure. Opening the passenger door, she shines the light against the seat, trying to find some sort of a clue. She reaches down and touches the upholstery. Runs her fingers along the area where the girl's back leaned against the cloth. It's still warm.

It isn't really much to go by, but it confirms that just a few minutes ago there was a girl sitting there—Molly—with her insanely long brown hair and funny outfit. And wasn't she sporting sandals? Who on earth wears those this time of the year? Tatum looks down at her own boots. She's only been outside the car for a few minutes, and already her toes are freezing. Sandals in the spring might work in Mexico, but not in Washington. Not even on a warm day.

Hippie clothing, her mother would call it. The type of stuff that you find in secondhand stores but that usually costs a fortune because it's considered retro and trendy.

Old-fashioned clothing. Out-of-date hairstyle. Sudden disappearance into thin air. This is too much like the movie she and Claudette watched last summer.

No, stop thinking like that. There's no such thing as ghosts.

But Molly couldn't be a ghost. Spirits are supposed to be cold. Isn't that what happens in movies? A chill goes through the room? Impossible. Tatum felt her. Molly reached out and touched her hand before she said those freaky things.

You're going to die. It will hurt and you'll be alone. And no one will help you.

What a horrible thing to say to someone. Was it a trick? Something that Claudette and the others came up with? A new way to torment Tatum even more? If so, where's the group now? Wouldn't they be hiding in the bushes, laughing their asses off at the chance to watch Tatum freak out?

Unless there's still more to come.

Tatum shivers and zips her hoodie up a little higher. Looking in both directions, she can't see any cars coming. Her car should be off to the side enough that someone won't hit her. Tatum stares into the bushes for a moment before stepping off the road and into the ditch. She can't help it; she has to double-check for two reasons: If this is a joke that's being played, she would rather die than let anyone think they scared her. And if

43

the girl really did fall out of the car, she can't drive off. Molly could be hurt, and Tatum could never leave someone by the side of the road if they needed help.

She didn't jump out of the car. You know this. You just don't want to admit it, because then you have to think of another answer. And you can't. You know these things don't exist. It's like believing in the boogeyman or Santa Claus. There's no such thing as ghosts.

The ditch is full of dew, and it soaks her jeans and boots. Tatum swears softly to herself as her foot sinks into the soft earth, making a disgusting squelching noise. The fog seems to close around her, circling her ankles, as if the earth is trying to swallow her up. She listens carefully to the night, for any sort of sound that might give her a clue.

Nothing.

She walks through the ditch, ignoring the cold as it crawls up her legs and makes her teeth chatter. Shining the flashlight in all directions, she spends a good five minutes before admitting that there is no girl there. No practical joke, either. Claudette wouldn't have done something like this without sticking around to get the last laugh. Besides, Tatum knows she wasn't followed because Claudette never knew about her Frog Road drives. That was the one thing Tatum kept to herself. Her secret mobile oasis, shared by no one. Not even her parents know she does this.

The bushes and trees to her left are thick and dark. The branches wind together, and dead leaves sway in the wind. Tatum definitely doesn't want to go there. Even if she could push her way through the brambles, she'd probably tear her clothing or scratch her face. What if she came across something even worse? For all she knows, there could be a decaying body hidden in that shadowy mess. Isn't that why ghosts haunt?

They're supposed to be unable to go on to the next world because of the way they died. Maybe this girl was murdered here, her body left to the coyotes and wolves. It's possible that it could have gone undetected for a number of years. Whoever owns this land hasn't done anything to it. It's never been farmed or clear-cut. No one seems to live there. She's never seen a house. At least not that she can remember.

Maybe that's why Molly appeared. She wants Tatum to help so she can leave this world and go on to the next.

Molly. No last name. That's not a lot to go by. Tatum turns and climbs back up to the road. If what happened tonight is real, if she really did see a ghost, there would have to be a record of it somewhere. Tatum can't be the only person to ever see her. And if she was indeed a restless spirit, murdered however many years ago, that would have made the news. Missing posters and all that stuff. Her smiling face on Walmart entrances. Parents out there somewhere, wondering what happened to their precious daughter.

Tatum climbs back into her car and starts the ignition. As she drives off, she keeps glancing at the passenger seat, wondering if the girl might reappear. But she doesn't.

She drives the car up and down Frog Road for the next hour, hoping to catch another glimpse, but Molly doesn't reappear. Finally, Tatum heads for home, all sorts of thoughts running around in her brain.

For the first time in weeks, she's thinking of something other than her own miserable life. She smiles to herself. Maybe this is exactly what she needs. A distraction.

* * *

45

It started in November.

"I've got a secret!"

Tatum closed her locker and turned to see Claudette grinning mischievously at her. Her curls, which Tatum was insanely jealous of, spread out in all directions; her hair had a real mind of its own yet always managed to look good. Wild and unruly, just like Claudette.

"What?" Tatum asked.

"I can't tell you." Claudette's eyes sparkled as she handed back Tatum's copy of *The Outsiders*. English period was next, and they'd been pretending to work on their assignments last night. Apparently Tatum must have left her book behind.

"Then why mention it in the first place?"

They turned and started walking toward class together.

"I can't talk about it here," Claudette said. "But I'm more than happy to give you all the X-rated details later. Let's meet up after final class and go over to my place. The 'rents are gone. But you have to promise to take it to the grave." She spun around and did a little dance step that made a poor freshman jump out of the way. "This is juicy."

"Let me guess," Tatum said. "It involves a boy."

"All the good secrets do," Claudette said.

They stepped into class just as the bell rang. Tatum took her seat and opened her book. Claudette was always finding new boys to fall in love with. It would only be a matter of time before she broke that poor boy's heart and went on to the next. Smiling, Tatum glanced over at her best friend before settling in to listen to Mr. Hawthorn, the English teacher, bore her to death with one of her favorite books.

* * *

Now that she looks back on it, boy was she wrong. When Claudette told Tatum she was going to go on a date with Mr. Paracini, Tatum was speechless. This wasn't some poor high school kid or the ever-forbidden college student; this was something that went way beyond that.

They were sitting on the bed in Claudette's room. Her friend had the school website open, Mr. Paracini's face enlarged across her screen.

"We're going to hook up on Friday night," Claudette said. "Nothing sexy, just hanging out. Hot kissing. Maybe some groping. Oh God, Tatum, don't give me that look." Claudette tossed a pillow at her. "Stop making that face."

"What face?" Tatum reached up to touch her cheek.

"Like you just found out your grandmother is running a crack house."

There was a pause while Tatum tried to rearrange her features, but the shock wouldn't let go.

"How on earth did you do this?"

"We're going to meet out of town. In Everett. Barry thinks that's the best way to do it. We need to keep this on the down-low. There are a lot of prissy people here." Claudette frowned. "That's the problem with small towns. Everyone needs to know everyone else's business. It's much harder to be discreet. Remember when I gave Larry Bronson a pity date? Thought I'd never live that one down."

"No, I mean, how did this happen?"

Claudette grinned wickedly. "That was tricky too. I hate

to brag, but I was a genius. I staked him out, of course. A few remarks. Some low-cut shirts. Tight jeans. No man could resist me. And you can't blame me. He's the hottest teacher around. Who wouldn't want a piece of him?"

Tatum grinned. Everything Claudette said was true. She was probably the prettiest girl at Hamilton and an absolute queen at flirting. No boy had ever turned her down for a date. She had the incredible knack of always knowing the right things to say and how to get boys to fall over themselves trying to please her. When Claudette put on the charm, the boys came a-running. And now apparently the men did too.

"We've been flirting back and forth all semester. Some of it's been hot and heavy; I'm surprised no one's picked up on it." She gave Tatum a glare that suggested Tatum should have known all along. She dug her phone out of her bag, pressed a few buttons, and then handed it to Tatum. "Sexting. Crazy stuff. Of course I've got him down under a different name. I'm not stupid. He's got two phones. One his wife doesn't know about. Keeps it on vibrate all the time." Claudette giggled loudly and pushed her hair back behind her shoulders.

Tatum accepted the phone but didn't really look. She didn't want to read her friend's X-rated texts. It would be too personal, like reading her diary. Yes, of course she knew Claudette flirted with Mr. Paracini. Heck, the entire female population at school flirted with him. He was incredibly handsome. Blond hair and blue eyes. Tall. Many a senior had spent time in his biology class ignoring her studies and staring at the way his jeans fit his body perfectly. Girls giggled about him in the bathroom during breaks. Tatum had even been a part of it. She remembered talking with Claudette and Juniper during lunch break, discussing how lucky Mr. Paracini's wife was to have snagged such a great piece of ass.

Tatum's face grew red at the memory. Now she was embarrassed. It was one thing to talk about how handsome a teacher was, but another to actually try and get a date with him. That was a rule that Tatum would never break. She wouldn't even know where to begin. But Claudette—well, she'd always been one to do whatever she wanted. Excitement and line crossing were what she dreamed of. The idea of dating a teacher would be something she'd consider a major achievement.

And Claudette loved a challenge.

"Don't you think this is a bad idea?" Tatum asked. "What if you get caught? Teachers aren't supposed to date students."

"What's the worst that could happen?" Claudette said. "It's not like they'd ever expel me or anything. All I'd have to do is tell them that Barry forced himself on me. Said I'd get a failing grade if I didn't do it." She widened her eyes and a hint of panic flashed across her face, making her look innocent and frightened at the same time. Not surprisingly, it worked. Tatum's heart actually skipped a beat.

"But Bar—I mean, Mr. Paracini could lose his job."

"That's only if we get caught," Claudette said with a grin. "And I don't plan on getting caught. It's all about the game. I've never gone all secret-agent with a guy before. I'm loving the whole idea. Oooh, maybe I could start wearing wigs." She grabbed one of her pillows off the bed and tossed it at Tatum. "Don't give me that look. I know what you're thinking. You need to lighten up. I'm going on a date with him! That's like everyone's fantasy. It's never going to lead to anything. Come on, Tatum. Even you can't deny his hotness."

Tatum agreed. She couldn't deny it. A good part of her was still weirded out; everything about it screamed wrong. But instead of criticizing, she smiled at Claudette and asked her what she was planning on wearing.

"Something really hot. And sexy. Oh man, we need to go shopping. Tonight! Text your mom and tell her you're staying for dinner." Claudette pulled her phone out and started pressing buttons. "I'll tell Mom I'm studying with you all night. Come on, if we leave now, we can hit Seattle with a few hours to find me a dress!"

* * *

That was the defining moment when Tatum stopped liking Claudette. She didn't know it at the time, but a small seed must have started in her brain. The weeks passed, and her anger grew as Claudette and Mr. Paracini continued to run around behind everyone's backs. And they were clever. Even in a small town, they still managed to pull it off without anyone knowing.

Anyone except Tatum.

She was the secret keeper. The excuse maker when Claudette's mom called. Tatum had no idea what lies Mr. Paracini was feeding his wife, but from what Claudette said about it, it sounded like the two of them didn't ever talk to each other.

"They're just married for the children," Claudette said. "She's apparently sleeping around on him, too. She thinks he doesn't notice, but Barry knows. He's putting together the divorce papers as soon as he can."

A web of lies.

After the proverbial crap hit the fan and all the ugly lies and blame had been shifted over to Tatum, she ran into Mrs. Paracini in the checkout line at Target. The older woman looked tired and disheveled, pushing around a red cart with two little children tossed in. If Tatum had seen her coming, she would have hidden longer in the stationery aisle. But instead she got in line right after her, not recognizing her from behind. It wasn't until Mrs. Paracini started tossing items on the counter that she turned and found herself face to face with Tatum.

At first she didn't say anything. She gave Tatum the iciest glare possibly known to mankind and slammed her shampoo bottle down hard enough to make it bounce. Tatum actually flinched, wondering how bad it would look if she turned around and ran. But there was already a bunch of people behind her; if she tried to leave, she'd really have to push her way through the crowd.

I'm not guilty, she wanted to say. *It wasn't me. Claudette made the whole thing up. I'm sorry.* So many words running around her mind.

She remembers everything Claudette said afterward, twisting the blame so no one would ever believe Tatum.

Tatum's been after him all year. She sent him love letters and asked him out on countless dates. I feel really bad 'cause she showed them to me. I should have told a teacher, but I didn't want to get her into trouble. She's got serious mental problems. She even told me she went to class early one day to surprise him. She took off all her clothes and sat on his desk. Mr. Paracini handled it well. He told her to get dressed and to stop it. He said if she continued her bad behavior, he'd have to report her.

Anything else, Claudette?

She told me that she wants to marry him. That the two of them

51

were destined to be together. She went to a fortune-teller or something like that, and apparently that's what they told her. She's really unhinged. I can't begin to tell you how much I've been dying to get this off my chest. It's horrible. I just want Tatum to get some help.

Tatum remembers staring at the magazines. Then at the candy. Anything to avoid looking Mrs. Paracini in the eyes. All she wanted was for that moment to be over so she could go home and hide in her bedroom till the end of the world.

The cashier ran Mrs. Paracini's items through without a problem. When it was over, the teacher's wife turned to leave. She pushed the cart about a foot and then stopped. She turned around and walked right over. Tatum stepped backward, bumping into the customer behind her.

"Psycho bitch."

Mrs. Paracini turned and walked off, her head held high, the red shopping cart squeaking.

It felt like the entire store had gone quiet. When the cashier finally broke the silence by asking Tatum if she wanted paper or plastic, Tatum fell apart. Instead of answering, she ran for the exit, ignoring the smirking checkout girl and the whispers and angry mumbles of the people waiting in line behind her.

She'd barely made it to her car when the tears came. Tatum sat there for a long time, bawling, thankful it was too dark for anyone to fully see what she was doing. Her hands felt like they would never stop shaking.

* * *

Tatum sits on her bed now, trying hard not to think about everything. She got home about fifteen minutes ago. She actually forgot to go to the coffee shop and buy the mocha she claimed she wanted in the first place.

She has her computer turned on, and her fingers hover over the keyboard. She's got Google open, but she's not sure what to type. She doesn't even know how to begin. The fact that she wants to do this is only making her feel even more foolish. Although she can't think of a single reason how, she's still positive she's the brunt of some stupid joke. But another voice nags inside her brain, louder now that she's alone, telling her that the whole thing goes far more mystical than that.

She types the words *ghost* and *Molly* and of course gets nothing. Lots of information on the movie *Ghost*. She's never seen it, but according to IMDb, it's good.

She adds to the search. She types in the proper name for Frog Road. She erases the name *Molly*.

She doesn't get anything on the first page. Wikipedia offers a list of famous ghosts throughout history. Who knew there were so many? The second hit is "how to tell if your place is being haunted." The third is a site full of people who claim to be victims of possession. The rest are listings for popular television shows and movies. Pictures of famous ghosts. The Brown Lady. The Headless Nun. Fun stories to scare your kids.

She moves her cursor across the results, reading each one, her inner voice laughing at her, calling her crazy for even trying this.

On the second page, she finds something. A forum set up to discuss current and past hauntings. She finds something under "American Hauntings—Share Your Stories."

GorgeousGus wrote: My friend saw a ghost in
Washington State. He lives east of Seattle and often

drives down this back road to get home. One night, he picked up a hitchhiker (yeah, I know, how freaking original). But he said that this girl, she called herself Molly, rode with him for about five miles. A total throwback from the sixties, massive hippie type. Totally outdated. Everything was fine until she started talking. She told him that his mother was going to die and that he should get her to show him where the will was. Then she disappeared right out of his passenger seat. He laughed the whole thing off, thinking he probably dozed off behind the wheel for a minute—until his mother keeled over of a stroke a month later. I kid you not! And he never found the will. They have no idea what happened to it, and now all the kids are fighting over the money. He should have listened! I've known this guy for years. He's not the type to make up these things. It took him three years before he even told me!

DumbEatingDonuts wrote: That ain't no ghost. Just those kids getting stoned on the medicinal marijuana.

MixMasterMic wrote: Oh man, I've heard this story. I grew up in that area. A young girl was murdered out there back in the late sixties I think. I remember my neighbor saying he picked her up one night. Almost gave him a heart attack. He's never driven down that road since. Goes miles out of his way just to avoid it. Why hasn't this been documented? This could be the real thing.

Oh. My. God.

That's her. That has to be her. Instant relief flushes over her body. If other people have seen Molly, that means she's not a figment of Tatum's imagination. She's not some sort of weird illusion designed by Tatum's brain because she's having a melt-down at school.

Molly is real.

And that means Tatum just saw a ghost.

A surprised yelp escapes her lips. No, this can't be real. She checks the dates on the forums, and the discussion occurred about two years ago. Tatum knows these things can be faked. It could still be some sort of joke being played on her. But why? She can't imagine what Claudette would hope to gain by making Tatum believe in ghost stories. They've known each other since they were in kindergarten. Claudette knows that she doesn't scare easily. If there's a logical reason behind this, Tatum can't think of it.

She needs to find out more. The Seattle library should have all the newspapers on the computer. But it could take a long time to go through them. Tatum only has a first name. She doesn't even have a date. The guy on the forum mentioned the murder happening in the late sixties. How many local murders could there be from that time period? Of course, it can't be that simple.

She wants to start looking tonight, but she can hear her parents coming up the stairs. If she gets going now, Tatum knows she'll be up all night. Yawning, Tatum decides that all the information will still be there tomorrow. After school, she'll head over to Bellevue and find a coffee shop to work at.

Turning off her laptop, Tatum can't help but grin. This is exactly what she needed. A mystery to keep her occupied. Something to make her forget that every other moment in her life is hell.

If what happened tonight is real, and she did see a ghost, this is something good that she can do. Molly's body must be out there somewhere along Frog Road. 'Cause everyone knows that's why ghosts haunt: they have unfinished business. She's probably buried somewhere in the fields around Frog Road. If Tatum can find her, she can help the girl reach the afterlife. How amazing would that be?

Just think of the possibilities! If Tatum died, she'd want her parents to have her body so they could put her to rest. Molly probably has family out there somewhere. Are they still waiting around the house, a small flicker of hope rushing through them every time the phone rings or someone knocks on the door? Is it possible they've been waiting over forty years for news of their wayward daughter? If Tatum can solve the mystery, she'll be a hero in their eyes.

And what about Molly's killer? What if there's evidence on the body that could bring him or her to justice? What kind of cool-ass justice could that end up being?

Crawling under the covers, she smiles to herself as she turns out the light. She's already forgotten the warning that the ghost gave her; the words *You're going to die* have escaped her memory.

That's her first big mistake.

MOLLY

No. Oh, no.

Please, God, no.

I can't get the images out of my mind. Even though I'm no longer in the car, no longer touching the girl's skin, the vision refuses to let go. It's gotten inside me, twisting and turning things around until I can't actually tell if it's happening to me personally.

It's like being tortured all over again.

I'm on the ground. There are multiple pairs of legs surrounding me. Some kick at me, sending me crawling around the circle in which I'm trapped. No matter which way I scramble, someone reaches out to push me back toward the middle. I feel something wet in my hair. A boy with a large nose and beady eyes hocks up another loogie and lets it fly. It lands on my cheek and I cry out, frantically trying to wipe it away.

Why are you doing this to me? Why do you hate me so much? I

told the truth. Claudette's the liar. She should be here, not me. Her!
Go after her!

These are not my thoughts.

From behind, someone grabs my arms and pulls them back.
I struggle, but I can't get free. I don't know who is behind me,
but their breath smells heavily of spearmint. They're breathing
heavily too. Air rushes in and out of my ear canal, making my
skin wet from the saliva. My stomach churns, food threatening
to escape. I can't help it. The smell is too overpowering. The
hot breath. Someone puts a hand across my eyes, yanking my
head up in a painful jerking manner. I bring my fingers up to
try and free myself, but I'm slapped away. Now it's my turn to
gasp for air. I wonder what my breath smells like. Crazy. I'm
going crazy.

When they finally release me, the tendons in my neck
groan in protest.

Why am I feeling this? I'm not alive. I'm not her.

I can hear girls laughing.

"Aww. Is the poor baby going to cry? Go ahead. No one
here to help you."

"I warned you. This is what we do to snitch bitches."

I won't cry. No. I refuse. I bite down on my lip and look up
at the black sky, refusing to let the burning in my eyes spread
across my face. Someone steps on my fingers, grinding them
down with their shoes. I hear it, the exact moment when my
finger cracks.

Funny. I cried with Walter. I bawled my eyes out. Begging.

But I won't beg this time.

Because it's not me. I'm the girl in the car. Tatum. This is
her future.

The reality brings me back. Closing my eyes, I remember who I am.

I am Molly.

When I open my eyes, I'm back at the lake. Parker is waiting for me. Or maybe he's just sitting still. It's hard to tell. He doesn't say anything as I reappear. He's studying the woods to the right. He spends a lot of time looking at the trees and the way they never move. He says sometimes he thinks all the answers are hidden in the valley and we just need to discover them. I'm often glad I don't have Parker's mind. He spends far too much time inside it.

I search around for Mary and spot her on the other side of the lake. She's chatting with the guy from South Africa. Throat slit open in his bed because he witnessed a murder. Now he haunts the dump where the landlord unceremoniously tossed his furniture after no one came to claim it.

"Something bad happened," I say.

Parker turns to look at me. "What do you mean?"

I tell him all the gory details. This is the first time I've ever foreseen someone's death. I even tell him how I slipped from my reality into hers, sharing her pain and torment. I give exact details to Parker until his steady resolve falters. His eyes grow smaller and smaller until he rubs his forehead with his long fingers. Mary comes by halfway through, and I'm forced to start from the beginning. Every time I relive this, part of me slips out of control. I'm wasting time sitting here. I need to get back to the real world. I need to save that girl.

"Are you sure?" Parker asks.

"Of course I'm sure," I say.

"It could have been a memory. One of the girl's, perhaps.

It might not even be real. It could be something she read in a book or saw in the motion pictures. We don't know if all your visions are real. There's no way we can test that theory either. I don't doubt what you saw, but it may not be true. Maybe you've just incorporated from your own death? Made things worse?"

"I didn't make this up," I snap.

"Never said you did," Parker says.

"And I can't think that way," I say. "These visions I get are real. They tell me things that are happening. I know things that these people have never told me. Secrets. I see the looks on their faces when I tell them."

"How could that girl's death be happening if she was in the car with you?"

"Because it hasn't happened yet!" I whip around in frustration, glancing back at the crowd of dead people on the beach. They're all quietly watching. Anger flares through me, although I know only I'm to blame. How can they not stare? The way I'm carrying on, they'd be hard-pressed to ignore me.

I want to scream at them. Run across the beach, hurling words, kicking up sand, and upsetting everyone out of their silence. Can't they see what's wrong here? Not just with the girl, but with the system. What good is being a ghost if there's no purpose? If there's no way to help the living? I want to knock over the wrought-iron tables and those stupid parasols that never change. Tear down the paper lanterns and toss them in the lake. I want people to speak up, sing songs, get drunk, and argue among themselves. I want them to feel things. What good is being dead if we can't be alive?

"But that's not the way your visions usually work," Parker

says, his voice calmer and far more quiet than mine. He's sitting on his log, his forehead wrinkled and thoughtful. If he's noticed the fire under my skin, he's pretending it doesn't exist. "Why are you now experiencing something different?"

"Someone changed the rules."

"That doesn't happen."

"There's always a first time."

I can't understand why he's arguing with me. Why can't he nod and pull me close, try and calm my anger and fear? If there were ever a time to be touched and soothed, now would be it. Just like my father used to pull me onto his lap when I was a little girl. He'd hold me tight, letting me smell his aftershave and sweat. In his arms, I could allow myself to calm down. Relax. But here, no such things exist. Touching is only something we used to do. We've forgotten. Instead Parker can only be logical. Why must he make me doubt myself?

"That's not really true now, is it?" Mary says. Her eyes are gleaming. I can always depend on her for a bit of drama. "Molly's foreseen the deaths of loved ones before."

"Yes!" I say. "Yes, I've done that!"

"I'm not saying it's not possible," Parker says. "I'm just saying it's different. Telling someone their elderly mother is passing is not the same as telling a young girl she's about to be beaten and killed. It's something we need to discuss. It won't do you any good to get worked up." He waves his hand around. "It's not like we can do anything. We're stuck. You don't even have a date. And time moves differently here. For all we know, it could have already happened."

"No," I say. "I refuse to believe that."

"I wonder why," Parker says. He pauses, staring off at the

water. Thirty seconds go by, and I start to think he's simply lost the words he meant to speak. "That many people against a young lady. Whatever might possess them to behave that way? How many did you say again?"

"I don't know for sure," I say. "About ten, at least. More. I could hear voices even if I couldn't see them all."

"All those people against a wee girl?" Mary says. "That's why I'm glad I'm dead. Stupid mentality of men. Cowards. They need to group together to attack. Don't have the tally-wags to go at it themselves. Why, back in me day there was this young bloke. Nicked some bread. You should have seen the way they hunted him down. Disgusting." She spits on the dirt, and the saliva instantly disappears. "Absolute cowards."

"That's not really the point," I say. "How can I stop this from happening? How could God show that to me and not allow me a way to help?"

"I'm pretty sure God has nothing to do with this place," Mary snaps. "If he did, he'd see how bloody boring it is and give us some jollies."

"There is a plan to everything," Parker says.

"Prove it," Mary says. "Find me the plan in this place. Sure, Molly's got that fancy little gift. But the rest of us just scare innocents every bloody full moon. There's no reason for all this. No purpose. We sit here every damn day and do nothing but stare at a bunch of water. What kind of afterlife is that? Where's our paradise? Where's my eternal rest? Instead I'm stuck here, occasionally showing my deathly knickers to a bunch of alley cats. And they don't care in the slightest. Have you ever tried scaring a cat? Bloody impossible."

I'm too restless, so I stand up. I walk over to the edge of the lake and look across the water. I love Mary and her observations and opinions. She's one of the only people here who can make this place seem like fun. But right now, it's not making me feel better. She's right. I can't do anything. I've never appeared to the same person more than once. I'll sit on this log for days or months, until finally I'm summoned back up again to warn someone about his or her wayward spouse. By then it'll be too late.

Being helpless is the worst thing in the world. And that's what I am. So are Parker and Mary and every other person who finds themselves dropped off in our little valley. Parker is right. If there is a universal plan, none of us can see what it is. And when we're stuck here, some of us for centuries, it's hard to imagine what purpose all of this holds.

But this. The ability to foresee Tatum's death. If I could find a way to prevent it, then I'd have meaning. My death wouldn't have been for nothing.

Parker comes over to join me. We stand together, listening to Mary ranting quietly to herself. She's really wound up. It'll take a while before she grows calm. This isn't the first time we've seen her like this.

"Maybe you'll see her again," Parker says. His shoulder brushes against mine. The thickness of his linen shirt presses against my skin.

"It's never happened before," I say.

"There's always a first time," he says. "You said it yourself: This is something different. You've never foreseen a death. Did you get a clue to when it'll happen?"

I think about it for a few minutes. Were there any hints to give away a time and place? "No," I finally say. "But soon. The weather was the same. Cold, but not winter."

"Let's wait a bit," Parker says. "Maybe you will go back. If not, I might be able to help you."

I look up at him. His brown eyes dart to the right, straight into the forest. "What do you mean?"

"I've been working on something for a while," he says. "Nothing concrete yet. Just ideas. But I may have found a way out."

I open my mouth to protest, but before I can, Parker starts to disappear.

Fade.

"My turn," he says. Then he's gone.

Poof.

* * *

One night, a few months after I turned fifteen, I pulled a small suitcase from under my bed and began filling it. I didn't need a lot, just a few things to get me through the next week. My peasant skirt, the love beads that Dad had brought home from a Mardi Gras trip to New Orleans, my two favorite blouses, and whatever else I thought I couldn't live without. I couldn't help but feel worried when I snapped the lock down.

"It's going to be great," Andrea, my best friend, said. She had her own bag, already in the trunk of her car. She sat at my vanity, rifling through the makeup on the glass stand, trying to find a color she liked.

"It's going to be amazing," I said. Noticing my hairbrush

on my nightstand, I reached over and snagged it. Wouldn't do me any good to accidently leave that behind.

I remember the heat that night. We were in the height of summer, and the humidity wasn't going away without a fight. There was so much moisture in the air that every time I inhaled, I felt as if I were trying to breathe underwater. The sweat stuck to my skin, dripping down my forehead and into my eyes. It pooled in the center of my bra. My clothing was still damp, even though the sun had gone down several hours ago. The window in my little bedroom was open, but there wasn't a breeze in sight.

Andrea and I were heading to Bethel, New York. It was 1969, and we were going to Woodstock.

I was more excited than I could remember. In my fifteen years, I'd never even been across state lines. My father was a trucker, so his idea of a vacation was cracking open a beer and sitting on the couch. The farthest I'd gone was an hour or two away to visit relatives when I was little. This was going to be my big adventure. And it would be better than Disneyland, more alluring than white sand beaches and faraway exotic lands.

Hendrix. Janis Joplin. Arlo Guthrie. Grateful Dead. CCR. The Band.

Andrea and I had spent our entire summer sitting on my porch with the music blasting. Thankfully, I had cool neighbors who often came over to join us instead of complaining about the noise. We stuck extension cords together so I could put my old record player out on the steps. Once the sun set, taking away some of the unbearable heat, we'd dance around the yard, our bare feet trampling the dying grass. People would bring over beers and lemonade. Even my brother would tear himself away from the television to come join us. It was the best summer I could ever remember having.

Andrea and I babysat to raise money for our addiction. We spent days cruising record stores, buying up all the new vinyl we could find. Weekends were memorable: sneaking into bars in neighboring towns and listening to local musicians play their hearts out. I bought a guitar from a pawnshop and began to teach myself a few chords, but I grew disillusioned, because no matter how I stretched my fingers across the fret, no matter how I tried to pluck the strings, I couldn't get the right sounds. I finally gave up and sold the instrument to my neighbor after coming to the conclusion that I didn't have to make beautiful sounds; I just needed to hear them.

The music couldn't get loud enough.

Music was life. The way I felt when the sounds surrounded me, carrying me away to far-off places that didn't exist. The way it made me forget all my problems, not that they were really worth complaining about. It was as if something had been lying dormant inside of me my entire childhood. Once it awakened, it was the only thing that mattered.

I never told my dad I was going. I knew he wouldn't approve, even though Andrea had her beat-up Ford car that burned blue smoke but still managed to be reliable. We scraped together enough gas money to get us there and back. I borrowed a tent from one of the families I babysat for.

We did all this under complete secrecy. Andrea's parents were relaxed and fine with her attending the concert. They'd even expressed interest in going themselves for a bit. They gave her the lecture about not doing drugs or drinking with strange men and then gave her twenty bucks for gas. But I knew Dad would be furious if he knew my upcoming secret. I was only fifteen, and he wouldn't want me crossing state lines. That's why I never asked him. I figured I could deal with the consequences when I got back. Even if he grounded me for the rest of the year, it would be worth it.

Lucky for me, Dad was on the road, spending long hours driving from one end of the country to the other. I was the good kid, never doing anything that got me seriously into trouble. My brother, Marcus, was two years older and had a job at the auto shop that kept him busy. Dad didn't think twice about leaving us alone for weeks on end while he worked. He knew he'd come home after each shift and find the house still standing. Besides, he didn't really have a choice. Mom had run away when Marcus and I were both still little. They'd gotten married far too young, and I guess she never could accept the idea of staying in one place for the rest of her life. One evening she packed her bags, called a babysitter, and snuck out in the middle of the night while Dad worked a double shift. No goodbye kiss. No letter. Just the babysitter, angry and annoyed the next morning when Marcus and I awoke.

Dad did whatever he could to try and raise us kids. Trucking brought in good money. We needed the income. From the time Marcus was twelve and I was ten, we'd pretty much been keeping the house clean and doing our homework by ourselves. Our neighbor would keep an eye on us to make sure nothing bad happened, and Dad often made it home on weekends to check that we'd behaved while he was away.

Marcus and I were both self-sufficient and there were no pets to take care of. Dad was allergic to dogs. The town we lived in was amazingly boring and predictable. Nothing exciting ever happened. The "bad" families were just poor; there hadn't been a murder in twenty years, not since two brothers got into a fight over who got to keep a prized horse.

Dad was delivering a load of foodstuff out to the West Coast and wasn't due back until three days after Woodstock ended. I planned on going there and coming back before he even noticed I was gone.

"Where are you going?" Marcus asked when Andrea and I came into the kitchen. I had the suitcase under my arm, and Andrea was carrying the tent. So much for hoping he'd still be at work and I wouldn't have to say anything.

"We're going camping at the lake," I said. I handed Andrea my suitcase, and she headed out the door, letting the screen slam behind her. I went over to the kitchen and grabbed a few items. "Where's the kettle? Do you mind if I take it? We might want to make coffee in the morning."

Marcus opened the old Frigidaire and yanked one of Dad's beers from the back. "Yeah, sure. I didn't hear anything 'bout camping. Who's all going to be there?"

"It's just us girls, so keep it quiet," I said. "No boys allowed." I grabbed the kettle off the counter and packed it, along with a few other things I thought would come in handy.

My brother put his beer against the counter and used the corner to catch the edge of the bottle cap. Beer foamed from the top, soaking his fingers. The cap rolled along the floor and went straight under the fridge.

"You better replace that before Dad gets home," I said.

"I will," Marcus said. He turned and headed off into the

living room, where he'd probably sit in front of the black-and-white television until he fell asleep. At seventeen, my brother was already getting old. Sure, he still liked to party and listen to music, but most nights he just wanted to relax.

When I look back on it now, I can see how easy it was to leave. I wanted adventure. I dreamed about it. Funny, when some of the ghosts around here talk about the choices that led them down their fateful roads, they often express regret, wishing they'd made different decisions. They wish they'd never left home and gone out on their own. They wish their spouses had been more attentive so they wouldn't have had to stray. If only they'd stopped drinking. Or not gone down that dark alley at night. Or never talked to strangers.

I never regretted leaving my house that night. No matter how short my life turned out, that time between the moment I left for Woodstock and the moment before I got into the van with Walter was the happiest in my life.

"Come on," Andrea said, sticking her head inside the door. "Let's get going."

I didn't stop to take one last glance at the worn-down kitchen before leaving. I was still under the impression that I'd be back in a week. And technically, I was. Julian drove me back so I could pick up more clothing and other personal items. But by then the place no longer felt like home. I'd already moved on.

I never intended to fall in love. But love is like that. It can easily slap you on the head from behind and you don't care.

* * *

We sit, our backs to the trees. Our faces stare dispassionately at the blue water.

"It hasn't happened yet," I say. I'm leaning against the log beside Mary, waiting for Parker to return. "I'm sure of it. This thing I saw. I'm sure I'm being given enough time to make a difference. Do you think we can change fate?"

"I don't know," Mary says. "We're puppets right now, ain't we? Being played on an imaginary string. Can't stop Fading."

"But what if we can do something?"

"Like what?" Mary arranges her dress and yanks at her petticoats. I catch a glimpse of slender leg before it disappears under all that ruffle. "If I could change anything, I'd like me a new outfit. It gets boring wearing the same dull thing all the bloody time. Christ almighty, I just want to breathe." She yanks at the strings on her corset.

"You don't breathe," I remind her.

"Well, it feels like I do." Mary finally lets the outfit settle against her chest. The way her breasts push up toward her chin, I can imagine that many a man found them attractive in her living days. Her brown hair falls gently against her chest, and she pushes it back aggressively. "What I'd like are some of those modern clothes they wear today. A pair of trousers! I'd kill to have that. Always thought dresses were too prissy anyway. When I was a wee girl, I used to run around naked. Always hid me dresses, I did. Ma was forever scolding me. She was constantly bending me over her knee. No wonder I turned out the way I did. If ever there was someone born to be a dance-hall girl, it was me."

I think of Tatum and her warm winter clothes. They are so different from the styles I used to wear. Of course, I wore pants

70

too: bell-bottom jeans with painted flowers across the denim. I also wore skirts, soft cotton that slid against my legs and spun outward when I twirled. As much as I'd like to see the way my breasts might rise up in a corset like Mary's, I'm thankful I'm stuck in my simple yellow blouse. But right now isn't the time to be discussing wardrobes, not when I have too many other thoughts on my mind.

"It hasn't happened yet," I say again.

"What?" Already Mary's lost the plot.

"The girl is still alive. Maybe I saw it wrong." I turn on my seat, my thoughts hopeful. "I warned her. She knows. She'll be able to protect herself. Stay away from wherever she's supposed to go."

"It'll happen," Mary says. "It always does. The living are too stupid to listen to warnings. Especially from a bloody ghost. I mean, come on, would you have believed it if some pale creature appeared to you and gave you a warning? No. You would have sauntered along, oblivious, like the rest of us."

"I don't know," I say, but I know she's right.

"It'll happen. And I wish I could be there, in all my finest ghostly getup, all cut and torn the way the bastard left me. No offense, chicky, you're too pretty a lass to scare anyone. But me? I'm the queen of gore. At least my killer had the decency to go after me alone. Of course, he was still mental. God-fearing bunch? I'll give them something to fear."

I don't say anything. I don't see the point. Instead I glance out at the water and wait for Parker to return.

TATUM

"I'm going to be late coming home."

Tatum sits at the table while Mom spoons scrambled eggs onto a plate. That's the number one rule of the household: everyone has breakfast. No exceptions. Mom's a dietitian. She spends her days at the hospital, teaching people the benefits of following healthy guidelines and making sure everyone eats the right amount of each food group. Because of this, the kitchen cupboards are filled with all sorts of crap. There's not a potato chip or piece of bacon to be found. And Mom is constantly going off on rants about the proper way to eat. Tatum has officially heard "Breakfast is the most important meal of the day" more than any other teenager in the world.

"Why's that?" The toaster pops up, and Mom grabs the slices of sunflower bread, shoving them onto the plate before passing it over.

Tatum takes the salt, ignoring Mom's frown, and heavily flavors the eggs. Her mother might be good at making everyone eat, but she's never been the best at cooking. "I've got a paper due. Thought I'd get some work done on it today. Going to head into Seattle and hit the library."

"Into the city? Tonight? Why don't you go to the library here . . ." The words get stuck in her throat.

Mrs. Paracini's sister runs the local library. The last time Tatum tried going there, the afternoon Tuesday book club, a group of middle-aged women, spent the entire time glaring at Tatum and talking loudly among themselves. And if someone tries to convince you that small-town people are always polite and friendly, they should spend a few days in Hannah. It ended with Tatum going home in tears, and the next day Mom got into a fight with a gossipy nurse while getting gas at the Shell.

Hannah is a town that Tatum no longer has any privileges in. No matter where she goes, people stop and stare. Then they talk. *Discreet* isn't a word in their dictionaries. Even Mom, with her "Ignore it and it'll all go away attitude," has grown weary of hang-up calls in the dead of night. What's worse are the emails suggesting Tatum be "hospitalized." She's become the town Lolita, the harlot, the girl everyone wants to see fail.

"Okay," Mom says. "But be home by seven. And keep your phone on."

"In the library?"

"There's no law against silent mode."

* * *

Tatum's day is blissfully uneventful. Sure, there are the whispers, the laughter, more red lipstick on her locker—but that's nothing she can't handle. She's learned to deal with all of that stuff like a pro.

Lunch is spent in an empty classroom, once everyone has already headed to the cafeteria. Experience has taught her that unless she eats with her back to the wall, she's an open target for all sorts of food-related attacks. These days she's better off finding a quiet corner somewhere and eating alone with a book.

Hiding isn't what Tatum does best. She's always enjoyed being surrounded by groups of friends. She'd much rather spend her weekends at parties and socializing than sitting at home pretending to study. In the past few months, she's read more than she did in her entire previous high school life. Books may help her escape, but they're not the reality she wants. She misses sitting in the lunchroom with Claudette, Juniper, and the others, gossiping about the boys, comparing teachers, complaining about assignments, and all those other important things that make high school so much fun.

Now, when the bell rings for her last class, she makes haste. She heads for her locker, uses some tissue to remove the lipstick drawing of her weighing roughly six hundred pounds, grabs her books, and practically walks right into Graham and Levi, who have decided to corner her for a laugh.

"Looked just like you." Graham tries to reach out and stroke her face, but she pulls back at the last second, nearly smacking her head into the locker.

Levi leers at her next. "I heard you go to Taco Bell every day and order twenty bucks' worth of food. No wonder the bio room smells so bad."

Pushing past the guys, she ignores their taunts. It's not

like she hasn't heard it all before. They're not exactly the most original when it comes to insults. Part of her always wants to respond—she's got some great comebacks for the never-ending fat jokes—but experience has taught her to stay silent. If she answers, they'll just follow her around. They're dogs that can't ignore the cat.

Outside, she makes it to her car without running into Claudette. All four tires are still full of air, and a quick walk around reveals no suspicious wet marks. Tatum jumps in and peels out of the parking lot. She drives carefully for the first few miles to make sure no one's tailing her.

All in all, it's been a good day.

At the Bellevue exit, she heads to the closest Seattle's Best Coffee and snags a good seat in the corner. She plugs her laptop into the wall and brings up Google. In another tab she loads the library website and puts in her PIN information. Accessing the newspaper catalog, she pauses.

There are so many. Hundreds of different papers in Washington State alone. Thousands throughout America. Quite possibly millions of articles to go through.

And all she has is a first name.

Suddenly Tatum feels foolish. What was she thinking? That she'd punch in a few letters and magically pull up all the information she needed to solve a murder? She doesn't even have a date. Sure, Molly did look like she was out of the sixties, with her long flowing skirt and love beads. But there are lots of girls who dress that way even now. The hippie style is always in. Even Tatum has a peasant blouse hidden away in her closet.

The odds of finding this girl are about as good as Tatum

waking up tomorrow morning and discovering that the past few months have been nothing but a bad dream.

A needle in a haystack.

Sigh.

But she has to try. It's not as if she's got a million other things to do. Taking a sip of her mocha, Tatum stares at the computer screen. She goes back to Google and begins to type.

Molly. Murder. Hannah, Washington.

Millions of hits.

Refusing to be dejected, she reads through the first few pages. There's nothing useful, mostly information about the ecstasy drug with the same name, the occasional person named Molly involved in an obscure murder trial, movie reviews, and a bunch of inconsequential stories, mostly involving people named Hannah. Why couldn't she come from a town that didn't have a female name? Towns like Bellingham or Everett would be a lot easier to Google.

Tatum spends the next half hour going through different words, trying to come up with something. Anything. The front door to the coffee shop has an annoying bell that sounds every time it's opened. Each time it rings and dings, she looks up just in case. After the twentieth or so time, she sees a familiar face. She almost spills her drink all over the laptop in surprise.

Scott Bremer.

Okay, not worth getting upset over. At least she doesn't think so. Scott isn't part of Claudette's crowd. He moved to Hannah a year ago from the East Coast, and he's a bit of a loner. He sits in the back row and never speaks up in class unless asked a direct question from a teacher. She's never actually seen him hang out with anyone. Sure, he talks to a few of the guys, but not in a chummy sort of way. At lunchtime, he's usually in the cafeteria, surfing the Internet on his phone with his headphones on. Scott lives two blocks away from Tatum. She remembers how the girls thoroughly checked him out the first month. He was new meat and not bad-looking, either. He's got this amazing spiky brown hair and piercing dark eyes. But if Scott wanted a girlfriend, he didn't show interest. He even blew off Claudette's flirts as if they were nothing more than polite conversation from his grandmother. It ended with Claudette declaring him probably gay or a eunuch, and he was pretty much ignored from then on.

Tatum has talked to him an entire two times. Once because he sat behind her in chemistry class and asked to borrow her notes after being out sick for a few days. The second time was a polite hello when they came across each other on the street. He was walking their family dog, a big, hyper chocolate-brown Lab. The animal jumped on Tatum, and Scott seemed really embarrassed about it. He couldn't get away fast enough.

Actually, she's talked to him three times. He was the one to give her the napkins yesterday when she was trying to deal with the urine on the tires.

Is it possible that Claudette has recruited him in her games?

No, it doesn't seem that way. In fact, it looks like Scott actually has a job at the coffee shop. He goes behind the counter and starts chatting to the girl at the cash register. Running his hand through his hair, he briefly catches Tatum watching him. A look of surprise crosses his face before he nods in her direction. Then he disappears into a room in the back.

Tatum finds herself exhaling in relief. Nothing but a coincidence. She goes back to her work.

Molly. Disappearance. Washington State. 1960–1969.

Six hundred fifty thousand hits.

Maybe she should try looking at the missing-children website. How many Mollys can there be?

Nope, that turns out to be useless. A quick search tells her she's not going to gain any ground that way. Unless she finds a last name, she's going nowhere fast. Besides, the records don't go that far back. They focus more on people who wouldn't now be in their sixties.

"Hey."

She looks up to see Scott Bremer standing over her with a broom in his hands. He's looking at her computer screen. His voice is soft and he doesn't sound sarcastic, unlike everyone else who talks to Tatum these days.

"Um . . . hi."

"Lost someone?"

"No." She closes the website instantly, feeling stupid. "Just doing some research for a project."

"Really? What one?"

Of course he'd have to ask. She pauses too long, trying to come up with a reasonable answer. "Just my own thing. I'm writing a story."

Scott leans on the broom. "Cool. Like a creative writing thing?"

"Yeah, something like that," she says. A part of her wants him to go away. Another part wants him to stay. It's been too long since someone her age has actually talked to her. "A ghost story," she adds.

"Very cool. What kind?"

"What do you mean?"

Scott looks back at the register to make sure it's still empty. "There's all sorts of ghosts. Poltergeists. Evil spirits. That paranormal-activity crap. Then there's the kind that are searching for something or can't cross over until their secrets are uncovered. True stories. Made-up stuff. All kinds."

Tatum grins. "True story," she says. "About a ghost named Molly. One I heard about recently. A girl who was murdered in Hannah."

"I didn't realize Hannah had its own ghost story."

"Neither did I," she says. "But like I said, I just heard it."

Scott tilts his head to the side and puts more weight on his broom. "So what does she do?"

"Do?"

Scott gives her a look as if to suggest that Tatum is way out of her league. "What's her ghostly shtick? Does she hang by the river and lure men to their deaths? Haunt castles while wearing a bloody gown? Freak out cats? All ghosts do something."

"Oh," Tatum says. "I think she's a hitchhiker."

Now it's Scott's turn to smile. "Ahh, the old standby. Hitchhiking. Gets into a poor unsuspecting stranger's car, rides along for a while before disappearing from the passenger seat."

Tatum's hopes soar. "You've heard about her?"

"Nah. But the hitchhiking ghost story is famous. An urban legend. She's always a local girl who gets killed by some crazy nutjob. There are different variations. My mom always uses hitchhiker stories to freak out my little sister and make sure she never accepts rides from strangers, that sort of crap. And my granny loves all that supernatural stuff. She's got tons of books."

"Is your grandmother from here? Do you think she'd know

any of the local stories?" Tatum can't help but think this could be a lead. "Molly haunts Frog—I mean, the road that goes past Evander, and it stuck with me. I found a forum with people who claim to have seen her. I thought it would make a good story. I do a lot of writing. Just me and my laptop." She swallows hard, trying to make her mouth stop moving. She's overdoing it. Scott is going to call her bluff. The last time she wrote something for fun was years ago. She's no writer. Tatum can barely keep up with a diary. What if Scott asks her more questions? Oh God, what if he wants to read her nonexistent story?

Thankfully, Scott is cool. "Not sure. What do you need to know?"

"A last name," Tatum says. "And some more information. I think it happened in the sixties. If your grandmother lived here then, she might have heard something."

"Yeah, she's been here forever. My mom grew up here too." Scott scratches his arm. "I'll ask for you. Like I said, Granny's really into all that spirit stuff. She's even gone to a séance before. She'll bore you to death if you ask about it. A ghost named Molly. Haunts the road by Evander. I can remember that."

"That would be great, thanks."

There's a bit of an awkward pause while they try not to stare at each other. The barista behind the counter starts up the espresso machine. The sound of milk steaming only intensifies the silence.

"Um . . . I didn't know you worked here."

"I started a few months ago. Saving for college. But I'm surprised. You're the first person from school I've seen in here." He absently kicks at the broom bristles with his foot. "It's a long ways to come for coffee."

"Yeah, well, sometimes I need to find a quiet place where I can actually get work done." She practically cringes at the lame excuse. And by the look on Scott's face, she knows he's thinking about Mr. Paracini. Of all the stupid things to say, she had to say the one thing that would bring attention to those horrible lies.

But thankfully, Scott doesn't go there. He just nods like driving forty minutes out of the way for a mocha is something he does all the time. In fact, he does, considering he's the one with the job way out here. There are plenty of places closer where he could earn a paycheck.

"Well, I'd better get back to work," he says as he looks over his shoulder, where the female server stares off into space. "I'll ask my grandma about the ghost. She'll love the idea of someone writing a story. She'll probably demand to read it."

"Thanks again. Have fun."

Scott turns and begins to walk away. Pausing briefly, he almost turns back to her, but then something must make him decide otherwise. Swishing the broom across the floor, he does a little dance step to the Nirvana song playing over the speaker. He looks back at her and winks. Tatum grins before she can stop herself.

Be careful.

No, maybe everyone in the world isn't out to get her after all. Maybe Tatum's been wrong about Scott all this time. Perhaps he isn't a loner, just more of the shy, silent type. She looks at the back of his Hendrix shirt and decides she likes the way his jeans fit. Also, he's wearing a kick-ass pair of Docs. Black with bright blue laces. Maybe if she hadn't listened to Claudette she might have given Scott the time of day much sooner.

But can she trust anyone?

Sighing, she slams her laptop closed and shoves it in her bag. Today's been nothing but wasted time. No, that's not completely true. Hopefully, Scott will be able to find out some information.

What she needs is a chance to talk to Molly again. She grabs her things and heads for the door. She'll be home early for supper, and Mom will be thrilled. And after it's dark, she's going to have to take a drive out to Frog Road again.

* * *

"What do you think?"

They were hanging in the bathroom during lunch. Claudette was staring at herself in the mirror, trying out a new lipstick. Dark red. She smacked her lips together a few times before applying a second coat.

"It's hot," Tatum said without really looking. Juniper had just sent her a text, wondering where the hell they were. She had snagged the good table, and the cafeteria was serving burritos that looked like rancid crap. Not a good visual. But it would have to do; she'd already tossed the lunch Mom packed for her. There was only so much tofu a girl could take.

"So Barry and I are going to spend the night together on Friday. His wife is taking the kids down to visit the grandparents, and he'll have the house all to himself. Can you believe it? An entire night together."

"What about last weekend?"

Claudette sighed dramatically and tossed the lipstick in her bag. Although she'd checked when they first came in, she bent down a second time to make sure the bathroom stalls were empty. A sure sign that something especially juicy was about to come from her lips.

"Last weekend we spent at that motel that smelled like dead fish," she said. "Sure it was fun and Barry bought me those roses, but it's not the same. This is going to be at his place. In his bed! Oh God, Tatum, I'm going to be lying right where his wife sleeps. How weird is that?"

"I thought you said they don't sleep together."

"They don't. Not *that* way. But I'm pretty sure they don't have separate rooms. Besides . . ." Claudette moved in closer until her lips were practically touching Tatum's cheek. "You and I sleep together all the time too. Does that mean you're my girlfriend?" She planted a big sloppy kiss on Tatum.

Tatum laughed and swatted her away. "Okay, point taken. But still, you're right. That is weird. I wouldn't be comfortable at all."

"Oh, I plan on being very comfortable." Claudette grinned. "And in the morning I'll make breakfast for him in bed. It'll be super romantic."

"You can't cook."

"That's so beside the point."

Tatum's phone beeped, but she put it in her bag instead of checking. Juniper would have to wait. "What are you going to say to your mom?"

"Mom thinks I'm spending the night with you," Claudette said.

"I don't know," Tatum said. "What if she calls?"

"She won't." Claudette rolled her eyes before turning back to the mirror. "We've had a hundred sleepovers. A thousand. She's never called once. You're worrying about nothing."

Tatum nodded. Claudette was right. That was one of the best things about having such a close friend. They spent so much time together, their parents didn't bother checking up on them anymore. It had worked to their advantage more than once: going to parties, staying out past curfew, using the whole *We were just hanging out watching movies* routine.

"I guess it's okay," Tatum said. She didn't add that they'd made plans for Friday night and Claudette had obviously forgotten. Tatum didn't blame her and wasn't angry; she knew how easy it was to forget when a guy was involved.

"Everything will be fine," Claudette said. "You'll see." She paused and looked Tatum carefully in the eyes. "Are you okay? You're not going to say anything, are you?"

"No. No, of course not." Tatum swallowed, worried that her face might be giving away her disapproval. "But . . ."

"But what?"

Tatum swallowed again. She had to tread carefully. Claudette wasn't always rational when it came to thinking things over. "Don't you think you're going really fast with this? I think it's cool and all, but what if someone finds out? You could get in a lot of trouble."

"No one's going to find out anything," Claudette said with a frown. "Unless you tell them. You're the only one who knows."

"What happens in the summer when Mr. Paracini leaves his wife? They'll all know then."

"I'll be eighteen," Claudette said. "It won't really matter what they think then."

"Yeah, I guess." Tatum thought that line of reasoning was blurry, but there wasn't any point in trying to convince Claudette. Turning eighteen and immediately going off with a man would give the impression that something had happened way before her legal birth date. And something like that could easily land Mr. Paracini in trouble. If he was taking all these precautions to keep the whole thing secret, why would he suddenly be open about it?

Tatum had her doubts, but she chose not to say anything. Why burst Claudette's happiness? Even if nothing ever came of it, hopefully her friend would find some new guy to attach herself to. Claudette wasn't exactly known for sticking with a guy for more than six months anyway. No, best to stay quiet and let her get it out of her system.

"But enough talk about me," Claudette said as she tapped Tatum in the chest. "We need to find you a man next. Someone mature. Super hot. None of these high school boys. I'm telling you, Tate, there's nothing like an older man."

"I dunno," Tatum said. "Mr. Paracini's almost old enough to be your dad. You don't find that weird?"

"The difference between Barry and other people my dad's age is that Barry is hot. He's Brad Pitt hot. There's something to be said about older men. They have far more experience. And they aren't going to leave you unsatisfied in the back of their mom's car. Really, Tatum, don't knock it till you try it."

Tatum shrugged. Claudette definitely had a lot more experience than her when it came to the opposite sex. But Tatum found boys her own age to be intimidating enough. She didn't think she could ever go after an older man. Especially someone like Mr. Paracini. Even if he was divorcing his wife, Tatum still felt like he and Claudette were doing something wrong. She remembered how upset Claudette had been when she'd found out Graham had cheated on her with a sophomore. It ended up being a huge fight in the parking lot, with Claudette almost slapping the braces off the poor terrified girl in question. According to Graham, they'd only kissed. But it was enough for Claudette to cause the scene to end all scenes.

Being married was a whole lot more complicated than simply kissing a sophomore. And even if they were no longer in love, Tatum was positive that Mr. Paracini's wife wouldn't be that thrilled about Claudette spending the night in her bed.

"Don't look so worried," Claudette said. "It's not like you have to date a man like Barry. You could go after a college guy. Then you can spend weekends cruising the dorms and kegger parties."

"Yeah," Tatum said. "That sounds more my speed."

"It'll be happening soon enough. Six more months till graduation. I can't wait to get out of this hellhole. No more small town. I sure won't look back. Just think of all the stuff we're going to do. You just have to get into UDub. Then you can come over on weekends and visit us on the boat. Did I tell you about that? We're gonna spend the summer sailing down to Mexico. Just Barry and I."

"Yeah, you might have mentioned it a few hundred times." It bothered Tatum that Claudette no longer included herself in the college talks. Since she started seeing Barry, she didn't seem to think she needed it anymore. All the discussions about courses and careers had been swept under the rug. Instead Claudette would launch into the boat story, about how she and Barry would live at the docks and spend their free time searching out white sand beaches. Tatum hoped it was a phase. Claudette always had a one-track mind. She was too busy thinking about summer to focus on fall. Things would change once she got it all out of her system. Tatum couldn't blame her. Sailing down to Mexico with the man of her dreams sounded pretty darn good.

"I'm just so excited. I love boats. Oh my God. Sailing and sex. That's my future, Tatum. Lots and lots of sex." Claudette tossed her hair behind her, looking like she'd just stepped off a runway in Milan. She spun around for Tatum, singing off-key, "If the boat's a-rocking, don't come a-knocking." She grabbed her friend by the arms and tried to bring Tatum into her dance.

"Nice."

The phone in Tatum's bag began to ring.

"Come on," Claudette said. "Juniper's gonna have a heart attack." She put her arm around Tatum and gave her a big hug. "Thanks so much for doing this for me. You're the only one I can trust. What would I do without you?"

* * *

Mom and Dad go to a movie that night. It's one Tatum actually wants to see, but she declines, saying she's got too much homework. She waits until they leave before grabbing her coat and car keys.

She drives up and down Frog Road about ten times before finally admitting defeat. Wherever Molly is tonight, it's not on the road.

MOLLY

Time may not be passing in our world, but I know the days are slipping by where I'm needed. I sit on the log and watch the Canadian girl appear and disappear several times. When she's here, she rocks back and forth, talking quietly to herself. I don't dare try and get close enough to listen. As I said, she's angry, and she might start a fight. She haunts her record studio every single night, or so everyone says. That means that since I've started watching her, almost an entire week has gone by.

Is Tatum still alive? I wish I could get a handle on this. I've spent all this time Fading back and forth, and I've never really wondered what happens after I disappear from people's cars. How many people did I actually help? Or hurt? I think back to the first: that nice salesman. I wonder if he went home and accused his wife of cheating. Maybe he decided that such things were beyond what he wanted to know. Either way, I hope I didn't hurt him. He was such a nice man. He deserved better.

We all do.

I try and think about what I know about Tatum. Sadly, it's practically nothing. She looked like an average girl. Pretty. Not the sort who might get herself into trouble. There's nothing to suggest she's a bad girl. Of course, I wouldn't have any way of knowing. I'm living in the past. I'm a relic. Back in my day, "bad girls" were the ones who wore too much makeup and hung around with the boys at the garage. There used to be one girl in particular—she was always the one parents used as an example when warning their children. I can't remember her name, but I met her once. She wore shirts that showed cleavage and she had a loud, harsh laugh. She used to smoke cigarettes and go out drinking with the guys on weekends. When I was younger, I remember trying to figure out what made her bad. She didn't seem like trouble. She seemed lonely to me. Like all she wanted in life was to be loved. She moved away when I turned thirteen, so I never found out what happened to her.

Is Tatum like her? "Bad"? Is she the girl parents lecture their kids about? No matter how many times I think about our short conversation, I can't see it. In a way, Tatum reminds me of myself. If you had told me I'd be the kind of girl to end up dead in a field, I wouldn't have believed it.

Did I become a warning? Was I the example of what happens to young girls who run away with the boys they love?

Parker came back a while ago. Before I could question him, he said he needed to go spend some time in the woods. He followed the path down to the right of the lake, and the trees swallowed him up. I want to go looking for him, but Mary talks me out of it.

"Who knows where he is. Them woods go on forever. You'd be chasing after your own tail. He'll be back soon enough."

"He knows something," I say. "He said so himself. That some things can be changed."

"Then you'll just have to wait till he gets his cryptic arse back."

I am too restless. I stand up and sit back down on the log several times. I even try walking around our little beach. I step around the wrought-iron tables, nodding at the people who occupy them. No one talks. They stand their guard, silent sentinels, waiting for their moment to be called back to the real world. Why? Is it because they believe they have no choice? Is there a choice? I reach up and bat at one of the paper lanterns, wondering why we behave this way. We can't all have been this quiet when we were alive. We lived. We loved. I know I'm not the only one to have raced across a meadow or played on the school swing set at two in the morning.

My fingers caress the paper of the lantern, and I get an idea. I swat at it, harder and harder, trying to tear through the tissue. I pause, waiting for someone to call out or ask me what I'm doing. Nothing. I swat harder. It's become a challenge. If I can make this stupid thing fall off its wire, maybe I can accomplish something. Finally my nails catch it and the lantern comes tumbling down to the ground.

I turn around to look at the closest faces. No one notices a thing. They're too busy stuck in their own emptiness. When I look back up, the lantern has replaced itself.

I've decided that I hate this world. I hate being dead.

* * *

We arrived at Woodstock two days before the event began. The radio had been talking about it for weeks, and Andrea and I knew we'd have to get there early or not get in at all. Already the roads were swamped with cars. The traffic went on for miles, and there was talk about shutting down the interstate. After being stuck in a car for what seemed like forever, Andrea and I were ready to have fun. But first we had to get situated. That would be the big problem. We'd heard on the radio that they were expecting hundreds of thousands of people in a location that would only accommodate fifty thousand.

The lack of space hadn't stopped anyone. Already there were thousands of people roaming about. We found a parking spot between a painted-up school bus and a group of motorcycles. Dozens of people sat around in the grass talking to each other. They passed around beers and smoked pot. Two girls flashed the peace sign at us as they wandered by. One of them seemed to have lost her shirt somewhere along the way. I blushed and turned away, which made a few of the bikers laugh at me.

"Should we even bother trying to set up the tent?" I asked as I climbed out of the car and stretched my legs.

Andrea stood up on her toes to try and get a better look. In the sea of people, we could see the occasional tent. But we'd have to walk for what seemed like miles if we wanted to find an open patch of land. "We might be better off sleeping in the car," she agreed.

"Probably drier," I said. The news reports were predicting rain. I glanced over at the group of bikers. One of them lazily massaged his leg and winked at me. His friends laughed a bit too loudly when I quickly looked away. "Safer, too," I added under my breath.

"Let's worry about that later," Andrea said, ducking behind me as two little kids rushed past. "Come on. Let's go check things out."

Andrea paused to ask the peace sign girls where we might find the stage, and the topless one pointed us in the right direction.

"Just keep walking. You can't miss it. It's huge. Stay groovy." She flashed the peace sign again and then lay down on her towel.

"Did you see her eyes?" Andrea whispered as we walked off. "I'd say she's been grooving all day."

"Probably most of last night, too," I said with a grin.

"So many people," Andrea said. Her eyes sparkled with excitement. "I've never seen so *many* in one place." She paused to check out the faded jeans of some gorgeous, long-haired young men as they walked past. "How come they don't look like that back at home? Seriously, I'm in heaven. That's got to be it. We died back on the road and now we're here."

I caught the eye of a guy with a straw cowboy hat covering his curly dark hair. He smiled at me. Andrea was right. The men from North Carolina weren't nearly as interesting as the ones we were now seeing. Of course, our town of Dixby only had about a thousand people, and the majority of them were over the age of thirty. Most of the guys our age were high school dropouts like my brother. Boys who spent their days working down at the factory, driving trucks like Dad, or hanging around the mechanic's shop, hoping to get a job fixing cars like Marcus. Going to college wasn't usually a viable option in our town. People didn't leave. They settled in and dug deep roots.

Me? I wanted to travel the world. I wanted to see all corners of the earth and everything in between. I didn't want to end up like my mother, trapped in a small town with a family she never wanted. Maybe if she'd gone off and experienced things first, she wouldn't have needed to run away in the middle of the night.

I planned on living life before I settled down. Being at Woodstock would be my first adventure in a string of many. I had plenty of wild oats to sow. A million lives to live. And so much music to hear.

Andrea let out a low whistle. Somehow, in the time it took us to park the car, the traffic seemed to have tripled.

Hundreds of parked cars blocked the roads. People set up shop selling all sorts of things. Thick, juicy slices of watermelon for fifty cents: green rinds littered the ground. Corn on the cob seemed quite popular: lots of people had kernels and butter smears stuck on their faces. Bare feet kicked around empty bottles of Coke. Love beads were passed around, beautiful bright colors in all sizes and styles. A few people sold clothing out the backs of their vans: Leather belts and bell-bottom jeans. Peasant shirts. Long, flowing skirts. Andrea and I paused a few times to feel the quality of the cotton and press the beautiful items against our skin to compare sizes.

And although no one straight-out advertised, several people whispered to Andrea and me as we walked by, offering drugs to sweeten our experience.

I smiled nervously, turning everyone down. It wasn't that

I was against weed; I'd smoked once or twice. But I'd never really enjoyed it the way others seemed to. People said marijuana was supposed to enlighten the mind. All it did was make me tired and paranoid. It made me want to curl up in a ball and hide away from the rest of the world. Hardly mind-blowing, in my opinion. And not the sort of feelings I wanted to explore that weekend. So when Andrea offered to buy some, I shrugged her off. She could do whatever she wanted, but I had come to hear the music. That was a natural enough high for me.

The closer we got to the stage, the busier things became. Soon we were elbow to elbow with all sorts of people. A group of feminists handed out pamphlets and I took one, putting it in my purse for later. We were women of the sixties. We had a right to get an education and a job. A guy screamed "Fight the power!" several times in my face, to the point where I covered my ears with my hands. "Don't let the man get you down. This is America! We need to let the government know we don't want to fight in their corporate war. Down with Vietnam. No draft! No draft! Girlies, support your men. Let those government pigs know you will march against Washington."

Thankfully, some elderly men stopped him from following Andrea and me farther.

I paused to look at some wooden beads spread out across a table. There were two men behind the table. The first had a bushy gray beard and matching long hair. He wore a tie-dye shirt and a bandanna. He sat on the back bumper of a Volkswagen bus, a cigarette between his fingers. He looked older than my father, and I couldn't help grinning to myself, wondering what Dad, with his crew cut and trimmed mustache, would say if he could see what I was seeing.

"Beautiful, aren't they?"

I glanced up into the most amazing pair of brown eyes I'd ever seen. I'd been looking at the old man and hadn't seen the young one standing across from me. Long sandy-blond hair spread across his shoulders and halfway down his back. He was tall and slender, and his shirt fit his body perfectly.

"Um, yeah," I said. That was it. One glance at him and he'd rendered me stupid. My conversational skills went out the window. I swallowed twice and gave him what I hoped was a nice smile.

The guy reached across the table and picked up a set of beads. They were brown and red. He lifted them over the top of my head and let them drop gently across my chest.

"They're from Mexico. We picked them up last winter." Tilting his head to the side, he squinted with a critical eye, studying the way the beads looked. Frowning, he removed them and tossed them back on the counter. "Wrong color," he said. He studied the collection and chose again, this time beads that were yellow and brown, the same color as his hair and eyes. "These are better," he said as he draped them down around my neck. "Yellow is prettier. Sunshine. They'll make you glow."

"Thank you," I said. He held up a cracked mirror, and I studied my reflection in the glass. They were truly lovely. "How much?"

"For you? I'd ask for a smile. But my business partner"—he nodded back in the direction of the man sitting on the bumper of the bus—"he's not going to be as generous. So I'll have to up my bid to a dollar."

The answer was so unexpected, I couldn't help but laugh.

I reached into my pocket and pulled out a bill. I could have turned him down. I wasn't so enamored by his looks that I would buy anything he might be selling. Yes, his smile was bright and genuine, and I loved the way his hair naturally waved around the collar of his shirt. I was sure a lot of girls fell for his charms. That didn't mean he'd be able to sell me just anything. But the beads were beautiful and the cost was reasonable.

He took my dollar and handed it over to the bearded gray-haired man, who nodded in my direction, but didn't say anything. He dropped the money into a rusted can and then stomped his cigarette on the ground beneath his shoes. I turned around to show Andrea, only to discover that the crowd had swallowed her up. Apparently she hadn't seen me stop and had kept on walking.

"Lose someone?" the young guy asked.

"Yeah, my friend," I said. "I could have sworn she was right behind me."

"Lots of pretty colors here," the guy said. "Plenty of distractions. It's not that difficult to get lost in the crowd. Want me to help you find her?"

"That's okay. If I don't catch up with her, I'll meet her at the car later."

"I hope so," he said. "In case you didn't notice, there's a major concert going on." He leaned in close to whisper in my ear. "I hear there's going to be a lot of people. Total party. Great bands, too."

"I hadn't heard about it," I whispered back. "But that explains a lot of things. Hope someone clued in the farmers. Looks like their fields are getting trashed."

"I hear some unpleasant wrongdoers have been raiding the corn," he said, "and then selling it back to the masses at inflated prices. Whoever said these guys are a peaceful bunch was lying. All those farmers better lock up their livestock next. And their daughters."

"One and the same?"

He gave me a charming wink. "I hear the livestock are smarter in these parts."

I laughed, fingering the beads, admiring the smoothness against my fingers. They were slightly cool, and I liked the way they felt against my skin. "I'd better move on," I said. "Thanks again."

"Anytime."

I got about two car lengths down the road before he caught up with me.

"You know," he said, "I've got some break time. I know this might sound forward, but would you like to get a Coke with me?" He held up the dollar bill I'd handed over. "You see, I've recently come into some money and am dying to spend it."

"Sure," I said.

"I'm Julian."

"Molly."

"Pleased to meet you, Molly. And I'm relieved, too. I was terrified that you'd turn me down."

"Oh, please," I said. "There are thousands of girls here. Even if I said no, I doubt you'd have trouble finding one to spend your money on."

"Good thing I found the right one on my first try."

* * *

Does it make me sad to relive these memories? I'd say no, because that's the easy answer. However, being trapped here, in this world, has left me knowing that there should have been a million more memories.

Julian made me feel alive. His family, the people he traveled with across the country, they took me in, giving me experiences I'd only dreamed about. They never judged me. They accepted me as one of their own. The time I spent with them was greater than the entire fifteen years I'd lived before. But if I hadn't stopped at that table and allowed Julian to whisk me away, I'd never have met Walter. I wouldn't have died, tied up and tortured in a moldy barn in the middle of nowhere. I would have gone back home to North Carolina, probably married some local boy, and lived out my life. Would it have been a good life? I don't know.

But it would have been a life.

* * *

Parker comes back after a while. He ignores Mary's immediate line of questioning. Brushing her aside with a wave of his hand, he sits down on the log beside me and stares out at the water for a few minutes before speaking. Mary stands in front of him, impatient and demanding answers, thrusting her chest out in a way that makes me think she's going to bust her corset.

"Let me talk to Molly alone," Parker finally says.

Mary opens her mouth to argue, but the look on Parker's face makes her change her mind. She glances at me, and I nod.

"It don't matter anyway," Mary says. "Molly will tell me everything once you're done."

"That's fine," Parker says. "But for now, I need just her ears."

Mary frowns and turns around, her petticoats swishing against her legs. She heads off and plops down on one of the French iron chairs. Even though she's out of hearing distance, I can tell she's watching us, hoping to read our lips or our minds.

"What if I said I know a way out?" Parker finally says.

"What do you mean?"

"A way back to the living."

"You mean being alive again?"

Parker shakes his head. "No, not living. You'd still be dead, and you'd have to return here. And it's not safe. There are others out there too. Dark souls. Remnants of people, crazy scary. Waiting to grab us if we sneak out."

"You're making that up," I say. "There's no way back. If there was, someone else would know." I wave my arm in the direction of the group; the beads around my neck tremble in agreement. Yellow beads, the color of the sun.

"No one else knows," Parker says. "Or if they do, they never mention it. But I discovered this a long time ago, in the woods. A way out."

I pause. "Why didn't you say anything about this before?"

Parker shrugs. "No reason to. Don't look at me like that. The dead have no business sneaking around pretending to be alive. Haunting is bad enough. Why else would anyone want to go back? Also, it's not safe. I said that. And if everyone knew, imagine how bad things could get? I don't think this pathway is supposed to exist. I think it's a mistake. Whoever created this place, they accidently put in an exit. If everyone goes there, it might disappear. I don't want to cause waves."

"How long have you known this? You could have helped people all this time."

"I couldn't have helped anyone."

"How do you know? Did you even consider trying?"

"Please be quiet."

My voice has steadily grown louder. I can't help it. Parker sits on the log, looking completely oblivious to the words coming out of his mouth. How long has he known? A few months? Years? Did he know about this place when I first showed up? What about the others? There are people who have come here, souls who could have used one last chance to go back and tell their loved ones they're safe. I look over at a six-year-old girl who sits in the sand a ways off. What if she could have gone back and told her mother she was okay? Couldn't that have ended years of grief? Does her mom still wake in the middle of the night, cursing God because her daughter isn't warm in her bed?

What if I could have gone back to Julian and told him not to cry over me? Would I have been able to do it? Could I have looked into his eyes one last time and then willingly come back here?

The truthful answer: I couldn't have.

I glance back at Mary. The Boston lady has come over to join her. She sits in the chair beside my friend, her poodle in her lap. She's trying to get Mary to converse, but mostly she just talks softly to herself. Mary glares at me. She's not happy in the slightest to be exiled from us, forced to listen to dog stories. I hold up a finger. One more minute. Or second. Or eternity.

"This place, does it let you go wherever you need to go?"

Tatum's face pops up in my mind. Even if I can manage to get back to the road, will I be able to find her in time? She could live anywhere. It's not like I managed to get her address or phone number.

"Yes," Parker says.

"Can you take me there?"

"I don't think you should do it."

"No," I say. "You can't do that, Parker. You can't offer me a chance and then take it away."

"I didn't say that."

"Then what are you saying?"

Parker frowns; his eyebrows move around on his face until they are practically touching. "I'll take you there. I'll show you how to do it if you want. But I don't think you should."

"Because . . . ?"

"It's dangerous."

"Yeah, you mentioned that," I say. "Dark souls. 'Remnants,' whatever that means. I'll take my chances."

"It's not just that," Parker says. "It's not easy going back. You may think it is. We Fade all the time. Some of us daily. But going back and haunting . . . that's a different thing. Being in the world, being a part of it again, can be addictive. Painful. Trust me, I know."

"Where did you go?"

"I don't want to talk about it."

Of course he doesn't. That's Parker. Throw him a bone, and instead of sharing his feelings, he buries the damned thing.

But I can't afford to get angry with him. I jump up off the log, trying to hide the anticipation building in my chest. We need to go.

I reach out to grab his hand, but my skin goes right through him. It takes me a second to process the fact that I'm Fading.

No. Not now.

I've got more important things to do.

Tatum.

TATUM

It's dark tonight on Frog Road.

Nine days. She's been out here every single night, driving the familiar stretch, searching for a young girl to appear out of thin air.

And for nine days she's seen nothing more exciting than a coyote.

Earlier today someone broke into her gym locker while she was running laps. They tossed her clothes in the toilet. Her favorite shirt—a black graphic from a popular Internet cartoon—is completely ruined. For the rest of the day, Tatum was forced to wear her old jogging pants. And she quickly realized she should wash her gym clothes far more often than she does. From now on she'll have to start bringing a second outfit to wear in case they do it again. And they will. Her tormentors aren't very creative. When they find something that works, they tend to repeat it over and over.

Starting Monday, she'll put a bag in her trunk with a pair of jeans and a hoodie.

Today Scott came up to her while she was heading into the library. He glanced down at her stinky gym clothes but thankfully didn't ask.

"I'm going to see my grandma this weekend," he says. "So I'll ask her about your ghost. I'm working Sunday night. If you don't mind the drive, I'll have some free time to talk about it. The shop'll be dead and I'm working alone."

"Okay, thanks," she said.

Now it's Friday night and Tatum should be out partying. She should be with her friends, sneaking beers and hanging out in a field somewhere, getting tipsy. That's what most everyone does on weekends. Back in the day, she attended her fair share of outdoor keggers. There's a place they often go when there aren't any house parties to attend. Usually someone lights a bonfire and everyone shows up.

She and Claudette used to go to all the parties. Tatum remembers one particular Friday night, only a few months ago. Christmas break had officially begun, and they were more than happy to have an excuse to celebrate. A bonfire night in the woods—right off Frog Road, to be exact.

They'd just arrived, and already Levi had pressed beers into their hands. He had a pair of reindeer antlers perched on top of his head. A bunch of the guys had pooled their money and gotten a keg. Someone's older brother had gone to the store to pick it up. They'd started out selling drinks for a buck a beer, but as the night went on, people forgot to charge. And everyone was a tad too drunk.

It was a cold night, but no one complained. They'd fed the fire until it blazed straight up to the heavens. Winter jackets were pulled out, although a fair number of guys and gals ran around in just their shirts. Refusing to submit to the elements, they'd simply inch closer and closer to the fire, their cheeks and arms rosy from both the cold and the heat.

Claudette wasn't drinking. It wasn't like Tatum was watching out for her; she just noticed because it was outside her friend's norm. Claudette loved a party more than anyone she knew. Always right in the middle of the action, her best friend often drank hard and heavy. Plenty of weekends had ended with Tatum holding Claudette's hair back while she puked. That was what friends were for.

"What's going on?" Tatum yelled over the noise. Graham Douglas had parked his truck close to the fire, and dance music blasted through the speakers.

"What do you mean?" Claudette asked. She waved to Juniper and a few others from across the way. They were standing in the truck's bed, trying to grind to the music. Juniper nearly fell out as she waved back enthusiastically.

"You're not drinking."

"I don't feel like it," Claudette said. She turned quickly, and half the beer spilled out of her cup. To Tatum, it looked like she'd done it on purpose. To pretend she was drinking when she really wasn't.

There was something odd in the way she said it that made Tatum pause. She wanted to ask more questions, but Graham came over and threw his arms around them both. He had some blinking Christmas lights wrapped around his neck.

"I ain't got no mistletoe, but you still have to kiss me!" he hollered. Beer dripped from his plastic glass and sprayed them both.

"Ugh," Claudette said, brushing him away. She pulled a tissue out of her purse and tried to mop up the spill before it soaked into her jacket. "You stink. And I'd rather kiss a rabid dog."

"I am a rabid dog," Graham said. Ignoring her protests, he kissed Claudette on her cheek. Then his lips brushed against Tatum's. "You're beautiful, babe," he slurred. "Why haven't we hooked up yet?"

"Tatum's got better taste than that," Claudette said.

"Bullshit," Graham said. "What's with you, anyway? You used to be cool. Now you act like you're all high and mighty. You've turned into a prude."

Claudette laughed. "You're so high school, Douglas."

"It's 'cause she's got that mysterious boyfriend," Juniper said as she joined them. "Some college guy. But Claudette won't give out details. Maybe she's afraid someone will steal him away."

Tatum frowned. The jealousy was thick in Juniper's mouth. She'd always been envious of Claudette's ability to drive the guys wild. Juniper wanted to be just like Claudette, but whatever queen-bee attributes Claudette possessed, Juniper lacked. So she spent her time clinging to Tatum and Claudette, bad-mouthing other girls behind their backs, and sucking up to any guy who paid her any attention. Claudette often said Juniper would be pregnant before graduation. As mean as it sounded, Tatum secretly agreed.

Tatum wondered what Juniper would say if she knew

Claudette's boyfriend was Mr. Paracini. How long would it take before Juniper would spread the news throughout the entire state of Washington?

"Who I date is none of your concern," Claudette said icily. She turned and wrapped her arm around Tatum. Holding up her empty cup, she waved it around. "Let's go get some more beer."

Funny, after Claudette tossed Tatum to the curb and destroyed her reputation, she and Juniper became the best of friends. It must suck these days for Claudette, unable to trust anyone with her secrets.

* * *

"I need your help."

On the drive home later that night, Claudette suddenly burst into tears. Not the pretty crystal tears reserved for sad animal-abuse commercials, but big whopping ones. This was the hurt that included snot uncontrollably running from her nose.

"What's wrong?"

"I think I'm pregnant."

A long pause filled the air, draining all the energy from inside the car. Tatum held on tightly to the steering wheel, her fingers white-knuckled as she tried to think of the right thing to say.

"I thought you were on the pill."

"Really? Really? That's all you can say?" Claudette punched herself in the leg. "Of course I was on the pill. I'm not a total invalid. Obviously *the pill* didn't work. These things happen, Tatum. Got any other great advice?"

"Maybe you should go to the doctor," Tatum finally said. Lame answer, but she couldn't think of anything better.

"I can't do that," Claudette said. "It'll get back to my mother. You know the receptionist and her are friends. They go for lunch almost every day."

"But what about that doctor-patient stuff? That's supposed to be confidential."

"Bullshit. Someone will find out. Someone always finds out. Everyone in this damn town is too nosy. And I can't let my parents know. Can you imagine what they'd say? Oh God, what if the school finds out it's Barry's? That could ruin all our plans. Barry told me that if I get pregnant, it's all over. He can't deal with another child. It'll be bad enough he has to support the ones he already has. I can't lose him. How could I let this happen?" Grabbing a tissue from her purse, she blew her nose loudly.

"That's not cool," Tatum said. "I can't believe you'd let him talk to you like that."

"It's not Barry's fault," Claudette said. "It's just that people wouldn't understand. It's one thing for him to leave his wife; it's another to get me pregnant. I'm not even eighteen yet. This could ruin everything. It's all my fault."

Tatum wanted to point out that Barry was just as responsible, if not more. He was a married adult who should have known better. But with Claudette's tears soaking up the passenger seat, she couldn't really lecture her friend about her choice in men. It wasn't the right time.

"If he leaves me, I'll kill myself."

Tatum paused. There was a certain panicky tone in

Claudette's voice, one she'd never heard before. Her friend, the confident, tell-it-like-it-is girl, was falling apart. And it was terrifying. Tatum's white knuckles grew uncomfortably cold.

"Don't talk like that," she said. "It's just a guy."

"Barry's my entire life. If he leaves me, I don't want to be alive." Claudette punched herself roughly in the stomach. "I can't be pregnant, I can't."

"Stop that." Tatum reached over and tried to grab Claudette's hand before she punched herself again.

"I don't know what to do."

"We could go to another doctor? Drive into Seattle."

Claudette shook her head. Leaning back in the passenger seat, she chewed on a fingernail until it bled. "It'll take forever to get in to see someone. I need to know sooner. Maybe we could hit up a drugstore. You could go in and get me a pregnancy test."

"Me? Why me? Why not you?"

"You know how embarrassed I get about this stuff. I can't even buy tampons. I have to get my mother to pick them up."

She obviously couldn't get condoms, either. Tatum gripped the steering wheel so tightly she worried she might actually break it.

"I'm not doing it."

"Please, Tatum. You're my best friend."

Of course she was. She turned on her signal light and took the next left toward the interstate. "Fine," she said. "But we're not doing it here. We'll head into Everett. I'm sure there's an all-night Walgreens somewhere. And I'll need to get some gas. The last thing I need is someone thinking *I'm* pregnant."

"You're the best," Claudette said as she wrapped her arms awkwardly around Tatum's chest, nearly forcing Tatum off the road. "I'll totally owe you."

What had happened to her friend? The scary moment had passed, and now Claudette sank into her seat and began chewing on another fingernail. But the crazed look that had crossed her face a few moments ago was gone. Had it even been there? It wasn't like her to be so all over the place. Claudette was the girl who managed to keep it together all the time. She'd never mentioned suicide before; in fact, she often made cruel jokes about people she thought might be considering it.

Again Tatum looked at her and wondered how on earth they'd ever stayed friends. "You can buy me a super-great Christmas gift," she finally said. It seemed easier to joke with her than to comment on her earlier behavior. And apparently it was the right thing to do because Claudette grinned widely.

"Deal. Something sparkly and sexy you can wear for New Year's."

It was in a Walmart where Claudette ended up peeing on a stick that ended the pregnancy fear. The results were blissfully negative. Claudette didn't bother thanking Tatum for doing the embarrassing checkout. She didn't apologize for Tatum's nerves when the salesgirl had given her a look that suggested Tatum had to be some sort of slut for sneaking around in the middle of the night buying pregnancy tests.

No, Claudette was too relieved to think of anything else, and of course Tatum let it go. She allowed Claudette to jump for joy in the bathroom stall and hug her several times. They drove back home, and thankfully Tatum's parents had gone to bed and never even noticed she'd missed curfew by an hour.

She lay in bed for a long time that night, trying to figure out what to do. What would happen if another pregnancy scare came up? What if Barry left Claudette? What if he decided it wasn't worth the stress to continue sneaking around? Claudette's behavior wasn't normal. She might end up doing something crazy. How would Tatum deal with it? If she told an adult, would that help?

The decision didn't come easily. But in the end Tatum figured she had to do something. She couldn't sit back and watch her friend destroy herself.

A week later, everything changed.

* * *

Tatum drives past the site of the Christmas bonfire and nearly misses seeing the girl walking out of the woods. She slams on the brakes, hard enough to make the car's tires slide to the right. With her hands on the wheel, Tatum exhales loudly.

She saw that. The girl.

Looking in the rearview mirror, Tatum scans the road behind her. The blacktop spreads out in quiet darkness. A red glow lights up the night as she keeps her foot on the brake pedal. She squints, trying to make out one shadow from another.

There. Movement.

She turns off the car and gets out.

Be careful. It could be a trap. You don't know who's been watching you this week. You've been here every damn night. Someone else might have noticed. And you still don't really know which side Scott's on. He could have told them all about your ghost story.

Tatum puts the voices in her mind on ignore. Keeping the driver-side door open, she stares out into the darkness. Slowly her eyes began to adjust, and the black shadows take on familiar forms.

It's her. The girl with her flowing skirt and long brown hair. The moonlight catches her movements as she climbs out of the ditch. She carefully wipes some dirt off her skirt before stepping up onto the road.

"Molly."

The girl smiles. No, that's not quite right. Her face explodes in emotion. Relief. Surprise. Happiness. The sides of her lips quiver and turn upward. "Tatum."

They both pause, looking at one another.

Tatum doesn't know where to go from here. There are so many questions she wants to ask, but suddenly they all seem stupid. Molly stands a few feet away from her, looking real and solid, not ghostly at all. What if Tatum's wrong about that? What if Molly is just some girl who happens to enjoy walking late at night along Frog Road? How dumb is Tatum going to appear if she starts going off like this is some sort of Halloween joke?

"I'm glad to see you again," Molly finally says. "Can we get in your car? I'm freezing."

Of course she is. Tatum looks at the girl's thin blouse and sees the goose bumps rising on her skin. Can a ghost have goose bumps?

"Sure," Tatum says.

They climb into the car. Molly doesn't say anything while Tatum turns it back on and puts the heat on high. She puts her hands against the vents to enjoy the warm air. Her fingers are long and elegant, the nails shaped into perfect ovals. After a minute or two, she stops shivering.

The silence fills the car. Neither girl says anything. Tatum opens her mouth twice, but uncertainty makes her stop each time. She's got to be wrong. Now that she's looking right at Molly, she's positive the girl has to be alive. She's too real-looking.

Finally Molly breaks the silence. "How are you doing?"

"Fine," Tatum says. She stares at Molly's skin. It's so real. Shouldn't it be more shimmery or something? She's seen all those images on the Internet. The ghosts seem to glow. They don't usually appear so . . . solid.

"Your friends. Are they still giving you trouble?"

"Ex-friends. How do you know that?"

Molly shrugs. "I just know things. You should start driving. That's the way it has to work. If you don't drive, I don't know what might happen. Stupid rules, aren't they?"

"So it's true, then." Tatum puts the car in gear and they start moving.

"What do you mean?"

"You. You're a . . ." There go those pesky words again, dying before Tatum can get them out.

"Yes," Molly says. "I'm a ghost."

She certainly doesn't have problems saying it.

"You're not afraid?"

"No," Tatum says. "Why? Should I be?"

"Not of me," Molly says. "Never me. All I do is a disappearing act. Aside from freaking people out, I'm quite harmless. And you seem to be handling this well, so I guess there's no fear of you losing your mind."

113

Tatum can't help herself. She reaches out and touches Molly's arm. Her fingers don't slip through air or pass through nothingness like one might expect when greeting a specter. No, Molly's skin is soft and cool. Very, very real. It's like touching her mother or even herself.

"You don't feel like one."

"What are ghosts supposed to feel like?"

Molly's got her there. "I don't know. Not solid. Isn't that how they show ghosts in the movies? But you feel real. I mean, like a person."

"So you'd feel more comfortable if you were able to stick your hand through my body?"

Tatum grins. "Yeah, no."

"That's a relief to hear." Molly puts her hands against the heating vent again. "That feels so good. It's cold tonight. I was afraid I might be stuck on the road for a long time. Cars don't always come right away. I once got stuck outside in a rainstorm for half an hour. When the car finally showed up, I looked like a wet dog. I remember the guy who picked me up. He had wandering hands. I hate it when they do that."

Tatum pulls her arm back instantly and Molly laughs.

"You can touch me," she says. "I don't mind. I'm really happy it was you. I've been thinking about you so much. But I've never gone back to the same person before. I thought I was too late with my warning."

Tatum barely hears her words. "How? I mean, how did you die?" she asks.

Molly shrugs. She's still smiling. "Does it really matter? I'm more interested in you. I'm here to help."

"I don't need help," Tatum says, frowning in confusion.

"But my warning. I see things. I saw you. You're in trouble."

"I'm fine. Nothing wrong." Tatum wants nothing more but to direct the conversation away from herself. She doesn't want to spend the few minutes they have discussing the queen bitch Claudette and the living hell her life has become. "I want to know about you. What happened? Why are you haunting Frog Road? Have you been doing this a long time? Is it a curse? Something you need to do? I can help. If you give me enough information, I can find your body and put you to rest."

"It doesn't work that way," Molly says.

"Ghosts haunt places because they have unfinished business," Tatum says. "I've been reading all about it. I can help. You have to tell me your story. How did you die? Is that too personal? Can you even tell me? Or does something prevent you? Oh God. Do you relive your death?"

Molly laughs, and the sound silences Tatum.

"That's a lot of questions. I'm more worried about you."

"This isn't about me." The conversation isn't going the way Tatum wants it to go. Tatum has an actual *ghost* in her car! The very thing that will make her forget all her problems.

"You're in trouble, Tatum. You need help yourself. Someone's planning to hurt you."

"They can't hurt me any more than they already have," Tatum says. Her fingers drum impatiently on the steering wheel. How much time do they have before Molly poofs? Molly said it herself—they need to keep driving. How long before she disappears? A mile? Two? Tatum needs to keep this conversation on track. "How did you die?"

"I was murdered."

"So is that it? Do I need to find your killer? Is he still alive? Or she?"

"I knew my killer," Molly says. She reaches out and picks up a gas receipt from the cup holder. She studies it in the dark. "Wow," she says more to herself than Tatum. "Julian used to earn less than that in a week."

"You knew the person who murdered you?"

"Yes, he was Julian's friend. Walter. He was my friend too. Never thought in a million years he'd ever hurt me. He used to play guitar for us in the evenings. He had a beautiful voice. Funny, I trusted him completely. He was like a father to me." It isn't hard to hear the bitterness in Molly's voice. She places her hands in her lap and stares at her fingers. They still look cold. On her left hand is a silver ring with a tiny diamond. An engagement ring? Tatum can't tell.

"Does Walter have a last name? I could track him down."

"They caught him. If he's still alive, he's probably still in jail. He bragged to me that I wasn't his first. He'd probably been killing for years. He knew what he was doing. That's why he was good at it."

So that can't be it. Tatum mentally crosses *Find killer* off her list. But maybe that's not quite true. Maybe Walter escaped prison or was paroled. It could still be Tatum's job to find him. And then what? Find a way to send him back to jail? Kill him herself? An eye for an eye?

"You're in danger, Tatum," Molly says. She reaches over and presses her fingers against Tatum's arm. "Listen to me. There's not a lot of time left. I'll Fade again and I can't do that unless I know for sure you're going to be safe. Someone is plotting to hurt you. I saw it. A group of others. You know these people. They used to be your friends. And the things I see, I think they come true."

"I'm fine, honest," Tatum says. She briefly thinks of Claudette and then brushes the thought away. Claudette may be a bitch, but she wouldn't ever hurt Tatum. Stealing her clothes is about as low as she'd stoop. Even Graham and Levi with their nasty comments wouldn't actually do anything physical. She's known these people her entire life. She'd know if they were into killing puppies or torturing grandmothers on weekends.

It's Molly who needs help.

"What about your body?" Tatum asks.

"What about it?"

"If you're buried in a field, I can dig it up and put your soul at rest."

Molly shakes her head. "You've been reading too many books. What I do, what I am—there's no way to stop it. I'm not the only ghost out there. If it were that simple to put me at rest, as you say, I'd like to think it would have happened to at least one of us."

"So you're in some sort of purgatory?"

"You could call it that."

"What's it like?"

"It's not important," Molly says. She turns around in her seat, and Tatum can see the pleading look in her eyes. She looks terrified. Why? Ghosts have nothing to fear. They're already dead.

"It's important to me," Tatum finally says. She glances at the road and sees that they've come to the end. She can see the town-limits sign not too far off in the distance.

"You. We need to talk about you."

But whatever conversation Molly wants, it's not going to happen. Already she's beginning to turn transparent. Tatum reaches out to touch her again, and this time her fingers slide through Molly's body. Nothing but cold air where her arm is supposed to be. Molly leans forward to get Tatum's attention just before she completely disappears.

"Help yourself," Molly says.

And then she's gone.

Tatum pulls the car over for the second time that night. She sits in the car for a while, letting the hot air build up inside until it feels like she's in a sauna.

The excitement spills over her, making it hard to think about anything except Molly. She's real. A ghost. How cool is that? There are thousands of people out there trying to prove spirits exist. There are entire television shows and people with silly degrees who use expensive equipment to try and find proof. She's seen these shows. Mostly they just run around in the dark and talk about how cold certain areas are. They pull out fancy machines and claim they're recording the voices of the dead. To Tatum, it sounds like static. Molly's voice is perfectly normal.

Tatum knows the truth.

Of course, she can't exactly scream it from the rooftops. People didn't believe her about Claudette; they certainly wouldn't believe her about Molly.

Not that it matters. Who cares?

Molly is her secret.

Tatum now has more information. She's got the name of Molly's killer. Walter. And Julian. She mentioned the name

Julian. That is helpful, but probably still not enough for her to uncover all the details she needs. What she needs is Molly's last name. Why didn't she think to ask?

She does a U-turn in the middle of Frog Road and heads back home. Sunday night she will head down to the coffee shop, and hopefully Scott will have talked to his grandmother.

Scott Bremer. She smiles at the thought. Is he just being nice to her, or does he actually want to help? Scott doesn't talk to Claudette; heck, he even straight-out turned her down when he first moved to town. Tatum doesn't think she's ever seen him at a house party or with Graham and his lackeys. Is it possible that Scott doesn't even know about all the crap that's become Tatum's life?

Not likely.

But maybe he doesn't care. Maybe he's heard everything and still wants to be her friend. He wouldn't have gone out of his way to be nice to her if he planned on brushing her off.

Sunday night. She can't wait.

MOLLY

"Dammit!"

I storm up and down the beach, kicking at pebbles, my bare feet barely making a mark on the sand. I've left my sandals somewhere back by the log, yanking them off in a fit of rage.

That girl. Tatum.

Parker and Mary sit on the log, watching me tromp back and forth. Both of them know better than to tell me to calm down. I can see it in Parker's eyes: he desperately wants me to stop. He can't understand why I'm getting so worked up by this. And I don't know the right words to make him care.

"How can anyone be that stupid? I practically hand her a warning on a silver platter, and she just shrugs it off? If someone had come up to me and warned me about Walter, I would have at least taken it into consideration. But no, she's got to get all weird about me being a ghost. Instead of worrying about herself, she's determined to put me to rest."

"That's the living for you," Mary says. "Bunch of giggle-

120

mugs if you ask me. Lucky you, though. They do tours in London where they found me body. You'd think at least one of those wankers would try and save my soul."

"How do you even know that?" Parker asks.

"I've seen it, I'll have you know," Mary says. "Got to scare the whole lot of 'em. Bloody idiots pulled out their cameras. I'll tell you, cats got better sense. At least they hiss and run away. Humans are dumb. They see danger and go rushing straight into it. They want the things that bump under their beds."

"That's not always true," Parker says. "I never went looking for trouble."

"That's 'cause you're boring, love," Mary says. "You never took a chance in your life, and now you're here. Even your afterlife is boring."

"Better than the alternative," he says mysteriously.

I let them bicker. My feet have sunk down into the sand. I remember being on the beach as a child. I used to stand right in the shallow water and wiggle my toes until they were covered. The moist sand was grainy and cushy against my skin. It made a wet sucking noise when I freed myself. Perfect for a hot day. Looking down at my ankles, I shimmy back and forth, trying to bury my feet and regain the sensation. But nothing happens. No wet sand squishing between my toes. No cool pressure against my skin. Not a single feeling. The lack of sensation only frustrates me. I shake myself free and continue to pace.

"You can't force someone to listen to you," Mary says after watching me go up and down the beach three times. "She's fascinated by you. Can't blame her. Appearing out of nowhere, all magical and ghostly. I'm surprised she ain't asked for your autograph."

"She wants to save me," I say with a snort. *"Me."* My voice is rising again, and I can't help it. I'm starting to get an audience. I can feel their eyes on my body. This is the sort of thing that never happens here. Loudness. Free speech. Reacting. Freaking out. All of this is unwanted. The invisible line we never cross.

"Did you explain that it's all nonsense? Fabrications?" Parker leans back, a soft smile on his face. Now I can't tell if he's being sincere or sarcastic.

"What do you think?" I snap. I turn toward the group, sitting in their eternal seats, and see several pairs of eyes turn away. So typical of them. Needing to mind their own business, sucked up in their own stupid afterlife. Heaven forbid they have to actually do or feel something. I can tell what they're thinking: *Why won't she just sit down? Stop making the living important. Be quiet and still. This is our afterlife too.*

"I don't know what to do," I finally admit. "I have to go to her again. Make her listen. I just need more time."

"Maybe you'll Fade again," Mary says. She still doesn't know about Parker's secret. I haven't had time to tell her, and she's forgotten to question me.

"It won't happen," I say. "I was lucky enough to get a second chance. Do you really think I'll get a third?"

"Maybe. The high and mighty up-above powers obviously decided she needed to be told again."

"I don't think so."

I look at Parker for help, but he's gazing out over the water. His face is dark with worry. I can't tell if he's regretting telling me about the way out or if he's trying sincerely to find an answer in that mysterious brain of his. Either way, all this talk isn't solving anything. Too much time is passing in the real world, and every second here is agony.

Why am I so obsessed with this girl? What is it about her that makes me sick with worry? I've never cared about the people I've crossed paths with before. Sure, I've thought about them sometimes, wondered if they solved their problems. But none of it has ever kept me this revved up before.

Does Tatum remind me of myself? Is that it? Do I subconsciously believe that by saving her, I'll be making amends for my own death? Would I have reacted the same way Tatum did if someone had warned me? Would I have protected myself or looked at Walter and laughed? He'd seemed so harmless.

"She's helpless," I say, more to myself than the others.

"Some things are beyond our control," Parker says.

"Not everything," I say.

"Especially everything."

I turn toward Parker, mentally reminding myself to take it down a notch. Yelling isn't going to accomplish anything. "She's going to die," I say. "And I can't make her understand. She's more interested in me. She doesn't get it. I'm already dead; I know what's waiting. What if one day she ends up here?" I pause and look around again, worried that my words may have already come true. More faces refuse to meet my eyes, but thankfully none of them are Tatum's. "I'll never forgive myself if that happens."

"Not all bad deaths end up here," Parker says.

"You don't know that," I say. "We're stuck here. How do we know there aren't other lakes? Other places where more of us wait? Ours can't be the only afterlife. There could be thousands of them just like here."

"There could be worse, too," Parker says.

"Prove it."

"I can't," Parker says. "I can't tell you if heaven exists either. But by your own logic, if places like this exist, then other places do too."

"I sure hope hell exists," Mary says. "It's the perfect revenge for the arsehole who did this to me." She places her hands over her throat. "Gutted me like a pig, he did."

"Yes, Mary," I say. "We all know. Your death was bad. So was mine. And Parker's. And that of every single person here. Get over it."

"I'm just saying—"

"This girl is still *alive*," I say. "Why can't we make it our business to try and keep it that way? Why does everything have to be about everyone else?" I turn and face the crowd again. "What's the matter with all of you? Isn't there someone out there you want to save? Why do you have to sit here, day in and day out, feeling sorry for yourselves?"

Parker gets up off his log and comes over to shush me. But I won't let him. I shake him off, twisting my body out of his reach so I can continue my angry speech.

"And how come none of you ever do anything?" My voice has grown dangerously loud. "Get up. Move around. Talk? Why does everything here have to be so quiet? There are no rules here. Who said we need to act like we're all dead?"

Because we are dead. I see the answer on all their averted faces.

Parker's wrong. This is hell. It's just cleverly disguised.

"It doesn't have to be this way!" I scream. "This world. We can make it better. But we have to do it together."

I'm greeted with silence. They're embarrassed by my outburst. It's so much easier to pretend I don't exist.

"Come on," Parker says, and he grabs my hand. "Let's go for a walk."

"And you," I say. The tears are flowing down my face now. "How come you only touch me when you have no other choice?"

* * *

When Sweetwater took the stage on day one of Woodstock, Julian kissed me.

It wasn't magical or mind-blowing. We weren't gazing into one another's eyes in adoration. I wasn't chewing my cheek in anticipation, waiting for that moment that might never come. He simply placed his hands on my face and our lips met.

That's when the magic began. Everything around me stopped moving. The screaming crowds and rock and roll disappeared into a fog. Butterflies pulled my stomach in all directions, and my legs actually turned rubbery. Thankfully, the crowd pushing against us kept me standing.

I hadn't known a kiss could feel like that. Sure, I'd kissed boys before. In fourth grade, Josh Beaumont had cornered me by the swing set for my first. I can honestly say it never made my insides quiver. The kiss had been awkward, and two days later, thanks to Josh, everyone knew about it. I never did give him a second. There'd been more than a few since that, with other boys. But none of them had ever knocked the breath right out of my body. None of them had left me desperately hungry for more like this did.

When Julian pulled his lips away, it took all my strength not to straight-out attack him. With my arms wrapped tightly around his waist, all I wanted to do was pull him closer. He looked down at me with his sparkling brown eyes, his hair tickling my cheeks.

Slowly I became aware of the noise around us. Someone slammed against me, sending me closer into Julian's embrace. The band's guitars wailed chords, and the bass beat a rhythm that vibrated across the fields and up into my feet. I was aware that Andrea stood a few feet away, probably watching us, dying to get me alone so she could grill me for all the glorious details.

"You're beautiful," Julian said. His words were soft, but I had no trouble hearing him over the noise. "I've never met anyone like you. I never want to let you go."

Everything was going so fast, like a big, gigantic blur. I couldn't keep up. Part of me was terrified; the other part wanted to run headfirst into everything. My father's lectures crept into my head, but I pushed them away. I knew that love meant getting to know someone better and that it didn't happen with a bang. I'd heard him tell me about how he waited three months before asking out my mother. And how they dated for four years before he asked for her hand in marriage. My father believed in taking his time, in making sure he made all the right moves. He constantly warned me about the dangers of going too fast.

But even with all his faithful patience, he'd still lost my

mother. Who knew how love really worked? I certainly wasn't an expert.

I'd only known Julian for two days, but it felt like a lifetime. Even when I look back on it, all these years later, it still feels right. In fact, nothing in my life had ever made so much sense. It was as if every single thing I'd done until then had been pushing me toward Julian. I would follow him anywhere if it meant never leaving his side. If the feminists and their pamphlets could have read my mind, they would have tried to drag me away.

Terrifying. But oh so right.

"Come on, you lovebirds!" Andrea shouted. "You're missing the show." Guitars rang out, and the singer's voice came through the microphone. "Oh man, that's my favorite song!"

Julian's hand trailed down my side, his fingers brushing against my arm, sending millions of sensations throughout my body. Taking my hand in his, he squeezed gently, his eyes never leaving mine.

I was in love. Completely, totally, helplessly in love. It had snuck up on me when I wasn't looking, and I was happily freaked. I didn't understand how such feelings could exist so quickly, but I wasn't about to complain.

We stayed together for a couple more sets. The musicians kept coming and coming. Finally, Andrea suggested we head off to find something to drink. The heat from the crowd was staggering, and we were all thirsty.

Andrea was the queen of moving through a crowd. She was short, barely five feet tall, but she had no trouble maneuvering herself around the masses. I trailed behind her, my hand still tightly in Julian's. I looked up at the sky, wondering if the people were right. The weather stations were forecasting rain.

"No more water," the lady said when we reached the closest stall. Her eyes were red and bleary from all the smoke, her hair piled on top of her head in frizzy knots. "We got nothing. Totally sold out. Try some of the cars down the road. They might still have stuff."

"Okay, thanks," Andrea said.

But no one had anything. We walked almost all the way back to our car, and everything was gone. Even the watermelon vendor had nothing but a pile of rinds. The crowds had depleted their sources. Everything was sold out.

"Great," Andrea said. "We've got food in the car, but no water. Who would have thought they'd run out of that?" There were small ponds over in the distance, and she gazed at them fondly. Even from afar, we could make out people skinny-dipping. "If we get desperate enough, there's always that."

I watched a group of naked children running down the hill toward the water. "Yeah, no," I said.

"Come on," Julian said. "I'll introduce you to my family. They're like pack rats. They may sell the clothes off their back, but they'll have plenty of water."

"You're here with your folks?" Andrea seemed impressed.

"Not my actual kin," Julian said. "They're on a farm in Idaho. This is my traveling family. I met up with them a few years ago and I've been cruising around ever since."

"Lucky," Andrea said.

"Why'd you leave?" I asked.

Julian looked down at me, and those pesky butterflies came back with a vengeance. "I didn't want to be a farmer," he said.

"That was good enough for my father and my brothers, but I always knew I was meant to do something different. I wanted to get out and see the world. I met Walter when his van broke down on the highway, and they took me in. There's a whole group of us. Twenty, twenty-five. Some people come and go. We settle down for the winter in a different town so the little ones can go to school, but we spend our summers touring around. Selling stuff we make. It's a great life."

"That sounds fantastic," I said. I tried to imagine being a nomad. Going from town to town, selling beads and shirts, moving on the second I grew bored. For a young girl who grew up in the most boring town on earth, it sounded like a dream come true.

"You should both come with us," Julian said. "We always have room for more. The bigger, the better."

"My parents would hunt me down and kill me," Andrea said. "I can't wait till I'm eighteen. Then I'm gonna give them the finger and take the first bus out of town. But Molly, her dad's way cooler."

"No, he isn't," I said. "You just think so because he's never home. Your parents were fine with you coming here. They even tried to tag along. I had to lie to my brother and sneak out in the middle of the night."

"You lied to come here?" Julian raised an eyebrow.

"She's crafty," Andrea said. "Made up this whole camping trip idea. You can't trust a single word that comes out of her mouth."

"That's not true!" I said in mock anger.

"See! All lies!"

I gave her a playful push, sending her into a long-haired

guy with glazed eyes. Andrea apologized to him, but he didn't notice. He stumbled away, looking up at the sky. I couldn't help but wonder if he thought it was falling down on him. Andrea and I caught each other's gaze and started laughing.

"You can travel all over the world if you want," Andrea said to me. "But make sure you take time to shower, okay?"

"Not a problem," I said.

"Speaking of water, I'm still dying of thirst." Andrea tossed her hair over her shoulders. "That stinky pond is starting to look good. Where are your people? I'm going to dry up before we find them."

"Just over there," Julian said, pointing to a VW bus. I recognized it. The back doors were open, displaying a few pieces of clothing. Most of the beads were gone from the table. Business must have been good. The older man still sat in his spot. He nodded at us as we approached, an unlit cigarette dangling between his lips.

"Who's that?" Andrea asked.

"Walter," Julian said. "He kinda runs the group. Him and his wife, Olivia. She's amazing. She makes the clothing we sell. All by hand. I've never seen anyone who can work a needle and thread like her."

A tiny older woman came around the corner of the van. Her blond hair was braided with beads and streaked with gray. The length almost reached her knees. She squealed happily when she saw Julian.

"Now, where exactly did you run off to?" she said in a booming voice. Her eyes trailed down to where Julian's and my hands were still entwined. "Never mind. I see. I gets it." She looked me over with a gigantic grin. Reaching out, she took my arm and pulled me forward. "Oh lordy, child. What do we have here? You're gorgeous. Absolutely gorgeous. Now I know why our little mousie snuck out of the barn."

"You got any water, Olivia?" Julian asked.

"Do I have water? What kind of mother hen you think I am?" She slapped at Walter's legs. "Go get the jug. We've got some thirsty chicks."

"Get it yourself, woman," Walter said. But he'd already climbed to his feet. He winked at me before he climbed into the van.

Olivia tugged on my arm and gently pushed me into the spot Walter had deserted. "Tell me all about yourself, dear. Details! Or I'll have to get them from him." She pointed at Julian. "And he's a guy. They never notice the right things."

That was how I met Julian's family: sitting in the back of the van, listening to amazing music as it drifted across the fields. Walter put some coffee on, and Olivia asked me all sorts of friendly questions. She was the kind of woman who didn't believe in personal boundaries. As long as I kept answering, she kept asking. I didn't mind at all. I wanted them to know everything about me. I wanted to belong.

A week later they became my new family.

No regrets. I'll keep saying that until the end of time. Eventually it'll mean something.

* * *

We climb. The forest swallows us up the moment we step off the beach. Ancient trees circle around us, enclosing Parker and me as we move forward through a multitude of green and brown. Moss covers tree bark and large leaves stretch above, closing us off from the blue sky. After the open beach, it's not long before I'm feeling slightly claustrophobic. I turn around, and already the lake has disappeared.

Up, up we go.

Straight into the mountains.

Parker walks ahead of me, his footing sturdy, his back relaxed. There are no trails here, but that doesn't deter him in the slightest. We go back and forth in switchback formation, alternating between heading toward what I imagine might be north and south. Every direction leads straight up. Parker never pauses to check out his surroundings. He's the only one who ever ventures out here, and the woods have probably become a better companion to him than the rest of us. I'm sure he knows them more than he knows me.

Parker doesn't once look back to see if I'm following.

If I still had muscles to worry about, they'd be aching. If my lungs took in air, I'm positive I'd be breathing heavily. If I still perspired, my shirt and face would be soaked with sweat. I've been sitting on that beach for over forty years; you'd think I'd be horribly out of shape. But I don't need to worry about these things.

When I was alive, I used to hike in the woods behind our house when I wanted some time to myself. It wasn't much, just a few acres of land that hadn't been developed yet. The trees were sparse and skinny, especially in the spring before the leaves began to grow. The wild grass yellowed as the summer took over, and the brambles would snag my clothing and leave red welts on my skin. But it was all I had within walking distance, so I didn't complain. All the neighborhood kids must have felt the same way because I often came across them. They loved the woods as much as I did; it was their escape from the adults constantly telling them what to do. They built small huts out of pilfered wood and rug samples from the local hardware store. The boys would hammer nails into anything they could use, and the girls would bring their dolls to have afternoon tea parties. Sometimes I'd take a garbage bag to collect the bottles and candy wrappers they left behind. Other times I'd let them convince me to play games. Hide-and-seek. Freeze tag.

The woods behind my house were full of life. Birds used to fly over my head, building their nests, warning me when I got too close to their young. Squirrels darted across my path, climbing the trees in a way that seemed unnatural. With their tiny hands and bulging eyes, they'd run effortlessly across the branches, chattering away as I walked beneath. Flies buzzed across my face, and spiders spun their webs in the evening, leaving dew-heavy designs to avoid the next day. Once, I picked up a Coke bottle to discover that a tiny frog had crawled inside.

My point being: A forest is a living thing. It's filled with life. This place, on the other hand, is just a shadow, a memory. Nothing but trees. No bugs, animals, or birds. No left-behind candy wrappers to show that someone once passed through. These woods are too silent. Too still. Not even the leaves move. And that's the weird thing. As we continue along, I begin to notice that there's no death in this forest. No fallen trees. No dried-up bushes. Everything is simply green and lush. Even the rocks look healthy.

"Why do you think this exists?" I ask as we walk along.

"Do you think the trees are stuck here too? Maybe they were cut down to make houses and their spirits came here. They never seem to die. Look around. Not a dead branch anywhere."

"You think too much," Parker says.

"It's weird," I say. "Unnatural."

"And you're surprised?"

"No, I guess not," I say.

Parker stops and sits down on an oversized rock. He looks up at the sky, and I follow his gaze. Nothing but blue peeking down at us. For the first time, I realize I've never seen a sun here. How strange. You'd think I might have looked. Where does the light come from?

"No sun," Parker says, reading my mind. "I've been as high as one can climb here. I've even swum out into the middle of the lake. No sun. I suppose that's why we don't get nighttime, either. I miss the stars. Sometimes when I Fade, I go over to a window and try to look up at them. But you can't see the stars in London anymore, even on a clear night. Too many buildings. They block out the night. What do they call it? Light pollution. Even the moon almost disappears. All that mystery and emptiness. Galaxies and universes that never end. Endless space. And this is where we end up. It's like being in a box. No matter how much I bang or claw, freedom stays just beyond my grasp."

Shocked is a good word to describe me. Parker sounds angry. In fact, he looks super pissed. His eyes narrow and his fingers tighten around a plant, tearing a leaf from its stem. He holds it up, turns it around so I can see its green veins, rips it in half, and then drops it to the ground. It disappears before touching the dirt. When I look back at the plant, I see it's returned to its full glory.

"This place is deceiving," Parker says. "When I first started exploring, the trees used to move around on me. I'd walk in a straight line for the entire day and never find myself on the other side of the beach. I'd climb over a mountain and come out on the exact same side. It only made me more determined to figure out its secrets. It had to be hiding something."

"And you found it?" I ask.

"Not exactly," Parker says. "But I did learn things. It changes because it's limited. There's only so far to go. Think of it like a snow globe, but without the glass walls. When I've reached the end, I simply start over again at the beginning."

"Endless time," I say. "Like a loop."

"Exactly," he says. "Whoever or whatever brought us here, they didn't plan on us leaving anytime soon."

"But you found a way out," I say.

"Have you ever talked to that Korean gent?" Parker asks. "The new one. Showed up not too long ago? Haunts a fraternity house at some university?"

I nod. Louis Chen. Our most recent crossover. Electrocuted by his roommate in the bathtub. Apparently they'd been designing a video game, and his friend got greedy over the royalties. Poor Louis. After one or two haunts, he discovered that his death had been ruled accidental. The game worth killing over became a bestseller, and the murdering roomie now lives in luxury.

"He spent a day explaining computers to me," Parker says. "You know what I'm talking about, right?"

I nod. Computers are foreign to people like us. Some existed in my day, but they weren't the kind that anyone would consider personal. A few Fades ago, I managed to get a look at my first. Some guy had left it out on his dashboard. Funny enough, my message to him was that his online girlfriend was actually a man. Stupid, I know, but he'd been planning on sending him/her thousands of dollars to come visit.

I think of the computers that helped launch the first astronauts into space. They were big and boxy, full of bright lights and fancy buttons. Back in the sixties, we were blown away by that technology. These days a computer like that would be obsolete and primordial. If Julian is still alive, I bet he uses one. Or maybe he has a fancy cell phone.

"Chen told me that computers often have back doors. Ways to get inside locked programs. Sometimes they're built by the inventor of the product; sometimes criminals—they call them hackers—get in there and change things."

"You think we're in a locked program?"

"No," Parker says. "But I think . . . maybe something else got inside and installed a back door. A way out. A chance to cause chaos."

"Why chaos?"

"Why not? If the afterlife is about being good and evil, then it makes sense that evil would want chaos."

"How do you know it's not evil that put us here?"

"I don't," Parker says. "But for argument's sake, let's assume it's not. None of us are truly bad. We're not models of perfect goodness, either, but I don't think it's that black-and-white."

I nod.

"You remember being alive. Did you believe in God?"

"Yes."

"Even though you never saw him. Or were given proof?"

"We know the afterlife exists," I say with a smirk. "Bit too late for that one."

"We don't know God is responsible, though."

"I guess," I say. "But arguing over a name is pointless. We still don't know, so unless you've got some firsthand experience . . ."

"It's irrelevant. What's important is that we didn't know back on earth. The afterlife is a constant guessing game for everyone. And with this back door, we'd have a chance to tell everyone willing to listen. Do you see my point? Whoever put us here didn't want us getting out."

"But we Fade."

Parker nods. "Trust me, I've spent decades thinking about that. I can't help but wonder if haunting was an accident. Maybe it wasn't something that was supposed to happen. A rift in the afterlife for those of us who don't cross over peacefully. We're the error in the computer program. We're not even a good mistake. No one really believes in ghosts, do they? The people who do see us, they make excuses. They talk themselves out of it. Think something's wrong with their eyes or that we're solar flares."

"Solar flares?"

"I don't know. Scientific excuses. Answers for questions they don't want to fully think about."

"So why not just shut this whole thing down?" I say. "Send us wherever we're supposed to go."

"I don't know," Parker says. "I'm just as ignorant as you. These are my thoughts and observations." He stands up and stretches. "Maybe that's the whole point. It's up to us to figure out the puzzle."

"That'll never happen," I say, thinking about all those people sitting on the beach, waiting patiently for all eternity. The thought makes me sad. Maybe there is some truth to that whole "finding closure" thing. Perhaps the answers to our questions aren't waiting back on earth. Maybe they're right here under our noses, but we've become too passive to find out.

"We should move on," Parker says. He gets up and stretches his nonaching muscles. "There's still a ways to go."

I can't help but think he's right about that, on more levels than one.

TATUM

Scott's wrong about Sunday night being quiet. From the moment she walks in the door, it's a steady stream of customers. Most of them look like students, with books spread out across tables and laptops open to Word documents full of notes or reference sites. Several look like they've laid claim to their spots and are refusing to move until midterms are over. Their study areas are covered with empty dessert dishes and half-drunk espressos.

Scott takes her order and promises to come over as soon as he has time. It doesn't happen. Caffeine-needy folks keep coming through the doors, and poor Scott, stuck on his own, can barely handle them all. It takes at least two hours before the crowd begins to thin out.

Tatum waits patiently in the corner, surfing the Internet, avoiding Facebook, and doing lots of "research." There are thousands of websites dedicated to ghost stories. Like Scott said, it's not just ghosts that fit the haunting bill. Poltergeists, banshees, and paranormal readings are in hot demand too. Want to talk to your loved one and find out answers from the great beyond? Talk to a spiritual medium for an outlandish amount of money. To Tatum, a lot of the real-life stories read more like crazed conspiracy theories. She finds a forum section for a haunting website and gets hopeful, but that changes quickly when she discovers it's mostly a bunch of people fighting over the best ways to record nighttime sounds or the best way to trap a ghost so you can take pictures. After several threads on how to tell if your house is being haunted, she begins to think most people are idiots. She finishes reading the comments from a woman who believes the ghost of a hamster possesses her dog, then closes her laptop and shakes her head. Of all the stories she read tonight, not a single one is similar to her own experience. Although plenty of people claim to have seen a ghost or, in a few cases, felt an icy-cold presence, no one has ever talked to one. Mostly they just seem to want to outdo each other on the Internet by bragging about who has seen or believed more.

"Hey."

She looks up and Scott is right in front of her. "Hey."

"We're closing. Do you want to stick around for a bit? I've got something for you. Sorry I couldn't stop by earlier. It's crazy." He points to a disheveled guy packing up his laptop and lowers his voice. "I thought I'd have to call the police on that guy. He nearly had a fit when I told him we're closing. I think he's downed enough coffee and Red Bull tonight to kill a large animal."

"That's okay," she says. "And yeah, I can stick around."

"Cool."

She waits as he ushers people out the door. The disheveled guy loudly demands the names and addresses of other coffee shops in the area. He then gives Tatum a death look as he heads to his car. She opens her computer and notices it's already nine thirty. Traffic shouldn't be too bad going home, but she's going to be late. For a moment she contemplates texting Mom to let her know, but then Scott reappears with a photo album in his hands. It's thick and stuffed with all sorts of papers.

"So I asked my grandma about your ghost," he says. "The girl named Molly. And yeah, she knew exactly what I was talking about. It was a murder thing back in the seventies. Big-time serial killer caught in Hannah. Apparently Granny was fascinated by it when she was younger. She even saved all the newspaper clippings."

"You're kidding me."

"Nope." Scott drops the album in front of her. "I guess her friend's father owned the land where they found the girl's body. Granny said she got to see it. The area where she was dumped, I mean—not the actual body. Granny collects all sorts of clippings. She's got an entire guest room filled with stuff. It took us nearly all afternoon to find it. But I managed to convince her to loan it to you for a few days."

"Wow, thank you."

"So you think this might be your ghost?"

Tatum holds on tightly to the photo album, almost too nervous to open it. "I don't know. I hope so."

"Even if it isn't, you should still be able to come up with enough for a story. I read some of the articles. The girl. Her name was Molly Bellamy. Horrible death. Ample ghost-story material there."

"This is incredible," Tatum says. She opens the album and begins flipping through it. The first few clippings are of no interest, just local stuff, but by the tenth page she finds the head-line. A front-page article dated May 1970. There are two large black-and-white pictures included. The first one is a farmer's field just off Frog Road. A group of small, blurred people move through the mucky acre, obviously police on the scene of the grisly murder. The second picture is one you'd find in a high school yearbook. A girl with long brown hair, smiling at the camera, wearing a peasant blouse and a beaded necklace.

Molly.

There's no mistaking it. This is the girl Tatum talked to. The reality hits her like a brick wall. She's real. Molly's *real*. Even though Tatum has seen her twice now, there's been a small part of her determined to believe she's losing her mind. But seeing this article confirms it. Tatum isn't crazy. She's really been communicating with a ghost.

How insanely amazing is that?

Tatum's hands begin to shake slightly from the excitement. If Scott notices, hopefully he'll think it's because of the three cups of coffee she consumed in the past two hours. Just in case there's potential for her and Scott to be friends, she doesn't need him thinking she's some sort of crazed Goth girl obsessed with death.

"I'm going to close up the shop," Scott says. "Feel free to stick around and read them. Shouldn't take me long. Half an hour, tops."

"Sure," she says. "Thanks again."

He wanders off, and she can hear the clinking of metal as he cleans up around the espresso machine.

Trying hard to suppress a grin, Tatum reads the first article. It's from the *Washington Post* on May 7, 1970.

The body found Monday in a shallow grave in Hannah, Washington, was positively identified yesterday as that of one sixteen-year-old Molly Bellamy from Dixby, North Carolina. Molly had been reported missing by the people she was traveling with when she failed to return home from a shopping excursion.

The police have no suspects, but are currently going through leads. Anyone with information should contact the local police department.

There's a bunch more to the article. The farmer who found the body is named. The cause of death isn't determined, but Tatum thinks it might have been too gruesome to talk about in the paper. Things were a lot tamer back in those days, or so her nana reminds her whenever she comes over and they see something violent on TV. Of course, Nana also has issues about girls who wear skirts shorter than knee-length and put on makeup. Thankfully Tatum doesn't see Nana often.

She goes on to the next *Washington Post* article. This one talks about how the police have been searching the farmer's field looking for more evidence. They've been putting in endless hours trying to find a lead. The body has been released and sent back to North Carolina, where Molly is to be buried in a plot beside her grandparents. There's another picture of Molly. She's sitting beside a young guy with blond hair the exact same length as hers. He has his arm draped casually across her shoulder. She holds up her hand to block the sunlight while she grins at the camera. The glint of a small diamond ring is on her finger. Tatum instantly recognizes the ring. Molly still wears it.

The caption beneath states it's the last known picture taken of Molly. She died a week later.

Tatum frowns. This can't be right. It goes against everything she's been led to believe all this time. If Molly's body was reclaimed and given a proper burial, why is she haunting? Why hasn't she crossed over or whatever it is ghosts are supposed to do? There's got to be something Tatum's missing. A reason right under her nose.

Tatum reads on. The next article is from October 16, 1971.

Walter Morris, dubbed the Commune Killer, was found guilty yesterday of first-degree murder in the 1970 torture death of Molly Bellamy, a sixteen-year-old from Dixby, North Carolina. Morris was the self-appointed leader of a traveling commune that had no fixed address and had moved across the USA several times over the past five years. Bellamy had joined the group back in 1969 after meeting them at the Woodstock music festival in Bethel, New York. She became engaged to Julian Lapointe, another commune member, a few months later.

Since his arrest one year ago, Morris has been linked to the deaths of six other young girls from across the country, and he is believed to be connected with at least fifteen more. Trial dates have been set for three more cases in Ohio, Tennessee, and Florida. If found guilty, he could face the death penalty under Florida state law.

There's a picture here. Tatum pulls it closer, trying to pick out the expressions in the grainy, faded paper. Walter Morris seated in the middle of a courtroom. His long white hair is pulled back in a ponytail, and he's wearing a prison uniform. He looks exactly the way she might have pictured an older hippie in the 1970s. Not that Tatum's an expert, but she went through a Beatles phase a few years ago and ended up downloading a ton of music from that era. She didn't listen to much of it—she found it old and boring—and she was mortified when her dad started singing along to Bob Dylan.

But she remembers looking at some of the album covers and news articles from back then. There was a lot of long hair. And beards. Walter Morris looks exactly like he belonged. And his face isn't that of a monster. His eyes are bright and friendly. His face suggests a friend's father, the kind of person you could talk to politely and never worry about.

He doesn't look like a killer at all.

Tatum looks at the picture again, this time noticing the people in the courtroom behind Walter. In the front row is a group of people who might have been part of the commune Molly traveled with. The expressions on their faces are full of grief. But one person really stands out. A young man, maybe a year or two older than Molly, wears a secondhand suit that's too large for him. Is this Julian? She narrows her eyes, squinting at the creased paper. She goes back to the earlier article, the one with the photo of Molly and the young man. Yes, it's the same guy. Molly's fiancé.

He's very handsome. Long blond hair falls across his shoulders. A slim build. The kind of guy Tatum would probably check out twice. He appears to be looking away from the camera, his eyes sad and longing. He's holding the hand of an older woman beside him. She glares straight into the back of Walter's head, looking as if she wants nothing more but to kill him herself.

"Is that your killer?"

Tatum jumps up in surprise. She didn't hear Scott come back to the table. He's removed his apron and is wearing a jacket. Tatum looks at her computer clock. Half an hour's already passed. It's time to go home.

"Yeah," she says.

"So does this mean you have enough to write your story?"

"I guess so," she says. "It's weird, though. I've done a ton of research on ghosts, and this story doesn't add up."

"Really?" Scott sits down on the chair across from her and picks up the first article. "What's wrong with it?"

"She has no reason to be a ghost. Her body was found. Her killer went to jail. Aren't ghosts supposed to have unfinished business? Every website I look at says that's the reason why they don't pass over. Something to do about being unable to enter heaven if your soul isn't completely at peace."

"Dunno," Scott says. "That sounds a bit vague. Wouldn't you think anyone who died young wouldn't be peaceful? I'd like to think I'd be angry if I get hit by a car on the way home."

"Yeah, no kidding."

"Maybe she tripped on her shoelace on the way to the white light."

"Or got lost."

"Had to stop and ask for directions?"

Tatum giggles. "Can you get heaven on GPS?"

Scott picks up the newspaper article and studies Molly's picture. His casual smile fades away. "She was really pretty. What a shame."

"She was engaged," Tatum says quickly. For some reason her stomach tightens when Scott mentions Molly's looks. Is she jealous? Come on. Of a ghost? What a ridiculous idea.

"Maybe that's her unfinished business," Scott says. "She's got to come back to get married. Wait, wasn't there already a movie about that? One with Johnny Depp?"

"It's possible," Tatum says. "Or maybe they got the wrong guy. No, that can't be it." She thinks about what Molly said to her. She mentioned Walter specifically as the person who did the deed.

"So do you really believe this stuff?" Scott asks. "Ghosts and unfinished business. Or is this just your writerly curiosity coming out?"

Tatum pauses. She knows she should laugh and say she finds the concept of ghosts to be completely stupid. Everyone knows there are no such things. But there's something in the way Scott is looking at her that makes her want to tell the truth. Well, not all the truth.

"Yeah, I guess I am a bit of a believer," she says.

Scott smiles. "Then I should tell you I totally lied."

"What do you mean?"

"About my grandma. Remember I said she was all interested in this stuff because it was her friend's farm? I lied. What if I told you that she claims she actually met Molly's ghost in person?"

Tatum nearly drops the cold cup of coffee that's halfway up to her lips. "But what about all these articles? They're all from the seventies."

Scott smiles. "She got them from her neighbor a few years ago. He was some sort of hoarder. Had an entire bedroom full of papers from all over the place. Magazines. Books. She kept a bunch of them and found all this stuff."

Tatum leans closer. She's practically on the edge of her seat. She's gone beyond trying to look cool and collected to impress Scott. Her excitement must be contagious because he can't stop grinning.

"So what happened then?"

"With my grandma? It's crazy, actually. I never knew this about her. She only told me this story the other night. I'm still kind weirded out. About five years ago, she was coming home from a bridge tournament. She saw this young girl hitchhiking on the road and says she felt compelled to pull over. She's never picked up anyone in her entire life, but she says she had no choice. It was like her body became possessed and she had to stop."

Tatum is nodding. She felt the same way when she first saw Molly. She remembers being wary, and then all that fear just went out the back window. There had been something magical about the girl on Frog Road.

"So she picks this girl up and they drive for a while. Have a bit of small conversation. She said her name was Molly and she seemed fascinated by the car stereo and the CDs Grandma had on the dash. Then the girl turned and touched her. She told Granny that she was missing something important and that she had to go back to her sister's house in New Hampshire. If she moved the bed in the guest room, she'd find her answer. Then she just disappeared. Granny said she nearly crashed the car into a tree. She was really shaken up over it. Wouldn't drive for a month. Made my uncle take her for groceries. Told him some lame story about the accelerator being broken."

Shivers slip across Tatum's skin. This is like what she read on the forum. That guy who insisted Molly had told his friend that his mother was dying and where to find the will.

"So what happened?"

"Granny got on a plane and went to New Hampshire. Her sister had died five years ago and they'd sold the house. But the person who'd bought it had turned it into a bed-and-breakfast. They'd kept most of the antique furniture, including the bed in the guest room. It was this huge mahogany oak thing—took three people to move it. But Granny insisted, and they found an envelope behind it with a safety deposit key in it. They went to the bank and found the box. There was all sorts of stuff in there that Granny thought had been lost. Jewelry. Pictures. Even some old stocks."

"That's amazing."

Scott nods. "Yeah, she told me all about this the other night after making me swear I wouldn't tell Mom she's senile and belongs in a nursing home."

"Wow."

"I know, right?" Scott picks up another article and glances at it. "I always thought Granny was kinda boring and old. Not anymore. Now she's kinda cool."

It's on the tip of her tongue to tell Scott all about her own experience with Molly, but she stops herself. She's not quite ready to share yet. Scott still isn't a friend, and a part of her still worries that she's being set up. Damn Claudette for making her so suspicious. It's not fair. Will she ever be able to trust people again?

Yes, she thinks. *The day I get out of here. I'll drive so far away, no one will be able to find me. Sure, I'll still have trust issues, but it'll be different. At least I'll be able to look at people and not immediately think they're on Claudette's side.*

"Well, I should lock up," Scott says. "I have to set the alarm. The owner will wonder if I stay behind too late." He stands and jangles the keys in his hand. "You can keep that stuff for a few days if you want. It'll give you enough time to copy it. Granny doesn't mind. Heck, she'll probably agree to an interview if you want one."

Tatum laughs. "That might be a good idea. I'll let you know how the story comes along."

"I hope you'll let me read it."

Tatum almost groans. She has no intention of ever writing it. All she wants to do is go home and surf the Net, looking for more evidence of Molly's activities. And Julian. Is he still alive? Is that Tatum's job? To find him? A love message from beyond the grave. How romantic.

She gathers up the loose newspaper articles and stuffs them back in the photo album. Tosses her empty cup in the garbage and waits while Scott turns off all the lights behind the counter and sets the alarm. He opens the door for her and locks it behind them.

"I'm working the next two nights," he says as they stand by the door. The parking lot is empty except for both their cars. "But I'd like to talk to you some more about it. This sort of thing is interesting. Maybe you'd like to get together for a coffee on Wednesday. A different coffee shop, hopefully. This isn't really my favorite place for my days off."

Tatum's stomach does a bunch of flip-flops. He's asking her out. More than anything else, she wants to say yes. But that pesky fear tickles the back of her neck. Can she trust Scott?

150

He's got to know about Claudette's accusations. He doesn't live in a cave and isn't immune to gossip. Claudette's managed to convince the entire town that Tatum's a psycho stalker chick. So why isn't Scott running away in fear?

"I don't know . . . ," she says lamely, hating the words as they come out of her mouth.

"Look." Scott reaches out and touches her jacket sleeve. "I know you've been through some hard times lately with all that crap that went down at school. It's a shitty thing that the others are doing. You'd think they'd get over it and move on to a new target. Find a new car to mark their territory on. Those guys are a bunch of morons."

"I can handle it."

"It's not right."

"I didn't do any of those things Claudette claims, either," Tatum says. "I really didn't. But no one believes me, so I'm stuck with it."

There is a long pause while Scott stares at the empty parking lot. In the distance, Tatum can hear the cars on the interstate. Her phone vibrates in her back pocket, probably a text from Mom wondering where she is.

"I know you're telling the truth," Scott finally says. "I saw Claudette and Mr. Paracini a few months ago, here at the coffee shop. They came in holding hands. I swear, when Claudette recognized me, I thought she was going to pass out. She whispered something to Mr. P., and he got all nervous and let go of her hand like she'd turned into a freak. They left right away. Couldn't get out fast enough."

"You knew?"

"Claudette came up to me a few days later and gave me

some stupid story about how Mr. Paracini was tutoring her. Of course I knew that was a load of crap. She was all over him. But she begged me not to say anything. Said Mr. Paracini would write me a great reference letter for college."

"And you agreed?"

"Sure," Scott says. "Come on, this was several months ago. To be honest, I didn't really care. If she wants to get into the teacher's pants, it's not my business. I never thought they'd actually hurt anyone."

"But what about later on?" Tatum's mouth has gone completely dry.

Scott looks down at his feet. "I'm sorry, Tatum. Really, I am. If I had known they were going to attack you that way, I would have said something."

"Then why didn't you?"

"I thought the whole thing would blow over. I never thought you'd end up getting bullied this way. In all honesty, I didn't want to get involved."

The words are like a slap in the face.

I didn't want to get involved.

Isn't that the way it always works? Who cares what happens to the other person as long as it doesn't happen to you? Tatum's lungs begin to burn and she inhales like she's been underwater. Her heart flutters in a bad way. She can feel the pulse at her temples. A panic attack. She hasn't had one of these in ages. She thought she had them under control.

Breathe. Breathe. Try and calm down. Focus on anything other than Scott. The panic recedes, but anger fills the empty space.

"You could have helped me." Any affection she felt for

Scott has disappeared. Tatum holds on tightly to her laptop, afraid she'll end up punching him if she drops it.

"What if I told you Claudette threatened to destroy me too?" Scott said. "I just got accepted into a bunch of colleges. UCLA has offered me a scholarship. In case you haven't noticed, I'm not working in a coffee shop for fun. My parents don't have the money to help me. I need a scholarship."

"What did Claudette say?"

"She came to me, telling me that Mr. Paracini would change my grade. Tell the schools that he made a mistake. Fail me in biology. She threatened all sorts of lies."

"It would have been us against them," Tatum says. "It's not too late, either. You could still go the principal. Tell the truth."

"Do you really think it would make a difference?"

The worst part is that she knows his words are true. Even if Scott did tell someone, the only thing it would do is bring up the whole ugly mess all over again. The damage is already done. Does she really want to go through it a second time?

But it's a chance to be redeemed.

If anyone believes Scott.

And Tatum has a strong feeling that no one is going to believe anything Scott says. No, more likely he'll get labeled a troublemaker and a liar. Then the others will start bullying him. He'll lose any chances of going to college. He'll be no better off than Tatum.

"I'm sorry," Scott says. But the apology isn't good enough.

"I've got to go." Tatum turns and fumbles with her key chain. She throws everything in her backseat unceremoniously.

Scott taps on the side of her car. She starts the engine and presses the button to lower the window. The radio begins blasting My Chemical Romance. She reaches over and turns it off so she can hear him.

"I can tell someone," he says. "I know it's selfish of me to think of myself when your life is such a mess."

"No," she whispers. "You're right. They wouldn't believe you anyway."

"I'm really sorry."

She knows he's telling her the truth. Unfortunately, the truth doesn't do much these days.

"I know," she says.

"Look," Scott says. He leans from one leg onto the other. "I'd really like to get to know you better. Take a few days to think about it. You'll have to give me back the articles anyway. Okay?"

"Sure." Her phone starts to ring. Her mother. She's going to freak if Tatum doesn't answer. Ignoring texts is one thing. Missed phone calls when she's almost an hour late are worth notifying the authorities.

"I've got to go," she says. She grabs her phone.

Scott steps back from the car. "Just think about it."

She makes no promises.

MOLLY

We climb.

Eventually Parker stops dragging me up the hill and we move across the terrain toward what I assume is the other side of the lake. I'm not even sure what direction we're going in. I can't see anything but trees and blue sky. I have no idea how long we've been hiking. Time means nothing here. If I could pin it down in earth hours, I'd say it's been more than a few.

"We're almost there," he says.

Things begin to change. Hardly noticeable at first. A dead leaf crunches beneath my sandal. I spot a fallen tree. We have to climb over it to continue moving. The bark is rough beneath my hands. Pieces fall off and onto the ground. They don't instantly reappear like they should.

I see footprints in the soft moss. Probably Parker's from the times he's been here before.

Then I hear it. The soft rustle of leaves above me. I look straight up.

Wind.

This place. This small area in the tiny corner of our snow globe. It's alive.

"How is this possible?"

There's moss on a downed tree beside me. It glistens with dampness. I reach out and run my fingers along the soft clumps. Pulling away, I see that my skin is wet. And it's cool. I hold my hand up to my face, shocked, my brain still trying to understand what it's feeling.

It's like I've escaped back to earth.

"I don't know," Parker says, but I can tell by the tone of his voice that he's got his theories.

"It's like a gateway," I say.

"Yeah, that's how I figure it too. A crossover between both worlds. This place, it's not very big. About fifty feet in diameter. There." He points to the right of us. My eyes follow his finger.

A cave.

A hole cuts straight into the mountain. It's about four feet high and wide enough to fit a slender person. It's so well camouflaged by the bushes, I probably could have walked right past it and never seen the entrance. I try and look inside, but all I can see is darkness. This is supposed to be the big escape from our prison. How does it work, and how quickly can I get out of here?

"Okay," Parker says. He stops, blocking me from moving farther. "I need to explain some things first. You need to understand what you're up against. There are . . . rules. Easy enough to follow, but trust me, you don't want to get trapped out there."

I almost want to laugh. It's inside here that we're trapped; being stuck on earth again sounds like a dream come true. How many times have I Faded to the road, only to wish I could spend a few hours doing my own thing? It always sucks when I see the headlights in the distance and know exactly what I have to do, what stupid mystical rules I have to follow, when I Fade back to this place. I am the ultimate puppet on a string. We all are.

"Fine, hurry up, then," I say, the words coming out harsh and slightly childish. After being stuck here for over forty years, I might have learned to be patient.

"Sit down." Parker points to a fallen tree. The one with the damp moss.

If I sit there, I'll get my dress all wet. Sadly, that sounds heavenly. I give Parker a look to suggest he needs to just get on with it, but he refuses to budge. Finally I sigh loudly and plop my butt down in protest.

"It's not hard to get out," Parker says. "Easier than I would think. It didn't take me long to work out the puzzle. You can go wherever you want. All you really have to do is think about it."

"Anywhere in the world?" Suddenly I'm no longer thinking about Tatum. I mean, once I save her, there's nothing off-limits to me. I could travel anywhere. See all the places I didn't get to visit before I died. Imagine. All I have to do is think about Rio and instantly I'd be in Brazil? How cool is that?

"Yeah, anywhere."

"So how come you don't use this all the time?" I ask. Parker might be cool with his overthinking, analytical brain, but surely even he can't resist such a good thing.

"I did, in the beginning. I was excited, just like you. But I learned quickly that there is a price to pay."

I pause. "Those . . . Remnant things?"

Parker nods. "They're dead, like us. But the similarity ends there. They're . . . I don't know how to describe it. Empty. It's as if their souls no longer exist. Empty shells."

"Okay," I say. "Avoid all empty Remnants. What else?"

"Be serious," Parker snaps. "This is life or death."

"How? I'm already dead."

"Not your soul."

I pause. Can my soul die?

Parker sits down on the log beside me and takes both my hands in his. His skin is cool against mine. I nearly pull back in surprise. I can feel him. The manly roughness of his touch. The pressure of his weight against mine. The outline of his bones. The blood coursing through his veins. Here, Parker is alive.

I try and think of all the times I've touched others in this world. Sadly, I can only remember a few instances. Once when Mary got me to untie her corset. Although my fingers struggled with the knots, I didn't feel anything. Another time, the crazy dog lady tried to read my palm to tell my future. She said I had a short lifeline. Hardly a fortune. Anyone here could have guessed that accurately. But I remember her skin felt no different from my own.

I've touched Parker before. I've never felt any emotional response with my body. No shortness of breath. No butterflies in my stomach. He's just something to touch against my unfeeling skin. But this, this is different.

This makes me remember:

A bright flash of sunlight. My brother and me, running through a field with baskets full of raspberries. My feet bare, toes digging into the spongy earth. Warm heat spreading across my head, my arms, my legs. Putting my basket down to do a cartwheel. Marcus laughing when I trip. The soft grass cushions my fall, and I can't help but join my brother in high-pitched squeals of delight.

Julian, holding me tight. Swimming out by the lake. We've wrapped a blanket around our bodies to keep warm. One of his hands caresses my skin; the other slips beneath my shirt, trailing a line of wetness along my side. Hearts beating. Breath heavy. Julian's lips brushing against my cheek. I tilt my head to kiss him.

My brain has turned into mush. A thousand thoughts rush through my mind. Part of me wants to throw myself against Parker, take in these new feelings as much as possible. What about his lips? Are they soft? Cool? Wet?

I open my mouth and gasp. Air rushes into my lungs, almost choking me. I can't remember the last time I actually tried breathing.

"It's amazing, isn't it?" Parker grins. He realizes he's completely derailed me by simply holding my hands. His eyes shimmer with excitement, and a bit of smugness, if you ask me. He's showing off a secret he's held on to forever, and if he weren't being so completely serious, he might actually enjoy it a bit more.

"It is," I say. I look down at Parker holding tightly to me. His hands are almost twice as large as mine. I have such dainty wrists. Parker's hands are rough but soft at the same time. I've forgotten how good a man's skin can feel.

"Now listen to me, Molly," Parker says. "When you go through to earth, it's got to be temporary. The Remnants will sense you. They'll be drawn to you. If you stay too long, they'll find you. And you don't want that. If they catch you, that's it. You're gone."

"You're not going to come with me?"

Parker is taken aback. "You want me to come?"

"Yes."

He pauses. For a moment I see a brief flicker of fear cross his eyes. "Okay."

I let go of Parker's hand and walk toward the cave. So much darkness beyond that doorway.

"All right, then," Parker says. He reaches out his hand again. "So you don't get lost. It can be tricky. And watch your head."

Nodding, I allow him to lead me inside.

We move carefully through the wet cavern. Both of us have to duck while we walk, and after a few steps the walls grow closer, until Parker and I have to move sideways. The light from the outside world quickly fades as Parker leads me farther into the dark. I reach out and touch the sides for leverage. The rock is icy cold against my touch, and my fingers become slightly slimy. But the cave quickly becomes super dark; I need something to press against so I don't lose my balance.

"It's not that far," Parker says. "Look ahead: you can see the glow."

He's right. As soon as my eyes adjust to the absolute blindness, I can see a faint glow from up ahead. It becomes brighter as we approach, and I'm surprised to discover it's the walls themselves that are giving off all that light. The air grows warmer, more humid, and breathing becomes difficult.

Yes, breathing.

Parker takes me around a corner, and suddenly we're there. The narrow walls open up to a small chamber. Everything glows, giving off a warm light.

"It's beautiful," I say. "It's like being on the inside of a diamond."

Parker nods. "No idea how it's even possible, but it is."

In the middle of the room is a clay bowl. Inside are dozens of tiny pebbles. Beside it are pieces of chalk. Parker goes over and picks up a piece. Moving back toward the left wall, he motions for me to come closer.

"Here's the trick. Write where you want to go with this," he says as he hands me the chalk. He points to a part of the wall that has a perfect smooth surface. "It can be a place, a person, whatever you desire."

I take the white piece of chalk from him and stare at the wall. This is happening. Parker's given me the thing I've longed for ever since meeting Tatum. A chance to save her. I still don't care if she thinks she's fine; I know in my heart it isn't true. All I have to do is write her name. But I hesitate.

I'm scared. And I know it's not because Parker's been filling my head with horror stories about the Remnants. I'm not worried about that—I'm positive he's overreacting, like he does with other things. I think Parker is trying to protect me from myself. And he's right. Going back to earth and not having to follow any rules is what terrifies me. This is the freedom I've been longing for. And now that I know it exists, how will I ever give it back?

What if there's a way to stay? To become human again? To live, grow old, and then truly die when I'm ready? What if this is my chance? Should I really be wasting it chasing down a girl who obviously doesn't give a damn about her own life? Why should I even bother? She's so determined to be right. Stubborn.

No, focus on the real reasons. I need to help Tatum. After that, I can deal with my selfish desires.

Carefully, I write Tatum's first name on the cavern stone. I don't have any other information. Hopefully the wall won't require it.

"Now pick up one of the pebbles," Parker says. "Put it in your pocket and don't drop it. You'll need it to get back."

"How did you figure all this out?" I ask.

"Roani showed me."

"Who?"

"A guy who used to be here. Like us. He learned from someone else, who probably learned from someone even further down the line. It doesn't matter. I'm the only one left who knows now."

"What happened to him?"

"He's gone. The worst part is, I don't think anyone remembers him either. One day he didn't come back, and no one ever asked about him afterward."

If the story is meant to scare me, it's not working. I'm even more determined to try this out. I reach down and pick up a small gray stone. Parker grabs one too. I slip it inside a pocket of my skirt and press my hand against it to make sure it's safe.

"Now what?" I ask.

Parker doesn't need to answer me. The walls instantly fade away. I close my eyes tightly, holding on to Parker to make sure he comes along for the ride.

* * *

I hear noises. Night sounds. Crickets singing away in the bushes. The faint rumble of a truck in the distance. The loud silence of being outside in a large open space. A cool breeze wafts across my face. Opening my eyes, I find myself standing on the sidewalk of a street I don't recognize. It's nighttime. Several rows of houses are in front of me. Most of them have their lights turned off. Cars sit in driveways.

"We're here," Parker says.

Where exactly are we? I look around, half expecting to see Tatum pop up in front of us. But the street is empty. There's not a soul in sight.

Except us.

I turn to face Parker. He looks slightly different. I can't explain or describe it. He looks more human. The wind blows his hair across his forehead. I've always wanted to run my fingers through his hair, and now I reach out and touch it. Parker smiles, enjoying my reaction. It must be stirring up old memories of his first time breaking free.

I step back and spin around, feeling the wind as it presses against my skirt. Looking straight up, I can see the yellow glow of a streetlight. I haven't seen one of those in forever. I'd almost forgotten about them.

"It's amazing," I say. A *town*. This isn't just Frog Road; I'm standing in the middle of a street, and there are people sleeping in those houses. I could run up and down the block and look in the windows. I could walk in one direction until morning. I could watch the sun rise.

"I want to do this forever," Julian once said, his lips pressed against my ear. We'd stayed up all night, and now the sun was about to rise. Sitting in the back of his truck, we'd piled blankets around us. The end to a perfect evening. Or the beginning to a new day. Where it began and ended never mattered.

"I want to watch the sun rise with you for the rest of my life," he said.

"Me too."

"Marry me."

No. No. No. Too many sad memories. Why can't I just shut it all out and move on? Why can't I make new memories?

I could if I stayed here, away from the beach with all those other souls who can't stop remembering.

"We can't stay long," Parker says, determined to destroy my fun. "Let's find your girl." He glances down the street. "She should be close. Any idea?"

I look at the dark row of houses. Only a few still have lights on, and most of them seem to be coming from upstairs bedrooms. "She must live here somewhere. I wonder what time it is."

"I don't know," Parker says. "Late, but not too late. Too many lights still on."

"Does this normally happen?" I ask. "When you write something on the wall, does it not always send you to the right place? Where did you go, anyway?"

"Now isn't the time to be asking," Parker says as he scans the block again. "Question me later. Right now, we have to find your girl. If the cave sent you here, she's here." He pauses, listening to the night. "There. An automobile. Hear it?"

I stop to listen. Sure enough, the roar of an engine grows

louder. A car turns the corner a bit too fast. As it moves along the block, I recognize it as being Tatum's. I step back toward Parker, wondering again if I'm doing the right thing. Suddenly I'm overwhelmed with the desire to jump in the bushes and hide like a pitiful puppy.

I don't.

I can see Tatum through the windshield. She doesn't see me at first. She seems to be distracted, barely even looking at the road. When she pulls over to park, her tire hits the curb. A pounding bass sound vibrates from the loud music inside. It's only after she turns off the car and climbs out that she notices Parker and me standing in front of her.

"Oh my God."

"Hi," I say. For the first time in all my Fades and haunting years, I'm at a complete loss for words.

"What are you doing here?" Tatum says.

"I came looking for you."

"How is that possible? Can ghosts travel? I thought you were spiritually bound to Frog Road." She reaches out and gently touches my arm. Her fingers are warm from being in the car. She withdraws her hand, looking somewhat surprised, as if she thought she might reach right through my being.

"Normally I'm stuck as a hitchhiker," I say. "But I found a loophole. A way to help you."

"Help! Yes! I have to show you this." Tatum holds up a large photo album. Her eyes sparkle with excitement. She's already over her surprise at seeing me. She barely even gives Parker a second glance. "I found a whole bunch of information about you. Tons of great stuff. My friend Scott's grandmother

165

collected it. You helped her once. She was the lady who found the bank key behind the bed. Do you remember?"

"I'm not sure," I say. "I don't always remember people when I Fade."

"Fade?"

"It's what we call it when we come here." I look at the album Tatum is waving around, and a sense of dread comes over me. Have all the people I've helped ended up with some weird determination to find information on me? How could they be successful? I try to remember the woman Tatum speaks of. If she is older, she might remember my death. Maybe she was young at the time of my murder and the news left an impression on her. Or she got lucky. Just like Tatum.

My death is not worth remembering. I should be long forgotten, not some mystery for a teenage girl to try and solve. But Tatum's got her mission. What I need to do is give her the answers she needs so we can move on and worry about her. Thanks to Parker, I'm going to get this extra time to spend with her.

"Cool," she says now.

"I can't believe you've gone to all this trouble," I say. Which makes me think this girl doesn't have a lot of friends to keep her occupied.

"Hopefully it'll give me the answers to help you."

Why can't she just let this go?

"You can't help me," I say, but I know my concerns are falling on deaf ears.

"Newspaper articles," Tatum says. "Pictures. And now I have names. Your last name: Bellamy. There's got to be other stuff on the Internet, too. I can help. I know I can. You know, help get you where you need to go. The bright light. All that stuff."

She's so excited. I wish I could share in her enthusiasm, even though I know it's misguided. I can see Parker behind her, amused and trying not to grin.

Most of us on the beach have experienced someone trying to save our souls at least once or twice. The Canadian girl is a great example. Several times she's appeared in the music studio to see a group of people trying to summon her away. They've burned sage in overwhelming amounts. She's had holy water thrown at her. The crazy dog lady says that the new tenant once tried to suck her up with a vacuum cleaner. None of these things have worked. No séances, exorcisms, or even plain old-fashioned begging. No over-the-top paranormal ghost shows with their psychic readers and scientific sound devices. No matter how many real-world humans try to remove us, we keep coming.

So although I know Tatum's heart is in the right place, I also know that I'm not leaving the lake until whoever put me there decides it's time. We've got people who have been there for hundreds of years. We all remember each other arriving, but no one remembers anyone leaving. Except for Roani, the mysterious disappearing person Parker just mentioned tonight.

Tatum's excitement about discovering my past isn't going to change that.

"Tatum, it's not . . ." I pause when I see her stiffen. She's not looking at me. I hear the footsteps from behind. Several pairs.

"Look who's out on a school night," a voice says.

I turn. Two boys around Tatum's age are walking toward

us. Neither of them appears very friendly, even though they're smiling. There's something aggressive in the way they walk, like they think they have a right to whatever is about to happen next. I remember guys like this. The type who thought buying a girl a drink meant they owned her for the night.

As they walk beneath the streetlight, I recognize them.

The vision I had of Tatum being attacked. They are both in it.

"Go away, Graham." Tatum's voice is cautious. Exhausted. Like she's had to deal with this guy more times than she cares to remember.

Graham. He's going to hold Tatum down. Press against her body, forcing the air out of her lungs. His breath will smell like spearmint. No matter how much Tatum struggles against him, she won't be strong enough to fight back.

Right now she doesn't seem scared of him at all. That's going to change if I don't make her listen.

"Where were you tonight? Sitting outside Mr. P.'s house? Peeking through the window? Writing love letters?" He reaches out to grab the album from Tatum's hands, but she's too quick. His fingers only touch air.

"Where were *you* tonight?" Tatum snaps back. "Waiting outside my house for me to come home? Just you and Levi hanging out? Stalk much?"

"Takes one to know one."

"Wow, witty," Tatum says. She looks straight at me and tosses her head slightly to the side, indicating I should follow. "I've got better things to do with my time. Go tip some cows."

Graham grabs her arm as she tries to leave.

"Hey!" I shout, and Parker steps between all of us, grabs

Graham's arm, and shoves him backward. The boy stumbles over his own feet, but only for a second. Regaining his balance, he gets right in Parker's face. Presses his chest against Parker's and bares his teeth. The other boy, Levi, reaches out and pulls his friend back. The silence grows heavy as the boys all face off against each other.

"Who the hell are you?" Graham asks.

He can *see* us? I open my mouth in surprise. I've spent too much time on the highway, only appearing to one person at a time. I honestly didn't think that anyone other than Tatum could see me. Until this moment, I wasn't even sure she could see Parker.

"I'm not your concern," Parker finally says.

"You are if I make you my problem," Graham says. From behind him, Levi snickers and sticks his tongue out in a lewd motion toward me. My eyes narrow, and I ignore the itch in my hand, the desire to punch away that smug look on Levi's face.

"I said get lost," Tatum says.

"What's with the costumes?" Levi says. "It's not even close to Halloween, hippie chick. The sixties sucked."

"And get a load of pretty boy here," Graham says. His voice goes high and stupid as he tries to mimic Parker's British accent. "Oh, golly gee, guv'nor. I like wearing prissy outfits. Got a fag for me, luv?"

"Really?" I say. "You're trying to give us fashion advice? I can see your underwear. And what's with the jeans? Can't you afford a pair that fits?"

"I think that's what passes for fashion these days," Parker says with a serious face.

"And they say my generation dressed weird," I mutter under my breath. I wonder what my dad would think of the kids these days. If he disliked Julian's long hair, he'd despise the way this kid's jeans look like they're constantly hanging at his knees.

"Is this the best you can do, Tate?" Graham asks. He's circling around Parker but keeping his distance. "A Brit queer and a drama-class dropout? Wow, who thought the reject could find kids even more rejectier than her?"

"That's not even a word, idiot," Tatum says.

"You should stay away from that chick," Graham says to Parker. He brushes some imaginary dirt off his jacket sleeve. "Don't believe a word that comes out of her mouth. Bitch is crazy."

"I think it's time for you to leave," Parker says. He turns around and steps in front of Graham. A threatening move. But neither of the two boys moves.

Graham smirks at Tatum. "Whoever these freaks are, they can't fight your battles forever. Kinda pathetic."

"Like you fight Claudette's battle?" Tatum asks. "Get out of here, Graham. Sucking up to her isn't going to get you laid."

Claudette. When I hear the name, my memory brings up a pretty girl with long curly hair. She's from my vision too. She stands over Tatum, enjoying her pain. Laughing as her foot crunches down on Tatum's fingers.

Graham steps forward, and Parker is there in a flash to meet him. Graham's hands shoot up, and he shoves Parker backward and right into me. Parker stumbles, his foot catching on the cloth of my skirt. I hear fabric tear. I look down, and I can see a rip in the bottom. Parker touches my arm in apology. I get out of their way before round two can begin.

Both boys glare at each other again. Graham finally backs down. I don't blame him. Parker is bigger than him by about twenty pounds. Taller, too. But it's not just that. There's something about Parker's attitude that's a little threatening. Otherworldly. Graham can't quite place it, but he can sense it. He knows better than to try and go after Parker. And I doubt his spineless friend, Levi, would help. He's too busy staying on the sideline.

"You're a mouthy little bitch," Graham says. "You'd better watch it. Mouthy bitches get shut up real quick."

Then Graham turns and walks away, Levi trailing behind as if nothing had happened. We watch them fade into the darkness. When they reach the corner, Graham turns and blows a kiss.

"What a jerk," Tatum says. She's holding her car keys in one hand and the photo album in the other. What's scary is that she doesn't seem to be bothered by the incident in the slightest. She looks annoyed, not worried. "Come on. If we're quiet, we can talk in my bedroom. I think my parents have gone to bed."

This isn't the first time Graham and his friend have verbally assaulted her. Obviously it's happened enough for her to build up some sort of immunity. But Graham. His eyes said it all. He meant every word that came out of his mouth.

Tatum really is in trouble. And I just met two of the people who are going to kill her.

"What was that about?" I ask.

"It's nothing."

"It didn't look like nothing."

"Let it go," Tatum snaps. "They're just a bunch of jerks who think it's funny to harass me. But they're harmless. They're all talk."

Tatum begins walking up the sidewalk toward the closest house. Parker reaches out and touches my arm, pressing his shoulder against mine. He's tense. I can feel the muscles in his arm.

"We're safer inside," he whispers.

Right. Remnants might be out and about. Or maybe he's thinking the boys might come back with more of their friends.

"Come on," Tatum calls back to us.

Growing up with these people has made Tatum blind. There are none more vulnerable than those who cannot see. If anyone should know that, it's me. Because we can never fully know someone, no matter how much they share. And the worst of mankind often wears the best masks.

I sigh. This is going to be a long night.

TATUM

She can barely control her excitement as she steps up to the front porch. Molly is *here*. In the proverbial flesh. And Tatum is about to sneak her into her house so they can have a talk. As she pushes against the door, she hesitates, hoping that her texts to Mom were enough to send her parents to bed without worry. She sent one off just after she left the coffee shop.

> I'll be right home. Sorry, got really caught up in my homework.
>
> Half an hour. I promise.

Mom replied, telling her she'd better be home as soon as possible or there would be hell to pay. But Tatum knows that once Mom gets an arrival time, she's less likely to worry. She's probably upstairs, tucked in with Dad (who is most definitely snoring), reading a book until she hears the key in the lock.

And if Tatum goes straight to her room, there isn't going to be a confrontation.

"Okay," Tatum whispers. "Follow me. We have to be quiet."

Molly nods. She steps across the entrance with that guy trailing behind her. Tatum's a bit more worried about him. She can easily explain a girl in her bedroom. All she has to say is that Molly is from school and Tatum is giving her a book for class. But a boy? That's the number one house rule being broken. Let's also not forget that it's after eleven on a school night. Tatum could get grounded until graduation if she gets caught. She thinks about asking Parker to wait outside, but doesn't. He's got a very guarded look on his face. The way he's monitoring Molly's every move suggests he's not going to let her out of his sight.

Thankfully, Tatum's bedroom is on the other side of the house. If they keep their voices down, there's no reason why her mom or dad should hear them. Tatum will turn on some music.

They climb the stairs quietly. When they reach the top, Tatum sees that the light is on beneath her parents' door.

"Tatum?"

She freezes. Points to Molly and Parker.

"Down to the end," she whispers. "On the left."

Molly nods and they move along. Once they're out of range, Tatum pushes open her parents' bedroom door. Sure enough, just as she guessed, Mom's got a book in her hands and Dad is snoring away.

"You're late."

"Sorry," Tatum says.

"Is everything all right? Nothing happened?"

No, everything is wrong. Don't pretend to care.

"I'm fine."

"Okay. Have a good sleep."

Mom places her book on the nightstand and turns out the light. Just like that. Nothing else. She's not even going to scold Tatum for being an hour past curfew. Like everyone else, even Tatum's parents don't care anymore. They'll be relieved when school ends and she leaves town. Their embarrassing daughter. Can't wait to get rid of her.

She's on her own.

Tatum closes the door quietly, ignoring the desire to slam it several times. When she reaches her room, she finds Molly sitting on her mattress while Parker browses the books on her shelf. The bedside reading lamp is turned on, leaving most of the walls covered in dark shadows.

"How much trouble are you going to get into if your parents find out we're here?" Molly asks.

"I won't if they don't come check," Tatum says. She turns on the clock radio by the bed, and music starts to play at low volume. "And trust me, they won't. They don't care enough."

"I'm sure that's not true," Molly says. "All parents care about their children."

"Not mine," Tatum says. "Mine think I'm a nasty little liar and a sociopath. They probably lock their door in fear of me killing them in their sleep." She sighs, knowing she's exaggerating, but the anger is there.

"Why's that?" Molly asks.

"I don't want to talk about it. Just forget I said anything." Tatum tosses the photo album on the bed. "You want to see the clippings? It's your life story. Well, some of it. It talks about

175

your killer, Walter. And about you. Did you really travel the country with a bunch of people?"

Molly looks down at the album. "My life is an open book, is it? Just a story for everyone to read. What a strange thought. Did they make me out to be some drug-crazed girl who deserved it?"

"No, not at all," Tatum says, hoping Molly doesn't see the editorial that pretty much blamed her for everything.

"I'm sure they were out there," Molly says with a sigh. "A girl living with a bunch of nomads? Sometimes people used to yell at me on the street. Once there was a preacher. Told me I was going to hell for holding hands with Julian."

"I'm sorry," Tatum says. "I didn't mean to upset you."

"You're not," Molly says. "It's not as if my death was like the Manson murders. I wasn't famous or part of some psychotic cult. I just find it surprising that strangers would even care. And for the record, I didn't do drugs. Never was into them."

Tatum plops down on the bed beside her. "How can you think that? I'll bet tons of people cared. There was a huge trial. I saw the pictures. Lots of people in the courtroom." Tatum reaches out and touches Molly's arm again. She can't get over how real she feels. If she hadn't already seen Molly disappear twice in front of her, Tatum might start questioning it. But no, Molly is the girl in the pictures. She's even wearing the same ring on her finger. She grabs a few of the loose articles from the album and shakes them for emphasis. "Your life is amazing."

Molly smiles. "Are you sure it's not the ghost part that makes you say that?"

From beside them, Parker laughs.

"Are you a ghost too?" Tatum finally fully notices Parker.

He looks to be a few years older than Molly, but it's hard to tell. The odd clothing he wears makes him look a lot older. An old-fashioned shirt with the sleeves rolled up. A pair of wool trousers. Definitely not the things the local boys wear. He looks like he's fallen straight out of a Jane Austen novel.

"*Ghost* is such an injudicious term," Parker says, and Tatum can tell he's clearly offended.

"Oh, stop it," Molly says. "You call yourself a ghost all the time."

"No, I don't."

"Yes, you do." Molly turns to Tatum. "And yes, he is. Parker haunts a hospital in London, England. We share the same afterlife. I guess that's what you'd call it."

"Wow, England. So you're looking for something too?"

Parker snorts in disgust. "This is useless, Molly. We shouldn't be here. She's too deaf to listen." He goes over to the window and peeks through the blinds.

"Just a few more minutes," Molly says. She turns to Tatum. "Parker's right. We don't have much time. What we did to get here, apparently we can't stay long. So we need to get down to business."

"Right," Tatum says. "Then you need to tell me every-thing about you. We have to figure out what you need to do to cross to the other side."

"No," Molly says. She reaches out and picks up a stuffed animal from where it fell off the bed. A teddy bear Tatum has had forever. Molly turns it over in her hands, admiring the toy. "I'm not here because of me. I want to hear your story. You need help, Tatum."

"I'm fine," Tatum says. She wants to grab that bear and

throw it across the room. Why can't Molly let this go? Tatum's life is dull as dishwater compared to Molly's. Can't she see this? If Tatum can help her, she'll get to be a part of something bigger. She'll accomplish more than getting Claudette to leave her alone.

"Those boys tonight," Molly says. "I've seen them before. When I first touched you in the car. I saw something. I saw them attacking you. They're going to hurt you."

"That's not possible," Tatum says. "I've known them my whole life. Like I said, Graham's all talk. He's just a jerk."

"Not this time," Molly says. She puts a hand on Tatum's arm. "I've seen it. And as you know, my predictions come true."

"How do you know that? Have you gone back to everyone you've talked to and asked them?"

"I know I'm right on this."

Tatum wants to argue, but hesitates. The fear in Molly's eyes is very much real. But she can't be right. Graham Douglas might do childish crap like piss on her tires, but he's not evil. He wouldn't actually hurt her. He's a football player who gets his aggression satisfied on the field. Aside from tonight, she's never seen him get into a fistfight. He may talk tough, but he's a softy. She knows Levi would never hurt her either. Levi might hide behind Graham, but he once brought Tatum flowers. Even though she only went out with him a couple of times, Levi has never shown the slightest hint of a grudge that she didn't want to date him seriously. He's more of a computer nerd. The only reason he and Graham hang out together is because they live next door to each other and both love to play video games all day long.

The more she thinks about it, the more Tatum convinces herself that this whole idea is ridiculous.

That leaves her former best friend.

Claudette may think it's perfectly fine to ruin Tatum's life to protect her own, but Tatum knows she'd never physically hurt her. They've been best friends since kindergarten. Tatum knows Claudette better than she knows herself.

No, that's not true. She was completely blindsided by Claudette. She'd underestimated how far her friend would go to keep her secret safe. The way Claudette managed to get the entire town of Hannah to think that Tatum is a monster.

But kill her? No. Molly's vision is wrong. Tatum looks down at her hands, surprised to see that she's been clenching them into fists. So tightly that her knuckles have turned white. If she's so positive Molly is wrong, then why is her body tensed up like she's about to ride a roller coaster with no safety bar?

"Tell me your story," Molly says softly. "I want to hear what happened. Tell me, and I'll tell you mine. All of it. My life. My death. Then you'll see: I'm not the one you need to be worrying about."

Tatum nods. "Okay," she says. "I'll tell you. And then *you'll* see. There's nothing to worry about."

She begins to talk.

* * *

After Claudette's pregnancy scare, Tatum found herself unable to fall asleep. She tossed and turned the entire night. It wasn't just the words that had come out of Claudette's mouth that scared her, but the tone.

If he leaves me, I'll kill myself.

That wasn't the Claudette she knew.

Claudette was confident. She knew exactly what she

wanted and how to get it. She always knew the exact perfect things to say to keep a boy's attention. She never had trouble getting guys to chase after her by the dozen. She was also a great friend. As far back as Tatum could remember, Claudette had been there for her. Whether it meant driving her home every day for a month when Tatum broke her foot, or hanging out all night when Tatum's old cat, Puffy Snuggleface, finally died, Claudette had always been her friend.

For Claudette to suggest suicide over a man, in Tatum's mind, only meant she'd finally gone in over her head. She'd gotten into a situation that she couldn't handle. Claudette needed help.

Tatum didn't know what to do.

She spent the next days in panic mode. Several times she almost spilled the secret to Mom. But every time she felt on the verge of opening her mouth, she'd think of Claudette and stop. What if she told an adult and no one believed her? Although Tatum was positive her own mother would, it wouldn't mean anything if the school refused to get involved. What if Mr. Paracini pretended the whole thing hadn't happened? It would be his word against Tatum's. And Claudette would be so upset about losing him, she might not tell the truth either.

This wasn't fair. The more Tatum thought about it, the more enraged she became toward Mr. Paracini. He was an adult; he should have known better than to mess up Claudette like that. He needed to be stopped.

Claudette would hate her. But once the whole thing blew over, she'd understand that Tatum was only looking out for her best interests.

She made it all the way through to the first Monday

morning after break. When Tatum got to school, she found Claudette waiting for her at her locker. Her friend's face was puffy under several layers of makeup. They ducked into the girls' bathroom, where they could talk. Claudette opened all the stalls to make sure they were empty before she started.

"About that other night," Claudette said. "I'm really sorry. I totally overreacted. I blame hormones. Forget about it, okay? Everything's good. Thank God! I totally promise to be über-careful from now on."

"Do you think that's a good idea?" Tatum whispered. "Don't you think this is getting a little out of hand?"

"Excuse me?" Claudette snapped. "So you're giving me love advice now? You?"

"No. But I think maybe you should stop dating him. You're getting too involved. You told me that night that you'd kill yourself. That's not right."

"I was being overdramatic," Claudette says. "You didn't really take that crap seriously, did you? Please."

"He's hurting you, Claudette. I think you should talk to an adult."

"I'm not talking to anyone, and Barry hasn't done a damn thing to hurt me," she said. "We're fine."

"He's taking advantage of you. What he's doing is illegal. He could go to jail."

There. The words were out. The temperature in the bathroom seemed to drop ten degrees. Claudette's eyes narrowed before she suddenly shoved Tatum back against the wall.

Tatum yelped as her head hit the mirror. Before she could regain her composure, Claudette pressed herself against Tatum, pinning her between the wall and the sink.

"Listen to me, you little bitch," Claudette hissed. "You better keep your big mouth shut. This is none of your fucking business. If you do anything to try and ruin us, I swear to God I'll make you wish you were never born."

"I haven't said anything," Tatum gasped.

"And if you're smart, you won't." Claudette relaxed her grip, leaving Tatum to grab hold of the sink in order to keep from falling. Her legs had turned to rubber.

"This isn't you," Tatum said. She waved her arm at her friend. "You acting this way. What happened to you? Can't you see you're not the same person anymore?"

Claudette laughed. "I've outgrown you. You can't handle that, can you? The fact that I can get a man like Barry to want me, while you can't even get someone like Levi to ask you out. You're nothing but a jealous, pathetic little girl."

The words stung. Tatum's eyes began to water. This wasn't her friend anymore. The Claudette she knew never would have said such vile things. Letting go of the sink, Tatum turned to head for the door. There was nothing more to say. But Claudette wasn't finished. Before Tatum could escape, fingers closed around her arm.

"You better not tell anyone," Claudette said. "Because if you do, I'll make you regret it."

Tatum shook her off and left without saying a word.

At lunchtime, she went to Ms. Dalian. As she took a seat in front of the desk, she could tell that she'd interrupted the guidance counselor at her lunch. A half-eaten sandwich rested on top of a paper bag.

"What can I do for you, Tatum?"

The tears came first. Then she started talking.

It wasn't easy. Thankfully, Ms. Dalian listened to her whole story without saying a word. She pushed the box of tissues in Tatum's direction and gave her all her attention. Her eyes widened when Tatum mentioned Mr. Paracini, but not once did she suggest Tatum was lying. And when the story was over and laid out across the table, the counselor reacted. She'd forgotten all about her lunch. The bell had rung for the next period, but she didn't tell Tatum to head for class.

"I just don't know what else to do," Tatum said. She'd stopped crying about fifteen minutes ago. There simply weren't any more tears to be spent. She sniffled and took another tissue. The garbage can was almost full of her discards.

"I think maybe you should skip the rest of the day," Ms. Dalian finally said. "Is your mother home? I can call her to come get you."

"She's at work. I can drive myself."

"Do you feel you can?"

Tatum nodded.

"I think that's best, then. You're in no condition to go back to class." Ms. Dalian looked at the phone on her desk and then stared at an imaginary space on her wall. "I'm going to have to talk to the principal about this. I honestly don't know what to do in this situation."

"Please don't get Claudette in trouble," Tatum said. "She's a good person."

"Honey, this isn't your friend's fault," Ms. Dalian said. "She's done nothing wrong. If anything, she's a victim."

"I just want her back to herself."

183

"That may not happen overnight. She's going to be very angry with you. And hurt. It may take a long time before she forgives you."

"I know that," Tatum said. New tears began to fall. "She's going to hate me. But I don't care. I'd rather have her hate me than let things stay the way they are."

Ms. Dalian nodded. "Okay, honey. Let's get you home. I'll figure out what to do next. I'm not going to mention your name, but if you're the only one she told, she's going to know. You've done the right thing here. Now go home and tell your parents. Everything is going to be all right."

"Okay."

Tatum believed her. She did because Ms. Dalian was an adult and she trusted that the guidance counselor would know exactly what to do.

How very wrong Tatum turned out to be.

Claudette wasn't at school the next day. She wasn't there the day after that. Tatum obsessively checked her phone and email every ten minutes, both hoping and dreading that Claudette would contact her. Several times she brought up Claudette's name, but she couldn't bring herself to hit the send button. So she continued to wait, but got only silence on her friend's end. Even Claudette's Facebook page was eerily quiet. She hadn't posted an update in two days. Nothing on Twitter or Tumblr, either. Claudette wasn't the type not to be online. People were starting to send posts wondering where she was.

Funny enough, no one messaged Tatum to ask her where Claudette was. She should have seen that as her first clue. If she hadn't been so preoccupied with her own feelings, she might have noticed that no one was really talking to her. She was so used to being in Claudette's shadow, it didn't alarm her that people were ignoring her. Or that, even worse, they were whispering when she walked past.

Hindsight is always 20/20.

Thursday came around, and everything was fine until after lunch. About ten minutes after class started, Tatum was called down to the office. The entire classroom seemed to hold their breath all at once. Tatum stood up, grabbed her books, and left without a second glance.

When she arrived at the office, she found a group of people crowded around the desk of Mr. Garrison, the principal. Ms. Dalian stood in the corner with a thick manila folder. Tatum's parents sat nervously in a matching set of chairs. Even worse, Mr. Paracini himself leaned against the wall.

Tatum's hands instantly turned to ice. What was Mr. Paracini doing there?

Ms. Dalian asked her to sit down.

They'd placed a chair right between her parents. When Tatum sat down, she saw her father turn his head, trying to hide his anger. When she looked at Mom, her mother cast her eyes to the floor.

What the hell was going on?

"We want to talk to you today about a problem that's come to my attention," Mr. Garrison said. "I understand you came to Ms. Dalian and told her quite a story."

Story?

"I'm sorry, I don't understand," Tatum said.

"We've talked to Claudette," Ms. Dalian said. Her eyes were hard to read. "The problem is, what she told us is completely different from what you told me."

"What did she say?"

"That you made the whole thing up for attention."

"That's a lie!" Tatum could feel the tears threatening to come. She blinked several times, trying to force back the burning feeling.

"And Mr. Paracini confirms it," the principal said. "In fact, he's told us some other things too."

What happened next would destroy her. Claudette had turned everything around so that *she* was the secret keeper and Tatum was the one chasing Mr. Paracini. Then the allegations about stalking were added. Weird love letters Tatum supposedly wrote. Confirmed evidence that Tatum had told several students how she planned to try and bang the hot teacher. Then a final lie from Mr. Paracini himself, about the afternoon that Tatum snuck into his empty class to wait naked on his desk.

"I should have done something," Mr. Paracini said. "I simply averted my eyes and told her to get dressed and leave. She kept talking, trying to convince me that she was a woman and not a little girl. I had to keep a distance of about ten feet while she put her clothes back on. I was horrified that another teacher might come in. Yes, I should have reported it. I just didn't want the poor girl to get in trouble."

Ms. Dalian nodded. She was still holding the manila folder and writing notes down on some paper.

"Up until then," Mr. Paracini continued, "I thought it was a teenage crush. I never expected that she'd try such a thing. Tatum's always been so quiet, she keeps to herself. She's not the first girl to send me love letters. I just toss them in the trash. My wife keeps warning me that I should be more careful. She's right. I guess from now on I'll have to report everything. I never would have guessed that a student would take a stunt this far. I'm glad I saved the emails."

"What emails?" Tatum demands.

The principal sighs and hands over some papers. Tatum goes through them. They're a bunch of letters addressed to Mr. Paracini from Tatum's email address. She reads part of the first one.

> I sit in your class every day and think about how I want to see you naked. You're so hot. I've been in love with you forever. Let's get together. Your wife never needs to know. Wouldn't you rather have a nice young thing?

She flips to another.

> I sat outside your house last night, hoping you'd come outside and take me. But your wife came home too early. Does she go out every Thursday? That could be our night. Love you so much.

The emails are time-stamped. The first one was apparently sent two months ago. But how is that even possible?

"I never sent these." Tatum tosses the paper on the table. "I didn't. They don't even sound like me. You can come over and check my computer. Claudette knows my password. She must have sent them. Or they're faked."

"That would take some elaborate work, to fake emails," Ms. Dalian says. "Isn't it time to come clean, Tatum? You made a mistake. You're confused. Maybe it's time for you to talk to someone. It's not unusual for young girls to develop feelings for their teachers. It's all about growing up and learning to deal with your emotions. We can get you some help."

"But I didn't do it. Claudette is the one."

"We've talked to Claudette. She says the two of you had a falling-out. You told her about what you were doing, and Claudette encouraged you to get help. People saw the two of you fighting a few days ago."

"She's lying."

"I'm in a difficult position here, Tatum. You must understand. There are a lot of people here who have a different story."

Tatum's parents were quiet through the entire ordeal. Her father kept making fists. Tatum wondered if he'd jump up in his chair and start punching people. Mom kept her gaze steady on the floor. She was wearing her dietitian's uniform, which meant they'd pulled her out of work. Her white shoes tapped nervously against the chair leg. There was a small, yellowish stain on her pant leg. She must have spilled something and was in too much of a hurry to clean it off.

"We recommend that Tatum get some counseling," Ms. Dalian finally said. She tucked the notes into the folder. "We can give you the names of some professionals, if you'd like. It doesn't even have to be local. It would be best if we keep this quiet. No need to start rumors. You know how kids can be. I'm sure Claudette will be willing to be discreet to help Tatum out."

Tatum nearly snorted in disgust. If there was one thing she knew best about Claudette, she couldn't keep something secret, especially if it meant hurting others. Claudette would see what Tatum had done as the ultimate betrayal. And the best way for her to get revenge would be to make sure everyone heard about it and no one forgot. And she'd find a way to do it without making it look like she'd been the one who started it.

The meeting ended with Mr. Garrison suggesting that Tatum's parents take her home and keep her there for the next few days while the school tried to sort things out. They weren't expelling Tatum, but a bit of time off was needed for everyone. Mom had to go back to her shift at the hospital, so Dad drove. Tatum tried talking to him, but he told her to wait.

"We'll talk about it later tonight. Until then, I want you in your room. No calls. No computer. Your mother and I love you very much, but we need time to think."

They didn't really talk about it. No one actually knew what to say. Tatum pleaded her innocence, and although her parents claimed to believe her, Tatum was positive they weren't fully convinced. Mom suggested she'd start calling psychologists in the morning, deciding that Tatum would feel more comfortable talking to someone who wasn't emotionally involved. Dad went to the garage and pretended to check the car engine for imaginary problems.

Tatum went to her room. She'd been defeated. She'd told the truth and no one had believed her. What else could she do?

Later that night, the text messages started.

Lying bitch. You should kill yourself.

As if Mr. P wants to see your fat naked body. Grooooooooooss.

Liar, liar, naked on fire.

Her Facebook filled steadily with nasty comments. Some of them were anonymous. Others came from people who had been friendly with her up until a few hours ago. Friends she'd sat with at lunch suddenly had changes of heart. People she'd never even met before, some as far away as New York and even New Zealand, were sending hurtful messages. Her so-called story was making the rumor circuit. Tatum changed her status to private after realizing the comments were coming faster than she could delete them.

Claudette's page, however, was filled with sympathy.

Juniper Hafner: I'm so sorry, Claudette. Who knew Tatum was such a crazed nutbar? You should consider suing her for slander. How could she say that about you? I feel so bad for Mr. P. She could have gotten him fired.

Graham Douglas: Claudette, baby. Just heard. That's messed up. Hope you are okay. Come back to skool. We're on your side.

Levi Tessier: Bitch b crazy.

The Omega Dude: Tatum better watch her back. She's gonna pay for what she tried to do to Mr. P.

Things continued that way for a very long time.

MOLLY

I'm silent while Tatum talks. The pain comes off the girl in waves, and it takes all my strength not to throw my arms around her and hold her tight. I can't even begin to imagine what she's been going through. In a way, her plight is almost as horrible as my death.

Almost.

"That's my story," Tatum finally says. "All of it. Your turn."

I don't even know where to begin after hearing that. Luckily for me, Parker has run out of patience.

"It's time to go," he says. He's been at the window the whole time, watching the street to make sure nothing goes bump in the night.

"No," Tatum says. "You can't go. You have to tell me about your murder. I have to help you." She jumps up off the bed. "I need this. If I have something else to deal with, I won't have to think about myself."

I understand that. Boy, do I. There have been countless

191

times I've sat by the beach, staring off into the lake, wishing I had other things to occupy my mind. But when you're stuck in a place that never changes, the same thoughts creep inside. Maybe I'm trying to do what Tatum thinks she's doing: escaping from myself.

If there's one thing I'm positive about, though, trying to help me won't take away her pain. It won't make her ex-friends hate her any less or stop bullying her. It won't make Claudette have a change of heart and suddenly tell everyone the truth. It also won't change the fact that the adults, people she's always been told she can rely on, have failed her.

And it won't change the fact that in the near future, her former friends are going to kill her.

But Parker is right. We've been here for too long. Parker is growing more concerned by each passing minute. As much as I believe he's overplaying this whole Remnant thing to keep me focused, I can't ignore that Parker is very uneasy. We have to leave.

"I can come back," I say. "I promise. I know how now."

"You can't make a habit out of this, Molly," Parker says. "You know it's not safe."

"Why isn't it safe?" Tatum asks.

"We're not exactly supposed to be here," I say. "We kinda bent some rules to come visit you tonight. So there are others looking for us. If they find us, it could be bad."

Tatum's eyes grow wide. "Really? You're risking, um, well, I guess not your life. You're dead. But you're risking something."

"It's okay, really," I say. "Give me a day or two. Time runs differently in my world. I can't accurately judge it. But I will return. I can't leave you like this."

Parker comes over to me. He's already reached inside his pocket and pulled out his stone. A large gust of wind hits the window, making all three of us jump. Tree branches scratch at the glass, sending creepy shadows across the bedroom walls.

"You have to be careful," I say to Tatum. I take her hand and squeeze it. "These people are not your friends. Don't trust them."

"I know," Tatum says. "But really, you're getting worked up over nothing. I've been dealing with it for months. I'm tough."

The twitch at the edge of her eyelid makes me think she's not exactly telling the truth.

"I hope so."

I pull out my own pebble and turn it around in my fingers. I look at Parker and he nods. Opening my hand, I let the stone drop to the floor.

Tatum's room instantly disappears.

* * *

Once I'd made my decision to leave home and run off with Julian, I grew nervous. How was I going to convince my father that this was what I needed to do? I was only fifteen; my birthday wasn't for another eight months. I could already envision the lecture. The fight I knew we'd go through. No matter how many imaginary scenarios played through my mind, I knew Dad wouldn't give me the answer I wanted. He would do everything in his power to try and keep me in Dixby. And that's why I knew I'd be leaving without his blessing.

Because nothing he could say would change my mind. Even if Dad tried locking me in my room, I'd still find a way to sneak out.

What worried me the most was if Dad called the police. I didn't want to get my new friends arrested for kidnapping. My main priority was to find a way to keep that from happening. If I got dragged back home, I'd never forgive him.

I spent a lot of time talking with Olivia over the last day at Woodstock. It was early Monday morning, and we were waiting around for Hendrix to take the stage. Because of the rain, the concert had gone over an extra day. Dad would be coming home on Wednesday.

"We have a good setup," Olivia said. "Just remember to tell your father. Sage is a teacher. She's fully qualified to help you get your degree. And we always find a place to settle down once school starts. You'll finish your education if it's important to you. We will make sure of that. Do you think it would be easier if we came along for support?"

"It would only make things worse," I said, thinking of Walter's wild long hair and Olivia's beaded skirts. Sage, the teacher, was a woman in her thirties who had spent most of Woodstock running around without a top. He'd take a quick look at their clothes and nonconformist hairstyles and pass judgment. The only reason Dad tolerated that stuff on me was because of my age. He figured I was just going through a stage. But fully grown adults doing the same thing?

"Stress the education. We firmly believe in it. Julian finished his high school degree a year early thanks to being with us. Don't let Sage's free spirit catch you off guard. Knowledge is power. It's the future."

I sighed. Education wasn't really a priority when it came to my dad. He'd never made it through high school himself. Back in my town, it wasn't uncommon for kids to drop out. I thought of Marcus and how Dad hadn't cared when he'd stopped going to class in his junior year in order to work at the mechanic shop. As far as Dad had been concerned, Marcus was old enough to make his own decisions. Somehow I had the feeling I wouldn't get the same respect. Dad was good at playing the "It's different 'cause you're a girl" card. Not that I wanted to drop out of school. I enjoyed learning. And I had to admit, as crazy as Sage was, she was smart. Andrea and I had spent a few hours with her discussing the Vietnam War. Sage may have enjoyed going braless, but her brain was anything but empty.

"Dad's going to think I'm foolish," I said. "That I'm too young and this all happened too soon. Maybe it's true." I gave Olivia the most pleading look I could muster. "Do you think I'm being stupid? I feel different with Julian. Like I've been waiting my entire life for this moment. Oh God, I used to laugh at girls who did the whole love-at-first-sight thing."

"If it feels right, then it's right," Olivia said. We were sitting under a tarp next to the van. The guys were off checking out the band schedule. By then, the rain had been falling for days. Everyone and everything was covered in mud. Olivia had pulled out her wash bucket and was trying to remove stains from some clothes. She even had an old-fashioned washboard. Her hands moved up and down it expertly.

"What about you and Walter?"

"I met him at a civil rights protest in New York. It's been almost ten years to the date. That's my Walter, always fighting for something or other. He asked me out for a walk in Central Park right as the police swarmed in for crowd control." Olivia laughed at the memory. "Inseparable from day one, just like you and Julian. Within a few months, he asked me to marry him," Olivia said. "And just like you, it felt right. I never doubted it. I knew by the end of our first date that he'd be the man I'd marry."

"That's very romantic," I said.

"Julian is a good man," Olivia said. "I've been raising him for the past four years. I know his heart. The way he looks at you . . . he's never looked at another that way. And when he says he loves you, it means he loves you. You could do a lot worse, but you're never going to do better. Mind you"—she gave me a wink—"I'm biased. If I was a good thirty years younger, I'd be chasing that boy myself."

Olivia's comments gave me strength. She was an adult and she understood. And she was willing to bring me into her family.

"Now come on," she said as a burst of distorted guitar echoed across the valley. "I think Hendrix is about to get down."

The day after Woodstock ended, Julian and I got into his beat-up truck early and headed back to Dixby. I'd offered to drive with Andrea, but she refused. Instead she drove behind us, honking her horn every now and then just to make sure we didn't forget. We made several stops along the road, pausing to pick wildflowers, buy snacks at gas stations, and pretty much enjoy that last trip back home.

Olivia, Walter, and the rest packed up and started heading south too. We'd agreed to meet up in Myrtle Beach the next week so that the children could go to the amusement park. From there we'd drive south, then west toward California. They planned on heading up to Washington State come fall, because they had friends and family there. Walter knew a guy who was willing to let them squat on his acreage for the winter. Olivia promised she'd teach me how to sew so I could help make clothing to sell to the shops.

On the outside, I was cool and calm. On the inside, I was a little girl, shaking and biting my lower lip to keep from crying.

The closer we got, the more outwardly nervous I became.

"It'll be fine," Julian said after I directed him to turn right. It was late afternoon, and the humidity had claimed the town. There wasn't a single soul on my street; everyone had retreated indoors to try and beat the heat. Curtains were closed tightly and blinds were drawn. The only sign of life was my neighbor's dog dozing in the shade under the porch. Julian reached over and put his hand on my knee, giving it a soft squeeze to reassure me he was there. I smiled back at him. From behind us, Andrea honked her horn to let me know she wasn't pulling over but was instead heading straight home. I waved at her, and as she passed us, she mouthed the words *Good luck*.

Dad's truck wasn't in the driveway. Neither was Marcus's car. I smiled to myself. If I could get all my stuff packed into Julian's truck before they got home, I'd consider it a small victory.

* * *

The cave is exactly the same as we left it. Parker and I appear in the middle of the strange cavern. The bowl full of pebbles mocks me. I start to reach down, to pick up a new stone, but Parker grabs my arm.

"You shouldn't go back."

I yank hard, pulling away from him. "Yes, I should, and I'm going to." But Parker gets between the bowl and me, refusing to relent.

"Listen to me, Molly. Just calm down and give me a few minutes of your time."

"You're not going to convince me," I say, trying to dodge left, but Parker is quicker than he looks. He grabs me by the arms again, pulling me close, right up against his body, where I can feel the warmth of his skin. His hands wrap around my waist, and if anything his touch grows hotter. When I look up at him, his lips are inches away from my own.

"I'm not saying you can't ever go back again," he says. "But you have to let the power recharge. Even if you pick up all those stones, you're not going anywhere for a while."

"What do you mean?" I look straight into Parker's brown eyes, trying to decide if he's lying or not. He seems sincere, but I can't really tell. In the dozens of years I've known him, this is the first time I've ever seen Parker so passionate. So motivated. So determined to keep me safe.

"It takes a while. Trust me, I know how this works. But you have to be more careful now. You've placed a trace of your spirit back on earth. The Remnants will be able to track you more easily now."

"Yeah, well, they didn't show up."

"They were coming," Parker says. "You heard the wind against the window. That was a sign."

"Or it was just the wind," I snap. "Come on, the rain was coming. Hardly a shock, rain in Washington State. Do you know how many times I've Faded only to get stuck in a downpour?"

"Why are you so determined not to believe me?"

His hands tighten around my waist.

"Why are you so determined not to believe *me*?" I whisper.

Parker's lips curl up into a sad smile. "Is that what you think?" he asks. "I never said anything of the sort. Do you think I would have shown you this place if I didn't think you could help? But saving that girl, it's not going to be easy. You've got to convince her to stop trying to free your soul first."

"Right," I say.

"Come on," he says. "We should head back down. Being here in this room isn't good for us. All these feelings and emotions. Trust me, we're better off not being around them for too long."

"Why?"

"Because they won't last. No matter how much you want them to, once we return to the beach, it's all over. And you can't stay here. Being here, it changes you. I already learned that the hard way."

There's a part of me that wants to suggest we stay in the cave forever. We could move some stuff around, maybe build some furniture, try and create a home. Sure, the beach is where everyone else resides, but does that mean Parker and I couldn't live here?

"It won't work," Parker says, as if he's reading my mind.

"Why not?"

"Because we're not alive. Being here, it's like pretending. Trust me, having this place, trying to exist in it, only causes pain."

Parker lets go of me and steps away. I'm instantly wishing he'd take me back into his arms, but instead he reaches out his hand to lead me outside.

* * *

Mary is waiting for us back on the beach.

"Where have you been?" she asks.

"Went for a walk," I say. I can't wait to tell her about the cave, but I need to find the right time. She'll be angry that we didn't include her. As much as I'd like her to come along, I know Mary can be a bit of a gossip. I agree with Parker that such a place is better left a secret. Especially considering that its power is limited. I can only imagine the fights that could break out if everyone started demanding to use it.

"Everyone is acting weird," Mary whispers to me. "After you left. I can't explain it, but your outburst got them all riled up. Like a bunch of peacocks fighting over a mirror."

"What do you mean?" I look over at the crowd of people, who are sitting in the exact same spots they've occupied since they crossed over. Nothing looks different at all. The black iron chairs and tables are still standing. The unlit patio lanterns still don't move. But when I look at some individual faces, they avert their eyes.

"People were talking," Mary says. "And guess what. Crazy

dog lady stood up for you. Called everyone a bunch of gits and said you've got the right idea. Became a loud ragger, she did. Gave this long speech about how just 'cause we're dead don't mean we can't actually have a good chat now and then. Added a bunch of rubbish about how we should be sharing our Fading experiences and being all nice and fuzzy friends. I swear, at one point even her little doggy started barking like he was agreeing with everything she was crapping out."

I glance over at the dog lady, but she's moved over to the far corner of the beach. She looks like she's talking softly to herself, but her dog is sitting on her lap, so she's probably rambling away to him. The more I stare at her, though, the more I notice that she looks terrified. She's rocking back and forth, stroking the dog's ears as if she's afraid he's going to disappear on the spot.

"And then get this," Mary says. "It started raining."

"What?" Parker and I both say in unison.

"It was the weirdest thing," Mary says. "No clouds or anything. But all of a sudden, rain came out of nowhere. Soaked the beach. Got everyone into a right ol' tizzy." She grabs my hand and leads me over to our spot. "There, look!"

It takes me a moment to notice what she's pointing at. Our wood log, the place where I've planted my behind for over forty years, looks different. It's *wet*. I touch the spot with my fingers. If I were to sit down right now, my skirt would most definitely get damp.

Then I remember Graham and Levi fighting with Parker. I lift up the corner of my hem and look at the stitching. There, along the bottom, is the tear in the fabric. Permanent. In the many decades I've been here, I've never even gotten a stain or a piece of lint. I poke my fingers through the hole, carefully, not wanting to let anyone else see.

This is a sign. But of what?

And how is this related to the fact that we just had our first-ever change in the weather?

"It can't be, can it?" I ask Parker.

"I don't know." Parker looks as stumped as the rest of us.

"Don't you see what this means?" Mary says. "We've been wrong. This place can change. Parker, you know this. Remember when the pretty tables showed up? I was so sick of those drab wooden benches. Reminded me too much of those nasty pubs in Whitechapel. I swear, I used to look at them and could almost smell them drunkards and remember the way they used to grope me. Kept bringing up bad thoughts. Maybe that's what happened. Someone else got so tired of the décor, they managed to change things without even knowing it. Imagine what we could do if we really started thinking about it. Could turn this place into the Queen's palace if we so wanted."

Mary can't control her excitement. She thinks she's onto something here, and the desire to make things different has taken over.

"I could get me a new dress, I could," she says. "Get rid of this damned corset once and for all. Something modern and pretty. Gonna have to find meself a magazine or something next time I Fade." She reaches up and tugs at her curls. "And a new hairstyle too. Something short and daring."

"I'm not sure that's quite what happened," Parker says. "If we could change this place that easily, don't you think we would have figured it out by now? Come on, Mary, you've been here longer than I have. You know how things work."

Mary pauses. She marches straight over to Parker. "You know something."

Parker shakes his head, but his eyes give him away. Even I can see it.

"Yes, you do," Mary says. "What do you know? Spit it out." She turns around and looks me over long and hard. "You know something too."

Close beside us, a group of people overhears our conversation. I can see them from the corner of my eye, listening intently.

"Not so loud," I say.

"Then tell me what you know. How did you make it rain?"

"It wasn't me."

"Of course it was." Mary throws her arms up in the air. "You're the one who was ranting and raving earlier. Then you and Parker disappear into the mountains and everything goes all wonky. You did something and you know it. I can see it all over your face."

"I didn't. At least I don't think I did."

Mary hoots loudly. More eyes turn in our direction. Parker shakes his head and starts walking away toward the trees. He nods at us to follow.

"Come on," I say. "Not here. Let's go somewhere more private and talk. We've got something to show you. You're gonna just die."

Mary does a little jig, her petticoats flying. She's acting like a little girl who just discovered Santa Claus is real.

Great. So much for being able to keep a secret. At the rate we're going, it'll be less than a few hours before everyone knows. And I need to get back to Tatum. I think of all the people on the beach and wonder what places they'd try and go if given a pebble and a bit of chalk.

No, it's not going to happen. Not until I save Tatum. I will not let them take that from me. After that, I don't give a damn if they use up all the energy, or magic, or whatever force keeps us locked away. They can travel to the moon or Mongolia for all I care. Once I've helped Tatum, there's nothing back on earth I need to see. Not really.

The Julian I used to know is gone. If he's still alive, he'll be a lot different from the boy he once was. He'd be even older than my father was. Would I really want to see him again? I may not have changed, but for him it's been a lifetime. No, some things are better left alone. I'm not that selfish.

Not anymore.

* * *

The day I left Dixby behind, I took the coward's way out. I went into my bedroom and gathered all my clothes. Julian packed up my albums and the battered old record player Dad had given me for my twelfth birthday. I grabbed my photo album and the few pieces of jewelry I'd collected over the years. Afterward, I looked at my bedroom and marveled over how empty it felt. Less than a week ago it had been my sanctuary. The hiding place I could go to when I needed to get away from the rest of the world. I'd painstakingly decorated it the exact way I wanted. The rock posters with the bands I loved.

The dresser I'd painted to look like a psychedelic rainbow. The thick blanket with the daisies, which kept me warm on cold nights. My old slippers, which always ended up pushed halfway under the bed.

I looked at all these things for several minutes while Julian took my possessions out to his truck. I studied the things I was rejecting. They no longer had a place in my heart.

None of it mattered. All these things I had once loved, I would leave them behind. I wondered what Dad would do. How long would he stand at the door, wondering when I might come home? When he finally realized I was gone for good, would he throw everything away and make the room into a spare bedroom? An office?

When Julian came back, he wrapped his arms around me and we stood in silence while I said my goodbyes. With the warmth of his body pressed against me, any last regrets and fears faded away. I was ready. I would not have a fight with my father while trying to convince him I was old enough to strike out on my own. I wouldn't give the neighbors the chance to listen to every heated word. I wouldn't allow Marcus to side with Dad and yell about how I was too young, too stupid, too foolish to believe that I was in love.

I was too chicken.

I wrote my father a letter.

I told him about Julian and how I was in love. I said there was nothing he could do to change my mind. I begged him not to try and find me or call the police. I pointed out several times that I was, in my eyes, an adult, and ready to make my mark on the world.

I cried as I wrote it. My tears blurred the ink at one point, and I had to scribble over the words and rewrite them. But as difficult as it was to leave my family and my life, I knew I was going where I wanted to be.

I wanted Julian.

I ended the letter by telling Dad I'd call him once I got settled and let him know where I was. I promised to keep in touch. I'd answer all his questions about Julian. I left the note on the kitchen table and walked out the door, hand in hand with Julian, embracing my new future.

You see, I said earlier I have no regrets. But I do have one.

I never spoke to my father again.

TATUM

There's a glaring A+ across the front page of her biology test. A grade that Tatum knows is bullshit because she deliberately answered four questions wrong. The answer to question three, for example: the flobberworm dying from too much lettuce is not a definition of biological structure. The zombie apocalypse isn't a good example of natural selection, either.

There was a lot of discussion about allowing Tatum to continue taking biology with Mr. Paracini. Some of the staff insisted she not be allowed anywhere near him; others argued that she shouldn't be denied the college credit. Sadly, Tatum's high school is small, and it wasn't as simple as placing her with another teacher. Mr. Paracini is the only biology instructor around for miles. Finally the decision came down that she deserved the chance. Rules were set in motion. Tatum is never allowed to be in the empty classroom with him. Heaven forbid she might get the idea to remove her clothing again and prance naked around the hamster cage. She can't meet him in private or in his office either. If she has something to discuss about her lessons, she is to do it in the hallways while other teachers are around to witness.

All this to protect the child-molesting monster.

Life is cruel sometimes.

It didn't take Tatum long to realize that her biology grades were suddenly improving. Her normal B average suddenly skyrocketed to the top of the class. She found bright red check marks next to answers that weren't worthy of anything other than a creative writing class.

Someone must be feeling awfully guilty.

Tatum contemplated her newfound academic status carefully. Part of her wanted to out Mr. Paracini, but at the same time she knew he would have a multitude of answers if questioned. He could say he simply made a mistake because he's been under so much stress. Of course, the easy answer would be that since Tatum is such a crazed hormonal mess, he felt that giving her a few good grades might boost her self-esteem. She did get slammed down pretty hard with her teacher crush.

Whatever the excuses Mr. Paracini might give, they wouldn't get him in any trouble. Teachers are allowed to give out whatever grades they want. It's not like Tatum is popular and loved enough to go bragging to her classmates. She's not going to win any awards for outstanding student anytime soon.

What upsets Tatum the most is the fact that her pervert teacher, the man who loves giving young girls pregnancy scares, seems to have a conscience, while her former best friend loses no sleep at night over destroying Tatum's life.

Is Claudette still secretly dating Mr. Paracini? Are they still planning their yacht tour over the summer once she turns eighteen? Or did he decide she was too much of a risk and he'd be faithful to his wife for a while? It's hard to tell. Tatum hopes he dropped her like a hot potato or, even better, found himself some poor ninth grader to harass. And if there is a god or goddess, this ninth grader will scream loud enough that everyone will learn the truth. All Tatum can hope for is that one day he does get caught and loses everything the same way she has.

And may Claudette die a bitter old hag.

With herpes.

Yep, a great leaking cold sore on her face would make for some good karma.

At lunchtime, Tatum decides to sit in the corner of the cafeteria, ignoring the corn dog on her plate. She's brought her laptop and is busy searching the Internet for information on Molly. Aside from some more newspaper articles, she can't find anything new. It's not surprising. Molly lived in a world without Facebook statuses. She didn't do anything extraordinary like walk on the moon. She wasn't a movie star or a model. She was a normal girl who accidently got murdered. Sadly, there's a lot more information on her killer, Walter Morris, than on her. Tatum finds his name on several serial-killer fan sites. He's lurking everywhere, being compared to the likes of Ted Bundy and the Green River Killer. He pops up in discussions about how Washington State has always been a hotbed for psychotic monsters. Criminology students have uploaded their term papers, and psychologists dissect his brain in detail. There are interviews with him, court transcripts, pictures of him smiling and waving at the camera. She even found a site that offers memorabilia. For $19.99, you can get a coffee mug with his photograph on it. Fifty bucks will get you a nice hoodie.

Molly's school picture comes up a lot, mostly in lists of the girls Walter killed. She is often labeled as girl number seven, or twenty-two if you count the ones whose murders he was suspected of but not charged with. Tatum finds it creepy, all these young ladies smiling in their black-and-white pictures, forever frozen in time. They'll always be remembered as victims, not as the promising people they should have become. They were high school and college students with hopes and dreams. They planned on being architects and secretaries. Two of them were married. One had a small child. Now they are nothing, just names for people to forget. Carol. Marcia. Annabelle.

Molly.

"Mind if I sit down?"

Tatum looks up to see Scott standing across from her. He's got his lunch tray in his hands, but the food is already half eaten. He must have been watching her for a while, trying to get up the nerve to come over.

"Yeah, sure," she says. "If you want."

Scott plops into the seat across from her. Tatum doesn't close her laptop. She doesn't need him to think she wants to actually talk. She hasn't decided if she's forgiven Scott or not. Yes, he's a jerk for not doing anything. Yes, he could have told the truth. But no, he probably would have been ignored. Tatum understands this.

But it still hurts.

Then again, what doesn't these days?

"How're you doing?" Scott picks up his fork and begins pushing cold French fries around on his plate. He's avoiding eye contact. Must be feeling guilty. Good.

Tatum shrugs. She clicks off the website of America's Worst Killers. Walter came in at number sixteen. The Commune Killer. The nickname doesn't really inspire the sort of fear to make the top ten. His long white hair and friendly dad-next-door smile don't inspire the disgust that Charles Manson's swastika-tattooed face does. He doesn't have crazy eyes. Or John Wayne Gacy's love of clown suits.

"How's the story coming along?"

Tatum shrugs again.

"Getting lots of writing done?"

"Not really."

"You know, you could try giving me a second chance." Scott picks up a fry and drenches it in ketchup. He pushes it around on his plate, leaving a red smear that could easily be mistaken for a bloodstain. Tatum watches with fascination and disgust.

"Yeah, I know," she says.

"I'm sorry for being such a douche bag," Scott says. He abandons the French fry and starts to fondle his empty Coke can. Anything to keep his eyes on the lunch remains so he doesn't have to look Tatum in the eyes. Guilt is funny that way.

"I know," she repeats.

"I have the night off," he says. "I was hoping you might want to hang out with me after school. I know a really cool place we can go. If you want to."

"You don't have to feel sorry for me." The words burst from her mouth, not exactly what she wants to say, but she still can't believe that Scott wants anything to do with her, except to make up for whatever guilt trip he's experiencing.

"I don't. No, I do, but that's not what I mean." Scott's hand tightens around his empty soda can, slightly crushing it. "I just want to hang. I've always wanted to, ya know. But you never even noticed me before."

"You're the one who doesn't talk to anyone. You blew Claudette off, big-time. She was pissed about it for weeks."

"Yeah, so?"

"I don't know. I just figured you didn't care."

Scott smiles. "So because I turned down your friend, you assumed I wouldn't care about you? Why do you think I'm always walking the dog down your street?"

"Guys don't usually blow off Claudette."

Now it's Scott's turn to shrug. "She's not my type."

Tatum grins. "Did you really walk your dog down my street just so you could talk to me?"

"Yeah."

That's so incredibly sweet. Tatum finds herself looking down at her computer so Scott doesn't see the blush burning its way onto her cheeks. She's never had a guy straight-out tell her he's interested before. Sure, there was Levi for a while, but they didn't exactly date. They hung around a lot with Claudette and Graham. Once they made out at a bonfire party, but the experience left Tatum feeling a little nauseous. Levi kissed her like he was trying to suck her teeth right out of her jaw.

It was Claudette who always got the dates. When she was around, Tatum became the invisible friend. When boys talked to Tatum, they usually just wanted to know if Claudette was available.

"It's not your fault," Claudette used to say to her. "You're really pretty, Tatum, but you've got no confidence. When guys are around, you just hide behind me and turn into a wall-flower."

"I never know what to say."

"High school guys are easy to talk to. They don't really care what you're saying. They just want to get into your pants. They'll listen to you for hours and not remember a single thing the next day," Claudette told her. "That's why older men are better. They've already copped a feel or gotten nasty. They don't have to be desperate anymore."

Older guys scared her too. She remembers when Claudette got her to go with her to a party at Seattle University. She spent the whole night leaning against the wall, watching Claudette make out with a freshman. The only guy who talked to her asked her where the bathroom was.

Scott is easy to talk to. Tatum is surprised at this, but at the same time she wonders if maybe it's because she doesn't have Claudette to rely on anymore. She can't relax and lean back against the wall and let her friend grab all the attention.

"So what do you say?" Scott asks her again. "Meet me after school? We'll take my car."

"Yeah, okay," she says. She has a quick mental image of her car being alone in the parking lot while she drives off with Scott. Talk about open hunting season. Graham and Levi wouldn't be able to resist. She'd come back and find it covered in toilet paper or pushed into a drainage ditch. "But meet me at my house instead," she says. "At four."

Scott nods. "Yeah, no problem."

She watches him walk off and notices that the others are watching too. Graham Douglas throws the last bit of his corn dog in Scott's direction. Claudette laughs and tosses her hair back. Even from halfway across the room, Tatum can see the hard glare in her eyes.

Tatum smiles to herself as she packs away her laptop. Claudette can be pissy all she wants. Tatum could care less.

* * *

"Your mother and I have been discussing things," said Tatum's dad not long after the meeting in the principal's office. "We think maybe you should go talk to someone. There's a good doctor in Seattle. You could go down once a week by yourself, or one of us can drive you. No one has to know."

Tatum sat at the kitchen table, Mom and Dad sitting opposite. They were all smiles and happy faces, but underneath the facade, Tatum could see the truth. There were dark circles under Mom's eyes. Tatum had heard them last night, whispering behind their closed bedroom door. A quiet argument, voices low, both of them determined not to wake their psychotic daughter. They'd been having these little talks every night, the light glowing under their bedroom door until the wee hours of the morning. Tatum knew this because she wasn't exactly sleeping well either.

"A doctor? Like a shrink?"

"No, no, not a psychiatrist," Mom said. "A psychologist. Dr. Bernstein. She's highly recommended. Think of her as a friend you can tell all your secrets to. Everything you say will be confidential. Your father and I don't have to know, unless you want to tell us."

"Yes, you can tell us anything," Dad chimed in.

"No, I clearly can't," Tatum said. "You don't believe me."

"Of course we believe you," Mom says. She glared at Dad and nudged him in the side with her elbow.

"Yes," Dad agrees.

"Really? Then why aren't you taking my side? Why aren't you insisting that I didn't do the things they said I did? Why aren't you trying to get Mr. Paracini fired?"

"You know very well that we stood with you," Dad says. "We've done everything we can, Tatum. We're lucky they didn't try to expel you."

"It isn't that simple, Tatum," Mom says.

"Yes, it is. Go upstairs and check my room. Go ahead. I dare you to find any evidence that shows I did that stuff. I keep my diary in the closet. Go read it. You won't find anything. I don't even have birth control hiding under my mattress. Claudette's the one who screwed all the boys, not me."

"Tatum!"

"Isn't that what you want to hear?" The tears were burning in her eyes again, and that only made her angrier. She was tired of crying. All. The. Time. She was done. She looked up at the ceiling, willing the waterworks away. If she could just make herself stop this one time, maybe she could be strong enough never to cry a single tear again.

"We want what's best for you. And it seems to me you need someone to talk to. Someone who doesn't know you. Dr. Bernstein is impartial. She won't—"

"Judge me? Like you do?"

"Yes."

"Exactly."

Mom frowned. "That's not what I mean. You're going through a difficult time. This will help you."

"I don't need to talk. I don't want help."

Dad slammed his fist down on the table. Everyone jumped.

"I'm done with this, Tatum," he said. "You can blame us all you want. You can say we're the worst parents in the world and pretend we hate you. But we have stood by your side this entire time. Do you really think for a second that we don't believe you? Give us more credit than that."

"I know."

"Then stop acting like we don't care. Your mother is right. Talking to that doctor is a good idea. If anything, you can learn better ways to cope other than screaming at us. We'll set up the first appointment for next week."

They tried. But Tatum didn't go. She refused straight-out. Mom and Dad could drag her there kicking and screaming, but they couldn't make her talk about something she hadn't done. Tatum was done talking. What was the point when no one bothered to listen?

Having her parents on her side simply wasn't good enough. They didn't count. They *had* to believe her; otherwise everyone would call them monsters.

The phone calls and text messages in the middle of the night continued. Tatum turned off her phone. She started to think she'd have to get a new number. If she tried hard enough, maybe she really could ignore everything.

* * *

After school, she finds the words *slut* and *I love you, five dollah* lipsticked on her locker. She doesn't even bother to wipe them off. At her car, she discovers that someone has blown up several condoms and attached them to her windshield wipers. She just pulls them off and tosses them to the side. She spots Scott's car and thankfully he's not in sight. She might not be able to look him in the eyes if she knew he'd seen the condoms.

By the time she gets home, Tatum wonders if Scott will keep his word. Part of her still thinks this is some sort of cruel joke. That's the problem when you get beaten down constantly. You stop believing that anything good can happen again. Every single person in Hannah has become a suspect. Even the little old ladies who shop at the dollar store seem to watch Tatum carefully, and she can't help but think they gossip about her by the cheap dishware.

At a quarter past four, she's convinced herself he's not going to show up. He probably got cornered by the others and bullied into changing his mind. He decided she's not worth it. If only she were prettier. Smarter. Less crazy. Who wants to date some freak who's writing short stories about ghosts? She probably stays home on Friday nights to play with her doll-head collection. All these thoughts go through her head, voices taunting her, but Tatum stays by the window, a small part of her wishing her inner voices would just shut up and leave her alone.

It's a shame. Why is the universe so against her? What sort of terrible deeds did she do in her past life to deserve this?

At 4:25, Scott's car appears in her driveway. Tatum rushes to the door before he has time to get out.

"Hey," he says when she climbs into the passenger seat.

"Sorry I'm late. I had to run home and grab a jacket, and Mom started talking. You know how it is."

"Yeah, it's cool," she says, trying to act like she didn't even notice he was late. "Where are we going?"

Scott puts the car in reverse and they pull out of the driveway. "I thought we'd grab some coffee first. After that, I'm not telling."

"A secret? I'm not a big fan of them."

"Yeah, I guess I wouldn't be either," Scott says. "But believe me, this one is good."

"Okay," she says. She's made up her mind to trust him. Of course, she's not exactly doing great in that department. She can practically hear Claudette laughing at her.

No, Scott is good. She's determined to believe this.

She has to.

Otherwise she'll spend the rest of her life unable to ever trust anyone again.

Maybe she'll tell him about Molly. Or perhaps it's too soon for that. Then again, he seems to believe his grandmother met her, so why wouldn't he believe Tatum? Of course, what if Scott's grandmother is a crazy cat lady who rambles on all the time and everyone just agrees to keep her happy?

Shut up, girl. Give your brain a rest for once in your life and have fun.

They drive to Starbucks because it's the closest. There's no drive-through, so they go inside. The place is packed with students she recognizes, and pretty much everyone turns around to look at them as they wait in line. Tatum takes a quick glance around to make sure she doesn't recognize any of her main tormentors. Thankfully, the coast is clear. Scott studies the menu, oblivious to the whispers and stares. He even ignores the laughter.

"I worked at Starbucks when I lived in Maine," he says. "It's not bad, but I like Seattle's Best better. Pay's about the same and the drive is longer, but at least no one knows I work there." He laughs. "Well, there are a few."

"I won't tell," she says.

"Hey, I'm not ashamed or anything," he says. "But this is a bit of a rich crowd. I can't imagine they'll have to worry about college tuition."

Tatum nods. It's no secret that the kids in Hannah are rich. It's not a typical small town in Washington. It's more of a rich suburb, the place where parents move when they want to own houses with pools and more bedrooms than they know what to do with. Even the more modest homes have a high-six-figure price tag. Her own parents are well-enough off; Tatum's always being told she can go to whatever school she applies to.

"Granny owns our house," Scott tells her. "She downsized and rented it to my folks so they could afford to come back. Otherwise we wouldn't have been able to do it."

"Why did you move back?"

"Dad lost his job last year and Granny got him a new one," Scott says. "He didn't want to do it, but in the end he had no choice. My parents hate it here. I think it makes my dad feel like a failure."

"That's sad," Tatum says. "Can't say I blame them, though. I can't stand this place either."

"I don't mind it," Scott says. "A place is just a place. It's what you do with it that matters. And I like being close to Granny. She's pretty cool. Way more interesting than my parents. She's fun to hang out with." He pauses, as if listening to the words coming out of his mouth. "Wow, I just became the lamest guy on the planet."

Tatum laughs. "Nah, I think it's cute."

"Great. Now I'll never be cool. Don't you know that calling a guy *cute* is a death sentence? That's pushing it straight into the friend zone. No passing go. Kiss that two hundred bucks goodbye."

She laughs again. From the corner of her eye, she sees some girls watching her carefully. They're all wearing red lipstick. Great. What's going to appear on her locker tomorrow?

Tatum and Scott grab their drinks and head back to the car. Scott is being elusive, refusing to answer any questions and promising to take her somewhere she's never been before. Tatum finds this hard to believe, considering she's lived here her entire life. But Scott's enthusiasm is catching, and soon she's loosening up and having a good time. She even finds herself laughing when Scott tells a bad joke about what the egg says to the boiling water.

It's a nice surprise when he turns left and heads in a familiar direction.

"Frog Road!"

"Why do you call it that?"

She explains the meaning behind the name, wondering if he knows that this is Molly's road. He must, but if he does, he doesn't say anything.

A few miles in and he pulls the car over. There's not a lot here. Farmers' fields. Off to the right is a marsh; she can see the water peeking out from behind the trees. An old train bridge is in front of them, casting shadows over the car. It's no longer used; in fact, she can't remember ever seeing a train cross in all the years she's been coming here. The bridge is small and plain, just an overpass over the road that looks like it's seen better days. Kids have spray-painted names and dates onto the wood.

"Come on," Scott says. He grabs his mocha frappe from the drink holder and turns off the ignition.

"Here? Your secret is here?"

"Yep."

She shrugs off her seat belt and gets out. The wind catches her hair, pushes it against her cheeks. It's nice out today. Overcast, but that's normal for Washington. It doesn't look like it's going to rain. In the distance, she can see sun peeking out from behind Mount Baker.

"Hope you don't mind getting muddy," Scott says.

"You're joking, right?"

He gives her a grin that suggests he might or might not be.

Beside the train bridge is a small path. It's narrow and steep, slightly muddy from all the recent rain. Scott leads the way. Tatum follows, keeping one hand on the wooden structure for support. She slips on a rock and almost falls, and suddenly she's laughing hard, imagining her rear end all nice and dirty for the ride back home.

"Careful," Scott says. Suddenly his foot slips out from beneath him and he goes down on one knee. He drops his drink, and thankfully the lid's on too tight for it to spill. But one hand goes straight into the mud, and Scott lets out a nice curse.

"You were saying?" she asks once she stops laughing.

They continue down the path, which travels alongside the

bridge and through the trees. There are signs of human life everywhere. Candy wrappers and potato chip bags. Cigarette butts. Empty beer cans.

Then the forest opens up, and they're down beside a pond.

The place is hauntingly beautiful. The water is a perfect circle, a mountain oasis in the middle of nowhere. Trees sink into the wet earth, covered in moss that drapes down from the branches. The water looks surprisingly clear and clean; Tatum can see the bottom. A few minnows swim by lazily. She even spots a tiny frog sunning itself on a log. From above, some birds scold them, cawing loudly, unhappy that their home turf is being invaded.

"Wow," she says.

"So. Have you been here before?"

Tatum shakes her head. She hasn't. She thought she knew every inch of Frog Road, and in a way she does. But when she drives down here, she doesn't usually stop to get out of the car. The local farmers own most of the land, and they can get a little moody when they find people trespassing. The only hot spots she can think of in the woods are places where she's partied in the past, and this place wouldn't make the cut. She can only imagine a drunken Levi falling in and drowning.

Actually, that doesn't sound bad at all.

"My grandmother used to take us here when we were little," Scott said. "There's an underground stream that feeds the pond. You can fish here. Not big fish or anything. Nothing you could eat. But we used to do some catch and release. A really big thing when you're five years old."

"I've never gone fishing," Tatum says.

"You're not missing anything," Scott says. "I once hooked

a fish in the eye, and that kinda ruined things for me. I got a little squeamish after that."

"I'll bet."

"I think it's funny that you call this place Frog Road," he says. "I used to go around and collect all the frogs. Thought I was some sort of amphibian king. I'd put them in my pocket and Granny would have to frisk me before we left."

"I used to do that too! I had such an obsession with having pet frogs. Wanted to take them to school for show-and-tell. Mom hated it."

Scott picks up a pebble and skips it expertly. Tatum finishes off her drink, taking in the lovely silence. This is the sort of place she could come to enjoy. Maybe she should pitch a tent and spend the rest of the school year living here. It wouldn't be so bad. She could get a cooler and a propane-operated barbecue. She tries to imagine herself doing her homework by firelight, curled up in a sleeping bag, enjoying the solitude, away from her nagging parents, who always give her that look when they think she's not watching.

Heavenly.

Of course, she knows this is nothing but a silly pipe dream. It wouldn't take long before Claudette's nosy body figured it out. Then she'd end up bombarded in the middle of the night with condoms filled with urine. Better to stay at home, where at least the walls protect her from some of the outside abuse.

Scott skips another rock, only this one falls in with a heavy plunk. He puts his drink down on a log and wipes at his dirty knee with some Starbucks napkins.

Tatum grins. The memory of him slipping is still strong.

It suddenly hits her. She does like Scott. In a way, she's

known for a long time, but this is the first moment where she actually allows herself the thought. There's no *but* afterward: *I like him, but Claudette wants him. I like him, but there's no way a guy like that would go out with me. I like him, but he should have stuck up for me.*

I like him. Period. And I think he likes me back.

As if on cue, Scott looks up at her and gives Tatum a big grin. "I think I'm starting to dry off," he says. "I definitely jinxed myself back there." Leaving the wet napkins by his drink, he comes over to her. "But I think my luck might be changing."

"Oh?" The word is heavy in her throat.

"Yeah." Scott leans in close. He's not a lot taller than her, just a few inches, and she enjoys the fact she doesn't feel as if her neck is breaking when she looks in his eyes. Scott's hair is short and spiked; she likes the way it still kinda parts down the middle although it's obvious he's trying to style it differently.

"I've been wanting to kiss you for a while," he says. "But I didn't know how to go about it. Do you think it's okay?"

He's asking? *Oh God. Just do it, already.*

Tatum nods.

Scott begins to lean toward her.

Behind her, Tatum can hear the crackling noise of people walking over dead leaves. Scott glances up, and all the color leaves his face.

"What the hell . . ."

MOLLY

I mark Tatum's name on the wall and we pick up our pebbles. Parker is pouting; he's doing everything in his power to make me aware he's completely against this. He's doubled his lectures on the dangers of spending too much time inside a world I can no longer be a part of. But he's the one who opened the door here; he can hardly complain when everyone wants to go through it. I hear his cautions, but they don't scare me enough. I'm far too determined to finish what I've started.

Mary, however, can barely contain her excitement.

"We have to get Tatum to take us shopping first," Mary says. "I haven't been to a proper dress shop in forever! Over a hundred years. Money. Where can we get some? Could always just do a quick pinch. It's not like they could call the coppers on me. Do you think I'd be able to bring something back?"

"I don't know," Parker says. "We're not going shopping. Be serious." He gives me a look to suggest I've betrayed him. I suppose I have, but he agreed to share the cave with Mary. I suppose I just pushed him into it. I didn't want Mary to be left out.

When we appear on earth, I realize quickly that heading to the mall will be the last thing we do. I appear straight out of thin air and into two feet of water. My feet begin to sink in the mud. Mary squeals, grabs the folds of her long skirt, and jumps backward, nearly tripping and falling into the cold water.

Parker stands on the bank, a satisfied smile on his face. He's the lucky one, and he's not going to let me forget it. It's my punishment for being so determined to go back to Tatum. He gets to stay dry.

Speaking of Tatum. We've interrupted something important. She's standing across from us, with a boy, and they look like they're about to lock lips. But our presence has already been noticed. Tatum looks thrilled, if slightly disappointed at the timing. The boy, however, looks like he's seeing a ghost.

Which, of course, he is.

"Molly!"

I manage to pull my foot out of the mud without losing my sandal. It's slow moving, and I'm the last to get to dry ground. Mud oozes between my toes, and a sharp rock gets stuck beneath my heel. I have to spend a bit of time in the shallow water, moving my legs around to try and remove the last of the muck from my skin. Mary is lucky with her leather boots; they don't get practically sucked off her feet in the quicksand. She sits on a log, using her hands to squeeze the liquid out of her heavy skirt.

Parker holds out his hand and I take it, allowing him to pull me out of the water and onto dry land. My own skirt is weighted with fluid and sticks tightly against my legs. Tatum rushes toward us and throws her arms around me. Behind her, the boy follows, a look of curiosity and shock on his face. It's almost comical. I think he recognizes me; perhaps Tatum has shown him a picture and told him my story. But his brain refuses to make the connection, so he's confused. *This can't be the murdered hippie girl from almost fifty years ago. It's not possible.*

"You're back," Tatum says. "It's about time."

"How long has it been?" I ask. It's only been a few hours on my end. Even though Parker warned me against going back too soon, apparently whatever energy keeps the cave active recharges faster than he thinks. Or that's what he's trying to make me believe.

"It's been three days," Tatum says. "I was hoping you'd come sooner."

Wow. Time really does fly. That's good to know. What feels like a few hours equals a few days. I wish I had a watch so I could experiment. But from what I've seen, people who Fade with watches often find them not working anymore. They always stop the moment the person dies. It's a horrible reminder, and such devices end up getting lost after a few days. No one wants that memory etched forever on their wrist.

"I know you, don't I?" the boy asks. He's staring straight at me. If he were a puppy, his head would be cocked to the side with one ear higher than the other.

"Scott. This is, um, Molly."

Absolute silence.

"Molly?" Scott glances toward Parker and Mary, taking in their unusual clothes and hairstyles. Mary has peeled off her boot and is holding it upside down, letting the last of the swamp water pour onto the ground. She's pulled her dress up over her calves, exposing her petticoats. Her shapely legs are very white from an entire life in the London rain. Hairy, too. She's not abashed in the slightest. Mary does what Mary wants.

"Hello," I say, trying to come off cheery and completely nonthreatening. It's not working. My voice sounds stilted and awkward. There's really no way of handling this situation without freaking him out.

"You're . . ." Scott's brain still doesn't want to give in without a fight. Tatum reaches out and touches him anxiously. She doesn't want to straight-out tell him, and I don't blame her. Because if she does, she's going to look like the crazy one.

"Molly's a friend," Tatum finally says.

"You look just like that girl. Molly. The dead hippie. The one my grandma saw." Scott turns toward Tatum. "Is this some sort of a joke? I don't understand."

"No," Tatum says. "Not a joke. She's real."

"You're doing this to get back at me," Scott says. "For keeping my mouth shut. It's some sort of weird revenge."

"No," Tatum says, "I wanted to tell you. I'm not writing a story. I made that up so I wouldn't have to tell the truth. I met Molly a few weeks ago on the road. I was afraid you'd think I was crazy because I was looking up all that ghost stuff. She's kinda my friend now."

I notice that Tatum doesn't say a word about my vision and how I'm trying to protect her from dying. She gives me a look, so I figure I better not bring it up either. I do like that she calls me her friend. It's been a long time since I've heard that word. I guess I could call Mary and Parker my friends, but with them the word doesn't feel right. Emotionless.

"That's not possible." Scott points in my direction. "You're dead. I've seen your picture. I read all those articles. Tatum and I talked about them. My granny! She claims she saw you."

"Who was your grandmother?" I ask. "Did I appear to her?" What a coincidence. I suppose it's not really surprising considering I've been haunting this area for all these years. And although most people probably don't say a word about the mysterious hitchhiking girl, there must be a few who've bragged to all their friends.

"You told her to go back to her sister's house in New Hampshire," Tatum says. "You said there was something important hidden behind a bed frame."

"Dorothy," I say with a grin. "I do remember her now." An older lady, a dozen Fades ago; she picked me up in a station wagon, admitting she'd never stopped to give a ride to a stranger before. She'd stopped because I reminded her of her own daughter, who was a lot older but had done some crazy stuff when she was a teenager that used to keep Dorothy awake late at night. Thankfully, the daughter turned out fine and didn't get into too much trouble, and Dorothy understood that sometimes a girl had to do things she didn't want to do, especially if times were tough. She had been lovely, and I was happy to give her a good fortune. No cheating spouses or death sentences for her.

Scott, meanwhile, has lost all coloring in his face. His grandmother's name must be Dorothy, because he nearly fainted when he heard me speak it.

"I've wanted to explain this to you," Tatum says to Scott. "But I didn't really know how."

Her words aren't convincing him. I can tell that's exactly what Scott's thinking. He's positive he's being made the butt of someone's bad joke. It's not every day a ghost catches you about to kiss the girl you like. Even worse that it's the same ghost his grandma claims to have seen. I get it, there must be at least fifty easier ways to explain this, but I'll be damned if I can think of one. Scott steps back, almost bumping into Parker, who isn't paying attention to us at all. Parker is staring off into the woods as if he sees something.

Then I feel it.

A slight chill. A wind brushes against my skin, seeping through the wet folds of my cotton skirt. A shiver rushes across my legs, making me tremble.

"We should leave," Parker says.

"We just got here," Mary says. "I'm not going until I've had my fill. Don't you give me that look, Parker. You've been keeping this from me all this time. I could have been romping down here, having a good time and getting me some drinks and men. Do you know how long it's been since I've had me a bitter? Some cheroots? Or bought meself some pretty things? I ain't gonna use this time hanging out in no swamp. We need to go somewhere else. Blimey, I want me a pie. Nice and proper, steak and kidney, none of that sickly chicken muck. I want one soaking with lots of jipper." She smacks her lips, stuck in her food fantasy, moving on to cakes and biscuits, but no one is paying attention to her in the slightest.

The cold brushes against my skin again. It's not quite a wind; it's more like the atmosphere has changed around me. Like the temperature has suddenly dropped several degrees. Tatum and Scott seem completely oblivious to it, but Parker's eyes are growing wide. Mary's skirts are so thick and plentiful, she probably wouldn't even notice if it suddenly started snowing.

230

"You can feel it," Parker says to me.

"What?" Tatum asks.

"I don't know," I say.

"I can see you shivering. You feel it," Parker says. He drops his voice, hoping I'll be the only one who hears. "It's the first warning."

"What?" Tatum asks again. She apparently has the ears of a bat.

"I'm freezing enough from landing in the bog," I snap. "It's not exactly summer."

Mary is searching her pockets. "I know I have some coppers in here. A few shillings at least. They've got to be valuable now, right?" She pulls out a few coins and holds them up to show Tatum. "Any idea where I can sell them? I want some new clothes." She tugs on the front of her corset, nearly exposing her breasts for everyone to see. "Can you imagine being stuck in this getup for all eternity? Driving me mad, it is."

"Molly." Parker says my name quietly.

I glare at him. What exactly does he want me to do? Freak out? Fall down at his feet and beg him to protect me from something I've yet to see? Head back to the hell that is my life and ignore the past few weeks? Let Tatum die because that's better than being afraid of my shadow? This isn't fair. At this rate, I'm never going to be able to help her. I can't run off every time Parker tells me to; otherwise I'll end up too late. And I'm not going to come back to earth only to find myself at Tatum's funeral. I'll never forgive myself.

How am I supposed to figure things out if Parker gets jumpy over every single gust of air? Every single time I go back, I lose time. Days pass. I realize that I'm going to have to start sneaking off to the cave without him. I'll have to find ways to leave him behind. And Mary, too. She's just going to have to go on her own if she wants to spend the day cruising the malls.

Already this is beginning to feel like a disaster.

Scott, meanwhile, is beginning to recover his dignity. He's watching me intently. His fingers keep going up as if he wants to touch my arm, but he pulls his hand back at the last second. I fight an insane urge to yell out *boo* and start laughing maniacally.

The wind blows again, pressing against my face. It's growing colder with each gust. The temperature is dropping steadily, and the sun doesn't appear to be going down anytime soon. Parker grabs my arm. Even I can see the goose bumps rising across my skin.

"Is your automobile close by?" Parker asks. "It's best we go someplace else."

"Somewhere I can get me a bitter?" Mary asks. "A drink is what I need to warm me bones."

"Will you stop talking about yourself for a single second?" Parker snaps.

"I can ask, can't I?" Mary growls back.

"Okay," Tatum says. "We're parked by the side of the road. But I'm not sure we can take all of you. It'll be a tight fit. And it's Scott's car. You'll have to ask him."

If she's feeling the cold, she's not saying anything. Actually, when I look closely, I can see beads of sweat on her forehead. She's warm. Her jacket is undone, and I can practically see the heat coming off her shoulders.

We all turn to look at Scott. "Um . . . sure," he says. He's still got a bit of that deer-in-the-headlights sort of look about him. I can tell he's dying to ask questions, but he's still not sure who or what to ask. Either way, I'm assuming they were here on a date and we've completely crashed their party. I feel bad for him; obviously he was hoping for something nice and normal, like a kiss. I try and conjure up the images I had the first time I touched Tatum. Faces flash across my memory: the girl with the curly hair, the boys I met the other night. A few others, people I haven't yet met. Scott's image isn't in my brain. I don't think he intends to hurt her. I hope not. Tatum's going to need him on her side.

"Molly." Parker is growing increasingly impatient. He's right. This cold isn't going away, and since I'm too stubborn to return to my prison, we'd better get out of here. At least someplace where it'll take a while to be rediscovered by whatever's lurking in Parker's imagination.

The wind stops. Cuts off in midblast. An eerie silence covers the area. Something moves through the bushes. Branches break and snap from the weight of bodies. Parker reaches out and grabs my hand. Fingers tighten, and he pulls me close. His eyes are wide and terrified.

"Oi! What's that sound?" Mary asks. She's paused halfway up the trail, but now she's turned around to face us. All those happy thoughts about drinking and buying new clothes have been pushed aside. Her nose wrinkles in concentration as she scans the area.

"What noise?" Tatum asks.

A groan adds to the air. From behind the bushes I start to see figures emerge. Shadows in human form. They're coming out from behind the trees. They're emerging from the water.

Bubbles rise to the surface. I whip around, and I can see blurry shapes in front of us, rambling down the path that leads to the road.

Wailing. The voices of a thousand dark souls fill my ears.

We're surrounded.

Parker's hand squeezes so tightly, it's as if he's trying to go right through my skin. "Don't let them near you," he says. "Whatever you do, don't get too close."

"Who is that?" Mary asks. She steps closer to us, finally understanding that something's wrong.

"Remnants," Parker says.

"What is it?" Tatum asks. She's squinting into the distance, trying to see what we're seeing. She's staring right at them; whatever these ghosts are, they're not visible to the living. They're here for us.

A Remnant steps into view. My blood runs instantly cold. I want to say it's male, but I'm not fully sure. It has no face, just bumps and shadows where the eyes, mouth, and nose should be. It wears clothing, faded and dirty, but I can't make out any distinct features at all. When I look straight at it, everything blurs, as if energy is pouring off its body in waves. It moves toward us, neither slow nor fast. The pale skin where its mouth should be pulses, and a gurgling wail fills the air.

"Oh, Jesus," Mary says. "Blessed Mother, protect us all."

"What is it?" Tatum asks again. I can hear the urgency in her voice. Her eyes dart around, scanning the area, seeing nothing. There's nothing for her to focus on. She moves closer to Scott, who puts his arm around her, protectively pulling her close.

One of them appears from behind a tree, reaching out

for Mary with blurred fingers. Parker recovers fast. He grabs Mary by the hem of her shawl and pulls her back. The Remnant's hands close around air. Parker lifts up his leg and kicks it squarely in the chest. The creature stumbles and falls, landing flat on its back, where it starts to sink beneath the surface.

"Don't let it near you," Parker says again. "We have to go. Your rocks. Get them out."

My hands tremble as my fingers close around my precious stone. I don't want to be the first to drop it. Not until everyone else is safe. I can't leave them behind. But Mary freezes. She stands perfectly still, unable to do anything as another creature closes in.

"Mary! Move it!" I scream.

She reaches her fingers down into the folds of her skirt pockets. "It's gone," she says. "I can't find it."

"It's got to be there," Parker says. "You can't have dropped it. Otherwise you'd be gone." He pushes his way in front of us both, spreading his arms out to try and protect us from the oncoming herd of Remnants. Two of them touch, their energy mixing together, making them look like creepy conjoined twins. The one on the right moans, a large lump forming where its mouth should be, tasting the air, tasting us.

"It's not here," Mary insists. She turns to me, desperation on her face.

"Check all your pockets," I say.

"What's going on?" Tatum asks. Her voice is a million miles away. When I look up, I can see one of the Remnants is almost at her. Will it walk right through her? Or will something happen? Just because Tatum can't see the creature, does that mean it can't hurt her? I find I don't want to take the chance.

There are too many of them. They're steadily closing in. Parker picks up a heavy branch and shoves the closest one back. Mary seems to have suddenly grown a dozen pockets in which to hide a pebble. We need more space. More time.

"Come on," I say to Parker. "We have to get everyone up to the road."

"What?" He looks at me incredulously.

"What if they hurt them?" I ask.

"They're human."

"That doesn't mean they can't be hurt, does it?"

Parker pauses, and I can tell he doesn't know the answer.

"We need to make sure everyone is safe," I say.

"If they catch you, you're going to die."

"I'm already—"

Parker grabs both my arms. "No, Molly. Not dead like what you are now. Simply put: no more you. There's no coming back from that."

I nod.

Parker turns and grabs Mary. "Come on," he says. "Let's get to higher ground. No, don't stop looking. Find that damn rock."

"What's going on?" Tatum asks.

"You don't want to know," I say. "But trust me, it's bad. You've got to get out of here. We don't know if they can hurt you or not."

"More ghosts like you?"

"Nothing like me."

Tatum seems to finally get it. Scott, meanwhile, has his hand on the small of her back and is already pushing Tatum up the path.

236

"No!" I scream. "Not that way. We have to go around."

Scott stops; a Remnant reaches out and misses him by inches. Scott pulls back and flinches. That's the first time I've noticed that Scott is shivering. He's looking right at the Remnant, and it's obvious he's not seeing it. But unlike Tatum, he seems almost aware of them. He gives me a questioning look, and I motion in the other direction. Nodding, Scott seems to have come back to his senses. Even though he's terrified, he's thinking clearly.

The Remnants come back toward me, where Parker is pulling Mary to the left, trying to find a way through the tumble of bushes. Mother Nature seems to be doing whatever she can to complicate things. The undergrowth is thick, and the only free areas are filled with the creatures. More and more appear out of thin air. There are about a dozen of them now, and they've almost got us surrounded.

Parker finally finds a small path. He ushers everyone through, and I scramble up the muddy slope, ignoring the wetness of the earth as it soaks into my skirt. Mary slips in front of me, cutting her hand on a sharp piece of stone. She cries out. Blood drips from her fingers.

I think it's the exact moment I see the blood that I realize I'm exhaling heavily as if all the wind's been knocked from my lungs.

Blood. Breathing.

In this state, we're humanlike. We can be hurt. And I've been so self-absorbed, I haven't even noticed.

I glance to the side and see the closest Remnant reaching out from behind a thin birch tree. Energy pulsates from its upper body, its skin rippling as if insects are just underneath.

Its hair is long and reddish orange, a stark contrast against its white-blue skin. If it touches us, will we become like it?

Panic shoots across my chest. For the first time since Walter brought the knife across my skin, I remember what absolute terror feels like.

It's slow going, but we finally reach the top of the slope. Everyone is covered in mud and dirt. Mary's fingers tremble as she tries to stop the bleeding. Her chest rises up and down in quick short gasps, her corset making it difficult to breathe in all that fear. I want to try and loosen it for her, but that will take too much time. Instead I reach into her closest pocket; if she can stand still long enough, I might be able to find her pebble for her. But I'm rewarded with only a wooden box full of matches and a couple of coins.

The thought is ridiculous. A stupid stone. How can something so meaningless suddenly become the most important essential for survival? I shove the matches and coins in my own pocket and continue the search.

"Come on," Tatum says. She's panting too. The scramble up the steep banks has set us all back. "The car's just over there."

"We don't need the car," I say. "But you and Scott need to get out of here."

"I'm not leaving you," Tatum says.

"Don't worry, we've got our own exit strategy." I've gone through both the skirt pockets. Now I'm reaching into Mary's blouse, sorting through a few more coins and whatever else she's managed to salvage from the past century. Parker joins me. Mary's become completely useless. She stands still, letting us search her, holding her fingers up and crying as the blood continues to seep away. For someone who was sliced apart by one of the world's worst killers of all time, she sure is having a hard time dealing with a little blood.

"Watch out!" Parker screams at me. I turn, and a Remnant stumbles straight into me. I fall, bringing Mary and all her petticoats with me, and we collapse into a heap on the road. Parker brings his branch up like a baseball bat and sends the Remnant reeling back into the woods.

I see Tatum rushing toward me with Scott trying to pull her back.

"Get out of here!" I yell at them. "Go. I'll find you."

"But—"

"Go! Scott. Get her out of here. Now!"

Scott holds on to Tatum's arm, forcing her toward the car. He opens the door and ushers her inside. Tatum presses her face up against the window, screaming words I can't hear. I don't care. As long as she's safe, that's all that matters.

"I found it," Mary says. With trembling fingers she holds up the tiny pebble, which she finally managed to yank from God knows where. "Now what do I do—"

Blurred fingers reach around her neck, squeezing tightly.

I think I scream. I'm not fully sure.

The Remnant's hand loops around Mary, grabbing a fistful of hair. Energy slithers along its arm, taking on a life of its own, pulsating away from the creature's body and wrapping tightly around Mary's. She opens her mouth to call out for me as currents squeeze her throat, cutting off the air. More energy encircles her chest, her legs and arms. It tightens, covering her, binding her to the Remnant.

I try to grab her fingers, which reach out toward me for

help. Then hands go around my own waist, Parker holding me back as I scream and struggle. Parker is stronger than me; he pulls me across the road, away from Mary, as she writhes under her invisible bondage.

"Let go of me," I gasp.

"You can't help her. She's gone."

But she's not. Mary is still there. She opens her outstretched hand, and I see her pebble drop to the ground.

She doesn't disappear. She doesn't Fade.

In the distance, I hear a car engine roar to life. Scott's finally listened to us. He's managed to find a way to keep Tatum inside the vehicle, and they're peeling out. Brake lights fade and tires squeal.

Parker's hand reaches into my pocket, and he's suddenly pressing something into my palm. A tiny rock.

"Drop it," he says. His voice is weirdly calm.

I look up at what used to be Mary. She's struggling to stay standing, her leather boots the only thing that identifies her for who she used to be. She's faceless now, swaying slightly, taking her first step toward us. Her beautiful eyes have disappeared. The mouth that always had such colorful things to say.

Parker's right. She's gone.

I open my hand and let the pebble drop to the ground. I Fade away and back into the cave, where Parker finds me. My legs tremble, and I collapse into the dirt, sobbing uncontrollably. Parker kneels down and wraps his arms around me, holding me until the shaking stops.

"You're safe," he says over and over.

He holds me until the end of time.

TATUM

Scott doesn't stop. His foot is embedded in the floor, and the tires squeal, filling the car with the smell of burned rubber.

The girl, Mary, just disappeared into thin air. But not in a good way. Tatum is sure of that. There's no escaping the look of horror etched across her face or the way she gasped as if something was starting to suck the last bit of air from her body. The way Molly screamed and tried to help her, Parker holding her back as if their lives depended on it. Something horrible happened. But what? Helplessly, she watched Molly and Parker fade away into the distance.

Scott turns a corner, sending Tatum violently against the passenger-side door. Her head knocks against the window.

Seat belt.

"Go back," she says.

"No way."

"GO BACK!"

Scott ignores her, so Tatum grabs the emergency brake and

pulls it. The car jerks, and the tires slip out from beneath them. Scott tries to keep control of the wheel while they spin around a hundred and eighty degrees. They don't end up in the ditch, but they come close. The engine sputters and dies, jerking to a halt. Scott slams his fist down on the dashboard.

"Are you nuts?"

"Yes. Now go back!"

"Molly told me to get you out of there."

"And you did. Now we go back. I need to make sure they made it. I have to be sure she's safe."

"How exactly will you know for sure?"

"Just do it."

Scott swears, but he starts the car again and turns around. Moving more slowly this time, they head back down Frog Road and toward the train bridge. The path is empty. Wherever Parker and Molly are, they're no longer there.

Scott doesn't stop, but he slows to a crawl as they drive by. Tatum looks out into nothing, searching for a clue, something, that can explain the craziness that just happened.

What did Molly see? What scared them so bad that they freaked out like that?

"They're gone. Are you satisfied?"

"I don't know."

Tatum lets out a steady stream of curse words herself, frustrated that she was just part of something horrifying and she couldn't see a damn thing.

Where is Molly? Did she get free? How long is it going to take before Tatum finds out for sure? How many days is she going to have to spend waiting before she can decide something terrible happened? A week? Two? Oh God, is this her fault?

"Come on," Scott says. "I'm taking you home."

* * *

Scott pulls up in front of her house. Tatum wants nothing more than to jump out of the car before it stops moving and run inside. But Scott wants an explanation; she can tell by the way he keeps opening and closing his mouth. When he stops, he turns off the car and waits.

"So this is what you do?" he finally says. "You're some kind of ghost hunter?"

Tatum laughs, although it's really not that funny. She looks at the driveway, where her car waits. Neither of her parents is home right now. Tatum wants to go up into the sanctuary of her bedroom, get into bed, and pull the covers up over her head until the cold feelings go away. Maybe a hot shower would help. Her hands are freezing. She stuffs them into her pockets, but it doesn't do a thing to warm them up. This kind of cold goes straight down to her bones.

"Care to explain what just happened?"

"I don't know," she says. "I really don't."

"You don't know how a bunch of ghosts turned up out of nowhere? Or you don't know why they called you by your name? Or that weird invisible attack? Was it an attack? Do we even know what happened?"

"You mean you believe it?" Tatum asks carefully.

"I have eyes, don't I?"

Tatum shrugs. Would she believe it if the tables were turned and she were sitting in Scott's position?

Scott exhales heavily. He taps his fingers absently on the steering wheel. "I don't know. I guess so. What should I say? That girl, Molly, she's a dead ringer for the girl in the photograph, and I know *it's* real. I gave you those articles myself. They weren't doctored or anything. Those other two looked like they stepped out of the Victorian era or something. Part of me wants to believe you're setting me up, but for what . . . I can't even begin to figure that out."

"Parker is the guy," Tatum says. "I met him for the first time the other night. I don't know about the girl. Mary. I've never seen her before. She really has a thing for food."

"I don't think you're crazy," Scott says. "If anyone knows you tell the truth, I guess it's me. So yeah, I believe you. Now I'm just wishing Granny was with us. She would have loved that, even if it did get weird."

* * *

Tatum tells him everything. Scott must be cold too because halfway through her story he starts the car up so he can turn on the heater. She tells him first about how she met Molly on the road. She tells him about Molly's strange warning only because she can't think of a better lie on the spot. Since Molly only gives premonitions to certain people, like Scott's grandmother, she knows she can't leave that out. She probably could have made something up about a lost cat, but Scott deserves complete honesty. She goes on, talking about how she's been doing all that research to try and find a way to help Molly, but how do you help a ghost who obviously doesn't seem to need it?

While she's talking, both her parents come home. They see her in the car and wave. Mom can't stop smiling, apparently thrilled to see Tatum talking with a boy her own age. Dad frowns, but thankfully doesn't do anything to embarrass her. They go inside after Mom points to her watch and taps it. Twenty minutes and then it's time to go in for dinner.

"So what do we do now?" Scott asks when she finally finishes.

"Wait for Molly to come back," Tatum says. "I hope she's safe."

"No, not that," Scott says. "What about you? If Molly says you're going to die, shouldn't you be more worried? She was right about my grandma. Completely right. Each little detail. And you said it yourself—you read that stuff online about other people she's spoken to. The things Molly says, they're true."

"Just because she knew someone was being cheated on doesn't mean she's right about this," Tatum says. "Come on, Claudette might be a big bitch, but she's not a psychopathic killer. She's never tried to pick a fight with me. She's having too much fun getting the guys to pee on my car."

"That doesn't mean she won't take it up a notch."

"She's not a killer," Tatum says. "I've known her my whole life. She never tortured animals as a child or crap like that."

"So you're just going to ignore the warning? Even though Molly keeps coming back? Did you not see that freak-out? It looks to me like she's taking a hell of a chance to try and make sure you're safe."

"What's that supposed to mean?"

"You didn't feel it?"

"What?"

Scott shudders and turns the heat up. "There was something in the woods. I couldn't fully see it. Blurred images out of the corners of my eyes. Things moving. A lot of them. And the temperature. It was so cold I could see my breath. But whatever it was, they saw it. It terrified them. It got Mary."

"Parker called them Remnants."

Scott nodded. "I think it was a different type of ghost. Something that came after them. If Molly found a way to escape her afterlife like she told you, maybe they're set up to make sure these things can't happen."

"If she comes back, she's putting herself in danger, then."

"Exactly."

Tatum doesn't want to think about that. These past few weeks have given her a purpose. Before Molly, she had nothing. She sat in her room and waited for everything to end so she could restart her life. It's been a horrible time; she doesn't want to go back to it. She needs Molly in her life. She wants to be her friend. Sure, that sounds stupid, but for the first time in ages Tatum feels good about herself. And then there's Scott. If it weren't for her ghostly friend, she never would have talked to him.

And thanks to Molly and to Scott's grandmother's stories, they're still talking.

"She's going through a lot of trouble to keep you safe," Scott says. "She's risking her own life. Wait, ghosts are dead, right? Does that make it her soul she's risking?"

"Nothing is going to happen," Tatum insists. She looks at the dashboard clock. Time's up. She'd better get inside before Dad comes out. "I've got to go."

"Okay. But do me a favor and think about it," Scott says. "Let's be careful over the next few days. Don't put yourself in a position where you're alone with Claudette."

"Fine."

She wonders if Scott might lean over and go for that kiss he missed earlier, but he doesn't. Instead he watches her as she walks up the driveway. It isn't until she reaches the door that he drives off. She goes inside, bracing herself for the barrage of questions that will be coming her way. Mom will most likely think that Tatum's being with Scott is the best thing in the world that could happen to her oversexed, older man–chasing daughter.

* * *

Tatum tosses and turns all night. No matter how much she tries to ignore it, Scott's warning keeps popping up in the back of her mind. What if he's right? What if she's completely under-estimating Claudette? Why else would Molly risk her soul to keep coming back?

She gets out of bed and turns on the computer to research Remnants, but finds nothing. She's not overly surprised, since humans can't see them and ghosts don't exactly keep blogs. Finally, around three a.m., she falls into a poor sleep that ends with nightmares in which she's being chased by shadow monsters with extra-large heads. In the morning, before she showers, her face in the mirror looks haggard. No amount of makeup can hide those dark marks under her eyes.

School is uneventful. No one looks at her or says a single word. She talks to Scott briefly in the hall before class, but that's about it.

Just before lunch, she gets called into the office.

The principal takes her outside to the parking lot without really talking to her. He hasn't said a friendly word since the last official office visit, months ago, when Tatum got called out for being a liar. Now his face is red and sweaty. He repeats that he doesn't have time for this nonsense. He wants to know where she was during first period. Was she in class? He is going to check with her teacher, so she'd better tell the truth. Tatum can't help but think he'd behave differently if it were any student other than her.

The damage is extensive.

They've broken all the windows in her car. From first glance it looks like they used a baseball bat. The fenders are dented in several spots. They opened the hood and tore out every single wire they could find. They removed the battery and smashed it open on the ground. Acid stains the asphalt beneath her feet. All the tires have been slashed. The seats cut and pulled apart. The CD player disabled and lying in pieces on the floorboards.

Someone used a key to scratch all sorts of nasty remarks in the paint job. Words even worse than what she normally finds on her locker. What's more is that they used something other than lipstick this time. On the hood of the car, the words are still drying. It's probably paint, but it looks like the words were written in blood.

DIE, BITCH, DIE.

The words make her shudder the first time she reads them. Scott is going to have a lot to say about this. Oh God, this is true. Claudette is capable of doing a lot more than Tatum's given her credit for. Maybe all that time spent with Mr. Paracini has done something to her brain.

There is so much damage that her car no longer resembles itself. It's more like a lump of gray metal now. Glass is scattered across the ground, along with bits of cloth from the seats. No amount of insurance money will put it back together. It's a write-off.

Dad's going to kill her.

The police are called in, although the principal isn't happy about it. He talks to the officers, and she knows he's telling them about her sketchy past. It's suggested more than once that she probably did this herself to get the attention and sympathy from the other students. One of the cops, a woman, gives her a compassionate glance, but the man obviously thinks Tatum must have brought this on herself. Still, he takes her statement and writes down everything she says.

No one saw anything. Tatum gives them a list of names, and the female officer assures her they'll follow it all up. But the odds are good that Claudette and her army will have alibis.

"If you did this, you should come clean," the principal says again. "I'm going to check with your teachers. If you so much as even went to the bathroom, I'll find out."

"They destroyed my car," Tatum counters. "There's blood all over it."

"It's just paint," the principal says.

"It smells like blood." She turns to the male cop. "Aren't you even going to test it to find out where it came from?"

"This isn't some stupid crime show," he grumbles. But he goes over to his car and pulls out a crime kit.

The lunch bell rings and students come out, curious about all the commotion. They stand around in the distance, and Tatum notices that Claudette and Graham are noticeably absent. Levi is there, taking pictures on his phone, laughing with Juniper. At least he's smart enough not to shout anything or get too close.

"Can you think of anyone else who might want to harm you?" the female officer asks.

"It's some sort of stupid prank," the male cop says. "Went a bit too far, but kids say this sort of stuff all the time. It's all that time on the Internet. Makes them feel invincible."

"Doesn't look that way to me."

"It had to be Claudette," Tatum says. "She hates me more than anything." As much as she wants the officers to believe her, she also wonders what the point is. None of this matters anymore. Her car is gone, and it's not like Dad's about to get her another, especially with college a year away. And now her salvation, the one thing she thought she could rely on to get her far away from this town, has been taken away.

Even with the small amount of insurance she'll get, it'll take her forever to save up for a new car. She'll be stuck working in town until she earns enough to run away for good.

* * *

At home, her parents are guarded. Dad thankfully doesn't scream at her for the damage done. Mom wants to call the police and demand answers, but Dad convinces her to wait until the morning. Might as well wait until they have more information so they can contact the insurance company. Mom's mouth is growing steadily tauter by the minute.

All in all, it could have been worse.

Afterward, in her room, she listens to Mom and Dad argue from behind the closed bedroom door. Mom wants to send her away for the rest of the semester, transfer her to another school. Maybe in Seattle. Maybe getting away from all this is exactly what Tatum needs to start over. Dad worries that sending her away will give the wrong message. Sending her away will only confirm her guilt. Maybe the insurance will be enough to get her another car. She's going to need one to be safe.

There's almost hopefulness in both their arguments. Tatum wants to believe that they are still on her side. Even with the ongoing talk about psychologists and getting help for her emotional problems, Tatum often doubts the support they claim to give her. But if Mom's suggesting that Tatum transfer schools, maybe she really does want to help. Of course it's pointless; even if Tatum goes all the way to Canada, Claudette will still find a way to stalk her. It will only be a matter of time before her past gets shoved down the throats of whatever new place she ends up in.

But if her parents believe her, maybe there is still a bit of goodness in this world.

More than anything, Tatum needs Molly. She has to find out if Molly is okay and made it back. But only a single day has passed, and she knows it takes longer than that. She's not sure how she's going to make it through the next few days without knowing.

She falls asleep on top of the bed with her shoes still on.

* * *

Glass shatters.

Tatum jerks awake, unsure of what she just heard. Is she dreaming?

An acidic smell fills her nose, making her throat instantly convulse, forcing her into an uncontrollable coughing spree. Something thick and bright assaults her eyes, forcing them to water. It takes a moment for her brain to register what she's seeing.

Her curtains are on fire.

Bright flames climb the fabric. An orange-and-yellow blaze spreads out across the carpet, dancing about, stealing all the room's oxygen. Her window is open; jagged pieces of glass stick to the windowsill.

Something sails through the air, crashing against the wall, sending an explosion of fire in all directions. A poster begins to crumple, charred paper dissolving at an alarming rate. Some of it reaches the bedspread, and black smoke fills the air, choking Tatum as she frantically jumps off the mattress and races for the door.

"Mom! Dad!" The only thing she can think about is making sure they're okay.

She gets halfway down the hallway before their door opens. They rush out in their pajamas. Mom starts to cough; already the smoke is spreading throughout the house.

"Where's the fire?" Dad yells.

"My room."

He doesn't say any more, just rushes down the stairs and comes back moments later with the fire extinguisher in his hands. Fighting the smoke and heat, he runs into Tatum's bedroom while Mom fumbles for her phone to call 911.

Thankfully, the fire is extinguished before the fire trucks show up. The rest of the house is fine, but Tatum's room is completely destroyed. Everything's covered in white foam. Her bedspread is ruined. The curtains are charred mush. The window frame is burned to a crisp. Everything smells like wet ash. Firemen traipse through the house with their big black boots, leaving muddy marks on the carpet.

Tatum and her parents sit in the living room. Outside, dogs bark and all the neighbors' lights are turned on. This is something that everyone will talk about for ages. A new chapter for the never-ending story of Tatum's life. The policemen and firemen have already walked Tatum through the events several times. There's not much to say. She woke up to the flames. On the floor of her bedroom, they discovered bits of broken bottle. Outside, they find another bottle in the bushes. Apparently the first attempt missed and hit the house instead, setting fire to the hedge.

No witnesses. No footprints in the wet grass. No strange cars seen fleeing the scene of the crime. Even though some of the neighbors are asked, no one saw a single thing. Everyone was too busy sleeping.

Tatum gives out the same names she gave earlier during the car incident. Her parents reconfirm it. They explain to the police that there have been problems at school and that some of the kids have been causing trouble. The police want to know which students are the worst, and Tatum repeats Claudette's and Graham's names. She mentions Levi, too. She is still having trouble believing that Claudette would take things to this level. But who else would do such a thing? Yes, Tatum is hated by everyone. No, until today, most of the bullying has been rather tame. Nothing she couldn't handle.

Now she's afraid.

Setting the house on fire? This has gone too far. Her father, whom she's been sure all this time secretly doesn't believe her, gets into a heated conversation with the policeman, demanding something be done.

"First my daughter's car, now the house," he says. "There's something wrong with these kids. Something wrong with their parents."

Afterward, Mom gets out some old blankets from the closet and makes up the couch for Tatum to sleep on.

"We'll get it fixed tomorrow," she says, referring to the window. "It might take a few weeks to clean everything up. You can use the office for your personal space until then. But you're stuck sleeping on the couch for a while."

"That's fine," Tatum says.

Mom gives her a kiss on the forehead. "Do you need anything? Set your alarm. I'm going to throw a load of laundry in before I go to bed. You're going to need clothes for the morning. Something that doesn't smell like smoke. Is there anything you want me to wash? Or you can borrow something of mine."

"My hoodie," Tatum says. "The blue one. And my yoga pants, I guess. Or I can wear yours. It doesn't matter."

"Done."

Tatum crawls onto the couch and Mom tucks the blanket around her like she's eight years old again. It feels good. No matter how old she gets, Tatum knows that now and then she still needs her mom to be a mother.

"You know," Mom says, "I'm going to say this. You know I believe you. If you can't have your parents on your side, then I suppose you've really got nothing. But this gang mentality. No matter what you did or didn't do, this sort of thing shouldn't be happening. This has gone too far."

"I didn't do it," Tatum says. "I really didn't."

"I know you didn't, sweetie. And I think by this point it no longer matters," Mom says. "But this, all this." She waves her hand around the room. "This needs to end. Tomorrow I'm going to personally call the school and all the parents. They need to know what their children are doing. This has gone too far. And I don't give a damn what your father says; it's time to find you a new school. You deserve a chance to finish out your senior year in peace."

"Thanks, Mom."

Dad comes down the stairs. Earlier he put his jacket on over his pajamas, and now he takes it off and hangs it in the closet.

"I'll call the contractor in the morning," he says. He double-checks the deadbolt on the front door and pauses, looking down at the shoe rack. When he turns, he gives Tatum a quizzical look.

"Your shoes," he finally says.

"What about them?" They're sitting in a pile by the couch. Soaked with foam, she had to practically peel the wet socks from her feet a few minutes ago.

"You said you were in bed when all this happened. But you were wearing your shoes."

"I fell asleep with them on," Tatum says.

"Are you sure?"

Oh God. No. Not again. Tatum looks to Mom for support,

only to discover that her mother is looking down at her hands. Just like that. No matter how much they claim to believe her. No matter how much they stand by her side. There will always still be that tiny seed of doubt.

Is this ever going to end? The suspicion? Or will all the family reunions for the next fifty years be full of questions about whether or not Tatum is torturing schoolchildren and robbing banks in her free time?

"You guys were arguing and being really loud," Tatum says, happy to see Mom look away and toward the floor. "It took me forever to fall asleep. I didn't even get under the covers."

There's a pause while Dad stares at her long and hard. "We'll talk about it more in the morning."

This time Tatum can't hear a single word when they both retreat to their bedroom. Tatum lies awake in the dark. Her parents have become strangers to her. It doesn't matter that they raised her, listened to her, watched her grow into the person she's become for the past seventeen years. They want to believe her, but with everything happening, maybe it's too much for them to process. When you hear something all the time, how long does it take to believe? There is something incredibly evil about false accusations. Tatum would never put her parents in harm's way; they should know that without question. In a way, this hurts her more than all the bad things Claudette has done.

In her mind, she silently calls out to Molly, hoping the other girl will hear her prayers and hurry back to her.

It doesn't happen.

MOLLY

I hold the pebble in my hand and write Tatum's name on the wall for the tenth time. Just like the other nine times, nothing happens. The cave is refusing to work. It mocks me, all that sparking light dancing around, sending shimmering slivers across Parker's face.

I throw the chalk as hard as I can, smashing it into several pieces. I kick at the bowl of pebbles, sending hundreds of tiny stones scattering across the floor. The dish cracks in two and then instantly re-forms. Everything in this cavern taunts me. All the things I can't destroy. The things I can't change.

Mary is gone.

And Tatum is going to be a goner if I don't get back to her. The worst part? It's all my fault. I've handled this badly. If anything, I'm putting her in more danger every time I appear.

I don't understand why. Whoever pulls the strings around here, why are they torturing me this way? What did I do on earth to deserve this? I'm the innocent here. The victim. I'm the one who was shredded into ribbons by a madman. My life was torn away before I even had a chance to begin it; I had to leave behind the boy I still love, and I never got the chance to say goodbye to the people I cared about. But I'm not allowed to think about that because the pain is still too strong. I'm the one who spends my now-endless days trapped in a world that has no emotions. No love. Just people who sit around waiting for a white light or a one-way ticket to a heaven that probably doesn't exist. A cursed afterlife that forces me to tell people things they don't want to hear.

Why me?

I want this to end. If I can't feel, then let me stop existing. Let me stop hoping. Let me die in peace.

Parker lets me rant; he leans against the wall, waiting for me to finish, letting me know he's here if I need him to hold me again. I do, but I won't allow myself the luxury. I don't deserve anything, especially not in this place where I can actually feel it.

"Do you think she's in pain?" I ask. I picture Mary, not the happy-go-lucky girl flaunting her corset and complaining about the various men she once knew in her life, but the faceless Mary now forced to wander the earth alone. I could swear she sensed me and all recognition was lost. She no longer remembers her friends. Now I'm just something for her to destroy. A new instinct she has to follow.

"I don't know," Parker says

"It looked painful," I say. "Maybe that's why the Remnants hate us. Because we can't feel anything, and they only . . . they only . . ." My voice trembles and I can't go on.

"I don't know if they hate us," Parker says. "I think it's

more like something they have to do. To balance everything. To remind the dead that we have no place with the living."

"Then why do we haunt?"

"To give people hope?"

"Hope?" The word sounds nasty in my mouth. "That's the stupidest thing I've ever heard. All we do is bring our own kind of pain, Parker. We remind the living that there's something out there that isn't paradise. All we do is scare and confuse them."

"It didn't sound that way to Scott's grandmother."

"She's the exception," I say. "I gave her a good premonition. Everyone else finds out their loved ones are cheating on them. Or that they're going to die."

"Not everyone."

"I hate what I am," I say. "I hate this place. I hate being dead. And most of all, I hate that my life was taken from me."

"You're not the only one allowed to hate here," Parker says softly.

He's right. I'm not alone in my hate. Maybe that's why this place lacks feelings. Perhaps all our hatred became too strong. It's easier to not feel anything than to be angry all the time. Is that what happened? Did all the souls here finally give up and shut down? Turn off their emotions because it beat the alternative? If so, Parker is right. This cave, this emotional turmoil—it's best not to be in it for too long. Because once the initial enjoyment is over, all I can do is remember the things I want to forget.

The things I've lost. And it's not like I can get past everything and move on with my life.

I reach down and pick up a piece of pink chalk. I go over

to the other side of the cave, where the glowing rocks aren't as bright. I draw Mary's name in elaborate script. I draw some pathetic-looking flowers. Parker comes over and adds to the monument. He draws a pretty girl dancing in circles, petticoats spinning and whirling, long hair flowing. Adding to my flowers, he draws a meadow with birds and willowy trees. A stream flows through the middle. I try not to get jealous that he's a much better artist than me. As a finishing touch, in the bottom corner I add a heart and color it in carefully.

"So no one will forget," I say. I wish I could draw music so that everyone who comes here could hear the songs she used to sing.

"Come on," Parker says after a while. "Let's go back down. It'll give you a chance to clear your head. We'll return the second you want, I give you my word."

I nod because there's nothing else to do.

* * *

"Marry me."

When Julian spoke those words to me, everything ceased to exist. I know, clichéd and stupid, right? But at that moment, I sincerely felt sorry for every other girl in the world, because they'd never get a chance to know Julian the way I did.

The word *yes* was the only one Julian wanted to hear. It was what I wanted to say more than anything else. But lying there in the back of the truck, covered in warm blankets, watching the millions of stars dance around in the sky just for us, I of course had to screw that one up.

"We're too young," I said.

"Not right now," Julian said. "I mean, not like this very minute. But somewhere down the road, once we're able to go off on our own. When you're done with school and I finish up this internship." Julian had recently started training with a guy who was teaching him how to work with precious metals. They thought he had a future creating jewelry. He had a special talent for design. The stores around Washington were asking for more and more. They couldn't keep his work on the shelves.

"But that will take two years," I said.

"You're the one who thinks we're too young."

I laughed and snuggled in closer. I wondered what my father might think if I called him to say I was getting married. I had a lot of guilt building up; so many months had passed, and I still hadn't done what I'd promised. Every time I came across a phone, I'd imagine him sitting in his chair, waiting for me to call. But the guilt wasn't enough yet to make me dial his number. I was afraid of his power over me. What if Dad demanded I come home? Or if he somehow figured out where I was and came to claim me? I couldn't bear to leave. So I didn't do anything. Selfish in my own happiness, I ignored the knowledge that my father and brother continued to live each day wondering where I was and if I was safe.

"I don't want to spend the rest of my time wandering around the country," Julian said. "It's fine for Walter and Olivia, but I'd rather settle down. We could have a nice house. Save up our money and travel. But I want someplace to call home. A white picket fence. A family."

"I agree," I said. Even though I'd been enjoying myself enormously, traveling across the country with my new friends,

I had to agree it wasn't always fun and games. The enjoyment of camping wore out quickly after I'd gone a week without a shower. And it wasn't that great to live with a bunch of people who didn't bathe on a regular basis. Sometimes the smells in our van could be strong. The people whose land we were squatting on had only so much patience when it came to sharing the shower. And I didn't like using the large basin we'd set up in camp. It took forever to heat the water on the campfire, and the bottom of the tub always left my skin feeling ragged. Also, Walter had a habit of coming around whenever I used it. As much as I loved Olivia and Sage in particular, I had to admit that Walter had started to seem creepy. I once caught him watching me when he thought no one else was looking. I didn't mention it to Julian, though, because he respected Walter and considered him like the father he'd never had.

"A small house," Julian said. "Not much; we don't need it. But it should have a yard. We can get a dog. I know you've always wanted pets."

"And a cat," I said. "Maybe some fish."

"We'll have to get a farm, then! The perfect place to raise a family once we're ready!"

It was wonderful, all this dreaming. How lucky I was to have someone to share it with. I felt complete. Ready to begin my next big adventure. I wanted that domestic bliss with Julian. I wanted that life. I'd only just turned sixteen, but none of that mattered. Dad had been seventeen when he met Mom. Marcus had had his longtime girlfriend since he was fourteen. And I was willing to wait two more years until Julian finished his internship and I finished high school. By that time I'd be eighteen and an adult. No one would be able to stop us.

"So what do you say?"

Julian reached into his pocket and pulled out a small velvet box. Opening it, he repositioned himself in the blankets so he was on one knee. Inside was a silver ring with a tiny diamond in the center.

"I made it myself," he said.

"It's beautiful." I held out my hand and Julian slipped it onto my finger. It fit perfectly.

"So that's a yes?"

I laughed and pulled him toward me. "Of course that's a yes. A million times yes!"

"I love you, Molly," Julian said. "I can't wait to spend the rest of my life with you."

Love. It's the most powerful motivator in the world. It makes people feel like they're invincible. It makes them imagine wonderful universes in which they live happily ever after. When two people are in love, they can move mountains.

I was in love. Life was mine for the taking. I had everything: a glorious future to look forward to and a man who loved me as much as I loved him.

Two weeks later I was dead.

* * *

We're not even at the cave entrance when I hear it: thunder. It vibrates within the cavern walls. The smell hits me as I push my body through the cracks: the scent of pine needles and fresh earth, intensified from the rain.

Outside, a storm has appeared out of nowhere. The clouds above us are dark and threatening. Lightning flashes, white-hot crackles of electricity, brightening the sky. I start counting: *one Mississippi, two Mississippi, three*—and there's the boom.

Thunder, loud and echoing.

"What the hell?"

Rain pelts down on us, soaking Parker and me. Within seconds, my shirt is plastered against my body. Water clings to my hair and trickles down my face; drops fall from my nose onto my lips. I open my mouth and raise my face to the sky, allowing the cool liquid to fall down my throat. I close my eyes.

Something is happening.

"Come on," Parker says. "Let's go find the others."

The path is muddy and slippery. We slide down, our hands sinking into the wet earth for balance. I lose a sandal and kick off the other, watch it fly into a bush. My toes sink into the soft earth, squishy and comfortable. My skirt gets filthy, but I don't mind. There's enough rain to wash away any amount of dirt.

It only takes moments to reach the shoreline. One minute we're slipping between the trees, high above the lake; the next I find myself toppling off a bank and into the deep blue water.

It swallows me up as I sink down. Kicking with my feet, I push to the surface to find Parker treading water beside me. He's laughing, and it's hard not to enjoy it for that brief second before I remind myself that there are more sober things to worry about.

We swim to shore, only to find ourselves close to the beach. My sandals are back on my feet the second I step out of the water. My skirt is clean again, but still wet. I automatically reach around to feel the torn hem; it's so strange to have something different after so many years of being static. Parker's hair is stuck to his forehead. I brush it away from his eyes so it sticks up in all directions. Parker grins at me, his fingers lingering beside my waist.

It's just a quick walk through the trees in this crazy world that now refuses to stay silent.

They're all waiting on the beach. Confused, the whole crowd of them, they're looking up at the clouds in fear. It's as if they expect the sky to open up and completely swallow them. A few of them had the smarts to cower under the French umbrellas. They look like tourists who suddenly got caught in the middle of a summer storm. Some of them, like the Chinese farmer and the rock groupie from Vancouver, hold their hands out cautiously, surprised to see the water splash against their skin.

In the center area of the beach stands the crazy dog lady. She's spinning about in circles, arms raised up to the sky, her dog bouncing along on his hind legs. He barks happily, his paws swinging up and down for balance. She's laughing hard, her eyes tightly creased, her mouth open to catch the drops. She twirls around one more time before seeing me.

"You," she says. "You did this!"

Me?

The dog lady comes dancing over, her faithful companion glued to her heels. "Thank you," she says. "You've done it."

"I haven't done anything," I say.

"Pishposh," she says. "Of course you have."

"How?"

The lady turns around and faces all the others on the beach. They're inching closer, wanting to hear what she has to say. The crazy dog lady is suddenly about to give a speech that makes sense.

"It's in all of us, you know," she says. "The ability to change things. This place hasn't defeated us yet. We've become stagnant. Forgotten who we are. Who we used to be. What we loved. But this girl"—she points at me—"she remembers. It's her determination to fix things that's bringing it all back."

"I still don't understand," I say.

"You need to go and save that girl," the lady says. "Get yourself back to the real world and make things right."

"How do you know about that?" I ask.

"What? You think just because we sit around like dead logs, we don't still have ears? I hear every conversation on this beach. So do the others. I know you're trying to save that girl. By doing so, I think you're going to save us all. Help us remember who we used to be."

It takes me a moment to notice that the rain has stopped. Now the clouds above us are drastically pulling away, revealing blue sky. Warm air presses against my skin, like I'm being covered by a cushy blanket.

"Is that what I think that is?" the lady asks. She's turned her attention away from the group. Even the dog suddenly sits back on its haunches, its crazy dance abandoned, mesmerized as the sky comes alive.

And then it's there, peeking over the mountain horizon like a lost child who has found her way back home. A bright white light as the sun slowly grows in the sky.

One by one, the others begin to move forward, stepping away from the safety of the umbrellas to come join us on the sand. Hands reach out to touch me, as if that might spread around more of what I'm offering.

"I remember this," Yuriko says. "It's been so long since I've felt the sun." When she touches my cheek, her fingers are cool and soft.

She's not the only one. Pretty much all of us ghosts appear in the real world during the night. Sunlight is a luxury everyone has forgotten.

"We have to remember," the dog lady says. "If we want to bring back our lives, we have to recall them. No more of this nonsense of sitting around and waiting for all that nothing to happen. This is our reality. Our emotions can fix things. Our memories. We need to bring it all back. The good, the bad, everything."

There are murmurs of people agreeing. Others start reminiscing, talking about things they've forgotten from being alive. A beach ball appears out of nowhere, and the Vancouver girl picks it up and tosses it into the air. A boy in rags runs to chase it. A fiddle appears in a blond girl's hands. She slides the bow across the strings, her braids bouncing as she begins to play an Irish melody. It makes me think of Mary, and I can't help but picture her bouncing across the sand. She would have loved this more than anyone.

Now we have a melody and everyone begins to dance. Louis Chen grabs my arms and pulls me in, bouncing in an offbeat way. He trades me off to an older gentleman whose hairpiece has gone askew. We spin around twice before I let go, and he's swallowed up by the music as several hands reach up toward the sky.

I spot Parker standing a ways off from the crowd. He's found his jacket and bowler hat by our usual spot. He turns the hat around in his hands before tossing it toward the lake like a Frisbee.

I sneak through the crowd and make my way toward him.

"You've done an amazing thing here," he says. "Feel it? All that energy and emotion. It's just like being at the cave."

I wrap my arms around him, pull him close. I run my fingers through his hair to feel the coarseness. It's soft, actually, different from what I expected. Our lips touch, and my stomach tingles and dances around for the first time in what feels like forever.

Love is no longer a memory.

Somehow it's been set free.

"I have to go back," I say to him once we stop kissing. "One more time. I have to finish this."

"I know." His voice is husky and filled with emotion.

"You don't have to come with me."

"You know I will."

He reaches down and takes my hand in his.

"Was there someone you loved once?" I ask. "A girl when you were alive?"

"Yes," Parker says. "Sophia. She was amazing. Brown hair. Big brown eyes. I used to rent the flat above the shop her father owned. She had the most beautiful voice. Very talented and a smart girl. She used to sit with me while I studied and didn't say a word. We could sit quietly for hours, reading by candlelight, happy to be together. I planned on marrying her, just like you and Julian."

"You never told me about her before. How come?"

"It hurt too much to talk about, I guess," Parker says. "Being here. The way things were. I tried not to think about it. Easier that way. I'm just as guilty as everyone else."

He moves in to kiss me again, but this time I pull back.

"Do you think we're betraying them?"

"No," Parker says. "Haven't you said you wanted Julian to move on? Find someone new to love? How is that any different to what we're doing here now?"

"I always thought Julian and I would be reunited, after he, well, you know."

Parker nods. "I used to think that way too. But I do know that wherever Sophia is, it's not here. And she'd be long gone herself."

"Scott would be a good guy for Tatum," I say. "Don't you think? He seemed very nice."

"Maybe," Parker says. "Let's give them the chance to find out."

* * *

Julian was gone that day; he'd been working five days a week with the precious metals internship. He'd bring home all sorts of books to study, spending his evenings reading by candlelight in the back of the truck. Weekends were spent together, making jewelry to sell so we could continue to put food on the table. Olivia helped by sewing clothing. Walter and a few others picked up odd jobs where they could. Sage taught me everything from her battered syllabus books. We managed to get by.

My job was to go around to all the shops and drop off the orders. I had a bicycle, a rusty red creation with a basket to hold everything. I'd found it in a ditch outside Portland and painstakingly brought it back to life. With Julian's help, I'd replaced the tires and handlebars. I'd painted it and attached streamers, which rippled and danced the faster I pedaled. I loved it, although the chain constantly slipped no matter how often I oiled it. That morning, I came out to see one of the tires flat, and I couldn't find the patch kit anywhere.

"I can give you a ride," Walter said. He'd been hanging near the campfire all morning, drinking lots of coffee. Olivia was around somewhere, but I wasn't sure where. Sage was spending the morning teaching the younger kids. We only got together for an hour or so in the afternoons because most of the required lessons I could do myself.

"I can wait," I said. "I'll get Julian to help me find the patch kit tonight, or we'll go into town and pick up a new one."

"Don't be silly," Walter said. "I've got nothing going on today—might as well make myself useful. Besides, I heard about a guy in town who's hiring. I can swing over and put my name in. We're going to have to save up some if we plan on bumming around this summer. There's going to be some great shows I don't want to miss."

"Yeah, okay," I said as I looked back at my bicycle. It really did seem to be on its last legs. Maybe I could stop at the shop and pick up a new tire, if it wasn't too expensive. I hated to give up on the poor thing so quickly. And it wasn't like we could afford a new one, especially when the van kept breaking down. Last week we'd had to put in a new transmission, and that had eaten up a bunch of savings. But Walter claimed he'd rather die than get a new vehicle. In hindsight, I think the reason he was so attached to the van was because of the things he did in it that no one else knew about.

Dark things.

I was about to find out.

The cave walls glow, and Parker and I spend a few minutes admiring our mural. No one asked about Mary back on the beach, and I'm trying not to worry they've forgotten her. Having the sun come out for the first time ever kind of trumps everything else. And besides, I'm the girl who brought it all back. Do I really want to be the one to let them know Mary's gone, too? That's all a bit much to handle for one day.

"Do you think enough time has passed?" I ask. The bowl sits on the floor, its never-ending pile of pebbles tempting me.

"Only one way to find out," Parker says as he swoops down and picks up a piece of chalk. He hands it to me, and I press it against the wall, writing Tatum's name for what will hopefully be the last time.

I will save her tonight.

I will keep her safe forever.

The walls instantly begin to disappear.

I don't know why, but I expect to come out on the other side in bright sunlight. Instead I find darkness.

I don't even have time to adjust my eyes to the change when someone slams into me, a heavy body shoving me backward and toward the ground. I hit hard, Parker's name on my lips. I see him reach down to help me, but he doesn't get the chance. A Remnant appears behind him, wrapping its blurry, energy-coursing arms around him, dragging him away.

"Parker!"

Smoke fills my eyes, causing me to blink back tears. The heavy, acrid smell is drawn deep into my lungs as I inhale. I

can't see anything. I try and focus, fixate on something familiar. Look for Tatum; she's got to be here. But where?

I see stars above me. A fire sends smoke billowing upward.
Bodies, dozens of bodies, stand around in a circle. I see Parker
struggling with the Remnant on the ground, trying to keep
the energy from overwhelming his body. His hand sweeps the
ground blindly; fingers close on a heavy rock. He picks it up
and smashes it into the Remnant's empty face.

Then I spot Tatum's friend Scott. He's lying on the ground
by the fire. There's blood on his head, and he's not moving.

I push at the person who brought me down, trying to get
the heavy body off me. Laugher rings in my ears as I scramble
to my feet.

"Welcome to the party!"

TATUM

Claudette corners her in the bathroom during second period.

Tatum's washing her hands when the other girl comes in. She's by herself, which is unusual. Most of Claudette's attacks happen when she's got her posse around to protect her. She talks mean, but she's all bark. At five feet nothing, she knows her limits.

Tatum stiffens when Claudette strolls in. It could be coincidental; she's not sure if something is going to happen or not. There have been a few accidental meetings that have gone fine. Usually Claudette just ignores her, and once she simply brushed past Tatum, shoving her against the sink.

When Tatum sees the smile, she knows there's going to be an altercation. Claudette is grinning like she's the devil and she's about to give a deadly Christmas gift to someone.

"You've got a big mouth, bitch," Claudette says.

"Get lost," Tatum says.

"The police came by my house this morning," Claudette

says. She intentionally bumps Tatum and starts messing with her hair in the mirror. Curls fly in all directions. "Wanted to know something about a fire. Are you becoming a firebug? Burning down your bedroom for attention now?"

"I hope they asked you where you were last night," Tatum says. "I'm sure you had a good excuse."

"What a poor, delusional girl you are," Claudette says. "The police sure seemed to think so. They wanted to know about your medical history. Of course I told them your parents were trying to get you professional help. And I told them about your infatuation. I'm surprised they hadn't already heard about it. They know now."

Tatum turns to go, but Claudette deliberately blocks her way, pressing up closely against Tatum, who's forced to take a few steps back toward the wall.

"What's the matter? Gonna cry?"

"I'm not getting into this with you," Tatum says. "I'd tell you to go pee on my car, but you've already gone out of your way to destroy it. You know how much I loved that car. What more can you do?"

"What's wrong with your car?" Claudette's voice is full of phony confusion.

"Don't play innocent. You suck at it. Go trash my locker if you're angry. Or get Levi to send me more dirty texts. Go spread your useless hate somewhere else. I've got to get back to class."

"Do you know how annoying it was having the cops at my breakfast table?" Claudette asks. "Your stupid big mouth is going to mess things up."

"I didn't do anything." She tries to push her way past Claudette, but the girl reaches out and shoves Tatum back. Hard. Tatum stumbles, almost going down.

"You just can't learn, can you?" Claudette says, and she shoves Tatum again. She turns around and faces the mirror, smiling at herself. She pulls out a lip gloss and starts applying a coat. "How dense is your thick head? You're never going to win with me. No matter what you do. Haven't I already shown you that whatever you say is useless? I've turned this whole town against you. Do you really think I can't do it again?"

"What's the matter, did Barry dump you?"

Claudette's hand slams against the mirror. Glass cracks beneath her palm. The lip gloss drops to the floor, spilling bright pink liquid across the tiles. Tatum takes a step back. Okay, that just qualified for the crazy round.

"I don't know what you're talking about," Claudette says in a very loud voice. "Stop making things up. Or maybe someone *will* teach you a lesson."

"Is that a threat?" Tatum shoots back. The bell rings, and suddenly the hallway is filling up with students. It's only a matter of time before someone comes in and finds them. Tatum's books are still in her second-period class. She's going to be late if she doesn't go get them.

"I don't need to make threats," Claudette says. The door opens and two freshman girls come in. They see Claudette and Tatum facing each other and pause. Tatum uses it to her advantage and pushes past her former friend. The younger girls scatter out of the way as she goes through the door.

She's made it to the hallway when Claudette catches up

with her and grabs hold of Tatum's arm, fingernails digging deeply into Tatum's skin.

"Watch your back, bitch. I'm coming for you."

Then she's gone.

Tatum's legs are still shaking after she retrieves her books and heads to her next class.

* * *

She never makes it home.

They must have planned the whole thing ahead of time. Waited patiently until Tatum walked by. They knew she'd be on foot. They'd gone out of their way that afternoon to make sure.

Scott had offered to drive her home after school. They stuck around for a bit by his locker, waiting for people to clear out. She told him about the altercation in the bathroom. She told him about the threat.

"She broke the mirror with her hand?"

"Yup."

"That's crazy."

"Yup."

"That's it. From now on, you're not going anywhere without me. And you need to tell your parents about this. Show them the texts and Facebook messages too."

She nods, relieved. There's no point in arguing anymore and trying to act tough. She shoves her hands tightly inside her hoodie pockets, hoping Scott doesn't notice the way they're trembling.

But when they get outside, they find all four of the tires

slashed on his car. Scott kneels down and checks. The cuts are wide. Whoever did this had a big knife.

"I'm sorry," Tatum says. "This is all my fault. I'll buy you some new ones."

"Don't worry about it," Scott says. "They were almost dead anyway. Nothing but thread. I've been saving up to buy some new ones."

"They have no right to include you in this," Tatum says. She looks around, hoping to spot Graham or Levi so she can give them a piece of her mind. The parking lot is empty. There are only a few students, and they're averting their eyes instead of gawking. Today Graham and Levi haven't stuck around to slap each other on the back. She doesn't see Graham's car anywhere. He must have destroyed and dashed. Claudette isn't present to call Tatum a slut and laugh, either. A typically cowardly thing for them to do: hide when their attacks focus on a guy who might actually fight back. They can do whatever they want to her; they know Tatum's not going to chase after them with her fists raised. This whole thing leaves her fuming.

Their fight is with Tatum, not Scott.

"Are you really surprised?" Scott asks. "I'm not. Don't look at me that way. I knew what I was getting into."

"Have they threatened you?"

"It's nothing, Tatum; don't worry about it."

"What did they do?" Scott tries to shrug it off, but she won't let him. She needs to know. "Tell me."

"Nothing major," Scott finally says. "A few remarks here and there. In gym today I got a ball thrown at my head. Bunch of immature stuff."

"Assholes!"

"It's okay, really. Guys say and do this sort of stuff to each other all the time. I'm not afraid of Graham. Or that little creep that follows him around."

"Levi."

"Yeah, him. Hardly threatening. He's kinda weird in a bad way. Not worth getting worked up over."

Tatum frowns. "You can't tell me not to worry. Not when you're telling me to be careful."

"I didn't get a ghost foreseeing my death. I'll walk you home. I'll get Dad to take me to the tire store tonight. I'm just glad it's my night off."

She hates that he's so nonchalant about it. She wants to scream at everyone in the parking lot, let them know that they're all just as guilty because they probably witnessed the whole thing and didn't do anything. All her classmates, the ones who glance away when she walks down the hallway. Her teachers who refuse to listen. Everyone who won't stand up for Tatum, because as far as they're concerned, she made her own bed. She deserves this. What's wrong with all these people? Even if Tatum had been guilty of falling in love with a teacher, would she really have warranted these actions? The whole thing is so messed up.

The police called the house this morning and spoke with her father. They said they'd talked to Claudette and she had an alibi for last night. They said they'd follow up with everyone else. When he got off the phone, he didn't say a word to anyone but retreated to his study. Tatum is positive her dad thinks she set fire to her bedroom. It's only a matter of time before he convinces Mom to send her to a private institution with padded cells where Tatum can't hurt anyone.

She thinks again about Molly's warning. It's not so

unbelievable now. Maybe there's some truth to it. Claudette has gone off the deep end.

Tatum decides maybe it's best that she keep a low profile for a while.

"Come on," she says to Scott as she shifts her backpack from one shoulder to the other. "Let's get out of here."

* * *

The attack comes a few blocks from home.

Tatum sees the SUV pulling over, but she doesn't register the danger until Claudette and Graham get out. Levi is driving.

"Look at the little bitch," Claudette says. "What happened to your ride?"

"You trashed it," Tatum says. "And you wrecked Scott's, too. You're going to pay for that."

"You should take better care of your things," Graham says.

"Go away, Claudette," Tatum snaps. "Take your monkeys with you."

Claudette stands her ground, moving slightly closer. Tatum notices that Graham is circling around so he's behind them. What's he going to do? Scott is taller, but Graham has at least twenty pounds on him. If a fight breaks out, Tatum isn't sure who will come out the winner. The street is empty. No one is outside puttering around in their yard or walking their dog. If she screams, someone might come, but Tatum isn't sure she wants to rely on it. People hear hollering teenagers all the time. They might just think it's some sort of joke. She puts her hand in her pocket, touching her phone, reassuring herself that she can call for help if need be.

"I think we should go somewhere," Claudette says. "You and me. For a drive. We need to talk things over."

"I think we've talked enough," Tatum says.

"But I have things to say to you."

Claudette's arm shoots out, grabs hold of Tatum's. Tatum tries to pull back, but she's still got her hand in her pocket. Claudette pushes Tatum down, yanks her hair. Tatum lands hard on her knees, tearing a hole in her jeans. Her teeth clamp down hard as Claudette manages a sharp jab against the side of her ear.

"Back off," Scott yells. He moves in to help Tatum, and suddenly he's lying on the ground.

Tatum manages to pull herself away and rushes to Scott's side. He gets to his hands and knees, dazed, blinking at the ground beneath him. Tatum looks up and sees that Graham is holding some kind of bat.

"What have you done?" Tatum screams.

"Going to do the same thing to you if you don't get in the car," Claudette purrs. "Now move."

She's being kidnapped in broad daylight on her own street. And not by some crazy guy offering her candy in a battered old van. Graham holds up the bat again as if he's going to take another shot. Whether he's aiming for Scott's head or hers, she's unsure. Tatum instinctively holds up her hands in defense. That allows Claudette to grab more handfuls of hair. She yanks hard, throwing Tatum off balance, and she tumbles onto her side. Tatum tries to fight her off, but she's pushed farther down to the point where she's practically crawling on her knees. Her scalp is on fire; it feels like every strand is being yanked out, one by one.

When the hell did Claudette get so strong? This is a girl who failed gym class because she couldn't even bench-press ten pounds. She's the one who always got Tatum to open jars of peanut butter when the lids were screwed on too tightly. Now she's managed to get Tatum into a hold that would make any pro wrestler envious.

It doesn't take her long to get Tatum pushed up against the SUV. Levi gets out and opens the door. He helps Claudette shove Tatum in. Her head smacks against the frame, and she sees stars.

"Bring the dweeb, too," Claudette says.

Tatum watches through watery eyes as Graham grabs Scott and drags him to his feet. She's not sure if Scott's conscious or not. He doesn't put up a fight, but instead leans on Graham, who half carries him to the SUV. Graham tosses him down beside Tatum. She crawls over to him, puts her hands against his face, calling his name. Scott groans. There's a large welt on the back of his head, and blood has soaked the back of his jacket. Head wounds always bleed the most; that's what her mother taught her. All she needs to do is apply pressure. Tatum spots a tissue box crumpled half under the passenger seat. She grabs handfuls and presses them against the back of Scott's head to try and stop the bleeding.

He might have a concussion. She can't remember what to do about that. Don't let him fall asleep, right? That's looking to be an impossible task considering his eyes have just rolled into the back of his head, showing only white.

"Come on," she whispers. "Don't pass out."

Scott mumbles something incoherent back.

Doors slam, and Tatum is stuck in the back with an

almost-unconscious Scott on one side and Graham and his bat on the other. Claudette and Levi get into the front, and he starts the SUV. He hits the gas and they peel out quickly.

The whole thing takes only a few minutes. No adults yelled out or came over to ask questions. No one saw anything.

Tatum finds her phone and pulls it out, but Graham is too quick. He snatches it from her and tosses it over to Claudette. She waves the phone in front of Tatum, mocking her by keeping it just beyond Tatum's reach. After Tatum makes a half-hearted grab for it, Claudette simply rolls down the window and throws it out.

At least Scott still has his phone. Tatum knows it's in his back pocket. Unless Graham tossed it as he was lifting Scott into the SUV. Tatum doesn't dare look. She doesn't want to throw that little bit of hope away.

They continue to drive.

After a few turns, Tatum realizes they're heading toward Frog Road. Levi has a heavy foot; they're going at least twenty over the speed limit. There's always the possibility that a police officer might pull them over. Tatum isn't being hopeful. With her luck, the cop would just smile and wave as they pass by.

The houses grow more infrequent as they head out of town. Levi turns a corner much too fast. Scott's semiconscious body is pushed against Tatum, and blood splashes against her shirt. She grabs more tissue, wondering how much fluid someone can lose before they simply bleed to death. The backseat has a large dark stain beneath Scott's head, but somehow she doesn't think Levi is too concerned about his upholstery. Maybe the SUV is stolen. She doesn't remember Levi having a car.

If they kill them, the SUV will be evidence. Tatum

carefully yanks at the silver chain around her neck and breaks the clasp. She lowers it down on the floor without the others noticing. There. Now if something does happen, the police will know for sure that Tatum was there. The others are leaving evidence all over the place. No one is wearing gloves or trying to cover their tracks.

They're now on Frog Road. The houses are gone, replaced by trees and fields. The sidewalks are gone too; if Tatum were to jump from the SUV, she'd land in the soft ditch. But at the speed they're going, she'd more than likely break something. Levi would just pull over, and they'd drag her back inside. Even if she were to get free, there's no way she could take Scott with her. Considering Tatum is the only reason Scott is here, she can't leave him.

Tatum decides it's best to wait till they get where they're going. Even though her imagination keeps picturing herself dead in a gutter or buried in a shallow grave, she pushes the thoughts away. No matter how intense the situation is, she still wants to believe that Claudette isn't the type who will go that far.

* * *

"Get out."

They've arrived.

They drove past the train bridge, past the place where Tatum almost got her first kiss from Scott. A mile or so later, Levi slows the SUV down and pulls over onto a private dirt road. They drive farther through the trees until they come to a field.

Off to the side is a dilapidated barn. Once it probably stood in the middle of a field, but trees and undergrowth have pushed their way around it, slowly reclaiming the building, one bush at a time. Red paint peels off the outer walls. The doors are crooked and slightly off their hinges. A tree has grown its way through the termite-damaged wood. Green leaves stick out of a hole in the rafters. The building looks like it's been around forever.

Tatum recognizes it instantly from the newspaper clippings Scott got from his grandmother.

This is where Molly died.

How does Claudette even know about this place? As far as Tatum knows, Claudette's experiences with Frog Road are limited. Tatum never told her about the times she drives down here. And she doesn't think she's ever been followed. The traffic is so nonexistent, she'd have seen if there were other cars behind her. With her paranoia mounting, she's spent a great deal of time watching her back in the past few months. Were Graham and Levi out scouting places to party and they found the barn? Are they aware of the murder? Does Claudette somehow know about Tatum's relationship with Molly? Maybe she found a way to hack Tatum's computer and look at her browser history. She found all the ghost stuff and put two and two together. This can't be random, can it?

A multitude of questions slip and slide around her brain, each more ridiculous and unlikely than the next, and before she knows it, Graham and Claudette are out of the SUV and opening the back doors. There might have been a short window there where Tatum could have jumped from the car and run for the bushes. She curses silently, wishing she'd been smarter and paid more attention to her limited chances to get free.

Claudette is losing patience. She reaches in to grab Tatum, but Tatum swats her away. If she's going to get out, she'll do it on her own. She's lost enough hair already. She checks Scott one more time. The bleeding seems to have stopped for now, but his face is completely drained of color. His eyes are open, but dazed. He seems to be staring at the spot right in front of his nose. She's still not sure he's conscious.

"Scott?"

"Now!" Claudette hisses.

As Tatum climbs out, she hears the roar of an engine. Hope floods through her, but it's quickly diminished when she recognizes the car pulling up behind them. Juniper is at the wheel, and there are a few others with her. Kids from school who used to be her friends but have long since sided with Claudette. Girls who like to wear red lipstick. Guys who play football with Graham.

"We're having a party," Claudette says. "You're the guest of honor. Time to have some fun."

Then she pulls her arm back and slams her fist right into Tatum's nose. Stars explode around her, her legs turn to rubber, and Tatum finds herself falling. Her head hits the ground, and she barely has time to recognize the shoe as it makes contact with the side of her face.

Things get hazy after that. Tatum can't seem to gain control of her senses. Thoughts are foggy, and thinking takes too much effort. Someone picks her up by her arms and drags her away from the cars. She can hear Claudette and Juniper laughing, but they seem far away. Voices are muffled, and she can only pick out words in the conversation.

The smell of smoke brings her back. Opening her eyes, she can see that someone has started a bonfire. One of the guys from school is tossing firewood into the flames. She knows this guy. He sits next to her in English class. He borrowed her notes a few weeks ago. And the girl behind him used to come over to Tatum's house when they were younger. They played Barbies together.

Slowly the fog lifts, and Tatum is able to process her surroundings. There have got to be at least forty or fifty kids standing around. Claudette must have invited the whole damn school. Some of them are drinking beers and chatting with each other. Juniper lights a cigarette and flicks ashes into an empty Coke can. She's chatting to Claudette about the biology test they took last week. She apparently failed it.

Tatum wants to look for Scott, but moving too much will only make them notice. It's better that everyone still think she's unconscious. Somehow she gets the feeling they're waiting until she wakes up. Then the party will really begin.

Tatum starts to take inventory of her wounds. Her nose hurts. Horribly. Claudette must have broken it. Wetness settles at the base of her septum, clogging her sinuses and giving her a strong urge to sniffle or sneeze. The pain has traveled up her entire face to settle in at her temples. Her stomach churns nervously. There are dried tears itching at her eyelids, but Tatum doesn't dare scratch them away. A branch is poking her in the side, making her want to shift, but even the slightest movement might give her away. Better to play possum for now.

She needs to get to Scott's phone and try to call for help.

But that's impossible; she has no idea if Scott is lying behind her or if they dragged him into the barn. He could be bleeding to death inside the SUV for all she knows. But the phone is her lifeline, the only way she can let the outside world know where she is. Just as when Molly died decades ago, this barn is not going to be the first place the police check when her parents finally get around to calling in a missing-person report.

And that could take days. Isn't there something about teen-agers? That parents can't officially consider them missing until after forty-eight hours? Will they just think she ran away? Oh God, what if Dad refuses to go looking for her? Maybe he'll be secretly happy she's gone and consider it a blessing in disguise.

The phone.

Tatum scans the crowd. It's getting darker. The sun has almost sunk into the hills now. Soon it'll be full-blown night. Good. Maybe a farmer will see the fire and come investigate.

All this hope is useless. There are too many variables, too many ways things can go wrong.

She's got to do something and do it soon. She can't just sit still and wait until it's too late.

Turning as slowly as she dares, she closes her eyes, trying to make it look like she's just rolling over in her unconscious state. Tatum counts to twenty before opening her eyes a crack.

Scott lies on the other side of the fire. His back is to her, and he's not moving.

"Wakey, wakey!"

Hands reach down and tighten on Tatum's shoulders. Graham's face appears, inches away from her own. Tatum shrinks back.

"Finally!" Claudette comes bouncing over. Shadows dance

across her face, making her smile look grotesque. She's grinning from ear to ear. But not in a happy way. More of an *I'm going to tear the skin off your back with my bare fingers* sort of way. Tatum closes her eyes before Claudette decides to poke them out with a stick. Claudette nudges Tatum's side with her foot. "Come on, faker. We know you're awake."

"Time to get this show started," Graham says. "You're on trial, Tatum. We, the people, have decided it's time you pay for your crimes."

"Guilty," Juniper giggles through a mouthful of beer.

"No," Graham says. "She's innocent until proven guilty. We have to have the trial first."

There are several shouts as people chime in with their opinions. Claudette slaps Tatum across her face, bringing a whole new wave of pain along the bridge of her nose. This time Tatum can't keep quiet. She cries out and the crowd cheers. Someone throws a beer at her head. The can slams into her ear, sending icy fluid down the side of her neck, soaking her jacket.

"I'm the victim," Claudette announces. "I say she's guilty."

"And her punishment?"

"Death."

Graham is suddenly behind her, grabbing her arms and pinning them to her sides. Tatum struggles hard; she won't make this easy on them. She still believes that if she can get free, she can bolt into the woods. It's dark and she's wearing her black jacket. It won't be easy to spot her, if only she can get a bit of a head start. But Claudette is putting her hands around Tatum's throat and starting to squeeze. Tatum takes a deep last breath before her air is cut off.

Somewhere in the distance, a voice calls out loudly. A voice Tatum recognizes.

"Parker!"

She's here. Molly. Tatum searches through the crowd. Some of the kids have spread out, moving toward the barn, where a commotion has begun. Tatum momentarily sees Parker as he's jumped by the boy in her English class. He goes down, but he's fighting hard.

Claudette's hands disappear from Tatum's throat, and Molly is reaching down to help Tatum up. Tatum inhales loudly, pain shooting through her nose, making her sound like she's breathing underwater.

"You're here," Tatum whispers hoarsely.

"We have to get you out," Molly says.

MOLLY

Someone tackles me and shoves me down, but I manage to throw her off. A red-haired girl tries to smash a beer can against my face, but it's empty and I barely feel it. With sharp fingernails, she tries to claw at my skin. I manage to bat her hands away before they do any serious damage.

"Welcome to the party," she trills. She's giggling like crazy, and I can't help but think she's put away several beers. She sways unsteadily on her feet, blurred eyes studying me. "Who the hell are you? You don't go to our school."

"I'm from out of town," I say.

"You shouldn't be here. I think you should leave," the girl says in that singsong voice. I dodge her claws again and push her straight into another kid. They both go down in a heap of flailing limbs.

And the cold wind pushes into me.

Parker! Just as I spin around to try and find him, he appears by my side, grabbing my arm protectively.

They're here. Remnants. It's not hard to spot them among the group of drunk teenagers. They've been waiting for Parker and me to come back. Somehow they've known that I would return to save Tatum. I wonder briefly which one is Mary, but that seems pointless. Whoever Mary is now, she's no longer the woman I once knew. She's not going to sit down with me and talk about corsets and whiskey. No, she's going to try and destroy my soul.

A Remnant appears before me, its arms stretching freakishly long, reaching out to grab my hair. Parker yanks me back, putting himself between the soul-sucking monster and me. The red-haired girl stares at me as if I've sprouted horns, and I instantly understand. She can't see the Remnants. To her, Parker and I must look like we're arguing with the night air.

I couldn't care less. Let her think I'm crazy. It might just give me the leverage I need to save Tatum.

"Parker!" I shout.

"I've got it!" he yells back, shoving his attacker against a tree, narrowly avoiding its energy as it stretches out, like semi-invisible worms trying to get free from a dead body. "Go get Tatum."

I spot Tatum over by the fire, lying on her back. The girl with the brown curly hair is straddling her, knees pinning Tatum down. It's dark, but the fire gives off enough light for me to see that Tatum is covered in blood. I see Scott, too, crumpled to the ground, and he's not moving. I run toward them both, praying that I'm not too late.

I grab Claudette by the back of her jacket and shove her straight toward the fire. She's momentarily distracted when her pant leg starts smoking.

"They've gone crazy," Tatum says. She tugs at my arm in a desperate attempt to get my full attention. "Claudette. She's lost her mind. She's not like this. She's not that mean."

"Looks to me like she is," I say, tempted to add *I told you so.*

Tatum looks at me blankly. "I think she really wants to kill me. Why would she do this? She's supposed to be my friend. Friends don't do that. They don't hurt each other."

"We've got to get you to a safe place. The Remnants, they're here. I don't know how much time I have."

"I've put you in danger," Tatum says. "This is all my fault."

"Not even close," I say. "Now come on. Let's go."

Something inside me wants to break. Poor, trusting Tatum. Even though Claudette has shown her true colors, put her through months of torment, told a terrible lie to save her own skin, and probably a lot more . . . after all that pain and betrayal, Tatum still wants to believe her former friend isn't *that* bad. I get that, I really do. For two days I sat tied up in the barn, bleeding, at first begging for my life to a man I still thought would change his mind and set me free. I didn't believe Walter would really kill me either.

Sometimes it's easier to keep the faith than lose trust.

"Come on," I say. "We've got to get you out of here." I turn toward Scott. "What happened to him?"

"He got hit on the back of the head," Tatum says. "I'm not sure if he's okay. He hasn't said anything since we got here."

I see the blood shiny and sticky in his hair. His eyelashes flutter when he hears Tatum's voice. That gives me hope. If I can get them into a car, maybe she can drive straight to a hospital.

"Where's your car?"

"Not here," Tatum says. "They brought us here."

That's not good. Maybe if we can get to a road, we can flag someone down. I pause, looking around, trying to figure out where we are.

Then I see the barn.

I freeze.

I remember being locked in there for days, tied to the wooden post, watching my bodily fluids slowly gathering by my feet. By the end my wrists were rubbed raw, almost down to the bone, blood and skin stuck to the coarse rope that kept me tightly bound.

The barn door is open, and I stare at the blackness, half expecting to see Walter step out any second with a knife in his hand, motioning to me to come back inside.

I can't do this. Not this place. Not here.

Memories hit me like rocks.

"You know where we are." Tatum's voice reaches my ears, but she sounds a million miles away.

"I know," I say.

"Come on," Tatum says. "Don't go back there. Not just yet. Stay with me."

But the barn is mocking me. It looks different from the last time I was here. Worn down as if nature's been reclaiming it bit by bit. I'm surprised it's still intact. If I were the farmer who owned it, I would have torn it down ages ago. How could anyone continue to live beside such a monstrosity? The ghosts that haunt this place are very different from the ones at my lake.

"Molly!"

I snap back to reality as Claudette tackles me from the side. Her pant leg is singed. Her eyes are focused on mine, and I swear I can recognize the uncertainty. She's crossed the line and part of her knows it. But she's come this far; she's not going back until she's finished.

"Who the hell are you?" she asks. "This is a private party."

I can't stop looking past Claudette's shoulder, where the barn looms over me. Tatum's voice breaks my trance, calling my name over and over like a broken record. My mind begins to clear.

"Really?" I give Claudette a strong shove and knock her off my chest. She falls back, stumbling. We both climb to our feet and the standoff begins. "That's the best you can do? You and I both know that Tatum doesn't deserve this. Any of this. She's innocent."

Claudette frowns. "What has the bitch told you? She's lying. She's a lying bitch."

"Keep telling yourself that. Stop, Claudette. Stay out of the darkness. You have a choice."

Something grabs me from behind and spins me around. I'm face to nonexistent face with a Remnant. And it's wearing a corset.

"Why?" I whisper. "You knew I'd come. You've been tracking me."

A whisper fills my ears. The creature that used to be Mary is able to talk. The spot where her mouth used to be vibrates in and out of focus. "Spirits need to stay dead."

"I am dead."

"You don't belong in this world, ghost."

"I don't belong anywhere."

The Remnant hisses. It might be laughter, though; I'm not fully sure. Energy begins to spread across its skin, moving through the air like invisible tentacles. I feel a jolt of electricity against my arm. I jerk back in pain; the touch is like silver fire.

"So now we steal your soul as a warning to those who come next."

The energy comes at me again, wrapping tightly around my wrist. Although the pain is burning, it's cold too. Memories, mostly feelings, start to fade. All the things I've ever experienced are being erased one by one. My mind is becoming a blank slate, and something old and horrifying is taking over.

Terror flows through me. I want to resist, but I can't. There's no fighting something this powerful. I can hear Tatum screaming my name, but I can't see her. My eyes are fixated on the red barn and the horrors that were inside.

Walter.

Standing over me. A knife in his hand. Smiling with the same crazed smile I saw on Claudette just now. Steel slips into flesh so easily.

I scream.

Pain.

Something else. A person standing in front of me. He's reaching out toward me. The one who brought me to Walter.

Julian.

No. I've fought too hard and too long to keep him. He's the one thing that's given me hope over the years.

No, that's not right.

Parker.

I jerk backward, throwing the Remnant off guard. The energy around my wrist loosens, and I yank hard until I'm free.

"You're not getting me," I say. "Not Parker, either."

I draw my hand back and make a fist. Just the way Marcus

taught me when I was little. I catch the Remnant that used to be Mary right on the bridge of the nose, and it gasps and falls backward.

The energy around my body disappears.

I wait, my fists up to protect my face the way my brother showed me all those years ago. The Remnant of Mary climbs to its feet but doesn't step forward to attack again. And although it no longer has a face, I swear it's grinning at me. I brace myself for another attack.

But instead of coming straight for me, the Remnant turns and shoves itself straight through the body of the closest unsuspecting teen. A boy with braces and bad acne stiffens as if he's been doused in icy water. He sways back and forth on his feet for a few seconds before shaking his head slightly as if trying to clear his mind. Then, without warning, he turns and punches the person next to him.

Uh-oh. That's not good.

It's almost as if the Remnants were waiting for a sign. I spin around, scanning the crowd. More Remnants step through unsuspecting teenagers. Suddenly everyone is turning against each other, and the field goes from drunkfest to crime scene.

I hear a branch crack behind me and turn in time to see the boy with braces coming toward me with his fists raised. I sidestep his advance, but he doesn't seem to notice or care. Instead he slams right into Claudette, who screams and falls backward into the fire.

I reach to grab Claudette, but Tatum beats me. She rushes bravely into the flames and pulls Claudette from the fire. Luckily, Tatum manages to get Claudette out before the inferno catches her clothing again. Claudette lies on the ground beside Scott, moaning slightly.

Parker. I have to find him. I scan the crowd, but all hell seems to have broken loose. The group of teenagers has turned chaotic. They're no longer standing around. They're beating the crap out of each other instead. Whatever the Remnants have done, it's made them hostile. But in the middle of their confusion, they've temporarily forgotten about Tatum.

However, Claudette is attempting to finish things. There's no thanks to Tatum for pulling her out of the fire. My words haven't gotten through her thick skull. She grabs Tatum by the hair and drags her toward the few teens who aren't fighting each other.

"What are you idiots doing?" she screams at them. "We have a trial to finish."

"But . . ." The red-haired girl stares at me. Whatever beer buzz she had is now gone. She's not so sure now that they should continue. Not when everyone seems determined to beat each other to death. A murmur goes through the crowd. A few of the teens step backward. This no longer feels like a game to them.

"This isn't over until I say it's over!" Claudette screams.

If I had a few minutes, I could talk to Claudette and the others. I'm certain I could convince them to stop everything. The party is out of control. It's time to go home.

But time is not on my side. Not when the Remnants are closing in. They have their own game to finish. And, Lord help me, I don't think I'm strong enough to fight them off again. Struggling with the one Remnant was by far the hardest thing

I've had to do since I died. I barely managed to get free. There's no way I'll be able to do that again, especially if they all jump me at once.

"Parker!"

"Molly." Parker brushes up against me. He's got something heavy in his hands. A baseball bat. He throws a wild swing at the closest Remnant, sending it flying back to the ground, where the dirt begins to swallow it up.

"Get them down!" Parker yells. "They can't seem to get back up. It's the only chance."

Easy for him to say when he's holding a bat.

"Tatum," I say. "We need to work together. Parker and I can hold them off. You've got to get Scott to a car."

"We need keys. I think Levi has them." She reaches down and tries to get Scott to his feet. Parker positions himself between the Remnants and the fire. He holds up the baseball bat, swinging whenever one of them gets too close.

"There are too many of them!" Parker yells. Every time he knocks a Remnant back, two more get in closer for the kill. He kicks at one and it grabs hold of his foot. That same strange blurred energy whips around his leg, pulling him off balance.

"Parker!"

I rush toward him, trying to pull him back from the swarming Remnants. They're closing in quickly now that they've got their opening. The baseball bat is torn from his hand as they bring him down. Hands wriggle around his neck. The skin around his mouth begins to blur.

I can't pull him back. The Remnants have him.

"You can fight it!" I yell at him. "Don't let them take away your memories."

A hand tries to snake around my wrist. I shake it away, determined to show Parker that he has the power to get free. I start pulling Remnants away from him, shoving them aside like they're weaklings.

"How?" Parker says. He's weak. I can hear it in his voice. Soon he'll be looking up at me and no longer recognizing my face.

"Fight it," I say again. "Look at me, Parker. Don't look away. You are strong enough to beat this." I shove one of them away, but not before it gets hold of the baseball bat. The Remnant holds it triumphantly above its head.

Parker fights. Hands drop away from his body, but more replace them. There are just too many of them now. They're not even going after me; the Remnants have made Parker their primary target. I suppose once he's claimed, they'll expect me to fall.

I have to do something. I have to stop them before Parker disappears before my very eyes. I can't lose him. Haven't I lost enough? Not here. Not in this place, by this damned red barn, with its memories that will never go away, no matter how many Remnants try and break my will.

I've been selfish, trying to sacrifice myself all along. I dragged Parker and Mary into my quest, and I'm not going to lose them both. Not when there's still one more thing I can do. I know Parker will blame himself, but that's something I'm going to have to live with. Or die with, as the case will probably be.

My hands dive for Parker's pants. No time for modesty now. Digging deep beneath the folds, I find it quickly. A small copper-colored pebble.

"No," Parker says. Suddenly he has renewed strength. He struggles again against the energy bands, but they're not loosening. I can barely even see his face now through the blur.

"I'm sorry," I say.

"Don't you dare, Molly! Don't let me go."

I turn my hand around and let the stone drop to the ground.

"Goodbye, Parker," I whisper.

He Fades away. The energy around him shimmers before dissolving into nothingness.

Parker is safe. My future is still uncertain.

TATUM

She manages to get Scott to the SUV, but of course it's locked. She scans the clearing, hoping to see Levi, but there's too much commotion. She can't spot him in the crowd. But she can see Molly and Parker, and it's not looking good for either of them. When Parker disappears, Molly stays down on her knees for far too long. From the way she's being banged around, there have to be at least a dozen Remnants there.

Is Parker gone? Claimed by the invisible creatures? Or did he manage to get back to wherever Molly and he exist? Tatum can't tell, and she can't see Molly's face to be sure.

She needs to help. But how can she fight something she can't see?

"Stay here," she says to Scott.

"I'm sorry," Scott says. He reaches out and takes a few of her fingers in his hand. He squeezes loosely, showing Tatum just how much strength he's lost.

She looks at him in surprise. He's finally coherent enough to talk.

"It's not your fault," she says. "It's mine."

Tatum tries to help him lean against the SUV, but it's obvious he's still in no condition to stand. All the moving around has reopened his wound, and blood is trickling down his neck.

"Not that," he says weakly. "You're right. It *is* your fault. Sorry. Horrible joke. But aside from that. Me. I'm useless."

"You're not," she says. "But I've got to go help Molly." She helps him slide down the side of the SUV until he's sitting with his back against the passenger door. "Crawl underneath if you have to, but stay out of sight. I'll be back."

"Be careful," he says. "Kick that premonition's ass."

She gets up after making sure Scott isn't going to just fall over again, and she makes her way back to the fire. Molly seems to have gotten to her feet too; she's moving toward the barn, maybe trying to lure the Remnants away. Whatever she's facing, it's clear she's not going down without a fight.

Claudette appears in front of Tatum. Her eyes are lit up in hatred. Graham and Juniper are behind her, along with a few of the other teenagers. The party has turned a whole new shade of weird. Levi, Tatum notices, is mysteriously absent. Maybe he's off puking in the bushes.

"Your freak-show friends aren't going to help you," Claudette says. Graham and Juniper and the others spread out, circling Tatum until she's trapped. There's nowhere to run. The showdown isn't finished. Tatum glances around, looking for Molly, but the ghost is nowhere in sight. She's too busy dealing with her own demons to help. Tatum is fully on her own.

"Why are you doing this?" It's the one question that

keeps going around in her head. Why? Why everything? At what point will Claudette realize she's reached the limit of horribleness?

"You're a psycho bitch."

Tatum decides she's going about this wrong. Claudette isn't going to listen. What she needs is someone else on her side. She looks over at Juniper and notices that the red-haired girl looks uncomfortable. Guilty.

"You know," Tatum says. "You know everything."

Juniper steps back, shaking her head. But Tatum can tell she's lying.

"We were friends," Tatum continues. "You and me. How can you stand there when you know I'm telling the truth? How long have you known? From the very beginning? You could have helped me. What did Claudette have to do to buy your silence? Become your friend? Look at me. How long till you end up in my shoes?"

"What's she talking about?" Graham looks between Juniper and Claudette.

"Nothing," Claudette says. "Don't listen to her. She's a lying bitch."

"Help me," Tatum says to Juniper.

"Shut the fuck up!" Claudette screams. She pulls her arm back and slaps Tatum hard across the face. "You couldn't stand that I was happy, could you? No, so you blabbed to the whole world. You tried to destroy me."

"I tried to help you. Oh God, Claudette. You weren't yourself. You were . . ." She pauses, looking for the right word. She can taste blood in her mouth. "Obsessed."

"You ruined everything!"

"So you have to destroy my life? Haven't you done enough? Okay, fine. I messed up. Is that what you want to hear? I royally screwed everything. And I can't take that back. I should have just left you alone and let you fuck up your life. Just let it go. Leave me alone."

"It's too late for that."

She wonders if that's true. Maybe. Have they come so far that there's really no turning back? Tatum doesn't think that's true. But if anything, maybe she can get Claudette to pause enough for Tatum to get Scott to a hospital. Tomorrow, Claudette can continue her revenge rampage, but tonight they need to pause for station identification. Otherwise Scott might die.

"Scott needs help," Tatum says.

"Oh, right. And then you'll just blab to everyone. Fool me once, bitch. Not this time."

It's become very quiet. Two of the others mumble something to each other and break from the group, walking away. After a moment, Juniper turns and follows them. Sadly, they don't make an offer to take Tatum with them.

"I have to get Scott to a doctor. Let us go. I won't say a word to anyone this time. I promise. You owe me, Claudette. You owe me big-time. Remember all the things I ever did as your friend. Forget about Mr. Paracini and all that other shit. Do this and we're even." Tatum tries to stand up taller, to make herself look a lot tougher than she feels. "I need the keys."

Claudette lunges at her, and Tatum braces herself for another smack. But Graham steps between them and shoves Claudette back. He reaches into his pocket and pulls out the car keys.

"Go," he says.

Tatum swallows heavily and takes a deep breath. She grabs the keys and turns, running toward the SUV before Claudette can compose herself enough to give chase. But something makes her stop.

Molly.

She can't do it. She has to find her. Tatum is the only reason Molly is there. They have to escape together. Turning, she runs off in the direction of where she thinks her friend might be.

The barn.

She spots Molly on the ground by the dilapidated doors. Tatum doesn't know what to do. How can she save Molly from something she can't even see? Maybe she doesn't have to. Remnants only go after ghosts, right? If she can put herself between Molly and them, maybe that'll buy Molly some extra time to get away.

"Molly! Come on, I've got the keys."

"Get away."

"Not without you."

She's about to grab Molly's hand when someone shoves up against her, pushing her to the ground. It's Levi; he's appeared out of nowhere. Grinning from ear to ear, he's breathing heavily and trying to grab her breast in the process.

"Get off of me," she hisses.

"I knew you were a slut," Levi sneers.

She manages to wrestle herself free and crawl toward Molly, who reaches for her to help her up. The only problem is that they're completely surrounded now. Molly has her invisible demons, and Tatum has Levi. They're going to have to fight their way out.

"Let's do this."

The second the words are out of her mouth, she feels something press against her body. Something trying to get inside. It's the strangest feeling, like she's being doused in both hot and cold liquids at the same time. One part of her feels like she's jumped into a lake after a sweltering day. The other half is snuggled up under a blanket while snow falls on the mountain outside her cabin window. The feelings are contradictory, but at the same time they make perfect sense. The presence pushes its way in, and suddenly her eyes are blinking without her permission. She watches her hand reach toward Molly. Struggling, Tatum forces it back down.

"Are you going to let her just do that to you?" someone whispers, but the words are coming from inside her brain.

It would be easy; all she has to do is walk over to Claudette and slap her. Fighting back. Why hasn't she thought about that before? Claudette may be strong, but so is she. Equal. The warmth is now spreading through her system, making her muscles spasm and weaken. It's as if someone has draped an electric blanket over her skin, tucked her in nice and tight. All she has to do is close her eyes and she'll be dreaming of better places than where she is.

Hit her. Hurt her. Get revenge. Make her bleed.

No, she thinks. The words echo in her mind. "NO!"

Mentally, she sees herself standing in front of the Remnant that's trying to invade her body. A young man, not older than twenty. Long hair spills across his shoulders. He's dressed in nineties grunge clothing: plaid shirt, steel-toed boots, dirty jeans. His chin has the beginnings of a goatee.

"You can't make me," she says. "This isn't about Claudette anyway. It's about Molly."

"Why do you even want to bother with that ghost?" the man says. His eyes are bright blue, almost neon. They glow inside his sockets. She half expects laser beams to come shooting out. "Give her to us and we'll go away. We don't want you or your friends. You're just playthings to us."

"You can't have her," Tatum says. "I won't let you."

"Why do you care?"

"She's my friend."

"She's a haunter. She has no friends."

"You're wrong."

It takes every ounce of energy in her body, more than any she's ever needed. She's never concentrated or wanted anything so badly before in her entire life. She imagines herself pushing this man, shoving him so hard that he flies back to the nineties.

Tatum's eyes open.

She's alone in her body.

And she can now see the Remnants. Dozens of them with their faceless souls watching her. The nineties Remnant is on the ground by her feet. She recognizes it only because of the stupid boots. The rest of it is slowly sinking into the ground. She turns to Molly, who is watching her with a look of utter surprise on her face.

"Did you know they can do that? Get inside us?"

Molly shakes her head.

"That's what they're doing to the others," Tatum says. "They're getting them to fight each other. They think it's funny. Can we stop them?"

"Yes," Molly says. "Knock them down. They have trouble getting back up."

"Let's do it."

They stand side by side, waiting for the Remnants to make the next move. The closest one, standing right next to Levi, steps to the side and through him. Levi stiffens and tilts his head as if he's listening. Slowly a grin forms on his face. His eyes stay on Tatum.

"That's not good," Molly says.

"I've got the keys," Tatum says. "Maybe it's time to split."

"Yeah," Molly says.

They turn together, pushing their way through the crowd, and it's almost too easy. The Remnants are backing off and not giving chase. They make it to the fire before coming to a dead stop. Molly reaches out and grabs Tatum's hand.

More Remnants are coming out of the woods. Dozens and dozens of them. But instead of coming straight for Molly, they're brushing up against the partiers instead. Tatum watches as one passes through one of the boys. He stiffens, turns, and punches the kid next to him.

"What the hell, bro?" The boy shoves back. Within seconds, they're rolling on the ground, punching each other while others cheer them on.

Tatum spots Claudette. She's screaming at Graham. Tatum can't hear the conversation, but she's pretty sure Claudette doesn't have as much support as she had a few minutes ago. Graham looks disgusted. Juniper is in tears.

Meanwhile, the frantic fighting of teenagers is getting out of control. Influenced by the Remnants, the kids are practically tearing each other apart. Tatum watches two girls team up against a boy, beating him down to the ground, where they kick at him. She spots one of the girls from her English class, bleeding from a cut above her eye and digging her hands deep into the hair of another.

These are the kids who have made Tatum's life miserable, but she can't run away and leave them. Not like this. She glances at Molly, hoping she might be able to offer a solution, but she can tell Molly doesn't have a clue what to do either. Maybe they can lure the Remnants away. Maybe if they leave, whatever spell they hold will be broken.

Juniper is suddenly beside Tatum, her eyes swollen with tears.

"I'm sorry. I'm sorry."

So not the time for an apology.

"She told me if I didn't go along with her, she'd do the exact same thing to me," Juniper says.

Tatum knows this is a lie. No, Juniper didn't need to be blackmailed into taking Claudette's side. She did it for the same reason everyone else did: Claudette is the popular girl. She's the princess. She's the one the lemmings follow.

But this isn't the time for a full-on confession.

"Take these!" Tatum tries pressing the keys into Juniper's hands. They drop on the ground and Juniper reaches down to pick them up.

"Get out of here, Juniper," Tatum says. "Go back to town and get help."

"But—"

"Just get Scott to safety. Get help."

Juniper looks like she wants to argue, but she notices that a group of angry teens is steadily moving toward them. She reluctantly nods, then loads Scott into the SUV before climbing into the driver's seat. She hesitates, but Tatum screams at her again.

"Go! Get help!"

Levi reaches the SUV first. His fingers scratch along the hood as Juniper screams. She puts the machine in reverse and peels rubber. Soon she and Scott are nothing but fading red lights as they head off toward the highway.

"Just you and me now," Tatum says as she turns to Molly. "We can't leave. You understand, right?"

"What a pair we make," Molly says. "And no, we can't leave. We're responsible. We have to finish it."

"Let's make them regret messing with us, okay?"

"Deal."

They stand their ground as the Remnants slowly move in.

"What happens if they get you?" Tatum asks.

"I become one of them, I think. That's what happened to Mary."

Tatum thinks back to the incident at the marsh when she watched Mary disappear. Now she knows the truth, and she's going to do everything she can to make sure this doesn't happen to Molly. But how? There have got to be at least a hundred Remnants closing in the gap. Tatum can only throw herself in front of so many at a time. Yes, she managed to keep the one from influencing her, but it took almost all her mental energy. She's not sure if she can do it again. If more than one of them comes at her at the same time, she knows she's going to be toast. She'll turn against Molly whether she wants to or not.

"Got any great plans?" Tatum asks.

"I'd suggest running," Molly says. "But I think we're beyond that."

"Wait," Tatum says. "You can go back, right? Get out of here. Leave them to me. They can't hurt me the way they can hurt you. Maybe they'll grow bored if you leave and they'll take off. The fighting might stop."

Molly turns and takes Tatum's hand. "I can't do that. You're in this because of me. If I hadn't taken that stupid premonition so seriously, I wouldn't have put you in any of this danger. Don't you get it? It was a test. Some sort of stupid test and I failed it. I made this happen."

"You didn't know."

"I should have known."

"How?"

"I don't know."

They both pause. There's not a lot of time left. In less than a minute, they'll both be fighting for their lives.

"I think the afterlife sucks," Tatum says. "Whether it's God or some flying monster who likes spaghetti."

"It was getting better," Molly says. "My world. We found everything we'd forgotten. It truly was improving."

"You never did tell me your story," Tatum says.

"If we get out of this, it'll be the first thing I do."

"I'm done waiting," Tatum says. She lets go of Molly's hand and picks up a thick stick from the ground. The edges are charred from being in the fire. "Time to fight. I'm not dying today. I have to get out of this hellhole of a town first."

Tatum charges. She rushes past the fire and straight into the crowd of approaching Remnants. She drives her stick straight into the chest of the closest one, trying to impale it. The stick breaks against the pale skin, but not before the Remnant stumbles and falls. It hits the ground and instantly begins to sink.

One down. Ninety-nine or more to go.

Tatum starts shoving. She doesn't look back at Molly, but she knows the ghostly girl is there when a Remnant falls beside her. It flails against the dirt, almost as if it's making muddy snow angels, before quickly sinking out of sight. Someone grabs the back of Tatum's jacket. It's the guy from English class. They're all influenced by the Remnants, all her classmates, and that makes her feel a little better. At least she knows it's the monsters making them behave homicidally, and not their stupid loyalty to Claudette. Tatum pulls away from him, dodging the punch he aims at her face. But she can't bring herself to hit him back; it seems wrong, considering he's not in control of himself. Instead she backs away, holding the stick above her shoulders to show she means business.

This isn't so hard. Once the Remnants are down, they don't get back up. But more are coming; it's getting harder to keep up. Tatum manages to do a double tripper, by pushing two of them against each other. A hand snakes around her waist, pulling Tatum tight. Trying to break free, she twists until she's down on her knees. Three Remnants fall upon her, and Tatum can feel them trying to invade her mind and body at the same time.

Go get the girl. Make her pay.

It's like a gigantic tug-of-war going on inside her body. All three creatures are fighting to take control first, mentally slapping one another, trying to force the others out. Tatum's head spins, her eyesight growing blurry as she fights for herself.

Then something miraculous happens.

Someone screams.

Tatum freezes. The Remnant holding on to her hair looks

up, just in time to get a baseball bat right across its face. It begins to disintegrate into the ground.

Strike!

More shouts echo across the clearing. Tatum manages to shrug off the last Remnant, mostly because it's too busy watching the scene unfold around them. It falls back and sinks, one more gone to wherever these monsters go.

There are people everywhere. No, not quite people. Ghosts. They rush through the bushes, spreading out around the Remnants and confused teens, forcing their way into the melee.

"Parker!" Molly gets up off the ground. Her skirt is covered in dirt, and she's got a cut on her cheek. "How is it possible? I made you go."

"I was wrong," Parker says. "It's not about the energy needing to recharge. It's about necessity. I hope you don't mind—I brought some friends."

A lady rushes past them with a white fluffy dog at her heels. She's got a leash in her hands and she's using it as a whip. She smashes the metal clasp right into the face of the closest Remnant, forcing its head to snap back in surprise. A girl dressed in a school uniform rushes in, flying straight into a pack of the creatures, screaming like a banshee in Japanese. Tatum's pretty sure she's using a steady stream of curse words.

These people are ghosts. From the look on Molly's face, she can tell her friend knows them. She's beaming at Parker like he's just done the greatest thing in the world. And from Tatum's perspective, it's true. The Remnants are starting to back off, overwhelmed by the number of ghosts pushing into the clearing. They pull back from the teenagers, leaving bewildered students to pick themselves up off the ground and look around blankly. A girl beside Tatum is alternating between crying with loud, ugly sounds, and mumbling about how her outfit is ruined. She's positive she's going to be grounded when she gets home.

A Chinese man picks up a smoking log and throws it like it's a pillow. A dark-skinned boy in rags grabs hold of a Remnant's arm and shoves the creature face-first into a tree. A group of Remnants manages to get a girl in eighties rocker gear to her knees, but before they can convert her, other ghosts come to her rescue. When she climbs to her feet, she screams in victory and plays some air guitar riffs.

The area in front of the barn has gone into complete overdrive chaos.

"They're falling back!" Molly screams.

And they are. The Remnants are retreating, heading toward the trees, running as if their afterlives depend on it. Tatum trips one that gets too close. It goes down in silent screams.

Tatum spins around, hoping to get another one before they're all gone. There are still plenty fighting. Instead she comes face to face with Levi.

"It's not over," he hisses.

Stabbing pain rushes through Tatum's body. She staggers back, away from Levi, looking down at her chest. Something silver is sticking through her shirt, right in the middle of her stomach. Suddenly she's falling, and she isn't aware that her legs have stopped working until she hits the ground.

Levi stumbles back, his hands covering his mouth, wiping Tatum's blood all over his lips. "You deserve everything you get," he says.

Lying on her back, looking up at the sky, Tatum is surprised that she can't see the stars. There are only clouds up there and a bunch of smoke from the fire. She tries to raise her head, but the pain is too severe. Using her hands, she feels along her body until she finds the end of the knife, sticking straight up. Tatum tries to pull it out, but the pain stops her.

Molly is down at her side in seconds.

"Tatum, no," she says. Molly presses her hands against Tatum's wound, possibly to try and stop the bleeding. It only makes things hurt more, but Tatum can't get her mouth open to tell Molly to stop. Wetness drips down her side, uncomfortably cold; suddenly her teeth are chattering, and she can't control them. The uncontrollable shivering only makes things that much worse.

"Ouch," Tatum whispers, unable to think of anything else.

Maybe they're drawn to the smell of blood or the fact that she's dying, but suddenly the Remnants stop their fighting and begin pushing their way toward Tatum and Molly. Even the ones that are slowly sinking into the ground start clawing their way back up to the surface.

"Hold on," Molly says. She gathers Tatum in her arms, surprisingly strong for being so tiny.

Molly drags her through the crowd, dodging Remnants and the fighting ghosts. Hands reach out and grab at her, tearing at Tatum's clothes, reaching for her hair. Molly tries to push them back, but it's nearly impossible without dropping Tatum. Then Parker appears at their side, sweat soaking his hair and fancy shirt.

"Get her somewhere safe," Parker says.

"Phone," Tatum mumbles.

"What?"

"Call for help. Phone. Kids."

"Yes," Molly says, finally understanding. "One of those kids has to have a cell phone. I've seen them. We can call for help."

"I'll take care of it."

Parker disappears.

"Come on, Tatum," Molly says. "Don't leave me."

Tatum wants to sleep, but Molly's voice is loud and clear through all that fog. Tatum closes her eyes for a prolonged period, just a small rest before having to deal with everything again. The pain is gone now, replaced by numbness. She's in shock, she assumes, and it's not really so bad. So much better than the stabbing pain tearing apart her stomach. Why does Mom always talk about shock like it's dangerous? She can't remember. It's actually quite refreshing, a nice change.

"Tatum, stay awake. Please."

She opens her eyes.

They're in the barn.

MOLLY

I place Tatum on the dusty floor, careful not to jolt her body more than need be. Her face is pale, as if all the blood has already drained away, pooling on the floor beneath her. Dust becomes disturbed, rising in a soft cloud up into the air.

My eyes quickly grow accustomed to the darkness. I look around, hoping to spot something I can use as a light. In the corner, hanging on a nail, is an old oil lantern. I rush over and grab it, give it a shake. A small amount of fluid swishes inside the metal container.

I have matches. I reach inside my pocket and pull out the small wooden box I took from Mary. I strike the tip and a flame sparks. Quickly, I light the wick. We used to have lanterns like this so we could stay up late into the night, listening to Walter strumming his guitar, or for when Julian and I would read books after everyone went to sleep.

The flame glows warmly from inside the glass, and I put it down beside Tatum. There's not a lot of oil left, but hopefully

I'll figure something out before we get cursed back into the shadows.

I don't know anything about wounds. I do know from Mary, a few of the others, and from my own personal experience that it can take dozens of stab wounds to actually kill someone. One of the bonuses of being a murder victim, I guess. It comes down to where the cut is and the amount of damage it does on the inside. A lot of killers are pros at making sure they don't nick arteries. They want the kill to last. But I'm worried that in Tatum's case, Levi didn't give a damn about prolonging her agony. No, his intentions were just plain old-fashioned death.

Hiding in the barn is the last thing I want to do, but it makes sense. I try and make sure Tatum is comfortable. I wish I had a jacket or something to use as a pillow. I go back to close the sliding doors. They creak and are unhinged, but with enough effort I manage to get them sealed almost all the way. I suppose a Remnant could squeeze its way through if it was determined, but thankfully enough of my friends have surrounded the door for our protection. Through the crack, I can see that they've formed a line, determined to keep the Remnants out.

Parker leads another group; he's got them going strictly after the teens, trying to find a phone to call for help. There's always the possibility that the red-haired girl or Scott has managed to send backup, but who knows how long that will take. Does either of them even know where we are to give directions?

There are still cars parked farther back toward the road. If we could get some keys, we could get out. Of course, I'm not actually sure if any of us can drive.

Too many questions, and time is running out.

I spin around, and my eyes fall upon the bicycle. I swear, my mouth drops to the floor. The bike is leaning against the wall, near an empty stall, as if no time has passed since the last time I saw it.

There's a lot more rust and dust. The tires are flat and I'm sure the chain wouldn't move, even if I greased it several times, but it's still my bike. The streamers hanging off the handlebars have long since lost their color. Walter must have moved it into the barn, along with the few pieces of jewelry I'd planned on delivering, the day he took me here. He wanted to make sure to erase any evidence of me having been in his van. The bag of jewelry is gone, but the bike remains. Maybe the police didn't put two and two together. Maybe they didn't feel the bicycle meant anything.

Either way, apparently the owners of this barn haven't cared either. They've obviously just let it sit for more than forty years. It makes me sad, remembering how much I loved that bike, to see it rotting away in this lonely place. A final piece of treasure to show the world I really did exist.

Off to the right, beneath the loft and hidden away in the shadows, I see a wooden post. It calls to me and I can't help but follow, running my fingers along the dry surface until I find them. There, about three feet above the floor, hidden unless you knew they were there. Tiny fingernail scratches. I place my own hand over them, and yes, it's a perfect match. The blood has long since faded away.

"Molly?"

"I'm here." I go back and kneel down beside her, trying my best to keep my expression calm. Her shirt is completely soaked through now. Tatum's teeth are no longer chattering; if anything, her face has taken on a peaceful expression and her body is relaxed. I tear off a chunk of my skirt and press it against the wound, hoping to try and stop some of the flow. Tatum winces slightly; her lips are pale and chapped.

"We're in the barn," she says. "I'm sorry."

"Why?"

"Because I'll bet you never wanted to see this place again."

"My bicycle is still here. Can you believe that? How weird. I wish someone had thought to take it away. It was meant to be ridden, not entombed." I'm rambling. I can't help myself. If I stop talking, I'll be able to hear the wheezing in Tatum's chest. Her death rattle.

Tatum tries to move her head toward the corner but gives up. Too much effort. "I'll bet you loved it," she whispers.

Outside, someone is shoved against the barn wall. The movement rattles the wood, sending dirt and sawdust raining down on us from the rafters.

"I did," I say.

"I'm sorry we're here," she says again.

"It's okay. Walter is gone. He can't hurt anyone ever again."

Tatum puts her hand out toward me, and I take it, squeeze gently. Her fingers are freezing. Her lips are turning blue.

"Tell me your story."

"We don't have time," I say. "Help is coming. They'll be here any minute."

"You're lying." She coughs weakly, and I can see blood on her teeth.

I shrug, because she's right. Or maybe she isn't. I simply don't know. Everything is out of my control, and there's nothing I can do. The barn doors rattle and I can hear angry shouts. I can't tell who's winning or if the fight is almost over. I realize that I don't really care.

I failed.

"Molly? Please. I need to hear it."

I sigh. This is a story I don't want to tell. It doesn't have a happy ending. It's filled with pain and struggle. It's not a parting tale to tell a dying girl.

But it is a last request.

* * *

I remember seeing a frog by the side of the road the day I was abducted. We'd barely gone any distance when Walter pulled the van over and turned us down the dirt road that led to the barn. I didn't really think too much of it; he'd said he had a few errands to run on the way, and he pretty much knew everyone in the area. That was one of the reasons Walter and Olivia came this far north in the winter: Walter had grown up here, and he knew enough people who were willing to take him in. He was liked by many of the local famers.

"You have to see this place," Walter said. "I've been in talks with Ron Kroger, the man who owns this land. He goes down south for the winters these days, and the local guy who watches his property had an emergency. Had to get out of town for a bit. But this place. We can't use the house, but the guy said we can use the barn. No animals or anything. It's been empty for a while, gathering dust and whatnot. It's big and we can damn sure make it cozy. I figure if we can get our hands on a wood-stove or something, we'll live like kings."

It did sound good. My tent had recently sprung a leak, and I had been forced to spread plastic all over the ground so I wouldn't wake up with a soaked sleeping bag. Even though we'd already made it through the worst of the winter, the nights were still hard when you were sleeping alone in a small tent with no body heat. Sometimes Julian would join me, but he shared a tent with Sage's two little kids. There simply wasn't enough room for me to crawl in there with them. We'd talked about getting a bigger tent, but in reality, Julian and I wanted to be alone.

Spending time together without other people was hard when you lived in a commune, especially one that shared everything from child rearing to bedding.

The barn stood at the far end of a large field. The area looked like it hadn't been farmed in a while. The soil hadn't been turned or planted for the new season, and lots of weeds and garbage covered the faded tractor tracks. Trees grew up around it, keeping it perfectly hidden from the road. As I got out of the truck, I could see the farmhouse in the distance. A good half mile away from where we stood, it was the only other building in sight.

I took a few steps forward and stopped, my foot in midair. Beneath my sandal was a tiny frog. I bent down and scooped it up into my hands, enjoying the soft rubbery feeling.

"You're gonna get warts touching a frog," Walter kidded.

"It would be worth it," I said, looking around. Beside the barn, partly hidden in the bush, was a small pond. I carried the frog over and released it.

"I used to keep tadpoles in a jar when I was a kid," Walter said from behind me. "Always died on me. My fault. I'd shake the jar or pencil-poke them to see what happened. Never had any patience when it came to living things."

"I love frogs," I said. "Any type of animal." I thought about the animals I wanted with Julian. I'd have to consider a fish tank so I could keep some amphibians. I stepped back from the pond, certain that my little friend would find his family, and joined Walter in front of the barn.

"Perfect, right?" Walter asked. "No one back until June. That would give us a little more than a month. Plenty of time to relax before hitting the road again."

I nodded. Julian and I still hadn't told Walter and Olivia that we wouldn't be heading off with them this summer. Julian had been putting money aside to rent a little apartment in Seattle. I planned on getting a job. We didn't know how to tell them yet. I knew Olivia would be very disappointed, but hopefully thrilled too.

"It's lovely," I said.

Walter went over and pushed open the sliding doors. They opened easily; obviously they'd been oiled recently. He stepped inside, motioning at me to follow.

I wish I could say I had an epiphany or my own vision that might have saved me that day, a weird feeling that raised the hairs on my neck or the sudden realization that Walter had ulterior motives, but I'm sad to say that I didn't. Even knowing that Walter occasionally had roving eyes that followed me when they shouldn't wasn't enough to make me think, *Oh hey, this guy's a killer. Find your bike and run.* I figured that if Walter made a pass at me, I'd brush him off, experience the awkwardness, and that would be it.

How blind I was. A foolish, foolish girl.

I followed him.

Inside, the air was cool, but not drafty. A bit of dust covered the floor, proving that it hadn't been used in a while, but nothing that Olivia, Sage, and I couldn't fix with a good wash bucket and a few rags. The wood boards creaked beneath my feet, but the foundation was solid. Strong posts held everything up, and a ladder in the corner led toward the rafters.

"We could hang blankets in the loft," Walter said as he shook the rungs to make sure they were nice and strong. "And make separate bedrooms. Could always pitch our tents round back for when we want some adult time." He gave me a leering grin, his eyes pausing a bit too long on my chest. I wrapped my sweater tighter around my body, thinking that we might be having that brush-off talk sooner than later.

"It's a good idea," I said, too cheerfully.

"What's that?" Walter leaned against the ladder. "Adult time?"

"Using blankets for walls."

"I like the sex part better." Walter grinned at my shocked face. "Oh, come on, darling. I know you're getting it on with my boy every night. I'm sure you ain't no prude. We picked you up at Woodstock, for fuck's sake."

"This isn't an appropriate conversation."

"You're a pretty little thing," he continued, ignoring how

uncomfortable I'd obviously become. "We share everything here. Everything. And it's about time you considered paying for your share of what I've given you."

"I think we should leave."

I turned to move toward the door, but Walter went over and planted himself between freedom and me. There was a long pause while he waited, as if he expected me to say something else. I didn't know what he wanted, so I made my way over toward the other side of the barn, keeping an eye on the door. I acted like the conversation hadn't fazed me at all and I wanted to check out the rest of the place. There were no other exits in the building. No side doors and no windows, except for the one up in the loft, where they used to store the hay. If I had to, I was pretty sure I could get there before Walter caught me. I was a lot younger and hopefully much faster. I was certain I could easily climb the ladder and get to the window. But how on earth would I get down without breaking a leg?

"I'm not a complicated man," Walter said. "I see something I want, I go get it. And I have desires. Different things, stuff I can't share with Olivia but I very much wish to experience with you."

"I want to go home," I said. I no longer cared about going into town to sell the jewelry. I couldn't understand how this had turned so dangerous.

"No," Walter said. "I don't think so."

I ran for the ladder.

Walter caught me before I even got my foot on the first rung. Grabbing my shoulders, he yanked me back, hard, and pulled me down to the floor. I kicked him and screamed as loudly as I could. I swung around, nails clawing at his face, leaving a long red welt down the side of his cheek before he managed to pin my arm beneath his sweaty body.

"No one's gonna hear you," Walter said. Bits of white hair had escaped his elastic band. Strands stuck up in all directions, making him look even crazier than I believed he already was. He panted heavily, his eyes wild and shining. He flipped me over on my stomach like I was a rag doll. I kicked and flung my arms uselessly, trying to swim away from him in a sea of dust.

"Please," I begged. "Let me go."

"You're like a little monkey," he said. "And I got some stuff to get from the van. Best you quiet down now."

He grabbed hold of the back of my head and slammed my face into the wooden floor. Everything went black.

When I came to, I was staring down at my feet. He'd hoisted me up against one of the sturdy posts and wrapped several coils of rope around my stomach and shoulders to keep me vertical. My hands ached behind me, tied tightly to the point where my fingers tingled. When I made a fist with my hand, I could feel the blood swelling beneath my skin. My feet were tied too, my sandals removed and flung into a corner of the room. I helplessly twisted my toes around in the dust.

Walter stood in the far corner. He'd brought in the oil lamp from the van, and the glow of the glass made me realize that a lot of time had passed. The barn doors were closed, but there was no light slipping between the cracks. Only darkness. Night had come. I wondered if Julian was home yet and if he was wondering where I was. Would he and Olivia even think to worry yet? Maybe not. They'd probably just assume we were still in town.

Walter had brought in a toolbox and was emptying everything onto the floor. Some of the tools were ordinary: pliers, a hammer, a rusty saw. There were also assorted knives, including butcher knives and scalpels. A long roll of plastic and some duct tape leaned against the wall beside a bucket. My bicycle was there too, along with the bag of jewelry I hadn't delivered.

"How's your head feel?"

I don't know how he knew I'd come around. I hadn't said a word, and he still had his back to me. I didn't answer. I might not have known much, but I knew my stirring would trigger some new event that I definitely wouldn't enjoy.

"I know you're awake. You're panting like a dog in heat. I can hear your heart racing from here, little birdie. Thump. Thump. Thump."

"Please let me go home, Walter."

"That's not gonna happen, Molly."

"Why not? I'm not going to say anything to anyone. They never have to know."

It's funny how people always say the exact same things when they're about to die. They beg to be released, make promises never to tell a single soul, anything to try and grasp for that last straw. That final desperation. The same words are always spoken, regardless of sex or age. Everyone in my ghostly world said those very words at one point or another. We all begged for our lives, hoping to get some understanding from our killers.

But that's the problem. There's never any empathy to be had.

Walter taught me that. He told me that every single girl he killed said the same things. They sometimes substituted and added extra: *My father is rich and will pay anything if you let me go. I have a husband. I have a child. I don't want to die.* All these women tried to convince Walter to give them their freedom, but none of it mattered. He wanted the kill more than anything else. The begging was an added bonus. Just another part of the ritual.

So I stopped begging pretty quickly. It was what he wanted, and I was determined not to give him that. I concentrated instead on freeing myself. I'd do whatever it took.

"I'm gonna have to go soon," Walter said. "Olivia will have my hide for missing dinner. And I'm sure there's going to be some excitement tonight with you not returning and all."

He picked up the duct tape and approached me slowly, a cat chasing his prey. I didn't look at him; instead I chose to keep my gaze on the floor.

"You're gonna have to spend the night here; I hope you don't mind. I'll be able to come back over tomorrow once it's safe."

When I didn't answer, Walter used the duct tape to cover my mouth. When he was finished, he leaned back and examined his work.

"Ain't no one gonna hear you anyway, but I need to be careful," he said. "Remember, there's no one around for miles. It's just you and me."

The knife appeared in his hand. He brought the metal edge against my skin, scratching a line down my arm without drawing blood. I tried to gasp in shock, but of course no sounds came out. Just a heavy whooshing of air passing quickly through my nose.

When the blade cut skin, my eyes grew wide. A slice along

my cheek, sending white-hot pain along my face. My mouth tried to open, but Walter had done his job properly. I couldn't scream.

"Now we're even," Walter said, pointing to his own face where I'd scratched him. "I'm gonna have a hell of a time explaining that one. But it should heal up before the police ask any questions."

He turned and went over to the lantern. He twisted the knob and the flame slowly flickered and died, sending us both into darkness.

"See you tomorrow, darling."

I waited until I heard the van start up and Walter drive off. Then I began to struggle. I twisted my limbs into as many positions as I could, desperately trying to free myself. But the rope was strong, and after a few hours all I'd managed to do was bloody the skin at my wrists and ankles. I thought the wetness might work in my favor by making the rope more slippery, but it didn't happen.

The tears came next. They rolled down my face, and my nose got all stuffed up to the point where I couldn't breathe. I panicked, thinking that I'd suffocate. Snot dripped down my face, sending a terrible itch crawling along my skin. It drove me mad, and I spent a good amount of time trying to make it stop by rubbing my chin against my blouse. It only made more of a mess and didn't give me any satisfaction.

Finally I gave up, exhausted, and closed my eyes. I wasn't going to get free. I'd still be there when Walter showed up bright and early. I'd just have to figure out a way to outsmart him.

I began to think about my family. I tried to picture Marcus

and Dad, sitting at home, watching TV, beers in their hands. Why hadn't I called home? All that ridiculous fear that Dad might try and take me away from my new family. I wished he'd actually found a way to track me down and do it.

When I got out of this, calling him was going to be the very first thing I did.

I pictured Julian and Olivia by the campfire, listening to Walter spin a tale about my whereabouts. I was sure he'd probably told them he hadn't even seen me that morning; he wouldn't admit to having given me a ride. He was probably pretending to be just as worried as everyone else. Dark hatred spread through my chest, making me wish a thousand different forms of revenge against him. When I got free, I was going to inflict every single one of them on him.

Poor Julian. He had to be so worried.

I stood all night long, legs cramping, wrists swelling, pain shooting through my body every time I tried to get more comfortable. I didn't think I'd ever be able to sleep, but eventually exhaustion took over.

* * *

"Rise and shine, darling."

I was already awake, had been for hours, dreading the moment I'd hear the van pull up to the barn. Walter had a thermos of coffee in his hands and a bag of doughnuts. He put them down on the floor before coming over to check how much I'd loosened my bonds during the night. He yanked and tugged, making my raw skin scream, before leaning back with a grin on his face.

"What can I say? I'm good."

Then he backhanded me across the face. My head jerked, slamming against the wood post. Not a sound escaped my duct-taped lips. Walter gave me another sadistic grin before he tore the tape free.

I gasped.

"You look terrible, darling."

My eyes were swollen from crying, and I could feel my cheek beginning to puff up from the smack. I'm sure I looked bad, but that wasn't exactly high on my list of concerns. Walter's face looked fine: the scratch I'd made had already begun to disappear.

"You'll never guess where I'm supposed to be right now," Walter said as he went over and poured himself some coffee. "I'm going around to all the shops to inquire about whether or not you showed up yesterday. What sort of answer do you think I'm going to get from everyone?"

I didn't say a word. I had my eyes on his coffee. My mouth was dry from crying all the liquid out of my body last night. As much as I loathed the idea, I considered asking him if I could have a sip.

"Your boy is devastated. I spent the whole night consoling him. Poor thing. He's at the police station with Olivia this morning. But I'm pretty sure the fuzz won't try too hard to find you. Not some little hippie chick. They don't care much for people like us." Walter noticed the longing in my eyes. He held up the coffee cup. "You want some of this."

I nodded in spite of myself.

He threw the coffee in my face. Thankfully, it wasn't hot enough to burn. Warm liquid dripped down my face, and I stuck my tongue out, trying to get the few remaining drops as Walter laughed at my predicament.

"Time to get this party started," he finally announced. He went over to his toolbox and pulled out some bolt cutters. Then he went over to my bicycle. "You love this rusty old thing, don't you?" Bending down, he cut through one of the tire spokes. Once it was free, he brought it over: a long, thick needle, which he held up and positioned right in front of my eye.

"Look at me," he said. "If you close your eyes, I'm going to stick this right through your socket."

I didn't blink. The spoke inched closer and closer, to the point that I could almost feel it pushing air against my skin. Never in my life had I wanted to blink so badly. Everything burned, and if I hadn't been so dehydrated, I probably would have been bawling. Finally I had no choice.

I blinked.

"No, not yet. I want you to see everything I'm going to do to you."

Walter pulled back his hand and drove the spoke into my shoulder.

I screamed. The first of many.

* * *

Tatum's eyes grow wide for a brief second before she moans and goes back into her state of semiconsciousness. I want to stop. I don't want to be having this conversation. Not now, not ever.

"He tortured me for several days," I say. "Going back and

forth between me and the family. He even joined in on the search when the police finally agreed to get involved. The day he finally killed me, he came to tell me that my father had flown in from Dixby."

Tatum's eyes flutter.

"I'm sorry," she says. "I wanted to hear it. I thought maybe it would give you closure. Get you to the light."

I smile down at her. "It's okay; I don't mind being a ghost. I get to meet some interesting people. And I have Parker. Just like you have Scott. I'm not alone."

"I'm tired, Molly."

"I know you are. Try and stay awake a little longer. Help is coming."

We sit in the darkness of the barn. The oil lamp is down to fumes, and the fire flickers as it steadily grows smaller. The noise outside has quieted in the past few minutes.

In the distance I hear a siren.

"Tatum. Hold on." I rub my hand along her arm. Her skin is clammy and cold. "Help is here."

The barn door slides open. Parker steps inside, looking frazzled. He comes over and joins us on the floor.

"Come on," he says to me. "The ambulance is on its way. I think it's best that we clear out. Too much we can't explain."

"The Remnants?"

"Gone. They scattered when they realized we weren't going down without a fight. For a bunch of scary ghost killers, they're nancy boys, don't you think? Either way, I don't believe they'll be bothering us anymore."

"Tatum?"

She isn't responsive. I instantly press my head against her

chest. The heartbeat is still there, but it's slow and weak. The siren grows louder, and red lights flash through the barn's doors.

"Come on," Parker says. "Let's go greet them."

We step out into the yard.

Most of the ghosts are gone or in the process of dropping their stones. The dog lady has gathered her pet into her arms. She waves at me and steps back into the shadows, disappearing in a poof of white fluff.

Soon all that's left is a bunch of confused teenagers. Whatever hatred seized them earlier appears to have faded. Some of them have already left, either by running through the woods or escaping to their vehicles. An ambulance and a police car have pulled up next to the few remaining cars. Red and blue lights make the trees glow, and a spotlight shines straight toward the barn.

I run over to the ambulance attendant as he climbs out of the van. "She's in the barn," I say. "She's been stabbed. Help her."

"Okay," he says. They grab their med kits and run.

"Come on," Parker says. "We need to go."

"But she needs me."

"You can visit her later. Right now we should make ourselves invisible. Before we get arrested."

Parker's got a point. I can see the police assessing the situation. They're trying to round up the rest of the teenagers, chasing two boys who make a mad dash for the woods. I can hear more sirens in the distance. It sounds like the entire squad has been called down. Parker and I have no identification; we're just a bunch of weirdos in period costumes. And the last thing we need to be doing is Fading in front of witnesses. The police are going to be dealing with some strange stories tonight, and we don't need to make it worse.

I go back to the barn for one last look. The ambulance attendants are hovering over Tatum, and it looks like they're doing their job. The only thing I can do now is wait and pray.

Parker touches my shoulder gently, and I nod. We step away from the glaring searchlight and move behind some bushes. We pull our stones from our pockets and face each other.

We drop in unison.

TATUM

She wakes in a haze. She's in the back of an ambulance, and there are blinking lights and machines everywhere. A woman smiles down at her and says something, but Tatum can't understand over the background noise. She watches while the uniformed woman prepares a needle and hooks up an IV. When she sticks the sharp into the soft fold of Tatum's arm, Tatum doesn't feel a thing. In fact, her entire body has gone numb. She can't make anything move. She can't even flinch when the IV is hooked up. She wonders if she's dead.

Another paramedic leans over her, mouth opening and closing, but Tatum can't hear. White noise. Her brain is full of fuzziness. A head full of bees. She tries to tell him to hush, that she can't hear him over the flashing red beams, but that makes no sense. Lights don't make sound, and if the sirens are on, she can't hear them either. The man continues to talk, his mustache moving up and down. It makes her think of puppets. It's almost comical, and she wants to laugh. Her lashes flutter, and her eyes involuntarily roll into the back of her head.

When she comes to again, she's in a white room. Everything is hazy; it's like being in the middle of a puffy cloud. Once again, she wonders if she's alive. The machine she's hooked up to is beeping, so she takes that as a good sign. At least the white noise is gone. What's returned is the stabbing pain coming from the middle of her body. Tatum tries raising her head from the pillow—she wants to look at her wounds—but she's lost all muscle control. All she can see is that her clothing is gone and there's a lot of white cloth and blankets reaching up to her chin.

From the corner of her eye, she can see two people sitting in the chairs beside the bed. Scott has his legs stretched out awkwardly; his head sports a large bandage. He's snoring softly, his mouth slightly open, and he looks younger than his years. Tatum's mother occupies the other seat, her eyes closed, an unread paperback in her fingers. She's dressed shabbily, in mismatched clothing, and her hair is sticking out all over the place. Tatum has never seen her mother look so disheveled. She wonders if Dad is nearby.

Light comes into the room. Tatum closes her eyes, pretending to be asleep, but she still peeks. A nurse has come in and injects a needle into her IV. It must be a painkiller of some kind, because the pain in her stomach lessens, and Tatum instantly goes back into a dreamless state.

The next time she wakes up, she swears Molly is standing over her.

"You're going to be fine," her friend whispers. "I'll be back. One last time. I promise."

When Tatum blinks, the room is empty, and she's left wondering if the whole thing was a dream. Or a mirage. Or heaven.

In the morning, when she finally wakes up without the clouds or fuzziness, she finds both her parents waiting for her. Mom throws herself around Tatum, nearly tearing the IV right out of her body, but Tatum doesn't mind. Then Dad is there too, warm arms holding them both, and he's crying.

They're all crying.

* * *

It's morning, about a week later, when Tatum wakes up to find Molly waiting by her side. It takes her a moment to figure out what's different about her ghostly friend; then she notices the change of clothing. Molly's gone modern. She's now sporting a bright blue hoodie instead of her peasant blouse. She's got a new skirt too, still kind of flowing and retro, but she's wearing a pair of soft flats instead of her sandals.

She'll have trouble convincing people she's a ghost in that outfit.

"Hey," Tatum says. She's doing a lot better now, and today they're letting her go home. She'll be spending the next few weeks in her own bedroom with a list of things she's absolutely not allowed to do. Mom has promised that her room is fixed and waiting for her. They've bought her a bed and duvet. New sheets. Deep-cleaned the carpet. Everything is new and smoke-free. Tatum can't wait to get back to her own room. The hospital hasn't exactly been the most comfortable place in the world.

"I wanted to come back," Molly says.

"One last time," Tatum says.

"You remember? Me coming? I wasn't sure if you saw me or not."

"I did. I thought you might be a ghost, though."

Molly makes a big show of rolling her eyes before sitting down on the edge of the bed. "Your parents are downstairs getting breakfast. I didn't want to disturb them. And you probably don't need to be explaining who I am to them."

"Yeah, I guess I still don't have a lot of friends at school. It's going to be different now, with the trial and everything. I'm sure there are still a lot of people angry with me."

"I heard."

As it turns out, her former friend Juniper had a massive change of heart. After she dropped Scott off at the hospital, the police picked her up. At first she denied everything, saying she had nothing to do with the incident in the woods. But as the other kids talked, and Levi got arrested for attempted murder, Juniper spilled. She came clean, telling the entire story, which ended up with Claudette's story compromised and Mr. Paracini in handcuffs.

It made the news everywhere. Teacher has affair with student and lies to cover it up. The married educator conspires with the minor he's dating and allows another girl to take the fall, by making up stories about how the fallen girl tried to seduce him. And then there's the part about the final party, in which the bullied girl is taken into the woods, where they try and kill her.

They couldn't arrest Mr. Paracini fast enough. The school couldn't wait to fire him either. Sweet revenge. Tatum guesses he won't be taking that boat trip anytime soon.

As for Claudette, Tatum hears she's been expelled, and there aren't a lot of places willing to take her. Whether or not she'll be charged with anything is anyone's guess. She's still claiming that she was under Mr. Paracini's spell. Half the town thinks she's an innocent girl; the other half screams teenage temptress. But the investigation isn't over yet.

Although Tatum is still a minor and the news can't identify her, the Internet is abuzz with gossip. It only took a day for her real name and picture to surface. Facebook fan pages have been set up in her name, and she's getting all sorts of attention. People have sent her cards, flowers, and gifts from all over the world. Her room began to overflow, and Mom started sending the presents to the children's ward. Then the cancer ward. Then anywhere else in the hospital they could find an empty table.

Apparently several magazines and newspapers have sent reporters to try and interview her. Dad has chased them away. But Tatum is certain she'll be able to convince him otherwise. The price tag they're offering is more than enough for her to go to any college in the world.

"It's weird," Tatum says. "I'm used to getting all sorts of negative attention. This positive stuff is kind of new; you'd think I'd be all over it. But I don't want to face it just yet."

"I don't blame you," Molly says.

"Mom says it'll die down, but it won't. Not for a while."

"Not until another story replaces it."

"Exactly. How long are you going to stick around?"

"A few more minutes. I need to make sure you're okay."

Tatum grins. "I'm good. Better than ever. And I've got a fancy scar. Scott says it makes me look cuter. But yeah, no more bikinis for a while. I might even have to have some plastic surgery. Yikes."

"I'm so happy for you . . ." The words trail from Molly's mouth.

"You told me your story," Tatum says. "Most of it. I remember that much. I guess it was enough. I don't think I want to hear the ending anyway. It wasn't a happily-ever-after."

"That's not true," Molly says. "My story isn't over yet."

"But you're dead. You died. Walter took your life and now you're a ghost, forever stuck on Frog Road."

Molly laughs. "It's not so bad. If it weren't for my hitchhiking, I never would have met you. My world now, it's better. We've been given hope, and it's you that brought it. And you saved me, Tatum. It may not have been the big white light you were hoping for, but you changed things in a way I hope you never know."

"Why not?"

"Because you're not going to die for a long time. The people I associate with, we all have a bit of a violent history. But not you—when it's your time, it will be different." Molly laughs again. "Old age. You hear me? You've got no choice now but to live to be a hundred. Maybe two hundred."

"No more murder for me," Tatum agrees.

Molly leans down and kisses her on the cheek. It's suddenly too final for Tatum. She doesn't want Molly to go. She reaches out and takes her friend's hand.

"Will I see you again?"

"Maybe," Molly says. She reaches into the pocket of her hoodie and pulls out a pebble. "It's been an honor knowing you."

"I'm glad I met you," Tatum agrees. "You're the best friend I've ever had."

"Give Scott my regards," Molly says, and the stone drops from her fingers, bouncing off the linoleum as she fades away.

In the distance, Tatum can hear her parents returning from the coffee shop. She presses the button to make her mattress move so she's sitting up. Hopefully Mom brought her a doughnut. It's true what they say about hospital food sucking. Tatum never wants to see lime Jell-O again.

nition, and I certainly added to it by refusing to give up, but now I see that there was a bigger picture for Tatum and me. Our determination to help each other was the most important thing. Tatum's days are changing too. I have faith that she'll be strong enough to move on. Her name is clear, and she's no longer being bullied. She has nothing to look forward to now except the future.

We saved each other.

As for the cave in the woods, I don't go back there anymore. There's no need. I have everything I want right here.

And when I do Fade, I try to enjoy the moment. I still enjoy stepping out onto that road as the headlights light up the earth beneath my feet. I get into the car or van or truck and give the person behind the wheel my best smile.

"Thanks for the ride."

This is the story of how I died.

Don't forget me.

I'm still here.

that never light up the sky. Now our beach is just that, sand and logs. There's a cabana off to the side filled with a never-ending supply of fresh towels and picnic blankets. In the daytime we can be found lounging around, drinking brightly colored drinks that appear when we want them. They taste heavenly.

In the woods surrounding our little inlet are dozens of cottages. I share one with Parker. They're beautiful little buildings with front porches and comfy chairs to sit on. At night—and yes, we have both sun and darkness now—we light candles and visit one another. Parker and I spend a lot of time with the dog lady. Her name is Grace, and she's fascinating. She used to be a dance instructor to some famous politicians. Whenever we come over, she serves us cookies that she baked during the day. I've even taught the pooch some new tricks.

We sleep and dream. We form relationships. We laugh and cry and support each other. I've really gotten to know these people I've spent so many years with. Who they are, not how they died. I now know how they lived. I share their stories. Their hopes and dreams. Their memories.

When new people arrive, we welcome them with open arms. They no longer have to sit themselves down quietly and wait for that first moment when they'll Fade. It's not easy: many of them come to us angry and confused, still hurting from the tragic way they left earth. But we all came the same way one time or another. And we're patient.

Tatum may never fully understand, but she did save me. She saved all of us. She made us remember that we deserved to feel the sun on our faces. That just because we died tragic deaths we didn't have to fade into memory.

The Remnants may have been involved with my premo-

MOLLY

The lake is cool and refreshing. I take my shoes off and step into the soft waves. My toes sink into the sand, which curls around my feet, giving me a wonderful feeling.

Yes, feelings.

Parker sits on our log. He's looking more modern these days, thanks to me. Our clothes took a real beating during our last encounter in the real world, so a group of us snuck into a mall late at night and did a bit of shopping. We left some of Mary's ancient coins on the counter for payment.

Parker wears a nice pair of jeans and a fancy top. He complained at first that the pants were too tight, but he's since grown used to them. His bowler hat has been retired, and I swear his hair has grown an inch or two. He looks incredibly handsome, and I can't help but admire him when he glances my way.

Our little world has changed. Gone are the French tables with the fancy black wrought iron. Gone are the paper lanterns